Tejas Desai was born, raised and
where he works as a supervising libı.
He is a graduate of Wesleyan University and holds a MFA in Creative
Writing and Literary Translation from CUNY-Queens College. He is the
author of the international crime series *The Brotherhood Chronicle* and
The Human Tragedy literary series. In 2012, he founded The New Wei
literary movement which seeks to promote provocative and meaningful
narrative artists. His articles and interviews have been published in
HuffPost, *Buzzfeed*, *The London Post* and other publications.

Praise for *The Dance Towards Death*

"If you're looking for a new young writer with a long breath and the
ability to create teeth-clenching suspense, you can't do better than Tejas
Desai and his epic *The Brotherhood Chronicle*. The third long awaited
installment is now a reality, but you'll want to start at the start and binge
all three."—Vincent Zandri, *New York Times* bestselling Thriller Award
winning author of *The Remains* and *The Girl Who Wasn't There*

"Desai's trilogy is a thought-provoking narrative on loyalty, hope,
crime, justice, politics, religion, and family. He uses the lineaments
of fantasy and fiction to relate the truth about societal differences,
customs, and the universal experience of life. Desai has created with his
trilogy a literary rollercoaster ride that will have you savoring its thrills,
and breathtaking adventure. It is a terrific story, eloquently told. *The
Dance Towards Death* is an absorbing and incisive expose of affiliations,
roots, race, and attachments to causes, countries, people and family."—
Authors Reading

"At once timely and exciting, Tejas Desai's *The Brotherhood Chronicle*
is a must-read and will keep you guessing."—*Queens Courier*

"*The Dance Towards Death*, the third book of Tejas Desai's *The Brotherhood Chronicle*, continues to engage the reader with remarkably
rich settings, swift dialogue, and a complex gritty plot. We find the

protagonist Niral back in Thailand, surrounded by beautiful beaches and plenty of vice, and later we are engulfed in an elaborate Hindu compound in India. The New York City borough of Queens sees plenty of action too. This series definitely stands out in independent publishing."—Matthew Allison, Librarian and Writer

Praise for *The Brotherhood*

#1 Amazon Bestseller

Winner of the Pencraft Award (Fiction-General, 2019)

"I picked up this book and quickly finished it within a day because it was so exciting. The plot is very fast-paced, so you won't want to put it down if you can avoid it. I think the highlight of the book was the characters though. The author creates realistic characters that each have their pros and cons, which makes choosing a side difficult at times. I also enjoyed the love that went into the setting. I've never been to Queens, but I feel like the author described it in such a way that I could have been there at some point in my life. I'd highly recommend this book to anyone that loves gripping crime stories set in the past. I certainly look forward to seeing where this series takes its readers in the future."—Amazon Vine Voice Review

"Tejas Desai's novel *The Brotherhood* has mesmerized readers due to the thrills it offers with twists and turns you don't see coming... Desai takes readers to the edge and beyond, and will leave you wanting more."—*Buzzfeed*

"Brilliantly conceived characters populate this engrossing novel... reading this novel is both entertaining and pleasantly educational, offering insights into Hindu culture and religious elements. Highly recommended."—*San Francisco Review of Books*

"What a well-written, intriguing not to mention engrossing story. Each plot point pulls you along building tension and drawing you into the life and goals of the main character. Characters are fleshed out perfectly, layered and flawed with excellent detail that make you love or hate them instantly. Story paces well and sub-plots enhance not detract from the main plot. A great mystery with the promise of more like it to come as the series progresses."—*My Book Abyss*

"A legit page turner...a spellbinding thriller."—*NYK Daily*

"Desai is especially gifted when it comes to taking readers on a thrilling ride, one that keeps them guessing until the very last page. His characters come alive in a way that gives readers an insider's view into a world loaded with raw emotion, greed, religious hypocrisy, and treachery."—*The London Post*

"If you want a thrilling read that will have you wondering what is going to happen every step of the way, and leave you wanting more when it's over, then *The Brotherhood*, by bestselling author Tejas Desai, should be on your reading list this winter. But be warned there is an excellent chance you will be reaching for *The Run and Hide*, the second book in this series as soon as you are finished....Desai is well known for creating characters that are intense and so realistic that at certain points you may well feel like they are in the room with you."—*LA Post-Examiner*

"Tejas Desai's novel *The Brotherhood* offers readers a rather epic escape, so much so it recently hit the bestseller list on Amazon. Desai is a wunderkind when it comes to crafting compelling characters that take you down a rabbit hole of betrayal, greed and hypocrisy."—*California Herald*

"With Niral Solanke, a private investigator, [Desai] created a protagonist that is both compelling and complicated and a book that hits all the sweet spots, so it will have readers hanging on for dear life."—*The New York Journal*

"Everything and everyone and anything aren't what they seem, and even as you adjust your logic to keep up The Brotherhood keeps you guessing all the way...The best way to describe *The Brotherhood* is simply this: a Mickey Spillane novel with a Bombay (or is it Mumbai...bloody hell) flavour...set in New York City. Betrayal, religious hypocrisy, greed, and sexual nastiness...it is nice warm cuddly pulp fiction with a nice global marinade."—*The Evil Parrot Book Club*

"The author writes with the power and conviction of personal knowledge of [Hindu] culture and [New York] City...Edge of the seat tensions and thrills, twists and the unknown leave the reader trying to guess the motive for Priya's suicide, or was it murder? This mystery thriller leads the reader to an expansive literary universe of noir fiction and is the first of an international crime trilogy."—*Authors Reading*

Praise for *The Run and Hide*

"Tejas Desai delivers another spellbinding, chilling, and complex page-turner novel...Desai has created with powerful prose a story that is timely, fascinating and told with a variety of nuances that keep the reader thoroughly engaged. *The Run and Hide* book two of *The Brotherhood Chronicle* ignites with diversity, immoral dilemmas, and a riveting look at the customs and ways of other cultures. If you want a peek at the Asian criminal underworld, this is the book to read."—*Authors Reading*

"The depth of writing here is admirable, the characters are nuanced and fully fleshed out, and the descriptions of the underbelly of the world are uncanny and often mesmerizing. The plot itself is intricate, well formed, and showcases the characters, their morality, their emotions, and ultimately their humanity. Solid book and highly recommend."—Amazon Vine Voice Review

"Tejas Desai's sophomore installation builds upon the rich tapestry of character and setting he wove in *The Brotherhood* in masterful fashion...It is refreshing and pleasurable to see so many greatly written, unique, and believable characters that capture the diversity of the human spirit."—Goodreads Review

"*The Run and Hide* is quickly becoming a reader's favorite."—*The London Post*

"Masterful use of pacing and tension...The settings are incredibly lively and the characters are memorable...The best way to describe this story is like a game of Jenga or Russian Roulette, where the reader is constantly apprehensive of when the sky will actually fall. I would recommend this novel to anyone who appreciates a thriller or mysteries."—Amazon Review

"There is strong ability in creating wonderful and fully realized settings which he shows throughout this book...If the author has not visited these places yet has written so eloquently about them, he is truly remarkable...He shows no plot holes that I can see; and the goals of his MC are met nicely, egged on by action, mystery and suspense...This author is one to follow and I highly recommend his books. I am very excited to read the next book."—*My Book Abyss*

"Tejas Desai nailed the underworld grit of Queens in *The Brotherhood*. With book two of the trilogy, *The Run and the Hide*, the story of Indian-American Niral goes international in scope. From debt, he enters a crime world that takes him to Thailand and India. The well-crafted settings and swift dialogue take the reader on an unforgettable journey. There are dark themes, but it contains hope for redemption for Niral, his family, and the Hindu Brotherhood organization."—Matthew Allison, Librarian and Writer

"This book is truly enjoyable. You should read it to learn more about different cultures and countries. It's a ticket to fun and suspense!"—Kacper Jarecki, author of *The Depression of The Blue Rainbow Sprinkle*

Praise for *Good Americans*

"Stories speak volumes about the human condition and modern life in America...a solid collection of rare caliber."—*Kirkus Reviews*

"A great collection of stories...from the oh-so-very satirical title, to the prologue, to each and every story, this book stands out on all accounts...the stories leave an indelible impression on your mind that makes you want to come for more."—*Vault of Books*

"Solid storytelling...incredibly thought-provoking...A very provocative, grimy, hard-hitting collection."—*Readers' Favorite*

"*Good Americans* by Tejas Desai offers devastatingly passionate portraits of individuals who represent today's jaded citizenry of American society. It's a collection of stories about the great diversity that exist in America and how it affects the very fabric of our nation. With the world reeling from bloody conflicts driven by the unacceptance of divergent views, nationalities, religions or skin colors—Desai's book is a great study of how we must learn to accept and embrace diversity or live in a world of chaos."—*Authors Reading*

"While ostensibly about the undesirable elements of society, the underlying question asked of readers by this collection is, what is a Good American? Or more pertinently, what is a good person? It is this question of identity-personal, cultural, societal, national-asked by this collection that poses much food for thought."—*Booklover Book Reviews*

"This cutting edge short story collection by Tejas Desai gives every reader a very unconventional approach to the contemporary American world...great detailed research done and the way the stories are penned shows it all...use of the perfect ingredients at the perfect place."— *Vanya's Notebook*

"A society variety show told through stories...The stories are compelling and real. A looking glass into society...If you are looking for a unique book that inspires conversation and thought, this is for you."—Amazon Review

"I greatly enjoyed the depth of the book and frequently found myself sympathizing with many of the characters. Tejas Desai has a talent for creating characters that you will find yourself rooting for even though they may not necessarily be 'good people.' I felt that Desai's depictions of New York City and its inhabitants are very accurate. The novel, while full of interesting stories on the surface also carries under that serious questions about ethnic identity, stereotypes, and personal integrity. I would recommend this to any young adult who feels like their identity is under heavy assault by the expectations of others or sudden independence."—Amazon Review

"A multicultural mirror of stories. Characters from different walks of life intersect and intercede on many levels much like in the underground tunnels of the NYC subway system."—Amazon Review

Other Books Released by The New Wei

The Brotherhood Chronicle
The Brotherhood by Tejas Desai (2012)
The Brotherhood by Tejas Desai (Second Edition) (2018)
The Run and Hide (2019)

The Human Tragedy
Good Americans by Tejas Desai (2013)

Independent Books and Blogs Recommended by The New Wei

A Brie Grows in Brooklyn by Brienne Walsh
(online blog, http://abriegrowsinbrooklyn.com)
Waiting for the Bomb by Richard Livsey (2013)
The Other Son by Allan Avidano (2014)
The Depression of The Blue Rainbow Sprinkle by Kacper Jarecki (2014)
Escape from Samsara: Poems by Vijay R. Nathan (2016)
*Celebrity Sadhana: Or How to Meditate With a Hammer (The Paparazzo
    Poet Meditations)* by Vijay R. Nathan (2018)
Death in Shangri-La (A Dotan Naor Thriller, Book 1) by Yigal Zur
    (2018)
Passport to Death (A Dotan Naor Thriller, Book 2) by Yigal Zur (2019)
The Return of TAU (Fortress of Time Book 1) by Dan Dwyer (2020)
Bell Hammers: The True Folk Tale of Little Egypt by Lancelot Schaubert
    (October 2020)

THE DANCE TOWARDS DEATH

*

THE BROTHERHOOD CHRONICLE

VOLUME 3

*

TEJAS DESAI

ΠШ
THE ΠEШ WEI

New York

The Dance Towards Death by Tejas Desai

Published by The New Wei LLC
PO Box 650411
Fresh Meadows, New York, 11365
September 2020

Contact the author at his website: tejas-desai.com

ISBN-13 # 978-1-7347278-1-4

Library of Congress Control Number: 2020909293

Copyright © 2020 Tejas H. Desai

Cover Design by Fena Lee

TABLE OF CONTENTS

Book One
Part I – Bangkok, Thailand; Near Khon Kaen, Thailand; Kings
      Point, New York; Bayside, Flushing, St. Albans, Long
      Island City, Broad Channel (Queens), New York

Part II – Near Chiang Mai, Thailand; Bangkok, Thailand;
      Sands Point, New York; South Jamaica, St. Albans
      (Queens), New York; Near Apex, North Carolina

Part III – The Road Towards Phuket, Thailand; Phang-nga,
        Thailand; Udon Thani, Thailand; Hunters Point,
        South Jamaica, St. Albans, Long Island City, Broad
        Channel (Queens), New York; Khon Kaen, Thailand;
        Sands Point, New York; Near Krabi, Thailand

Part IV – Phang-Nga, Thailand; Near Krabi, Thailand; Udon
        Thani, Thailand; South Jamaica, Broad Channel,
        Long Island City, Astoria (Queens), New York; Surat
        Thani, Thailand; Kanchanaburi, Thailand; The Road,
        Thailand; Near Udon Thani and Nong Khai, Thailand;
        Sands Point, New York; Near Erawan National Park,
        Thailand

Book Two

Part V – Bushwick, Bay Ridge, Greenpoint (Brooklyn), New
York; Near Udon Thani, Thailand; Chiang Rai,
Thailand; Sunnyside (Queens), New York;
Near Chiang Mai, Thailand; Bangkok, Thailand

Part VI – Chiang Rai, Thailand; Near Udon Thani, Thailand;
Bushwick (Brooklyn), New York; Near Kanchanaburi,
Thailand; Bangkok, Thailand; Forest Hills,
Fresh Meadows (Queens), New York

Part VII – Tomkinsville (Staten Island), New York; Mumbai,
India; Surat, India; Outside Chiang Mai, Thailand;
Mae Hong Son Province, Thailand

Part VIII – Outside Udon Thani, Thailand; Surat, India; Long Island City, St. Albans, Flushing, Sunnyside, Forest Hills (Queens), New York; Mae Hong Son Province, Thailand; Yam Gam, India; Bushwick (Brooklyn), New York; Near Nong Khai, Thailand; Near Chiang Mai, Thailand

Book Three

Part IX – Yam Gam, India; The Road, Gujarat, India; Dwarka, India; Near Lamba, India; Mae Hong Son Province, Thailand; Nong Khai, Thailand; Outside Vientiane, Laos; Karen State, Myanmar; South Jamaica, Forest Hills, Sunnyside, Flushing, Long Island City, St. Albans (Queens), New York

"Performing the duty prescribed by one's own nature,
one incurreth no sin."

−Krishna to Arjuna, the *Bhagavad Gita*

"Long is the night to him who is awake; long is a mile to him who is
tired; long is life to the foolish who do not know the true law."

– Gautama Siddharta

ORIENTATION

The third volume of *The Brotherhood Chronicle* continues the turbulent story of former private investigator Niral Solanke and several survivors of a complex international criminal world. Niral is returning to Thailand from India, still indebted to the Dragons despite living with Bhai in Dwarka, participating in the violent events in Yam Gam and speaking with Manu about his daughter in Mumbai.

Duncan is preparing to go to Chiang Mai to be with his wife Lamai, but first needs to pick up Niral at the airport while avoiding Nam and the arrival of Dragon reinforcements from New York. Mr. Hong is increasingly paranoid about loose ends and an impending war with Sumantapat, but he prepares to go abroad while leaving the dirty work to Nam. Nat and Rob are in Isan searching for Apsara, while Pom, after taking Sumantapat's tip and following his own hunch, has walked into a trap in Bangkok.

In the New York City area, Vince Stevens has just outed Hemraj and Ashley's association with Ashok, leading Bob and Sveta to change their residence from Kings Point to Queens in order to ally with Lance and Carty. In India, Manu does Niral's work for him as The Brotherhood tries to assuage the caste divisions in Yam Gam. Bhai and Talim continue to plot for Shri Diwali, and Niral continues to balance his divided loyalties to all parties while figuring out how to get out of the complex situation in which he finds himself.

BOOK
ONE

PART I

†

Bangkok, Thailand; Near Khon Kaen, Thailand; Kings Point, New York; Bayside, Flushing, St. Albans, Long Island City, Broad Channel (Queens), New York

---

1

In the bathroom of the Bangkok airport, Niral took off his shirt, removed his janoi, balled it up, and stuffed it in his pocket. He stared at his scarred chest for a long time, half white and half red from the differing burn levels he had suffered. He remembered the actions in New York that led to getting burned and the aftermath that led to what he was now. The killing of Satish, the new orientation of Yam Gam under The Brotherhood organization, his new pact with Bhai and his alternative pact with Talim. The ultimate truth that he was still indebted to the Dragons despite all of his other entanglements. He laughed to himself about how a Dragon tattoo would have looked with the scar, especially on his back, where some skin had been grafted.

At the exit of the arrivals concourse, Niral was immediately accosted by Duncan.

"Come with me, man," Duncan said, his eye twitching. "We've got to be careful."

"Why? Is someone trying to kill me?"

"Something like that. Hurry up."

He shielded Niral's head with a newspaper. Wearing sunglasses and a hat, Duncan looked around frantically as they scurried along. Once they reached his sedan, Duncan shoved Niral inside the backseat, then pushed Niral's bags in too, forcing Niral to move to the far side.

"Don't we have a trunk?" Niral asked as Duncan closed the door. Niral noticed a crack in the window next to him. Duncan got into the front seat, threw the newspaper, sunglasses, and hat on the passenger seat, and began to drive.

"What happened? Is Sumantapat onto us?"

"Not exactly. But things have changed. We have to implement a new strategy."

"I was only gone for two weeks."

"Rob's out of the picture. So is Apsara. I'm out of the picture soon too. So it'll be you."

"What are you talking about?"

"I'm going up to Chiang Mai with Lamai. She'll have the baby within the next couple of months. It'll allow me to lay low and reboot our operations there. Remember, I said we'd move there one day, once you were free?"

"So you're paying off my debt?"

"Yes, once you pull off Bhai's assassination. Otherwise, we'll owe the old dealers."

"There are new dealers?"

"Kan put me in touch with someone who can get us an endless supply of drugs through Burma. But I've got to meet with him and set it up. Meanwhile, you'll handle operations here."

Niral shook his head. "Thanat, Talim, now some other guy? Isn't it enough?" he asked, referring to all the other figures Duncan had created business deals with in the past.

"Not if you want your freedom. You want to be Mr. Hong's slave forever?"

"If I'm down here, I am Mr. Hong's slave – or Nam's. And what happened to Rob and Apsara?"

"I'll explain later. We've gotta get to Same Same. But first I'll drop off the car at the warehouse. Then we'll ride over on my bike. Yours is missing, but I'll buy you another one."

Niral raised his hands to stretch, but they hit the roof of the car.

"Well, at least Mr. Hong's not trying to kill us," Niral said, shaking his hands.

"Mr. Hong just went abroad this morning. But we'll have to talk to Nam and whoever Mr. Chang brought over."

"Mr. Chang?" Niral asked, but Duncan didn't respond.

Duncan parked the car in the warehouse garage. They both got out. As Niral took out his bags, he noticed a red stain on the floor.

"What's that?" he asked, pointing at the blotch.

Duncan pushed dirt over it with his foot. "Nothing. Leave your bags in the car. We'll get you to Khao San later."

"Okay," Niral said, wondering if Rob was 'out of the picture' because he had been eliminated on that spot.

They locked up the garage and rode over to Sukhumvit. As they drove along, Niral realized he missed the smell of steaming noodles from the Bangkok street carts.

They parked near the Skytrain station. Niral looked for the day's disabled beggar and Indian men flirting with ladyboys, but he didn't see either. Instead, surrounding the entrance to the club were rows of Chinese and Korean men. They wore various hairstyles and dressed in dark suits.

"What's up?" Niral asked.

"Reinforcements," Duncan responded. "Things have gotten heavy. Remember, no mention of India, and let me talk. You're taking over, but you're not aware of details."

"Well, I'm not," Niral replied, shrugging.

As they approached the entrance, the men shifted to block it. Duncan spoke to them in Thai, but they did not comprehend. Suddenly, Nam emerged from the entrance. They shifted to let him pass and bowed.

"Such loyal soldiers," Nam said. "Nothing like in Bangkok. And they just got off a long flight!"

Duncan rolled his eyes. "Can you tell them that..."

Nam laughed. "Sure. They're okay," he said in English, waving. The men continued to stand aside. Duncan and Niral followed Nam up the stairs, Duncan first. As Niral entered the second floor, he saw Mok behind the bar. Without warning, he felt something cold and metallic

3

against his cheek, then he heard a gun cocking. He froze. He thought it was the end.

He heard a maniacal cackling. Instantly, he recognized it. He turned to see Ricky, his former friend from junior high school and Dragon associate who had saved his life in New York by pulling Vishal's knife out of his stomach, and had helped him, along with Wan Kim, find Roberto Tragliani's home. He was bald-headed, a little fatter now, and wore a wife-beater.

"Fucking herb," Ricky said, still holding the gun. "Can't believe you fell for it. Should've seen your face!"

Niral cleared his throat. "I see you haven't changed."

Ricky faked like he was firing, clicking with his tongue. Niral flinched but held his ground.

"You do look different, Niral," he said after another laugh. "More mature. Maybe?"

"You look the same. Can't believe they sent you."

"Man, the balls on this brother," Ricky said, dipping his gun into his waistband. "Disrespecting me after I saved his life. Your ass might have a future in this outfit after all."

"Where's Wan?"

"Brother Wan's a busy guy these days. He's working with Mr. Yoon. He's directly under Mr. Chang. You know, the Big Boss?"

"Isn't Wan on parole?"

"Sure, he goes to his PO once a month. Doesn't do the dirty work – hangs with the legit crowd when possible to keep up appearances so he can't get logged in as fraternizing with known criminals."

"He moved past you. You must be pissed."

Ricky shrugged. "Hey, I like grinding in the muck. Getting my hands dirty."

"Sure. No jealousy."

"Wan's my brother, brother. You might be too, with the right attitude."

"Still sending money to the cabby's widow?" Niral asked.

"Whole story behind that. We'll catch up later."

"Niral, where have you been? I am glad you have met your old friend,"

Mr. Hong said, emerging from the back room. "He told me he knows you from high school."

"Yes, we go way back," Niral replied. "Junior high, actually."

Duncan stared at Mr. Hong like he was seeing a ghost. His eye didn't twitch as it often did. Mr. Hong smiled.

"I don't know if Duncan told you, but we have new developments. We need to be extra careful, which is why we have brought in more people and why I canceled my trip abroad. Come inside, we will tell you what we would like to accomplish."

2

Nat stood on the porch with the other officers until Khon Kaen detective Chak emerged.

"Grandmother confirms the description," he said. "Looks like the same farang did this job."

"And the boy?"

The detective shook his head. "Dead. Blood and body parts all over the room. The grandmother is shaking. It's almost unspeakable."

Nat choked up and began to cry.

"What's wrong, detective?" Chak asked. "I don't want to speak out of turn, but I'm sure there are gruesome murders in Bangkok, too."

Nat shook his head as he wiped his tears with a handkerchief.

"Those murders didn't happen to my son," he said.

"Your son?" Chak asked, amazed.

"Yes. I had him out of wedlock. I abandoned his mother. That was many years ago. What a coincidence. Do you believe in karma, detective?"

Chak nodded. "I believe in Buddha. Reincarnation."

"This is my penance. I sinned long ago. I've never visited him. I never took upon myself the duties of a father. Instead, I lost myself in my profession. Now, I will never know him. Except perhaps in another life."

"I understand. What a terrible blow. Not just to your heart but to your conscience. Listen, why don't you go back to Khon Kaen and rest? We will take care of the investigation."

Nat shook his head. "I've come too far. I must find this farang."

"He is very dangerous. We will release the sketch you made to the media. And we are having the grandmother make one, too. It can't be that hard to find a tall farang in Isan."

"If he stays in Isan. What if he runs for Laos?"

"We have patrols along the roads heading up to Nong Khai and other cities, though he can still get through local roads or trails."

"Do what you can. May I speak to his grandmother? I know her from many years ago."

"The sketch artist will soon be done with her, so yes, you can go in. Don't worry – everything has already been photographed and the body parts removed and placed under one cloth, which we will soon move to the medical examiner's office. But there is still blood everywhere. The grandmother may be in shock. I warn you."

Nat nodded. He donned gloves and entered the room. Through his one good eye, he saw blood on the floor, the walls, and the bedsheets. He almost threw up but put his hand over his mouth and, controlling it, swallowed the vomit. The acid stung his esophagus.

A mound was in the corner of the room. He approached the bed. The grandmother lay there, sitting against the bedpost, answering questions from the sketch artist.

She looked up at him.

"Do you remember me, Khun Yai?" Nat asked.

Her face contorted. She began breathing heavily and put her hand on the sketch artist's arm.

"Oh my. Is this a nightmare?" she asked.

Nat knelt before her and greeted her with a wai. The sketch artist got up, excused himself, and left the room.

"I am sorry, Khun Yai, for abandoning your daughter."

The grandmother began laughing. "My daughter is having fun in Sweden with her farang husband. She wasn't any more loyal than you."

"So you raised him alone? I am sorry," Nat said.

"I wonder if I am dreaming. Are you truly Natthew?"

"Yes, Khun Yai."

"You never called me Khun Yai back then."

"I decided to rename you after I fled. Even if I was not a part..."

"Your parents are dead, Natthew. Do you know?"

"That's not possible. Piti didn't tell me," he said, referring to the go-go dancer from his village who had helped him on his search for Apsara in Khon Kaen.

"That whore who slept in the same bed with her pervert father, Dang, not wearing a shirt even after she had breasts? She was only a girl when you left."

"Yes, but I would write to her on the internet."

"Figures. You perverts are all the same."

"How did my parents die?"

"I don't know. They moved out of the village. Piti didn't tell you?"

"She never mentioned they moved out."

"Of course not. Now she lives in Khon Kaen with Dang. How would she know? Yes, your parents won the lottery and bought some land in the next village. I only know because old man Prasong has land in that village too and visits sometimes. He told me they died a few months ago, but not how."

Nat stared at the floor, shocked. "How could they both die? And nobody told me?"

"Maybe they didn't know there was anybody to tell. You can find Prasong and ask him."

Nat closed his good eye. He tried to process this news.

"What happened to your eye?" the grandmother asked, pointing to his patch. "Did you lose it?"

Nat opened his good eye again. "First, my son, now my parents. Who will I lose next?"

"Is Som dead?" the grandmother asked. "Oh God. I haven't seen him."

Nat pointed. "He is in the corner. All in pieces. Don't look."

"That is his friend, Wat. Another pervert with his whore Boonsri. The farang took Som out, saying he would throw him off the porch. But he didn't. He came inside, holding Som by the neck, and took Boonsri, too. He laughed in my face, said I was a good woman. I wanted to strangle him, but I stayed silent to protect Som. Then the door closed, and they were gone. I wanted to head to the door, but I had no energy.

Finally, Prasong came by in the morning and called the police."

"So Som is not dead?"

"I hope not. You have not found him?"

Nat smiled and rose. "No other boys so far. Let me tell the detective. My son might be alive!"

3

Bob and Sveta took a cab to Bayside, where they got out on the corner of Northern and Bell Boulevard.

"This is nice neighborhood," Sveta said, looking around.

"Yes, but this isn't where we're staying, darling," Bob responded. He heard a honk from the gas station behind him. A beat-up Hyundai Accent pulled up.

"Get in, brother," Lance said. "See you got Heidi with ya. Good looking out."

Sveta gave Bob an anxious glance.

"Who is this?" she asked. "Uber?"

"I be Uber for you, baby. I give you a ride any day now."

"Don't worry about him," Bob said. "He is a friend. Let's put our bags into the trunk and get in."

Lance opened the trunk with a latch, and Bob put the bags in. Sveta could feel Lance watching her legs from the rearview mirror.

Bob got in the front seat, and Sveta crawled into the back.

"Where are we going, husband?" she asked.

"Secure spot, baby," Lance said, pulling off. "No one'll find you there."

"We need to be careful, darling," Bob explained. "Until this deal goes through."

"Hope you avoided the cameras, Bob," Lance said. "Otherwise we got complications."

"We got out in time. Hemraj, too. Back on his way down south."

"Reformulating that plan. I like the way that archrival thinks."

"Not for long, I hope. I'll find out what he's planning, and we can beat him to the punch."

He heard Sveta dial something on her phone. He turned around.

"Who are you calling?" he asked furiously.

Sveta glanced away. "No one. Just Rob."

"Give me the phone," Bob said, holding out his hand. "I don't want you calling him."

"Why not?"

"Darling," he said, trying to make his tone sweet again. "We can't trust anyone right now."

"Not even Rob?"

"Not even Rob. Will you hand me the phone?"

She put it back in her pocket. "I'll keep it. Don't you trust me?" she asked, crossing her arms.

He rolled his eyes and turned back towards the front.

"Women," Lance said, shaking his head.

4

"This is the situation, Niral," Mr. Hong said, finishing his explanation at the back table. "Duncan is going up to Chiang Mai so you will have to buy, drop off, negotiate, and sell the merchandise yourself. I will have him increase your salary so you can pay your debt more quickly. Meanwhile, I have another assignment for you."

"Yes?"

"Go with Nam to Apsara's place. Talk to her roommate. Figure out where she is. We need to find her and Rob. They are liabilities and must be eliminated."

"Why do you need me?" Niral asked, hiding his relief that Rob and Apsara appeared to be alive.

"Her roommate will trust you and allow entry without force. But we may have to use force to get what we want."

Niral swallowed.

"You don't feel attached to these people, do you?" Mr. Hong asked. "They are our enemies now."

Ricky approached. "That guy Mok says you should watch the TV. Looks like Rob's being hunted in Isan."

They got up and proceeded to the bar outside, where Mok was

watching the news on TV. It showed a short interview with a detective, a shot of a home near Khon Kaen, and a draped mound of what was probably body parts being carted off. The announcer explained the horrific murder and that the alleged perpetrator was being sought for other crimes. Then, the sketch of Rob's face came up.

"Damn it!" Mr. Hong screamed. "Nam, move now."

"I'll go too," Ricky said, bowing to Mr. Hong. "Our men will protect you here. I wanna get involved."

"Sure," Mr. Hong said. "The more, the better."

Duncan approached Niral and handed him a smartphone.

"It's yours," Duncan said. "I'll call you later. Keep the Indian phone for now."

5

Nat circled a bush near Prasong's home, smoking a cigarette and wondering how to search for a son he never cared for until now. He never imagined these two halves of his life would intertwine. And now, considering the news of his parents' deaths, he decided to visit Prasong and inquire about both.

Prasong still lived in the same hut he had lived in for years. It was on stilts and much bigger than Khun Yai's or his parents'. He had been known as the village elder, even when Nat was young.

Nat passed cement storage jars which usually contained drinking water, removed his shoes, and climbed up the wood stairs to where he saw a man sitting on a mat in low lamplight, eating rice wrapped in a banana leaf. As the man noticed him against the dusk, he seemed scared. But he spoke calmly in the Isan language.

"Are you the police?" he asked. "Have you come about the murder?"

"Yes," Nat responded. "I am the police. But I am also Natthew. Home at last."

The man took the lamp and held it up towards Nat.

"Why do you wear an eye patch? Have you become a Muay Thai boxer?"

Nat entered the room. "No. I am a detective in Bangkok. Homicide."

"In Bangkok? Yet your family brings you back."

"My son is not dead. I expect to find him."

"Som is a tough cookie. Too bad you never knew him. You disgraced your family and ran away. And you were a son, the only child. How do you think your parents felt?"

"You told Khun Yai they died. Is this true?"

"First, your uncles and aunts moved down south to live with the Dai people. Then a tall farang arrived and took your girl to Sweden. Everyone was happy and thought she would send for her son and parents, that the family would immigrate, but she never did. She disappeared too. Maybe she did not want the drain of the Isan family, everyone from third cousins on demanding more and more. Even I call up my grandniece in Bangkok when I need some extra money. It is the way."

"That's why I wanted to avoid this life."

"You escaped your responsibility. How can a good Thai lead his life that way? You had a child. You had parents. If you moved away for work, fine, but you should have contributed. Instead, Som grew up with an ailing grandmother who couldn't work. If not for his uncle and aunt sending money from his mother's farm and turning up once and a while to check on him, he would have starved. At least the bitch did not take that."

Nat sat down on the hard floor, his feet behind him out of respect. "My parents. How did they..."

"Committed suicide together. They drank poison."

Nat looked up. "Suicide? Why?"

"According to the note, it's because your mother found out she had cancer, and they didn't want to go through procedures. Who can afford it? They wanted to die together, alone, in peace. The complications of maintaining their new land was trouble anyway. Why put up with the hassle? So they went out."

"Do you think if I had been here...?"

"How do I know? Now things are past us. Try to find your son and make it up to him if you can."

Nat nodded. "I will do my best. This farang is a personal demon. He is the very reason for my existence now. He is—"

"I would think your son would be. In the past, a man like you would have been shunned by the village, maybe even punished. But now it is commonplace. At least you are not a woman."

Nat stood. "Yes. My son. I will make him my light. If I find him, I will raise him right, into a just man."

Prasong laughed. "I am glad you have changed your mind, for now. Look, visit his uncle and aunt before you leave on your crusade. At least have that decency."

6

Bob and Sveta entered Lance's home, Bob carrying his bag and Lance Sveta's bag.

"My momma bought this home in 1973 when there wasn't a black man around. Now it's reeling with brothers. Too many."

"This is where we stay, husband?" Sveta asked.

"It's homey, sugar," Lance said, stacking the bags in the living room corner. "There's even a basement where you can hide out if someone starts popping. By the way, Bob, our boy Niral never gave me back my 9mm. I got a new one, though. And plenty more downstairs."

"Someone will shoot at us?" Sveta asked.

"Don't worry, darling," Bob said, giving Lance a nasty look. "Don't take him seriously."

Lance rolled his eyes. "Look, my daughter Shoquanda's in NC. I sent her down so she'd stop hanging with the animals. So now one room upstairs is empty. Ya'll can stay up there, but we gotta get a cot, cuz the bed's small and only fits one. Or you can both stay on the couch down here."

"Do you have cot?" Sveta asked, folding her arms.

"Sure, but I gotta get it from downstairs, sugar."

"Go upstairs and make yourself at home, Sveta," Bob said. "I'll get the cot. We will be right up."

"First room on the left, baby," Lance said. "Feel free to rummage, but don't touch Shoquanda's dolls or her pics now. She likes 'em like that."

"Okay," she said, shrugging, then slouched up the stairs.

Lance stared at her ass, then went around to an alcove by the living room and opened the door. He pulled a string to turn on a dim yellow bulb and descended. At the bottom, he flipped a switch, and a bright white light illuminated the room. It was filled with brown cardboard and wooden boxes.

Bob closed the door behind him as he carefully descended the creaking wooden steps.

"What is wrong with you, talking to her like that?" Bob asked.

"Like what, brother? I'm just being me."

"Well, be more professional. She doesn't know anything about the plan yet."

"Why not? She involved."

"I'll ease her into it. Meanwhile, remember she's my wife."

"Or what, my brother? What you got in your repertoire to be making threats?"

Bob swallowed. "I'm just saying we're in it together."

"You damn right we are. But you remember this: you in my crib now. I'm CEO in these parts. You're not even CFO. You're Executive Assistant, brother. So you best act like that. Now, I ain't taking my right of first night or nothing—that's some medieval shit. I'm just complimenting a fine piece. Nothing wrong with that."

Bob rolled his eyes. "Whatever. I'll call Vishal and figure out what they're planning."

"Hold off on that til we check the news. Maybe Lauren Conrad step down. Then I talk to Mr. Carty and tell him Hemraj went down south. That could inform Carty and Vishal's thinking both."

"Fine. So where's the cot?"

"Peace, my brother. It's behind these boxes. My old Marines cot. Got it shipped from Saudi Arabia. Just kidding. But it's a replica. You ever in the Marines?"

"The Air Force, actually."

"'Nam?"

"That's right. Gulf War?"

"First one. Long time back. Saw people burned to a crisp, guys with their heads blown off. War ain't good for nobody, but you gotta follow orders, right? Semper fi and all that crap."

"Yes. All that crap."

"We might get along better than you think," Lance said, holding out his fist.

7

Niral and Ricky got into the back seat of Nam's car and drove towards Klong Tuey.

"Is it far?" Ricky asked.

"No, we just take a right on Soi 22 and go down," Nam replied.

"I didn't know you had a car, Nam," Niral said.

"You learn something every day," Ricky replied.

Niral turned to him. "Since when are you guys buddies?"

"I never met Nam til today. But we've talked on Skype."

Nam turned onto Soi 22 and then immediately onto a side street, stopping his car at a dead end. Ricky took out his gun and pointed it at Niral.

"What the—"

"Don't worry, Niral," Ricky said. "Just listen."

Nam turned and looked over his shoulder at Niral, smiling.

"We know you're selling ya ba," Ricky said. "We want in. We've got orders from Mr. Chang, so don't think it's just us."

"Then why are you—"

"Mr. Hong doesn't know. You know his deal with not dealing drugs here, just sticking to the safe rackets to keep from making waves. The bosses in China and Korea think he's a pussy too. He won't last long. We've been wanting in on this trade for a while. If Hong won't deliver, you can."

"We've hardly got a big network," Niral explained. "And our product is limited and contingent—"

"You've got the highest quality shit on the market, far as we know. You can charge higher prices now that you're set up. And with Duncan out of the picture, you've got it all to yourself. Look, we could've just followed you, found the shit, stolen it, and whacked your ass. We wanna work with you."

"Because you wouldn't know how to get it, distribute it..."

"But you do. We hope so anyway. Look, all we're asking for is tribute. You're a Dragon, tattoo or not. A good 10 percent to start. More later when you grow."

"Duncan will think I'm skimming. We're not making such amazing profits that he wouldn't know."

"We're wary of him because he's Hong's man. He might have to go, too. But you're our man. You'll deliver, right?"

Ricky pushed the gun against Niral's cheek.

"Do I have a choice?" Niral asked. "I'll try my best."

"All we ask. Now, let's go bust some ladyboy head," Ricky said, putting his gun away.

"You ever see a ladyboy before?" Nam asked Ricky, speeding down the alley in reverse.

"No, but I'm looking forward to it. You ever fuck a ladyboy, Niral?"

"He *was* a ladyboy," Nam said. "This guy was gay. This Apsara chick said she fucked and reformed him. But I don't believe it. Maybe you're still sucking cock, Niral."

"Didn't think you were that much of a herb, Niral," Ricky said. "Can't wait to tell Wan you turned queer."

"This place does that to you," Niral said. "But I'm straight now."

"Better be, brother," Ricky said, waving his finger at Niral. "Better be."

8

"Som was a troubled boy. What would you expect when both his parents abandoned him?" Som's uncle said as he spoke to Nat in his kitchen. He was eating larb with pork, blood, and offal. His wife placed some more sticky rice on his plate. Meanwhile, Nat dined on Som Tum.

"I'm sorry, Udom," Nat said. "I was young, stupid, and irresponsible."

"Yes, but now you are responsible. A police officer in Bangkok. While we continue to slave away on the farms. Yes, you are responsible now."

"I want to find Som."

"If this farang chopped up Wattana, why do you think Som is alive?"

"I am hoping. The police are doing their best."

"What will you do?" Udom asked, pointing his fork at Nat.

"Find him. That's why I want to know what places he knows of. What if he ran away from this farang? Would he go to another village, a city? Could he convince this farang—?"

"Som lived with his grandmother. She couldn't walk half the time, let alone work. We would drop off food three times a week from the farm. He even cooked for her sometimes, on burning wood behind his home. He went to school, but he understood you need money in this life. So I've heard about him and Wattana and this Boonsri."

"You knew?"

"I didn't have time to care. If Boonsri's father found out, he would have killed Som and Wattana, not because he didn't want his daughter pinched, but because they didn't share the earnings with him."

"Udom," his wife said. "Do not talk that way."

"It's true. You know it's true, Nat. What they say about Piti and her father is also true. What is the point of going to Bangkok when you can do it here? And did that Swedish farang who married my sister pay tribute to our family? Sure, he paid for food and beers the first few days, but then he disappeared with her, and like you, they didn't even send money back. Absurd. Meanwhile, we have stupidly stayed here and endured on the farmland. We treated Som like a son. Now he is gone too."

"Where else did he make money?"

"What do you mean? He was a boy. I think you should find out more about this farang if you hope to find him."

"Did he have any other friends?"

"Ask at the schoolhouse tomorrow."

"Did he ever go to Khon Kaen? Udon Thani? Nong Khai?"

"You might as well ask about every city in Isan. I think he's been to Khon Kaen. He took a couple of trips up to Udon Thani with Wattana, I think. I wouldn't be surprised if Boonsri went too."

16

9

"After careful consideration, I think it is prudent to resign from the Council on the Future of Long Island City," Ashley Simmons said, speaking into a TV reporter's microphone at the entrance of her home in King's Point. "I want to emphasize that I did nothing wrong and merely followed my heart. I've known Hemraj Patel for many years. Perhaps I should have recused myself when his company decided to bid for the contract, but since we are not married, I did not think this was necessary. Our personal relationship would not have affected my vote for the good of Long Island City. Nevertheless, even the appearance of impropriety can be damaging to an organization. I am on many other boards and foundations, and I do not want to negatively impact them either. Therefore, I am leaving the CFLIC, not because of wrongdoing, but because I think it is in the best interest of all involved."

The report switched to Vince Stevens, the city councilman who represented an area that included the Long Island City Project, who was being interviewed at his office in Long Island City.

"While I do think something fishy was going on, I'm glad she did the right thing so we can all move on," he said. "I hope another member will be appointed who is as impartial and will think only about the interests of the people of Long Island City, as I do."

Alicia Tragliani clapped her hands with slow, bold snaps. Uncle Jerry, her father's brother and top advisor, laughed. They were sitting in the living room of her modest home in Broad Channel, watching TV.

"They know how to talk, don't they?" he said. "That's why they're not living down here in Broad Channel."

"They're in the thick of things, stuck between the City Council and the Queens Borough president," Alicia said. "But we're free."

"If we can get the contract."

"Brendan Carty's the only other major bidder. He retook Ledacorp and was Vishal's boss once. They should disqualify him too. Have our man call the Daily News."

"He's not implicated in Vishal's schemes, though. Or in your father's."

"The media can twist anything and make it big. Look what they did to us."

"Our people were on trial. Which brings me to my second point, Alicia. This could backfire. They could trudge that up again. They could find out about our interest in DeKalb Construction."

Alicia turned off the TV and eyed a picture of her father, Roberto, and herself on top of a drawer adjacent to the TV. The photo had been taken on her wedding day, the day before he was shot right in front of her while eating dinner at their home in Maspeth, a bullet zipping through the window of their dining room. Juan Garcia, the triggerman and Vishal Patel's chauffeur, had been hunted down and killed, but it wasn't clear if he had received an order from Vishal Patel or had acted on his own. Her marriage had failed in the turmoil that followed her father's death, and many of her relatives along with associated Lucchese soldiers had been imprisoned for a variety of crimes related to the Coleman Investments scheme for Long Island City, aided by the testimony of Bob Macaday. She kept the picture not only to remind her of her father's murder, but also everything she had lost as a result.

She stood up. She was a big girl with strong haunches. She wore a white dress covered with rose petals.

"So what's your plan, Uncle Jerry?"

"Keep trying to influence the CFLIC and the Community Board. I told you; the Queens Borough president is on our side. She wants the housing developments, which will allow us to pinch construction money and squeeze prostitution and gambling inside. But we need approval of the CFLIC first. So they need to appoint a new voting member who's on our side and can influence the others."

"Several members must have been bought by Hemraj Patel, not just this blond," Alicia noted.

"Yes, but with the press going crazy about him being Vishal's cousin, they're buyable again."

"How are we going to influence who gets appointed?"

"Unlike the local Community Board, where we do have substantial influence with half the members appointed by the Queensboro president, the appointments on the CFLIC are handled internally, by the members themselves. So if we could influence the right members, they could appoint someone who could swing things in our favor."

"Which is the opposite of what you said before. Seems like an uphill climb."

"So we'll climb, Alicia. Do you think your father would have given up?"

Alicia walked over to the drawer, picked up the picture frame, and then put it down again.

"My father was naïve. He trusted Vishal Patel. He saw an Indian hedge fund manager and thought we could use him. He didn't realize the man was sick, manipulative, and evil."

She opened the drawer, removed a gun, and rubbed it with her hands.

"Vishal Patel is dead too," Uncle Jerry noted.

"Yeah? Well, who gave the order to kill my father? Juan Garcia didn't think it up himself. He couldn't have been that loyal."

She lifted the gun and looked at it.

"This is the gun that supposedly killed Vishal. So Niral Solanke told him. That's what his bodyguards told me. But what if he's still alive? What if he's behind this cousin of his?"

"We can send somebody down to Carolina to investigate. Or we can send someone to talk to Niral in Thailand. But that might trigger a war with the Dragons here, since he's under their protection. And we're short-handed, Alicia. We're vulnerable. We can't risk a war, not out in the open. You know everything today is underneath, couched within legitimate transactions."

"So we just forget the bastard that murdered my father, ruined my marriage, sent our relatives and friends to prison, stole our money, and decimated our city? Is that what you mean?"

"I simply counsel brains over brawn. What I've always counseled. If he's alive, I want Vishal's head too. And certainly the money he stole."

"We couldn't find Bob Macaday. We've searched for years."

"We had no idea where Bob ended up, and we couldn't take on the US Marshals. Here, we know there's a lead in Carolina. If nothing else, maybe we'll stumble upon a new market. NYC is no good for organized crime anyway. Hasn't been for decades."

"It's still home, though. Even Broad Channel," she said, putting the gun back in the drawer. "Fine, send a man down to Carolina. See what you can dig up."

10

"Carty says with Ashley out and Hemraj exposed, it should open the pathway," Lance told Bob. "Vince Stevens can work the local membership to get another sympathizer on the CFLIC. No way they'll give it to Hemraj's company now. And with the artistic restoration being the preferred development of the City Council and the protesters, Carty's company should get the support of Hemraj's former supporters on the CFLIC. Alicia's company only wants a housing development, not a mixture. So with the two votes still in our pocket, we'll win. At least the rec from the CFLIC anyway."

"You sure a dark horse won't come up and bite us?"

"Not likely."

"So what do I tell Vishal?"

"Show shock, brother. Say: 'What do we do?' That kind of thing. And see what he reveals."

"All right."

Bob called up Vishal. He picked up right away.

"I've been waiting for your call," Vishal said.

"You could've called me. You gave me this cell phone."

"I wanted to see how long you would take."

"So what's the plan now?" Bob asked.

"I had a Plan B."

"What's Plan B?"

"We'll get another contender with no connection to me."

"You don't expect me to create a construction company, do you?"

Vishal laughed. "No, Bob. Don't worry, when the time comes, I'll tell Sveta how to vote. Meanwhile, I'll have to work via other avenues."

"What avenues?"

"You'll see, Bob. You'll see very soon."

11

Nam had a wire around Buppha's neck while Ricky rummaged in Apsara's room next door. Buppha was making choking sounds, and blood was leaking out of her neck.

Meanwhile, Niral sat uncomfortably on a chair, watching Nam torture the ladyboy.

"Bitch, you're gonna tell me where Apsara went, or I'm going rip your neck out," Nam told her in Thai, releasing the wire and pushing her forward. She crumbled onto her hands and knees, holding her neck and breathing deeply.

Ricky came out of the room. "Niral, help me look. There are a million hiding spots in here."

Niral stood and approached Buppha instead.

"What are you doing, Niral?" Nam asked.

He knelt down, took Buppha by the hair, and lifted her head up.

"You know where Apsara is?" he asked. "Tell us now."

She shook her head vigorously.

"You understand you're going to die if you don't tell us?"

Buppha nodded.

"Did she ever mention a village in Isan?"

"She never tell me where," she said between coughs. "Just Isan."

"She's lying," Nam said. "Let me at her."

"You sure she didn't?" Niral asked again.

"Yes. Yes. Please. You know Apsara never tell anyone anything."

Niral released her head and stood. "She's right. She didn't. I don't think she knows anything."

"Are you psychic?" Nam asked.

"We're wasting our time," Niral responded. "Torturing her won't get us anywhere."

"I found something," Ricky said, coming out of Apsara's room. He handed two slips of paper to Nam.

"They're in Thai, I think," he said.

"Yes, one is a bus ticket to Udon Thani from a few months ago,"

Nam said. "And the other is a wire transfer from a month ago to a bank account in Udon Thani. It's for 100,000 baht to a person named Prem Pramangchun."

Buppha suddenly gasped, and her head rose. Niral knelt by her.

"Do you remember something?" he asked.

Buppha nodded. "That is name she called him."

"What name?"

"The Thai man. She call him Pornopat too. That detective ask. I couldn't remember the name."

Niral appeared surprised. "She called Pornopat, or Thanat, Prem? He was here?"

Buppha nodded. "Many times."

"What detective came by?"

"He said his name was Pom. He asked me about Apsara's boyfriends."

"And you told him about Duncan and Rob?"

Buppha nodded, coughing.

"How about me?"

She shook her head. "No, only them."

"She's talked to the cops," Nam said. "I knew we should have gotten rid of her."

He took a knife from his pocket. Niral stood up.

"No," he said. "We need her alive. In case this cop asks her again. She could lead him astray."

"She could squeal on us, too. She's probably already made a deal with him. Get out of jail free."

"If you kill her, we'll have to clean up the mess," Niral reminded Nam. "If he finds her dead, this could get worse for us."

"She's got the mark on her neck. He'll ask about that."

"So she'll lead him astray. Maybe to Sumantapat."

Nam put the knife back. "You already fucked up by letting that tourist, Bob, live," he said, pointing at Niral. "If she talks, your head's on the pike."

"You're soft," Ricky said to Niral, walking to the door.

Niral bent down. "Remember Buppha, if that detective comes back, say a client strangled you and make up a description. Say he asked about

Apsara and mentioned Sumantapat, but you didn't know anything. Don't say anything more about Duncan or Rob, and don't mention Prem either. You got it?"

Buppha nodded.

"Okay, go rest now. I'll be back another time," Niral said.

"Soft," Ricky commented, shaking his head.

12

Back at the police station in Khon Kaen, Nat called Pom's cell phone. When he didn't pick up, he called the station and spoke to Chan.

"Pom hasn't showed up today," Chan said. "Probably working hard on a case. Or dozing off after last night's hangover."

"More likely driving his kids to school," Nat said. "Did he get the DNA I sent? Or the passport fax?"

"You'll have to ask him. You wanna talk to General Toon?"

"No, that's okay."

"You sure? You should probably update him on your case. Seems like a lot's been going on."

"Yes, but I'm no closer to finding this girl Apsara, or whatever her name is. I can recount incidents, but I don't know yet how they add up. Anyway, I want to talk to Pom first."

"Okay, your call."

"Another question, Chan. Have they released Robert Murphy's picture down in Phuket?"

"I don't know. I hear a manhunt's going on in Isan, though."

"Look, I'll call back later. Tell Pom to call me if you see him."

13

Wan took the elevator up to the sixteenth floor of the municipal office building in downtown Flushing, New York. As the doors opened, he bowed to Mr. Yoon, then followed him towards the glass office doors. Mr. Yoon nodded at the young Korean secretary, who picked up the phone and dialed. Wan smiled and winked at her.

As the doors slid open, they saw Mr. Chang putting a golf ball towards a hole. He had a mini-golf unit in his office near his desk, with the backdrop of Queens and the Freedom Tower of Manhattan in the distance.

"You called, Big Boss?" Mr. Yoon asked as they both bowed deeply.

"Yes, yes. Please, sit down. Would you like something to drink?"

Both declined. They sat on a soft, black leather couch.

Mr. Chang picked up a glass of Sazerac and drank it down. He sat on the edge of his desk, still holding the golf club in his right hand.

"I hear Ricky and his friends are enjoying themselves in the Land of Smiles. Is this true?"

"I have not heard from him, Big Boss," Wan said. "I've heard good things about Thailand. I wish I could go myself."

"Do you want to go back to prison, Wan? I need you here. You are my best man."

Wan looked at Mr. Yoon. "You flatter me, sir."

"I don't mean that Mr. Yoon is not solid, but I think it's time I gave you a new assignment. Extortion from Chinese and Korean spas in Flushing is decent money, and running the money laundering schemes through Korean businesses is better, but there are certain tasks that are bigger and require more sophisticated methods. Do you know anything about the construction business?"

Wan shook his head. "I wish I did."

"Well, let me tell you something about construction. The mafia has run this racket for years, but after the prosecution of the Tragliani's construction company, the Lucchese has a lighter footprint. Still, they've got interests. I'm looking to go into the same business, and I need a man to oversee it. For years, the mob has made money controlling the unions who worked for a construction companies, slowing down work unless the company paid a tribute. Or they might demand hiring a larger number of men than the company needed, getting the payments, and then distributing less to the workers; or having workers not show up or even making them up on paper. They also have interests in the raw materials and employ similar shenanigans. Sometimes they run the companies themselves and drive up the prices. Or they do all of the above. And when they've bought off the people awarding the contracts, that's the ultimate steal."

Wan nodded. "So you want me to control a union? Or a company? Or both?"

Mr. Chang smirked. "I've had control over Ozone Construction and a union for a few years. Where the Traglianis left off, we stepped in. And even better, now we have influence over a board in Queens that will hand out a contract to a new project they are pushing. So if everything goes as planned, we'll get the contract, and we can start construction. In terms of area, this is the largest single project we'll oversee."

He pointed to a map of Queens that stood on a stool next to his desk.

"See, we already have projects in Flushing and Elmhurst. This will expand our reach to Long Island City, and it might even lead to projects in Sunnyside. Sure, the Lucchese still have interests in Brooklyn, southern Queens, and some parts of northeast Queens, but our reach is expanding."

"This is a great honor, Big Boss," Wan said, bowing while he was seated. "I—"

"You haven't heard yet what I want you to do. We have paid professionals running the construction company and the union. But I need a man to lean on them, to make sure tributes are paid and work is slowed when necessary. You'll also have to clean up any messes, including incursions by competing factions. Word is that Alicia Tragliani's construction company is one of the bids for the contract. She doesn't own the company, but her men lean on it. She wants this project badly so she can get back at Vishal Patel, who murdered her father. It isn't just about money for her, so she will try anything to get it. But our pockets will be dry if we don't get it, so it's even more important to us. Mr. Yoon has been overseeing the project for me, but I want to give you greater responsibility. Will you do what it takes to secure this bid and navigate any trouble spots?"

"Of course, Big Boss." Wan stood suddenly, then awkwardly stumbled to his knees, bowing.

Mr. Chang smiled and drank his Sazerac.

14

At Same Same, Nam, Ricky, and Niral met with Mr. Hong at the back table. Ricky smoked a cigarette while Mr. Hong drank Johnnie Walker.

"You let another witness live, Niral," Mr. Hong said. "Should we kill you now?"

"I'm the legitimate man now, remember?" Niral replied. "Your men let her live."

Nam smacked him in the head.

"How dare you talk to Big Boss that way?" he screamed.

"No need for theatrics, Nam," Mr. Hong said, smiling. "You are right, Niral. It was their job."

For the first time since Niral met him, Nam appeared to be afraid.

"Look," Niral said, "killing Buppha eliminates any chance of getting information from her in the future. If anything, we should use her. Sumantapat has an inside connection with the cops. If she has an inside connection with a detective, we can use that to our advantage. Isn't sinking Sumantapat the ultimate goal?"

Mr. Hong leaned back. "My ultimate goal, Niral, is to not get into trouble, and we have our own sources in the Royal Thai Police. But I agree, another will not hurt because Sumantapat has more contacts. I will let you work on this Buppha, but she's your responsibility. Now, back to the immediate problem of Apsara. Do you think this Prem is Thanat?"

"Why would Apsara send him money last month?" Nam asked. "Unless Niral didn't kill him."

"I saw the head," Mr. Hong said.

"But you never met him yourself."

"It was him," Niral said. "I'm sure."

"It could've been a setup," Nam replied. "You kill someone else, make it seem like..."

Niral glanced at Nam nastily, and Mr. Hong interrupted.

"The police have confirmed Thanat is missing, and our sources tell us his DNA was discovered at the gem store," Mr. Hong said. "Of course, it may be possible he wasn't killed and that he is living in Isan with Apsara. Anything is possible..."

"Are you saying—" Niral started, but Mr. Hong held up his hand.

"Don't worry, poo noy, I'm not saying you have done anything wrong. Point is, Nam, you need to figure this out. Investigate her bank account here in Bangkok, then go up to Udon Thani. I don't want you back until you kill everyone who is a threat to us: Apsara, Rob, and Thanat, if he's alive."

"Should I bring up some men?" Nam asked. "And who will protect you here?"

"Take Ricky. I need our best men on this. The other men from abroad will stay here. We're coming closer to a bad situation, and we need numbers."

"Sure, I can tag along with Nam," Ricky said. "I wanna see Thailand anyway. I can't speak for the Shanghai and Seoul boys, but my men from New York are good, and they're loyal."

"I have no doubt," Mr. Hong responded. "I won't go back to Shanghai or anywhere else until I make sure this situation is stable. That is what leaders do."

"So I'll head to the bank?" Nam asked.

"First, drop Niral off at Duncan's apartment," Mr. Hong said. "He wants to give Niral final instructions."

Nam licked his lips as he stared at Niral. "Sure, Big Boss. We'll drop him off."

15

"We've blocked off the routes to Udon Thani and Nong Khai, stopping all vehicles that pass," Detective Chak said. "But we can't block every side road. If they go east or west or south, they're gone. We've done raids on nearby villages, but we can't search every village, and without leads..."

"I need to find out more about this Rob Johnson," Nat said, smoking a cigarette. "Why does he do what he does?"

"We've broadcasted the sketch in the media. We're handing out fliers in the surrounding villages, in the cities, and all over Isan. If he appears, we'll catch him."

"Pom mentioned the Dragons. This might be connected to drugs. Do you know...?"

Chak's eyes widened. "The grandmother said the assailant took ya ba before the murder. I thought maybe he was an addict. But maybe he sold it too?"

"There's a high-quality breed being distributed around Bangkok," Nat confirmed. "Maybe he came up here to distribute. Or maybe just to find his girlfriend."

"What girlfriend?"

Nat took out his phone and showed him the photo of Apsara.

"Where is she?" Chak asked.

"I don't know. I've been looking for her."

"Can you email this to me? We'll give it to the media. If we find her, maybe we find him."

"I will. Thank you."

"Maybe you should head back to Bangkok," Chak suggested. "We've got things covered here. You've been banged up enough. Your eye, your arm..."

"My partner, Pom, is handling that end. I've been trying to get in touch with him."

"Two is better than one. But we've got an entire force on it."

"My son. I need to find him."

"Honestly, Detective, he is probably dead."

"I refuse to believe that."

"I was told you abandoned him before."

Nat became angry, but he showed cool heart and controlled himself.

"Yes, once was enough," he said, putting out his cigarette. "I should go to the schoolhouse and talk to his classmates. Yes, I should do that."

16

"Here you go, faggot," Ricky said, pointing his gun at Niral. They were in the backseat of Nam's car, parked in front of Duncan's apartment building.

Nam turned around. "While we're away, remember to put aside our tribute. We'll collect when we get back."

"I can't believe you suggested that I didn't kill Thanat," Niral said.

"You're not a killer, you pussy," Nam said. "But you are a drug dealer. So remember who you work for."

Niral got out of the car, then leaned into the open doorway.

"Don't hurt Buppha," Niral insisted. "I told you, we can use her."

"You're the legit guy, remember?" Ricky said. "It's our choice."

Both Ricky and Nam started laughing.

"I thought sending money to that cabby's widow showed some class, Ricky," Niral said, slamming the door. "But I guess nothing's changed since junior high."

"I told you, Niral, the situation's complicated," Ricky responded through the open window. Then Nam drove away.

Niral rushed up to Duncan's apartment and rang the bell. Lamai answered.

"Niral!" she screamed when she saw him. She reached out and hugged him. "It has been so long!"

He hugged her back with one arm, being careful due to her pregnancy.

"Come inside and sit," she said, letting him in. "Duncan is on the phone. He'll be out soon. Meanwhile, let me make you a shake."

"Thank you, Lamai. I am thirsty."

"How have you been?" she asked, moving to the kitchen. "Duncan told me you went to India?"

"Yeah, reconnecting with my roots," he said, sitting down.

"You should come to Chiang Mai with us," she said, placing chopped up fruit into a blender.

"I wish I could. But I have to run things while Duncan's gone."

"Of course, I forgot," Lamai said, slapping herself in the head. "We'll miss you. I hope it's not too much work."

"Me too," Niral said, laughing. "I do want to visit, though. See the heart of Buddhism. I've visited temples here, but it never stuck."

"If you came, you could talk to a monk. I took Duncan to one here, but it's so much better there. Believe me, you will find peace in Buddhism if you learn it in Chiang Mai. That is the cultured place of Thailand. Bangkok is the trash."

"And yet, you live here."

"More opportunity, Niral. But Chiang Mai and Chiang Rai—they are the heart and soul of Thailand. The home of the true Thais. The Lanna people."

"I wish I could, Lamai. I do want peace. My life has become complicated again, after years with no complications."

"What complications?" Lamai asked, bringing the shake. "Where's Rob, by the way?"

"Gone."

"Duncan fired him? The monk advised him to take a moderate approach. But I guess I knew he wouldn't listen to that..."

Niral took the shake. "It's complicated, Lamai. Just relax and have your baby. Our issues will bring you down."

Duncan came out of the room, his eye twitching.

"Niral, come on," he said. "We'll be a few minutes, Lamai. Let me know if your sister calls."

"Sure," Lamai said without joy, staring at Duncan.

Niral got up, winked at Lamai, and strolled into Duncan's room.

Duncan closed the door. Niral sat on the bed.

"I don't have much time," Duncan said. "Lamai's sister, Malai, is coming down to pick us up. You keep my car and bike for yourself. Sell the last bit of ya ba in the car to Kan in Kanchanaburi, then go down to Phuket to get the next advance of drugs from Rahmat. Your flight to India is in six weeks, and I've got your ticket here. Whether I'm back or not, you better be on that plane. We need the assassination to go down because we'll get the second payment of product after, and we'll be free of our debt to the Muslims at the same time.

"Meanwhile, I'll take a small stash to Chiang Mai and meet a man up there. If that works out, we'll have a steady supply and network for the future. After the assassination, I can pay off your debt to Mr. Hong and sell him my part of the diamond business. You move to Chiang Mai, and we live happily ever after. How's that sound?"

"Pretty good, I guess."

30

"I'll give you the key to this apartment. You can use it while I'm gone. Now, look, where are the diamonds?"

"What diamonds?"

"The diamonds you got from Talim."

"That's the thing, Duncan. I lost them."

"You lost them?"

"Lot of shit went down in India. After I got the diamonds, I drove up to Dwarka, then out to the villages. I got close to Bhai. He believes I'm dedicated to The Brotherhood, so coordinating Bhai's assassination with Talim should be no problem. But in the process, the diamonds got lost."

Duncan rolled his eyes. "All right, no big deal. Only costs us money. But that means you better sell our shit while I'm gone, both drugs and diamonds."

"Where do I sell the new batch from Phuket?"

"I'll give you a list of contacts. You can always call me. I'm trusting you with the empire, man. This is what I always anticipated. Making you a partner. So make me proud."

He slapped Niral's arm. His eye was twitching again.

"What happened to Rob and Apsara?" Niral asked. "I thought they were part of the team, too. But Mr. Hong wants them dead?"

"Apsara disappeared. Maybe she got hit by Sumantapat, maybe she got scared. Rob went to look for her. Now he's wanted for assaulting a cop in Isan. They might as well be dead."

"They had no loyalty. No discipline."

"And no brains. We have brains. That's why we'll survive."

Niral turned towards the laughing Buddha and turned the picture around.

"Okay, Duncan," he said, holding out his hand. "Give me the keys to the kingdom. And my gun, too."

17

Nat strolled around the schoolyard of the local Matthayom 1-3, the lower secondary school, surrounded by kids in white-shirted uniforms.

He smoked the last of a cigarette, inhaling deeply into his lungs, while watching kids tease and fight each other, steal smartphones, and text each other's friends. He recalled his attendance at this same school, where he had met Som's mother, Hathai. They were in the same circle of friends and eventually began to go out. There had been no smartphones then, but he had been just as reckless when, at fifteen, he had made the mistake of impregnating his girlfriend right before he had graduated.

If he could have gone back in time and changed things, he would have. She would have been childless when she met the farang, and her move to Sweden would have been tainted with one less dishonor. He could have gone to a Matthayom 4-6, become a civil engineer or computer programmer, and lived in a skyscraper in Bangkok. But given the situation, he felt he had made the best choice for himself. With a child and wife at fifteen, he would have been destined for a miserable existence on the farm, like Som's uncle Udom. He had never regretted running away to Chiang Mai, finishing his education, and becoming a cop. His profession had its pitfalls, but it made him feel worthy and alive. But the shock of his son's disappearance, someone he had shunned until now, woke him up to the possibility that he had committed a grave sin when he had run away from his personal responsibilities to take on the responsibilities of a nation. Now, finding his son was the only way he could come face to face with his choice and redeem himself, and his profession as a cop could certainly help him.

He ground the cigarette butt into the dirt, marched inside, and asked for the principal. He was directed to the office of his old friend Gamon. Gamon was happy to see Nat. They joked around like in the old days, and Gamon didn't say anything about Nat's abandonment of his family. In fact, he expressed sadness at Som's death and had heard about Nat's parents too.

"You must be reeling," he said. "I don't know what I would do if my parents and son died."

"My son isn't dead," Nat said, "just missing. That's why I came. I want to speak to some of his classmates. Figure out where he might have gone."

"I'll ask his teachers and call his friends into the office."

Tejas Desai

Several minutes later, children filed inside Gamon's office.

Nat learned his son was often in trouble, influenced by the older Wattana, the school bully. Boonsri's reputation was well-known. Some girls admired her, others shunned her. The boys wanted her but were scared of Wattana, so they kept their distance. Everyone kept their mouths shut about their illegal activities, but after Wattana's death, they didn't mind spilling the beans. They told Nat that Som, Wattana, and Boonsri had gone up to Udon Thani several times.

Nat asked to speak with Wattana's friends. He didn't have many. One kid told Nat he had accompanied the threesome to a spot in the woods where Wattana took Boonsri for trysts when her house was off-limits. They met a man who paid for sex with Boonsri under a tree. Wattana recorded the copulation and blackmailed the man, who gave them all his money and ran away. The four celebrated by drinking papaya juice laced with rum that Som had stolen from his uncle.

The boy agreed to lead Nat to the spot in the woods. Nat was surprised at how forthcoming and helpful the boy was, almost proud of his involvement. But then he remembered his own teenage years and the antics of both boys and girls, and he wasn't surprised at all. Guys would gang up on weaker kids, and girls would slash tires and worse.

Nat thanked Gamon before he left with the boy.

"No problem, Nat," Gamon responded. "Listen, one more thing. Your parents' bodies were never claimed. No one wanted to pay for the funeral. Before you return to Bangkok, visit the village and cremate their bodies. Make sure they are reincarnated."

"Prasong didn't do it?"

"If he did, I didn't get an invitation."

"Of all people, why wouldn't he?"

"Prasong is not your family, Nat."

"But why he didn't tell me about it?"

"I don't know," Gamon said with frustration. "Maybe he assumed you didn't care."

18

Buppha heard a loud knock on the door. She picked up a kitchen knife, but her arm shook enough that the weapon was probably useless. She considered jumping out the window instead.

The knocking became louder. Then she heard Niral's voice.

"What you want?" she forced out, her voice low and raspy.

"I won't hurt you," Niral said. "I'm glad to hear your voice."

"I don't have a voice left," she said softly in Thai, approaching the door. "Are you alone?"

"All alone."

"That's what you said before I was choked," she said, her free hand feeling around the fresh scar.

"I'm sorry," Niral said. "I had no choice."

"What you want now?"

"To protect you. I was afraid they came back."

Buppha unlocked and opened the door an inch. She saw Niral's gun. She shut it again.

"I have it to help, I swear," he said. "I could shoot you through the door if I wanted."

She opened the door again. Niral rushed inside. Buppha closed and locked the door.

"No one's in here?" he asked, looking around.

"Why?" she replied. She still held the knife, not sure how or if to use it. "They come with you?"

He checked Apsara's room, then Buppha's room. "They might have instructed you to say that."

"I remember when I see you first time," Buppha said. "I try to boom boom you, but you don't care. You go to Apsara. Now you care?"

"I fucked her and I failed her, Buppha. Just like the first time. It won't happen again."

"Maybe she kill herself after that bad man with tattoos give her ring. Maybe I kill myself too. You think I get clients now? It is too much."

"Don't do that. I'll protect you."

"How? You Indian. They Thai."

"I'll take you somewhere safe."

"I don't go anywhere with you."

"That man with tattoos will come back and cut you up. You want that?"

"I am Kathoey. No one cares."

"Well, I care, okay, I care," Niral said, pointing to his chest.

"Why? You don't want to boom boom me."

"No, but I want to save you. Is that a bad thing?"

"I pray to Buddha. He save me."

"Pray later," Niral said. "Don't worry, Buppha, you can pray later."

19

Nat searched next to the spot in the woods where the man had fucked Boonsri, but he didn't find anything significant. It was another dead end. Perhaps Chak had been right. He should let the Khon Kaen police handle the search in their neck of the woods.

Nat took out two cigarettes and offered the kid one if the kid would light the match for him to make things easier. The kid obliged.

"What happened to your arm and eye?" the kid asked as he lit his own.

"Police business," Nat said, puffing.

"Som would have thought it was cool that his father was a cop."

"I think it's cool too."

"So what will you do now?"

"Go cremate my parents. Then search for Som in Udon Thani."

"They loved Udon Thani. They told me about the girls there. Lots of farang go there."

"How about ya ba?" Nat said. "Did they buy any up there?"

"I don't know what you mean."

"Don't lie to me, you asshole," he said, pushing the kid. "They were buying ya ba, right?"

"No," the kid insisted. "I swear."

Nat took out his gun and pointed it at the kid.

"I'll give you one more chance to come clean. If you lie to me again..."

The kid's legs shook, and his pants became wet. Nat saw the urine pour down his shoe.

"What the fuck," Nat said as his phone rang. Keeping the cigarette in his mouth, he reluctantly put the gun away, then answered his cell phone. The kid continued to stand there, shaking.

It was General Toon on the phone.

"Nat, we have a situation here," he said. "I need you back right away."

"Back to Bangkok?" Nat asked, trying to balance the cigarette in his mouth while he spoke, then allowing it to drop. "I was going to search Udon Thani for the farang. Let Khun Pom handle it."

"That's the thing, Natthew," General Toon said after a pause. "Pom's body was just found by the Chao Phraya River. He was murdered."

20

Buppha plopped down on Duncan's couch and turned on the TV.

"Yes, this better than Klong Tuey," she said.

Niral peered out the window of the 77th floor apartment.

"Your neighbors probably saw us leave, but I doubt anyone saw us arrive here," he said. "Just don't go out unless you tell me first."

"I get used to this apartment. Is it yours?"

"No, but I have it for a while. Believe me, it's better than Khao San Road too."

She began watching the news. Niral saw Rob's picture again.

"That is Rob?" Buppha asked, leaning forward. "He is in trouble."

The report described the attack on Wattana.

"Oh my," Buppha said. "All Apsara's boyfriends are bad."

"Yeah," Niral said.

Then, Apsara's picture appeared, too, saying she might know Rob's whereabouts or be in cahoots with him.

"Apsara is in trouble now too," Buppha said. "You are with bad people, you become bad."

Another report came on about the murder investigation in Phuket. Robert Murphy's picture appeared as a missing witness. Sources indicated possible evidence linking Rob to that murder, but in an interview, General Chaow confirmed Panit was still their man. However, they suspected Robert Murphy had witnessed his wife's murder or was killed himself, so ascertaining his whereabouts was important.

"Apsara's boyfriends are busy people," Buppha said. "Busy killing people." She turned to Niral. "You are sure you will not kill me?"

"You shouldn't watch so much TV," he said, walking toward the remote.

"I am learning," she said, keeping the remote from him.

"We know they're bad people, so we need to find Apsara before they get her. That detective probably knows more than he's saying. If he calls you again, find out what he knows about Apsara."

"You said tell him another man is bad."

"I said that so Nam wouldn't kill you."

"They say you let tourist live. That is this Murphy?"

"I'll tell you everything once this is over."

"Will it be over?"

"I hope so."

Buppha gave Niral the remote and slunk back on the couch. But before Niral turned off the TV, another story ran.

"Detective Pomrachat Katankug was found murdered on an isolated bank of the Chao Phraya River in southern Bangkok today. Police are scouring the scene but so far they have no leads..."

"Holy shit," Niral exclaimed, turning to Buppha. "Is that—?"

Buppha shook her head. "Bad people," she said. "Very bad people."

PART II

Near Chiang Mai, Thailand; Bangkok, Thailand; Sands Point, New York; South Jamaica, St. Albans (Queens), New York; Near Apex, North Carolina

---

21

A tuk-tuk driver drove Duncan deep into the Chiang Mai countryside. They stopped at an elephant camp, where Duncan was grabbed and blindfolded. He was forced to sit sideways on what felt like the back of a motorcycle, both hands bound behind his back and tied to the back handle of the cycle. He was driven for another twenty minutes. Duncan enjoyed the fresh air of the countryside as he was whisked along, so different from Bangkok, but he began to question his decision to move up north.

They stopped suddenly and the driver told Duncan to dismount. Duncan jumped on the ground, stumbling. Then the driver cut the rope that tied him to the motorcycle. He heard the motorcycle drive away.

Birds chirped. He waited nervously. His hands were still tied behind his back.

"Hello?" he shouted.

"Shut up," he heard someone whisper to him in broken English. The blindfold was ripped off violently. The sunlight blinded him temporarily, but his vision soon clarified and Duncan saw he stood in the middle of a deserted, grassy field surrounded by forest. The man next to him was dark-skinned, about his height. He wore a white shirt and a red bandana covered his head. He carried an AK-47.

"Come," he said, taking Duncan by the elbow. They trekked through

38

the forest, crossed a log bridge that hung over a raging stream, and finally approached a large wood building, where women were jarring honey in an open restaurant. A light-skinned man in a red shirt and blue pants was sitting alone on a long bench next to tables, sipping a fruit drink. He stood as Duncan approached.

"Ah, you have arrived," the man said in English, folding his arms. "Good morning."

The dark-skinned man pushed Duncan forward. The light-skinned man yelled at the dark-skinned man in S'gaw Karen.

"I apologize for his manners," the light-skinned man said. "I am Thon."

Thon yelled at the dark-skinned man again. Duncan could feel the rope being cut, and after only a few swipes, the rope gave away, and Duncan's hands were free.

"It is just a precaution," Thon said.

Two men came out. They also wore red bandanas and carried AK-47s. Thon led Duncan to the table.

"Would you sit, please?" he asked. "Have you ever had nya u?"

"No, what is it?"

"It's a dish made of fermented fish, rice, and vegetables. Would you like some?"

"Sure," Duncan said.

The three men with bandanas looked angry at Duncan. Thon spoke to them.

"Don't mind them," Thon said. "In our culture, it is polite to refuse a dish before ultimately accepting it. This shows modesty. But I explained that you don't understand. And I am sorry for the blindfold and the rope. It is not exactly hospitable, but we need to make sure our location remains secret. I hope you understand."

"Of course," Duncan said.

Thon said something to one of the women.

"She will get the dish," Thon said. "Thank you for coming. Kan is an old friend. I am glad you are in business with him. He says your product is very good. Can I ask where you acquire it?"

"I wish I could tell you, but it's a secret. The quality is very good, but the supplier only delivers down there, and I want to base my operation up here now."

"Hmm...that is too bad. I've wanted to expand our operation to Bangkok and the surrounding cities."

"Bangkok and Pattaya are already saturated, as you can imagine. The Kanchanaburi province and Hua Hin have been hubs. I want to sell locally, using your product but expanding its reach here. But you won't do business with me?"

"I did not say that. But the south would be a better market. We already sell to local distributors here. Much of that product makes it to Bangkok anyway. If we cut out middlemen, we will both make better profits."

"Can I ask you where your product comes from?" Duncan asked.

"Burma, of course. We work with our Karen partners in Kayin State. They get their heroin from Afghanistan, and the ya ba is produced in factories in Bangladesh and India. So I am told."

"My product has a similar origin, I suspect, but the delivery method is different."

"Let me ask you: how much do you wish to purchase, and how do you want it delivered?"

"Right now, I don't have a ground game up here. My man might come up later, and he can help expand the market up here. I'm willing to pay more if I can use your distributors and dealers for now."

"I don't understand," Thon said. "We only supply product and sell to distributors. You don't add anything. With due respect, of course," he said.

The dark-skinned man looked angry. The woman came back with the dish of nya u, but Duncan didn't touch it. His eye began twitching as he tried to explain.

"I came up here to get my footing. In the long run, I can pay a lot more for your product than your current distributors because I will develop a network that is more efficient and will make more profit. I can expand the market here locally so the product isn't just going down to Bangkok. We'll both benefit in that case. But right now, I need to set up that network, just like I did in Bangkok and Pattaya, and you can help me with that. We can expand to the Bangkok area at a later time. Maybe Isan and down south, too, where I have connections."

Thon looked at the dark-skinned man. "If you are so good at making networks, why abandon your operation down there and with such superior product?"

"It is more trouble than it is worth," Duncan answered. "Our trade is more volatile in Bangkok. Up here, we can relax and make money all at once. I have a family, and I want that life."

"We Karen who have been running all our lives can understand the need for a peaceful life. But again, what can you offer us now? You want to buy our product that comes through our network and use our distributors too. So you want to replace us?"

Duncan thought. He realized he wasn't convincing Thon, so he would have to promise something big, even if he wasn't sure he could deliver on it. "Okay, here's a better deal. I can get our superior product delivered through your channels," he said. There's already a hunger for it in Bangkok and beyond, so we can create market for it here too. And later if you want to switch to using it instead of your current supplier, it will help you expand if you want to purchase and deal it yourself."

"If we both sell the same product in the same places, won't there be a conflict?"

"I don't think so. We can sell in different places at first. In the long term, I plan to expand our reach. I'll start here. We can work together on that if you want. We can become rich together."

"So as I understand it you won't buy our current product. In that case you will pay us to use our network through Burma to get your superior product here? You will be the middleman to this supplier. Then you will have to tell me how and where you get this product."

"Revealing that wouldn't make me much of a middleman, would it? Anyway, I still have to work it out with the supplier, but I don't think it will be a problem."

Thon looked at the dark-skinned man again. "We need to make sure there is no conflict with our current operations. As I said, we don't work with dealers directly, but we can put you in touch with our own distributors, who you will also have to pay, if you are serious about this plan. Our delivery network is intricate and won't be cheap. I cannot give you an answer now, Mr. Duncan. We make our decisions by consensus, so I will have to speak to our elders. They may want to discuss this more with you, so we can come to a more complete arrangement. But I will be in touch either way, through the man who picked you up."

"Where will you be in touch? I don't have an office up here."

"Our man will text you and meet you somewhere. Don't worry; we don't disrespect your space in Chiang Mai or your in-law's home in Chiang Rai."

Duncan swallowed, his eye twitching. "How do you know where my family lives?"

"We do our homework, Mr. Duncan. Please, enjoy the nya u before you go. It is a wonderful dish."

22

Almost two weeks had passed since General Toon's phone call telling Nat about Pom's death. The autopsy had taken several days, then the funeral another week. Nat had finally met Pom's wife, Anong, and his children, the two boys now fatherless like Som had been. He wondered if he should take a father role for them instead of looking for Som, who was most likely dead. The Khon Kaen police had not located Rob Johnson. They hadn't found the missing teens either. And Nat hadn't returned to Isan to cremate his own parents, even as he had witnessed the cremation of his partner.

But after witnessing burnings, spiritual releases, processions, chanting sessions, and prayers at Pom's funeral, he still identified as a detective. His arm had fully healed. He no longer wore an eye patch. He was rejuvenated and primed, he thought, to figure out this crime.

He set up a meeting with General Toon in his office. To his surprise, Detective Chan and another man were there. Chan and Nat nodded to each other. General Toon introduced the other man as Colonel Nopasit Limwat, a member of the Narcotics Suppression Bureau. Nat greeted him with a deep wai.

"Please, sit, Mr. Nat," the Colonel commanded. "I have heard of your bravery. Shot once, beaten. You have kept going on this very complex case."

"Thank you, Khun Colonel," Nat responded as he sat next to a clearly uncomfortable Chan.

"I want to express my condolences for Detective Pomrachat," the Colonel continued. "I hear he was an expert detective."

"With all due respect, Khun Colonel, I would like to proceed to business," Nat said. "Khun General, have you received the autopsy results for Pom?"

General Toon looked at the Colonel, who flashed a cool heart smile to this slight. General Toon did not rebuke Nat, and instead, said, "Yes, Detective. He was shot twice with a rifle: once in the back, once in the front shoulder. The body was moved, so he was not shot on the riverbank. The night before he disappeared, Sumantapat said he told Pom one of the victims of the previous murders, Boy, had followed a go-go dancer to a warehouse on the river. So Colonel Limwat's men are searching all the warehouses on the river for possible leads."

"Detective Nat, a police detective's murder is a serious matter," Colonel Limwat stated. "And the level of violence associated with it leads us to believe this is related to a struggle over this new strain of ya ba in the provinces. Yet, many of the murders and disappearances have taken place in Bangkok. So some Bangkok-based gang must be involved. Have you heard of the Dragons?"

Nat glanced at Chan but didn't respond.

"They are an international gang we have begun to watch," Limwat continued. "Their leadership is primarily Chinese, but they employ all types of people, including Thais, Koreans, Europeans, and others. They are present in many Asian countries and the West. We believe their main boss here is Fan Hong. He is Thai-Chinese, born and raised in Bangkok. He owns a couple of clubs here but also in East Asia. We need proof he is leading the Dragons and this ya ba scourge."

Nat remembered Pom had mentioned Fan Hong to him over the phone, but he didn't say anything. He wanted to know what his superiors knew. "Is the farang who kidnapped my son also a member of this gang?" Nat asked.

The Colonel glanced at General Toon. "Kidnapped your son?"

"A detail I forgot to mention," General Toon said. "Coincidentally, the farang Maric, who I believe might be known as Rob Johnson, might have seized or assaulted Detective Nat's son in Isan."

"I'm sorry to hear that," Limwat said. "Then it is doubly personal for you, Detective Nat." He paused, then continued. "We have not tied this crime in Isan together yet with the other crimes in Bangkok and Phuket, but we are investigating."

"Did you get the DNA sample of Maric I sent to Pom?" Nat asked. "Did you test it?"

"I received it for Pom," Chan said. "I sent it down to Phuket for analysis against the mattress from the hotel room where the tourist was killed. That is what you wanted, right? And to see if there were any outstanding warrants on Maric from other cases, or if he has used a different alias than this 'Rob Johnson'?"

"Yes," Nat said. "Thank you, Chan. I hope they received it in Phuket."

"It will be tested," the Colonel confirmed. "The Phuket police also received the DNA results of the woman killed in Phuket from Texas. This Linda Murphy has been confirmed as the victim. Her husband Bob Murphy has not been found. We are assuming he is dead. Killed by either the Thai Panit or this farang Maric. We will check outstanding warrants for Maric and hits in DNA databases around the world from the sample you acquired. You see, Detective, we are devoting our full resources to this investigation under the assumption that these crimes may be related to the ya ba scourge."

Nat breathed a sigh of relief. "I'm so glad," he said. "I had this dream the other day that Pom was close to cracking this case open, and that is why he was murdered."

"Very possible," Limwat said. "He was a noble detective. We will not let him die in vain."

"One thing I want to make clear, however," General Toon stated, "is that we also must devote our full resources here in Bangkok to the investigation of the Dragons. The Khon Kaen police will continue their search for Maric, but you must gather evidence against Fan Hong's gang here. You cannot return to Isan at this time, Nat."

"But Khun General, I must cremate my parents," Nat said. "They must go to heaven to wait for reincarnation. And my son..."

"As I said, the Khon Kaen police are working to find your son," General Toon responded. "You can always go up some weekend to cremate your parents. Many Buddhists wait a year. You can wait."

"It is the best way for the good of this case, Detective Nat," Colonel Limwat said, smiling.

"You will team up with Chan now," Toon continued. "I've reassigned his partner. Find out about Fan Hong, his relationship to this case, and the new product. The Colonel's team will search the warehouses and do the proper work on the distribution side. Together we will stamp out this scourge."

23

Maem stormed into the office at Go-Go Rama. Sumantapat was counting baht.

"I told you involving the police would backfire," she said. "Two cops just asked for double the payoff for the club after mentioning the drug investigation General Toon is pursuing. They say the Narcotics Suppression Bureau is involved too. Next time they will ask for a higher commission on the ya ba too."

"They've already asked. I said fine. If they can eliminate this new product for us, it is worth it."

Maem shook her head. "This is more about revenge, isn't it? You just don't like Fan Hong?"

"It is about many things. They don't concern you. Go back to running the club. If the cops ask for more commission, you have my permission to give it. This is why I look at the big picture and you run the whorehouse, bitch."

24

When Niral arrived at the diamond supplier Shekhat's warehouse with a duffel bag full of money to exchange for a new batch of diamonds, a gaggle of cops were already there, combing around and through it. A few had dogs.

Niral parked his motorcycle and kept his distance. Through the door, he could see Shekhat was inside the warehouse, speaking to a couple of detectives. His brothers were near the entrance. Niral positioned the bag against his waist so the police wouldn't notice his gun, then proceeded towards the brothers.

"What's going on?" he asked in Gujarati.

"They say a cop was killed," one brother responded, his fingers encrusted with dried dal. "They have a warrant for every warehouse along the river."

"Every warehouse? How far from the river does it have to be?"

"That's what they said when they handed the warrant to Anil. I don't know how many warehouses they're checking."

"What are they looking for? Bullet casings?"

Shekhat excused himself from the detectives and approached Niral. He was shaking a bit.

"I am sorry for the disturbance, Niral," Shekhat said. "These damn Thai police."

"What are they looking for?"

"They are from the Narcotics Suppression Bureau. So I guess drugs."

Niral swallowed. "I see. Why do they think there are drugs here?"

"Apparently, some detective was murdered by the river."

"Right," Niral said. "I think I saw that on the news."

"I just hope they don't ask for a bribe. Sometimes they pretend to find drugs and demand a payment. My business can't afford that."

"I imagine not," Niral said, noticing out of the corner of his eye that the two detectives were looking at him. "Listen, I'll come back later."

"Actually, would you mind counting the diamonds now?" Shekhat asked. "I could use the money."

"If they see diamonds and money, they'll be tempted," Niral said. "I'll come back later today. Hopefully they'll be gone by then."

Niral left without making eye contact with the detectives. He drove past Duncan's warehouse and around it to make sure no cops were there. He parked his motorcycle near the Muay Thai boxing school, then ran over to the warehouse and hopped upstairs to the office. He wiped down the desk and stripped the office of Duncan's possessions. Then, he ran down the internal staircase to the garage. He drove the car to Duncan's apartment building and parked it in the lot. He called Duncan.

"Nice to hear from you," Duncan said. "How's the work going?"

"I'm making progress. Sold the last batch to Kan, who says hi. I'm going down to Phuket tomorrow to get the next batch of drugs from Rahmat. We've gone over the assassination procedure with Talim by encrypted messaging, and I think we're set. Meanwhile, Bhai has every confidence in me, so he won't suspect a thing."

"Great. I met with Kan's friend here. I think I made a good impression. We're working out a solid deal."

"How's Lamai?"

"Enjoying the quiet life. She's a different person up here."

"Awesome. I called to tell you I found cops at Shekhat's. Apparently, they're checking every warehouse along the river. Don't know if ours counts, but I took out your personal shit and wiped down the desk. Can't do much about fingerprints and DNA on other stuff, but hopefully they won't check."

"We don't have a criminal record, so I'd worry less about that. I don't know about Rob."

"I'm not sure. He's never divulged much. Maybe he has one from Australia. But they might have DNA from his altercation with the cop in Isan."

"What are they searching for?"

"They say they're working on the case of the murdered cop they found on the riverbank. But they're drug cops."

"Shit!" Duncan yelled. "You've gotta get the car..."

"Don't worry, I took it and parked it in the lot here. The ya ba's all sold, but they could bring dogs to sniff the odor. Plus, I'd lose access to the car if the cops dropped by today or tomorrow."

"Good thinking. Shit, though. Can you check for dried fluids in the garage?"

He realized he had forgotten about the red stain Duncan had spread dirt over. "Why? Something go down there?"

"Lots happened while you were gone. No time to explain it all."

"Okay, Duncan. I've also gotta go back to Shekhat's to make the diamond transaction, then drop the diamonds off to Mr. Hong himself so I can inquire about the Apsara investigation."

"All right. Thanks for your hard work. Keep in touch more often."

"Sorry, I've been busy juggling all this shit. No wonder you got both me and Rob."

Duncan laughed. "By the way, I called the apartment yesterday and some girl answered. She sounded familiar."

"I've had some giks over. You know, girls from Scandal."

"No prob. Just make sure they don't steal anything. And don't keep the merchandise around."

"Of course, Duncan. You know I'm careful. Always careful."

25

Brendan Carty sat at the head of a long table in his dining room at Sands Point as maids brought in trays of hors d'oeuvres. Bob and Lance sat across from Brendan's two sons, Lachlan and Seamus. His wife, Judith, and his younger daughter, Siobhan, were in the drawing room, chatting with Sveta.

The maids departed and closed the doors. Brendan said, "I love family. And extensions of families. That's why I take backstabs so personally. You know who I mean, Bobby?"

"I assume you don't mean me?" Bob replied. He had grown a goatee in the last two weeks, something he was proud of.

Brendan laughed. "You've been forgiven, Bobby. You're not even Bobby anymore, you're Franklin Stewart III, aren't you? Only we know your true identity."

"So forget Bobby. Call me Franklin from now on."

"Sure. We'll sweep away the past. Now to the future. Seems like I was wrong. We've got new competition. Maybe another Vishal front. They call it Ozone."

"Can they bid this late?" Bob asked.

"The Chairman of the CFLIC received it. It's been swirling around the council members. They're including it in the vote at the next meeting in two weeks. Looks like it has teeth. I'm not sure if a Vishal henchman persuaded them or if it's the proposal itself."

"Yes, Sveta got it via email," Bob confirmed. "Two council members called my phone to discuss it."

"So you've seen the bid," Brendan said. "Are they swayed by the proposal or politics?"

"Probably both. The proposal emphasizes a duplicate of the Spray Mecca, which acts as a museum and charges an entrance fee. It includes a colony for would-be artists, who are admitted via a competition that grants them fellowships. These fellowships are set up by a non-profit organization funded through donations. The majority of the donations will pay the competition staff, with a minority set aside for the artists. Rent-control residential units will be built where Gigglies once stood. But the units will be smaller so it will house a higher capacity than the other proposals.

"A higher-end commercial development will be built where The Dock stood, complementing the skyline. If the same developer owns both, they could balance the high rents at the latter with the lower rents of the former. Plus, the proposal promises to use union labor at all three sites, even identifying the particular unions. So the proposal seems more efficient on all fronts. It provides the high capacity, low income housing the borough president wants, the artistic restoration and union labor the people want, and the revenue and status the City Council wants."

"Our plan does the same thing," Brendan said. "It has balance too."

"Yes, but it isn't as efficient," Bob replied. "You can tweak your proposal before the meeting, but I don't know that members will have time to reread it."

"Fire that old man who drafted it," Lachlan said. "Get Goldman instead. He'll fix it."

"I told you to get the Jew in the first place," Brendan scolded.

"Seamus's call."

"The old man had more experience," Seamus explained. "It was the right call at the time. We've just gotta one-up it."

"Goldman will one-up it," Lachlan insisted. "That's what Jews do."

"Enough with these generalizations," Bob said. "My ex-wife was Jewish."

"It's a compliment," Lachlan said. "I'm just saying, we should've got Goldman from the start. But the old man invested with Seamus's side of the firm, so he wanted to give him business in return."

"Look, why don't ya'll fight about something worthwhile," Lance interjected. "Jew or no Jew, ain't no proposal gonna get by this council without influence. We got Stevens. Let him work some magic behind the scenes. He had our back before."

Brendan smiled. "I like how this man thinks. That's why I got him on my team."

"We'll be multi-faceted," Bob said. "I'll have Sveta put together a dinner with some CFLIC members, and we'll get him on our side. With Stevens influencing the Community Board and Goldman fine-tuning the proposal, we can still beat Vishal to a pulp. Easily."

26

Sitting calmly in his office, Sumantapat told Nat and Chan what he had told Pom.

"Ah, this violence, for what?" he exclaimed when he was done. "We should be happy with this life. Don't you think, detective?" he asked Nat.

"Yes," Nat agreed. "The middle way of contentment."

"Thailand is confused," Sumantapat continued. "Sure, we still smile, we still wai, we still talk about sanuk, we still say we respect the monks, but when was the last time you prayed at a temple?"

"I did at Pom's funeral," Nat said.

"Of course you would pray at a funeral. But we should follow Buddha more closely. You know, I trained to be a monk before I went into business."

"Sounds like you were more privileged than me," Nat said. "I missed that stage."

"It bestows great prestige on the family. But I was not born into privilege. I grew up in a small village near Mae Sai. And you are from Isan?"

"How did you know?"

"Your look."

"Are you Burmese?"

Sumantapat laughed. "I don't know my heritage, honestly. Now listen, if your partner was the latest victim of the drug disease, and Fan Hong is the spreader, perhaps I can help."

"Tell me, why would Fan Hong target your men: Pornopat, the gem dealers, Boy?" Nat asked. "Are you competing with him in the drug trade?"

Chan glared at Nat. Nat didn't seem phased. Sumantapat laughed heartily, displaying cool heart and a half.

"My dear detective, do I look like I want a death sentence? Fan Hong doesn't like me. I bought his only nightclub in Pattaya and ruined his dreams of an empire in that city. Now he only owns two clubs in Bangkok. That is like nothing for a Dragon, especially as he is Thai-Chinese, born and raised here. So perhaps his insecurity led him to the drug trade and his bitterness, towards murder. But that's merely a theory. I don't know his mind. And Bangkok is a big city. My men could do things I don't know about. Maybe they sold on the side. More likely, they knew things that got them killed. Boy pursued that duplicitous hussy, Apsara. That, I suspect, is why he is dead."

"And Pom?"

"It seems he also pursued the hussy and was killed."

"We need evidence, not just speculation."

Sumantapat took a wad of baht and pounded it on the desk. "Last I checked, detective, it is your job to pursue and secure evidence, not mine. But I do have more information. I recently discovered why Boy suspected the hussy. Through his associates, he learned she worked at Fan Hong's club Scandal under the name of Ploy. So there is your connection. Fan Hong to the hussy, to the murders of Boy, Pom, Pornopat, and his fellow gem dealers."

"So while looking into Apsara, these men were killed on orders from Fan Hong?"

"Ah, that is what I am suggesting. And maybe he had her killed too."

"If Apsara was involved in the gem scam with Pornopat, and he found out about the drug connection, that could make sense, too."

"That is possible, detective. I must reiterate that I know nothing about a gem scam."

"I couldn't find Apsara in Isan," Nat continued. "Instead, I ran into the same farang who killed the wife of the man who may have witnessed the gem store murders. The same farang who butchered a boy and kidnapped my son and a girl. This farang seems to be the key."

"The Dragons employ farang. He is eliminating loose ends for Fan Hong. Why else would he be in Isan? He's looking for the hussy. It seems she ran away after Boy's murder, perhaps horrified by all the bloodletting and thinking she might be next. Probably she is already dead. This is how it looks to me. General Toon told me the Narcotics Suppression Bureau is raiding warehouses by the river. You may find a drug stash this way but I doubt it will connect you directly to Fan Hong. He knows Bangkok well and can cover his tracks. But this hussy, Apsara, may connect him, and this farang may connect him."

"So you are saying I should return to Isan?"

"No. I am saying you should find a stronger connection through research. Maybe your senior detective friend found one. It did not die with him. It is still there to be found. By the way, he did ask about farang names when he visited."

"Do remember them? Were they Rob Johnson, Borisslava Maric?"

"I don't remember. I am not interested in farang. But go back to the basics. How does a farang come to Thailand? Who pays his way? Why does a dancer keep several names and why does her boyfriend call himself both Pornopat and Thanat? Perhaps Buddha should have made me a detective. Might have been a good life."

"A poor one," Nat corrected, standing.

Sumantapat shoved the wad of baht towards them. "A gift for General Toon," he said. "And nuggets for you."

Chan picked up the wad. Then Sumantapat took out another wad and shoved it towards them.

"And a brick too," he said.

27

Since Niral had left his motorcycle parked near the Muay Thai boxing school, he took a motorcycle taxi back to pick it up. He still held the bag of money. It was dark outside, but inside the school, he saw lights and heard the crowd. Peeking in, he witnessed one of the boxers dressed in flaming colors of red and yellow praising Buddha with an ornate dance.

Niral ran toward the warehouse and slipped into the courtyard. He could not see well, but he found the garage door and tried to slip the key into the lock. After struggling, he was able to open it.

As he flipped the light switch, he heard a siren outside, then running. Quickly, he shut off the light and closed the door. In the darkness, he crept towards where he thought the staircase was.

The door to the garage slid open. Several flashlights swirled around. He used their scant light to find the staircase and ascended to the fifth floor.

Upstairs, he took out his gun, crept to the external staircase, and peered over the railing. He saw the two detectives from Shekhat's warehouse and police officers holding machine guns. He realized he should have cleared the garage before eating dinner and warned Buppha not to answer the phone unless the caller ID indicated it was him.

He wracked his brain over an escape route as he observed officers climbing the external staircase. Suddenly, he recalled a drainpipe on the side of the building which he could slide down. He risked falling to his death, but he would risk more if caught here with a weapon. He ran to the adjacent window and spotted the pipe. He would have to leap and hope he caught one of the rings encasing it.

He didn't see anyone below. He cursed a building made without fire escapes. The last time he had run for his life, a drainage pipe on Amrat's roof had saved him. Now, as he climbed the window railing, bent, and positioned himself, he hoped he would have the same luck.

28

Wan took a couple of buses from Flushing to the neighborhood of South Jamaica in southeast Queens, walked to the side of a house, and descended a narrow staircase to a locked door. He knocked three times.

A panel slid open, and a pair of suspicious eyes regarded him.

"Who you? We didn't order no Chinese."

"Here to see Tyrone. Tell him it's Wan."

He heard him say, "You expecting some chink?"

There was a pause. Wan wished he had brought his gun. He was about to leave when he heard multiple locks releasing.

The door opened, and a large, muscular black man wearing a gray t-shirt motioned him inside and patted him down. Several young men sat at a round table, smoking and playing poker. They watched him like they were stalking deer.

A substantially dark-skinned man, about thirty, approached him from the side. He wore a Carmelo Anthony Knicks jersey and red sweatpants.

"My nigga," he said. They clasped hands and hugged with one hand, then did a complex handshake and patted each other's chests.

"You know this motherfucker?" the man in the gray t-shirt asked, closing and locking the front door.

"Yeah, this my prison buddy, Wan. We mad tight. He came in with extra muscle when we fought the Aryans or the Latinos."

"Not enough Asians in Sing Sing," one of the poker players said. "So they man up with us."

"Aight," the man in the gray t-shirt said, bending over and sizing up Wan. Then he returned to the poker table.

"Don't mind these cats," Tyrone said. "Let's go inside my private room and discuss old times."

Wan followed him into a large boiler room fit with a laundry machine and small desk.

"My office, nigga," Tyrone said, sitting behind the desk. "It ain't Fifth Avenue or nothing, but it'll do."

"You'll get better digs once you start working for me," Wan said, closing the door and sitting across from him.

"Man, how long it been since I've seen you? Maybe once since you got out."

"Probably. I been busy, working for the man. He's been promoting me."

"Yeah? Sounds like you doing good, dog. Even being on parole."

"Exactly. Because I work for a good organization. They take care of their people. It isn't just a bunch of knuckleheads sitting around playing poker. We could have done that in the joint."

Tyrone laughed. "See how this nigga talk. Like he Don Corleone. I got a set-up here. We fix OTBs, bookie shit, loan sharking, extortion when needed, nothing that'll rock the boat. Not like niggas down here got much. But it's rising. Forget about the immigrants, even white folks moving in now. Cheap real estate. Think we might move to prostitution soon."

"I'm looking for a killer. You don't have to do it yourself."

Tyrone watched him, nodding his head lightly.

"Aight. We hire out, at times, for the right price. But don't you got killers of your own? Like thousands? You got the organization, as you so eloquently express."

"Yeah, but the job's down here. I'd rather have someone who knows the area, the community. In and out, quiet. No robbery, just murder."

"Hmm. Assuming you ain't double-crossing, I got someone for you. He's a young kid, but he's rising in our ranks, and he's got blood on him. Never been caught. These young killers, they're savvy."

"If this works out, we'll have more projects for you. Real money-making ventures."

"Aight. Gimme the details, and we can negotiate the price."

29

Nat and Chan returned to the police station.

"I can't believe you took that bribe," Nat said.

"Just delivering it to General Toon. I don't know what he'll do with it."

"Yeah, but you took some off the top. Double."

"Well, you didn't want your share."

Nat shook his head. "Let's just get to the computer. You sure we have access to immigration information?"

"Normally, we'd have to subpoena the Immigration Bureau for the documents, but we have a database accessible only to us. It doesn't up-date the immigrant's activities, like their entry and re-entry status, but it will list when the immigrants first entered the country, if they had a visa, and who their sponsor was if they have one. Plus renewals."

"And Pom knew about this database?"

"Yes. He used it in the past when farang were implicated in crimes. Very rare, but it does happen. The prosecutor can't use this in court, since we are not supposed to have access to it. General Toon was able to get the password through his contacts. But it makes our job easier, and we can get the official info later via subpoena."

"Good. Would it tell us if Pom accessed the database before he died?"

"There probably is a way to tell, but I don't know how. Our administrator already went home."

They logged on the computer, and Chan accessed the database. They looked up Borisslava Maric. It appeared he had entered the country on a one-year, multiple entry, non-immigrant business visa. He had been sponsored by a farang named Duncan Smith for his company Emblem Jewelry and had flown in from Malaysia a year and a half before. He had renewed his visa once.

"Duncan Smith," Nat said, remembering suddenly that Pom had told him about his interview with Duncan. "Where does he live? Where is his office?"

"Here's a copy of the application. It lists the company address. You know what, I believe it's near that Muay Thai boxing school. It's an old office building where there was a fire many years ago. Now it's an abandoned warehouse."

"Close to the Chao Phraya River?"

"Not right next to it, but it's close."

"That could be the warehouse where Boy followed Apsara. How about his home address?"

"We can look that up on another database. But first, let's look him up on this one. Duncan Smith is now a permanent resident. He entered the country seven years ago on a tourist visa, but he then received a work permit and renewed it with a non-immigrant visa. He worked for a jewelry-making factory. And guess who owned the factory and sponsored him?"

"Fan Hong."

"Exactly. Looks like we have the pieces."

"For a warrant, maybe. We can check tomorrow."

"Let me call General Toon now. See what he says."

"Nat, that warehouse has been raided," Chan said as he spoke to Toon. "They found money, plus traces of drugs, blood, and flesh. Could be Boy's murder site and the drug hub."

Chan told General Toon about the connection they found to Fan Hong. Nat was shaking, wishing he could smoke a cigarette.

Chan turned to him. "He says that should be enough for a search of his home."

"He can get a judge to sign off on that? Tonight?"

"He's General Toon. He can get anything."

"I don't know if it's enough."

"We don't need enough," he said, smiling.

30

Niral had climbed down the pipe a few stories, then fell a couple of stories. He was shaken up, but he recovered fast. He hid in the brush and made his way around the warehouse. Then it began to rain, making a bad situation even worse.

He scurried carefully while crouched over, his gun out. When he finally reached the Muay Thai boxing school, he realized he didn't have the bag of money with him. He must have dropped it, but he wasn't sure when or where.

He cursed as he fastened his gun, mounted his motorcycle, and drove away. Despite not having the money, he drove towards Shekhat's warehouse.

The rain drenched him. It wasn't a torrential downpour, but he had to maneuver carefully. His visibility was impacted as his headlights hit the fog and shafts of rain. The constant honks by tuk-tuks annoyed him. When he got to Shekhat's warehouse, he parked his motorcycle and rushed inside, holding the gun.

Shekhat's brothers were eating in the corner. They always seemed to be eating. Shekhat was brooding near the table. One of his brothers muttered to him, mouth full, and Shekhat turned.

He didn't look happy. He stood and approached Niral, hands on his hips.

"Sisterfucker, you've come to collect?" he asked in Gujarati.

"Yes," Niral said. "Give me the latest batch."

Shekhat stared at him. "You think you can command me? That you are so superior? I know what you did in your village in India. Don't think…"

Niral brushed his wet hair from his face.

"What do you know?"

"I know what happened."

"It is now a Brotherhood village. It's been saved from caste influence."

Shekhat laughed. It began softly, but it became a deep laugh.

"Caste influence? You must be joking. Do you see what makes the world go 'round? Even the police ask for huge bribes. Do you know what I had to give just now or they would have put me in jail?"

"So what, you're ruined?"

"I will be. But it will be far worse for you if they know what you did. Murdering a young man…"

"Don't think I wouldn't do it again," Niral said, holding the gun steady. "I'll give you one last chance to give me the latest batch. I'll pay you back, fair value. Nothing more."

"Now you demand an advance without payment? What gall! Niral, you have The Brotherhood's money behind you. All I ask is a good piece of the pie, and I, too, will convert to The Brotherhood."

Shekhat put his hands together, a namaste and wai in one. He stood perfectly still, almost mockingly.

Niral shot him four times. He heard the brothers scream. He could feel a tear trickle down his cheek, or maybe it was just a drop from his hair. He wiped it and pointed the gun at Shekhat's brothers. They stared at him in shock, one with his mouth full, the other with his hands up.

"You can be smart and live," he said, trying to keep his voice measured. "You can even profit from this. But keep calm. And do what I say."

31

From the terrace outside his bedroom window in North Carolina, Hemraj peered at the bushes at the edge of their property. His sister, Dharini, holding a martini, joined him.

"Sightseeing, brother?" she asked.

"Thought I saw someone in the bushes. Fucking niggers."

"Get off your high horse, Hemraj."

"Sorry sis, but I fucking hate them. Just take out the lynch ropes."

Dharini shook her head. "Why do you hate them, Hemraj? Enlighten me."

"Let's see: they've got no role in society, and everywhere they go, there are problems."

Dharini put her arm next to his, contrasting his dark skin to her light tone.

"I think you should check out the color of your own skin, brother."

"Hey, I'm not black, okay!" he shouted, pounding his palm. "I mean look at us. One generation, and bam, we're in the one percent."

She pointed her finger at him. "Those black people make our motels run. They clean them, they fix the pipes, and they maintain the electricity. Do you think that gets done by magic? By little oompa-loompas? Too bad Dad never made you work in one. You would have turned out socially conscious, like Krish."

"That little ass-kisser. He thinks he's such a patriot."

"Well he is. Our brother fought for this country. What do you do? Build crappy buildings with hick labor and illegal Mexicans? Follow around some blond, blue-eyed heiress who's never worked a day in her life? Ashley's just playing with you. She'll never marry you. She'll get a white guy eventually."

"You don't know anything," he yelled. "I know my girl better than myself. It's complicated, that's all. Anyway, if we did get married, I'd have to move to New York. I'd leave you."

"Since when do you care about me?"

"You better shut your face, bitch."

"Now, now, ladies and gentlemen, what is going on here?" Ashok asked, coming out onto the terrace holding a glass of Sazerac in his left hand, his right hand shaking while holding a cane. "We're not having a family feud, are we? I've already healed the divide between uncles. We don't need another chasm."

Hemraj flicked his fingers at her. "She's being herself, as usual. Criticizing me, as if she's contributed anything. I run my own company, bitch!"

"Dharini will contribute more than you think, Hemraj," Ashok said. "She'll do plenty."

"Hasn't done shit yet. Fucking lush."

Dharini took a drink. Her eyes were still flirtatious.

"I've got plans for you, Hemraj," Ashok said, pointing the cane at him quickly. "This family will go places, but first you've got to get mired in the dirt. Dharini's right, you haven't been tested yet."

"Tested? After all I've done..."

"I don't mean building buildings. That won't raise you spiritually. Let's look at other options. Let's push you over your hatred of this land's most valuable race."

"Valuable? What value..."

"As I understand it, you attended a public elementary school on the other side of town."

"Yeah, and never again. Fucking drug deals and shootings on the damn playground. That's what Dharini and Krish never endured. We'd moved by the time they were old enough for school. They just knew Hedridge. They don't understand the real world."

"You were young then. Your reaction was strong. Now you're old. You can revisit the teenage years you missed and gain a new understanding."

"What the fuck are you talking about, A? I'm not following at all."

"Yes," Ashok said, drinking the Sazerac. "That's the point, Hemraj."

32

Bob climbed the steep, creaky stairs at Lance's house and found Sveta lying on Shoquanda's bed completely naked. Her dress, earrings, hair clips, and underwear were on the floor. She held Bob's cell phone.

"You want Lance to see you like this, is that it?" Bob asked, sitting on the bed, his knees almost touching the cot next to it.

"I've been calling Rob, but he won't pick up. I miss him."

He took the cell phone from her.

"Forget him. You're Julie Stewart now. You've got a better life. How'd you like Carty's wife, Judith, and his daughter, Siobhan?"

"They're like Ashley and those board members, fake and stupid. Those annoying girls with braces in Thailand were better."

"There's a freedom in being with the common people, I know. But you've been there all your life. You don't want to go back. You want to be Julie Stewart, don't you?"

"I don't want Sasha or Boris or Alex. No, but do I want Bob either? This is slavery too."

"You'll have nothing unless we pull this off. You're going to set up a dinner in Hunters Point with the CFLIC Chair, Kirk Cortland, and his wife. We're going to talk them into accepting Brendan Carty's plan. That's our mission now. Forget Rob, Ashok, Hemraj, and Ashley. We've switched sides."

Sveta squinted.

"Switched sides?"

"Yes. Rob is on their side. Not ours. Got it?"

Sveta sat up. "What do you mean, he's on their side?"

"It's complicated. Just don't call him anymore. He's lost interest anyway, obviously."

Sveta stared at Bob. Then she began slapping him, yelling loudly.

"Crazy Russian bitch," Bob said, trying to grab her arms.

"Damn," Lance said, peering in. "Shit's going down in rich-boy land."

Bob gave him a murderous glance, something Lance had never seen before.

"Close the door, you baboon!" Bob shouted.

Lance frowned and did as ordered.

"Like that brother in The Jinx," Lance said. "Damn."

33

As the rain poured down, Niral sped towards Patpong, then realized it was approaching two a.m. Scandal had probably closed. Mr. Hong might have gone to an auction or an underground club. He might have left for his apartment. Or perhaps he had never left Same Same. After all, his protection was there.

Niral wanted to deliver the diamonds to him directly so he could discuss a new plan before he left for Phuket. And he wanted to know what Nam and Ricky had unearthed in Khon Kaen. They'd been gone for two weeks already.

The rain continued to pound as he sped through the streets of Sukhumvit. No crippled boy this time as he pulled up, but he could see the Indians and ladyboys in the doorway to the next bar. Still flirting, despite closing time.

Chinese and Korean gangsters guarded the staircase leading up to Same Same. But as he locked his motorcycle, a bevy of vehicles pulled up. Niral hid behind the staircase to the Skytrain. Uniformed men in riot gear rushed out of the cars. The Indians and ladyboys ducked; the men carried machine guns.

Maybe a gangster in the stairway fired first. Maybe not. But a hail of bullets sounded. The first line of defense in front of the Same Same club fell as rain, fog, and blood mixed and formed red clouds like at a Holi celebration. Niral crouched and put his hand on his holster. He checked the street. The street vendors hid under their carts, and the tourists eating late night noodles hid under their tables. Then he heard gunfire upstairs, as if the gangsters further up the staircase were firing back. A few uniformed men lined the entrance, occasionally firing up, then taking cover, while a larger group of commandos prepared to rush up. Then the shooting ceased, and the men conferred with each other.

As he unlocked his motorcycle, Niral noticed someone near the vehicles staring at him. Perhaps a detective from Shekhat's warehouse, although he could not see clearly through the rain. He turned his motorcycle around and prepared to draw his gun. But a shot or scream never came. As he rode away, he noticed the commandos charging up the steps: a yellow flash, a hail of fire, unceasing.

PART III

†

The Road Towards Phuket, Thailand; Phang-nga, Thailand; Udon Thani, Thailand; Hunters Point, South Jamaica, St. Albans, Long Island City, Broad Channel (Queens), New York; Khon Kaen, Thailand; Sands Point, New York; Near Krabi, Thailand

---

34

Niral parked the motorcycle outside Duncan's complex and took the elevator up to the apartment. He woke Buppha, and they gathered their things quickly. As they left the apartment, heavy voices in the elevator spooked him. and he decided to descend seventy-seven flights of stairs.

Exhausted at the ground level, he saw the police outside but slipped into the parking lot. As he drove the car to the gate, however, Niral was stopped by a police officer who asked for his passport or working permit. Still drenched, he handed over his passport, making sure he blocked the officer's view of Buppha's neck. If asked to pull over, he was prepared to shoot his way out. But the cop, despite radioing Niral's name to headquarters, apparently did not connect it to Mr. Hong, nor did he ask to inspect the car, and Niral and Buppha were allowed to leave.

A couple of hours later, they stopped in Phetchaburi, outside of Hua Hin, to eat at a food court. It was six a.m. Buppha was shaken up but in decent spirits. Niral called Duncan but there was no answer.

They continued to drive. About five hours later, they reached Chumphon where they stopped at a seafood restaurant, and for the first time, Niral saw women wearing Muslim headscarves in Thailand. He'd never seen that sight on his trips to Phuket or nearby islands like Ko Pha Ngan or Ko Samui, and this wasn't even that far south.

By now it was noon, and Niral called Duncan again. This time Lamai picked up.

"Where's Duncan?"

"He's in the shower. Sorry, was I not supposed to answer?"

"It's okay. Just tell him to call me back right away."

"Is something wrong?"

"No, no, just need to talk to him about something. How are you? How's the baby?"

"He's healthy. It will be a boy, just so you know. My sister and I went to the doctor and saw the ultrasound. Duncan was distracted when I told him but happy to hear it. Less than two months away for the delivery!"

"Great. Listen, just tell Duncan to call me, okay?"

Niral checked the news reports on his phone for the incident in Sukhumvit. The article said the Narcotics Suppression Bureau had a violent exchange with a brutal drug gang around two a.m. at the Same Same club outside the Skytrain station. The Bureau intended to take the perpetrators alive, but in the fire fight the entire gang was killed, including owner and mastermind Fan Hong. Hong's nightclub Scandal was also raided and arrests had been made without any casualties. The Bureau was looking for additional suspects, but it did not name them. Nor did it directly connect the raid to the new ya ba or the murders in Isan or Phuket.

Niral continued to drive towards Surat Thani. About halfway down, he received a call from Duncan. Buppha answered. Niral pulled over and took the phone.

"Did you see the news reports?" Niral asked. "Same Same just got leveled."

"What?"

"Mr. Hong's dead. Gang's gone. And they raided your apartment, Duncan."

Duncan was silent for a solid minute. Then he said, "Where are you?"

"On my way to Phuket to pick up the last shipment. But maybe I should lay low for a while."

Duncan sounded resolved now. "You're right, Bangkok is too hot right now. Phuket's not a good spot either. Maybe stay with Kan in Kanchanaburi when you come back up. I'll figure things out on my end." Niral heard Duncan crying. "I don't know what to do, man. I can't just leave Lamai and the baby."

"They'll find out where you are, and soon," Niral said. "You've got to lay low somehow."

"I know. I know," he said. "Look, they'll probably track my phone. I'll get a new one and call you back with the number. See if you can get another one too."

"Okay, Duncan. Stay safe."

"Oh, and who's that girl you're with? Sounds like the same gik from before."

"It's Buppha, Duncan. Apsara's roommate."

Duncan hesitated. "Are you serious?"

"Don't worry about it. I'll handle it."

They stopped again briefly in Surat Thani. By the time they left, it was four-thirty p.m. By six they reached Phang-nga, where Niral got a cheap hotel room and turned on the TV. The reports had magnified. Now, they said an international drug gang called the Dragons had infiltrated Bangkok and surrounding provinces, selling a more addictive version of ya ba. Fan Hong was dead, but his associates were still being hunted. Among them was a farang named Duncan Smith, and they posted Duncan's picture. They believed this scourge was related to killings in Isan and Phuket perpetrated by another farang named Borisslava Maric, and they posted his picture too.

At a news conference, Commissioner Prongchat said that while the raids were concerning, they were also a testament to the resolve of the Royal Thai Police in ridding Thailand of the poison of addictive drugs. He was happy the drug dealers had been killed and others were on the run. He said the government should consider stricter monitoring of foreign visitors so vicious gangs like this could not infiltrate Thailand. Someone asked him about the farang woman killed in Phuket, for which a Thai, Panit, was being tried under penalty of death. Prongchat said it was possible the Thai was innocent but that they would continue to investigate.

Niral called Duncan again. Duncan immediately gave him a new number.

"When you call, make sure it's from a different phone." Duncan said. "You shouldn't have used your phone there, but it's too late."

"Your picture's..."

"I know. I can't go home. It's too risky."

"Where are you? What are you going to do?"

"Still figuring it out. Just go ahead with the plan. Same steps."

"Okay. And I guess Malaysia if there's too much heat?"

Duncan sounded angry. "That's not an option. We need to finish what we started. Just stick with the plan. Call me with your new number when you get it. Stay in touch."

35

They were drinking champagne in the office. A rare sight at this division, but everyone was ecstatic about the decimation of an international drug gang, even if they had nothing to do with it. The division's honor had been confirmed, General Toon was a hero and so were Nat and Chan, kind of. Pom was praised as being a martyr of sorts, having the courage to follow the track of killers and thugs, even in the face of certain death.

The gangsters and dancers rounded up at Scandal were being questioned by agents in a secret location run by the Narcotics Suppression Bureau. But Colonel Nopasit Limwat was at the party, drinking champagne with General Toon Tomechrin. Both approached Nat and Chan.

"Why aren't you smiling, Nat?" Toon asked. "You'll get a medal. Maybe a promotion from the Commissioner."

"I keep thinking about my son," Nat said. "May I return to Isan and search for him?"

General Toon looked Colonel at Limwat.

"There's still work to be done," Toon noted. "We need to capture this farang Duncan Smith. His wife is from Chiang Rai, so he may be holed up there. We need to send someone."

"The Narcotics Suppression Bureau will take care of it," the colonel stated. "I will go myself."

"We don't have jurisdiction there, do we?" Chan asked.

"The crimes occurred in Bangkok," General Toon said. "I can speak to Khun Commissioner."

"We will handle it," the colonel confirmed. "Detective, if you are sad, go home and think there. You are ruining the atmosphere."

Nat took the hint and, ignoring Chan's pleas, left. But instead of going home, he found himself on the doorstep of Pom's apartment in Thonburi. Pom's wife, Anong, answered the door, and Nat broke down. Anong had to help him inside. Pom's two sons sat at the dinner table, eating noodles.

"I've wasted my life, discarded the people who mattered," Nat said while sitting on the kitchen floor, delirious. "Fighting for justice was a lie, a tool to help others acquire power and fame. What else can I do with my life other than end it?"

Anong held him by the shoulders, then slapped him in the face.

"My husband would be ashamed of you! He would call you a coward!"

"I am a coward," Nat said. "I abandoned my son. My entire life has been cowardice."

"So change it. Change it for Pom."

Nat looked up at her. "Pom? I barely knew Pom."

"So why are you here? Get out and leave us in peace."

"Your sons," he said. "They need a father."

Anong held his stare. "You want to be a father to them when you could not even fulfill your own responsibility?"

Nat didn't respond. He held the stare too.

"Or are you saying something filthier? That you wish to make me your wife so you can have my body? What a shameful man! Get out before I call the police on you!"

She tried to pull him up, but he pulled her down. She struggled and got out of his weak hold. She ran to the phone and picked it up as a threat. He didn't wait around. He jetted towards the door.

36

"What will we do?" Nam asked, sitting on the bed in their hotel room in Udon Thani, his hands on his head. "Mr. Hong is dead. All my men were killed or arrested. We can't go back to Bangkok."

"No," Ricky said. "But I talked to headquarters. They say stay on the mission."

"What mission? It's pointless to find Apsara now."

"Looks like it matters to Mr. Chang. Not sure why, but it does."

"We've been watching the bank for two weeks. Our contact in Bangkok says no one's withdrawn from the account. Nobody in Udon Thani's heard of this Prem Pramangchun."

"So we cruise the villages."

"Which one? There are so many."

"Better than sticking around here. Even getting laid by young girls gets old. Let's rummage some villages, choke some old ladies. You never know what an old lady'll spill."

Nam stood up. "I don't know who is sicker, you or me?"

Ricky laughed. "Believe me, you don't wanna find out."

37

"Nigga, you ready to roll?"

"How many cats we gonna catch?"

"T. tells me three. One nigga, two white dudes."

"Gonna kill a honey too?"

"Nigga said dudes. Don't know 'bout the bitch."

"Yeah. But it be cool to kill a bitch."

"Your Bangladeshi ass got no respect for women, nigga..."

"That's right, I'm gaming for a catch. No violatin', just a smooth ride."

38

"An excellent pitch, Mr. Stewart," Mr. Cortland said, shaking Bob's hand outside the restaurant in Hunters Point. "I like the way you think. I wonder if we could get you on the council too."

"Much too busy, I'm afraid. My wife takes care of our philanthropic endeavors."

"And a beautiful woman she is. Well-spoken and cultured too. I imagine Russia has a better education system than the US."

Bob smiled. "Yes, I have no doubt. We're always lagging behind."

Sveta kissed Ms. Cortland's cheek, then wished Mr. Cortland good night too.

Mr. Cortland asked Bob, "Do you live in Forest Hills? Perhaps we can meet closer to home?"

"We live in Bayside, but sure, one day," Bob replied.

As the Cortlands waited for their car to be delivered by a valet, Bob claimed their own driver would come around. This wasn't untrue, but the Cortlands drove away before Sveta called Lance to pick them up in his beat-up Hyundai Accent.

"How was that dinner, brother?" Lance said over his shoulder as he drove them around the corner.

"I think it was a success, don't you?" Bob prodded Sveta.

"I am glad it is over," she replied, putting the phone in a small purse that she placed on the seat. "I want to take shower and get the fake rich sweat off me."

Bob smiled. "It was a good idea to invite only the chair and his wife. Get to the board a little at a time. Better than some huge pitch to fifteen people. And he can influence more members."

"True, brother," Lance agreed. "Very smooth."

They drove across the gentrified area of Hunters Point, passed the waterfront and some warehouses, and then slipped onto the Long Island Expressway.

"They really set up this spot," Lance noted. "Used to be rail yards and projects and nothing else. I'm thinking way back, brother."

"I remember that too," Bob said. "I'd see the rail yards if I took the seven train in. That's why I was excited when Vishal pitched the LIC project to me. I wanted to build something in Queens."

"You used to take the subway, brother? Man like you? I pay my respect."

Bob smirked. "I wasn't always a rich man. I used to be like you, Lance."

"And what are you now?" Sveta asked, folding her arms. She had been cold to him since the other night, when he had forced himself on her to show her his power.

"No, brother," Lance said, ignoring her. "I don't believe it. You were never like me, were you?"

"I sure was. Used to take out the trash. El Paso wasn't no aberration or nothing," Bob said, resuming the accent he had adopted in Texas and Thailand until his fateful interaction with Pornopat.

"So that's where your ass was, El Paso? Funny place to put a wit. Right across from Mexico."

"What are you talking about?" Sveta asked. "You lived in El Paso, baby?"

Bob shot her a cold look. "You've never bothered to ask about my past, darling. Always about you. Always about Russia and Australia and how lonely you are here, how much you miss Rob, who treated you like shit and sold you away, darling. Did you know that? He sold you to me."

Sveta saw Lance's eyes in the rearview mirror. He was staring at her, but he didn't say anything.

"Did you hear me?" Bob continued. "He sold you. He didn't want you anymore. If I had to guess, another girl was more important to him."

She turned to him. Tears were in her eyes.

"How are you so mean? After all..."

"After what?" Bob thundered. "What have you done for me? You're on the council? I could do a better job than you."

"So why don't you? And tell them your real name."

He slapped her across the face. She cried.

"You bitch. Why do I always pick 'em?"

Lance didn't say a thing. They were all silent for a while. He took the Grand Central Parkway.

"Tell me about your past, husband," she said finally, wiping blood from her lip. "I do care."

71

"Maybe I will. But you've got to forget Rob. I'm sorry I said it that way, but it's true. He sold you to me because he didn't want to help you anymore."

"What is difference? I will never see my brother Kolya or my mother again. Who cares if it is Rob or Bob?"

Bob swallowed. "You're right. I'm sorry. You didn't deserve that. You've been a better wife than I could have ever hoped for."

"I am better than the whore you worry about. Lauren?"

Lance looked at Bob through the mirror.

"Sveta, you're better than her and my ex-wife combined," Bob replied. "I can trust you, can't I?"

He put his hand on hers and gripped it tight. She looked at him.

"You are bastard, but you are good bastard," she said.

They began to kiss passionately. Lance shook his head. "White folks, man. You can never predict 'em."

He pulled off the Grand Central, drove on some side streets, and parked in front of his house. Bob got out and Sveta slid over to get out with him. Lance checked the door light, which didn't seem to be working. As Bob put out his hand to take Sveta's, a masked kid emerged from behind a tree. He pointed his arm at Bob, a rolled-up shirt covering the boy's hand.

Two shots fired, the noise deadened by the shirt. Still, Lance heard it loud and clear. He jumped out of the car. Sveta screamed as Bob fell on her as she sat in the entrance to the back seat. The kid pointed the gun at her, hesitated, then ran away. Another kid approached from the left and pointed his gun at Sveta too, but Lance shot him point-blank in the head. Sveta continued to scream. The lights turned on at neighboring houses. Lance fired three shots at the other kid, but he disappeared into the nearby park.

Lance cursed loudly. People were watching through the windows now, afraid to come out. Bob was shaking violently in Sveta's lap, trying to say something, but she couldn't make out what he was saying. Then his shakes became quieter, and he was still.

Sveta was still crying, covered in blood, her arms around Bob when

Lance told her to get in the car. But Sveta wouldn't listen. She was hysterical.

"Then help me get him in the car," Lance urged. He started to lift Bob up, but then a siren sounded in the distance. He cursed again.

"If you don't get in the fucking car, I'm gonna leave you or shoot you. I don't give a fuck," Lance said, pointing the gun at her. This time, she complied, placing Bob's body on the ground and slipping further into the back seat. Lance shut the door, ran over to the driver's side, and sped away.

39

After destroying his phone and buying another at a local store, Niral decided to rest. He ate a simple dinner of noodles and khao yam with Buppha, then held her in his arms and kissed her lightly as they slept. The next day, Niral told her he had to go out and gave her money to spend on whatever she might need.

"How long will you be?" she asked.

"Maybe late. Don't worry too much."

She hugged him. "I am alive because of you, Niral. I should reward you."

"Have a good time. But don't be showy with the baht."

He drove a short distance to Pasat's restaurant. He parked and passed the tour groups.

"Tourism makes Thailand," Pasat said, giving Niral a menu as he sat. "Where are you from? India? I love India."

"I'm from Rob Johnson, actually."

Pasat considered him. "I did not know they would send an Indian. Where is Rob?"

"He's busy. But I'm on the case."

Pasat stood still. "I always got along with Rob until the last time he came. I felt he was disrespectful. But I did want to see him again."

"Maybe another time. I was told you would give me directions?"

"Always down to business with you Indians. All liars and cheats."

Pasat entered the kitchen, came out, slapped a folded piece of paper onto the table, and returned to the kitchen. Niral took it, a bit flabbergasted at Pasat's changed attitude. He was looking forward to eating quality southern Thai cuisine, which Rob had raved about in the past, but it didn't seem to be in the cards. He left the restaurant and, passing the tourist entourage again, returned to his car.

40

When Piti motorcycled back to her house from school, she found Nat sitting on the steps leading up to her home. He appeared disheveled and drunk. He held a half-empty bottle of Johnnie Walker in one hand and a gun in the other.

"What are you doing, Natthew?" she asked, trying to raise him by his shoulders. "The neighbors will see you."

He tossed the bottle into a shrub and stood on his own, waving the gun at her.

"Is your father home?" he asked in Thai. "I want to see that sick fuck."

"No, Natthew. You will make us lose face if you stay out here."

"Tell me about Udon Thani. Everything you know. Then tell me why you never told me my parents died."

"Your parents died?" Piti asked.

"They are lying between heaven and earth, between one life and another, you incestuous slut. And my son is missing and being tortured. Maybe he is dead, but does it matter? I lose face all day and no one cares."

He began to laugh like a hyena. She looked at the other houses. He pointed his gun in the air. She was afraid he would fire but he didn't.

"Let's go inside, Nat. Nothing good can happen here."

"Nothing good has happened here. Yes, let's go inside. Tell me about Udon Thani. Tell me about my parents and my son. Tell me about me, okay?"

41

"I can't believe this shit," Lance said, pacing around Carty's drawing room. "Bob's dead and they gonna figure out he's been living in New York."

"Yes, I wonder who that will anger?" Carty asked, dressed in his robe, holding a white Russian.

"Who would hit Bob like that? Who even knew he was—"

"Only one man."

"But how'd Vishal know Bob was with us?"

"Maybe Bobby's cell phone. A tracker? Possible."

Lance thought. Then he closed his eyes. "Course. Motherfucker. And we still got that phone too. It's in Sveta's purse."

"Don't worry. This might work in our favor."

"How? Sveta's a mess. Even Siobhan and Judith can't put her back together. I can't go back home cuz I blasted that kid, not to mention they'll ask me about Bob."

"Yes. You're both runaways. We'll get rid of your car and that phone. I'll have Lachlan put a man on it."

"Why you so calm about this, brother? What you taking when I ain't looking?"

"Think about it. It also might be Alicia Tragliani. She wanted Bobby dead too."

"Yeah, but you're saying it was Vishal."

Carty shrugged, then began to strut around, sipping his white Russian.

"I don't know. But I imagine we will know soon."

"How?"

"Vishal will howl. Or Alicia will."

"Why'd Alicia do it? That mob don't got no steps. They slide."

Seamus rushed inside the room, carrying an iPad.

"Father, I just got a random call on Skype. You won't believe who it is. And what it shows."

42

Niral followed the directions down Route 4 towards Krabi. He took a detour towards the coast, then followed deserted, narrow roads between tall stalks of grass and wheat. He felt like he was driving through the side roads of Gujarat again, except it wasn't raining, and certainly not flooding, and he was driving, not Manu.

He tried to make the correct number of turns, but he began to worry he had messed up the directions Pasat gave him. Then he approached an alcove whose perimeter consisted of houses and ended with a forest. When men came out carrying AK-47s, he knew he was in the right place.

One of the men, who had a facial scar, jumped in front of his car. It surprised Niral, and he had to slam on the brakes to avoid hitting him. He considering backing up, but another man slipped behind the car. A third man studied him through the window, squinting. Then he waved for Niral to get out.

As Niral emerged from the vehicle, a man wearing a salwar kameez and topi approached.

"Mr. Niral Solanke, is it?" The man then greeted him with a wai and said, "As-salamu alaykum."

Niral repeated the greeting. "Yes, that's me."

"I was anticipating Mr. Maric, but they sent you. The assassin. The true hero."

"Well, I'm not a hero yet."

"In a month, you will be. You will accomplish an essential deed for the furtherance of humanity under Allah."

"Do you have the merchandise to pay for that?"

"Right down to business. I would rather have some tea first, like they do in India."

Niral shrugged. "Sure."

He stepped forward, but two men surrounded him.

"I'm sorry, they must check you for weapons first."

They felt him up and took Niral's gun from him.

"I imagine this procedure will occur at the temple complex in India too," Rahmat said.

"Yes, they've got the security down. But we've got the plan set. Bhai will die."

"I am sure he will," Rahmat said, leading Niral inside a small, deserted coffee shop. He had Niral sit down across from him.

76

"I never bothered with such formalities with Mr. Maric. Or Mr. Johnson, as you call him?"

"Rob. We call him Rob."

"What an Australian name. Fake, short. No history to it."

"It's derived from Robert. I'm sure there's history to that."

"Borisslava Maric must have a history too. They all have histories. But are they blessed by the true God?"

"I don't think any of us know that," Niral said.

"But do we not?" The scarred man brought two small cups of tea, holding the saucers underneath them. It looked like Indian tea, light brown with dark fat on top. "Tell me, why would you act like these farang? You are Indian. You have lived in Thailand for many years."

"I am a farang. I'm American."

Rahmat laughed out loud. "American! You are not American. Remember always that you are an Indian. And not just any Indian but one dedicated to Allah."

"I'm not dedicated to Allah. But I don't see how that matters."

"You are interested in procuring drugs. An advance for the assassination. But why the assassination? Because you hate Bhai for what The Brotherhood did to your loved ones in New York?"

"The Brotherhood didn't do anything. The situation was manipulated within. I realize now you can't blame the divine, or some organization, for the actions of a few."

"So your motives are strictly financial. But how much will you truly make?"

"Duncan told me you'll send us more drugs once the assassination takes place."

"Yes, but if it does not, then you owe us. And we will collect."

"Don't worry, it will happen."

"Because you want money."

"I want to live in Thailand not as a slave but as a master."

"Of Duncan Smith?"

"Of myself."

Rahmat waved his finger at Niral. "Here you are mistaken. You become master of yourself only when you embrace God. Then you understand

The Dance Toward Death

your true path. You will never do so through money or independence, as the farang call it. Your friend Maric did not understand this. He was even emptier than I thought, twisted inside. This is why he is running from himself up in Isan."

"You know?"

"He is doomed. I would have killed him myself if he had come here."

"Why?"

Rahmat poured the tea into his saucer, then cupped the saucer with the tips of his five fingers like an Indian and sipped.

"He killed an innocent boy when he was here last. I guess it was an act of frustration after we showed him he was not invincible. He cannot kill children and think there is no consequence, in this life or the next."

Niral hesitated. "So you don't mean the kid up in Isan?"

"He is addicted to killing innocents. He murdered a poor woman in Phuket too. How can you associate with a man like that?"

"He's out of the picture now. It's just me and Duncan."

"Except Duncan is wanted too. He will probably be caught. Your drugs will be worthless if you cannot sell them. So you must have a deeper reason to kill Bhai than money, independence, or even fame. What is your motive?"

"You guessed revenge, right?"

"Yet, you say you are not angry at him. Perhaps your experience in New York shook your faith but not your confidence in Bhai."

"Why don't you tell me why you hate Bhai? You seem to know him."

Rahmat laughed. "Niral, I don't know Bhai, but I can tell you why I detest him. I was born a Buddhist here in Surat Thani province. I was raised to believe that if I prayed to Buddha, I would make merit for myself and my family. So I prayed, and my early life was good. I had nice parents who owned a small restaurant. I had decent grades in school. I studied hotel management in college, but before I got a job, I was told by my parents to join the monkhood for a few months so I could make ultimate merit for my family. So I went to a monastery. I was told to follow the five precepts, such as not taking what is not given, false speech, avoiding intoxicants, etc.

"Yet, I found monks doing all these things, Niral, and then pretending they were gaining merit. Only one monk I knew was honest, and he told me to go to India to study the true origins of Buddhism. Before that, I did not even know Buddhism derived from Hinduism, or that Buddha was a Hindu first. I went to an ashram in Andhra Pradesh. There, I learned the true nature of Hinduism was selfishness. I learned that if I prayed and dedicated myself to an idol or God, I would gain things for myself. I felt, in my heart, that this was wrong. How the true purpose of prayer should not be gaining material things or merits for oneself but sacrificing for God's greater plan and purpose. I was confused and depressed. I walked out of the ashram. I felt like Gautama, wandering from a lie. And that's when I entered a mosque. I was welcomed, and I learned the true path of humanity and the Lord. What arrogance I had before!

"To wish that one receive individual rewards for serving God. Serving God itself is a service. That can be the only purpose of life. Now I serve Allah and his messenger. People like Bhai, the hypocrites, the idol worshippers, are moving the world against Allah's vision. That is clear. He gives people things for accepting his religion. Peace, security, money, the promise of equality. Yet, the only equality lies in Mecca, of a brotherhood of man under Sharia. What is freedom's value if it is spent in sin and vice, like your disgusting friend Mr. Maric?"

Niral rolled his eyes. He hadn't touched the tea.

"I'm not sure what kind of monastery or ashram you went to, but neither Hinduism nor Buddhism teach that you can get things simply by praying. That's the layman's version, just so you know," Niral responded. "You talk about not benefiting or sinning from service to God. But you are selling drugs. You are making money."

"For the greater good. No one said sacrifices did not have to be made. Ultimately, we must ensure that all mankind is under Allah's law. But if some people or some principles must be sacrificed, they must be. Remember, it is different than at the monastery because those people are doing it for themselves, whether it is correct or not. We are doing it for Allah."

"But Talim has a selfish purpose. He wants revenge for the murder of his family."

"I am in no position to judge Talim's faith or his reasons for killing Bhai. But he doesn't dictate my reasons for supporting the plot. The ultimate result should be a switch in the direction of India and of this part of the world. If the assassination is done right."

"We'll do it right."

"You are keeping the operation very quiet. Even I do not know the plan, and I often know everything. Talim wanted you to use poison at first, but that is not how you will do it now?"

"No. Not theatrical enough, he says."

"Yet, you stayed with Bhai for weeks to learn his movements. Why would you do this, if not to kill him yourself?"

"I guess you will see."

Rahmat smiled. "A magician. Maybe your motive is pride in your skill to deceive and accomplish?"

"Why do you care about my motive so much? You don't care about Talim's motive."

"Even if Talim's motive is partially personal, I know he is loyal to the greater purpose. You say you are not, so I would like to delve into it further, because perhaps your reasons and your consciousness might expand. And anyway, I admit I am partial to Talim's motive. Muslim brothers and sisters must be avenged. Allah does want that."

Rahmat finished his tea. He looked at Niral's.

"It is not poisoned," he said. "And it is boiled. Do not worry. We need you, Niral Solanke."

"I don't want to drink caffeine this late," Niral responded. "It will keep me up."

"And why not stay up, Niral? Sleep here tonight. Stay with us for a few days, even weeks. Share the plan with me. We will help you prepare. Then, even if Duncan has been arrested or killed, we can get you to India."

"And forget the drugs?"

"Yes. We will smuggle you into another country after the assassination, give you a wife and a life. Will Bhai give you a wife? Will Duncan?"

Niral chuckled. "Look, why don't you show me the shipment first? Then I want to talk to Talim, in private, and make a few other calls. It's a complex operation with lots of players."

"Sure, call Talim. I feel he does not trust me now, but so be it, Mr. Solanke. We will show you the merchandise, then leave you to your phone calls."

43

Piti gave Nat some water to drink. They sat at the kitchen table as she consoled him. She told him she hadn't heard about his parents' passing.

"My father will be home soon," she said. "I don't think you should meet him."

"He's a rapist. The kind of man I joined the force to stop."

"He's never raped me. He's never raped anyone."

"He didn't touch you for all those years when you slept with him without a shirt on?"

Piti closed her eyes. "I don't want to talk about that. If you think your son is in Udon Thani, we can go up there. I know some girls who work at bars and massage parlors around town. Some hotel concierges too. If they know this Apsara, maybe we will find your son. Then tomorrow, we can claim and bury your parents' bodies. I can call off work tonight. I don't think one night will be a problem. Do you think you are okay, or will you get sick?"

"I want to go tonight," he said, glancing at the gun he had placed on the table. "After I kill your father."

Piti slapped his hand.

"You should be ashamed to say that. After you didn't do anything as a father..."

Nat got up in frustration. He reached into his pocket for his cigarettes. They fell on the floor. As he bent over, he heard a voice at the door.

"Piti?" the voice asked. "Who is this?"

Nat looked up. Piti stood quickly and grabbed Nat's gun.

"What is going on? Who is this?"

Nat stood up too. "I am taking your daughter away to Udon Thani, sir. For the night."

Piti's father stood motionless, then smirked. "You will pay extra for that, my friend. Piti, don't forget to charge extra," he said, waving his finger and moving into the living room. Then, with a groan, he continued, "Haven't I told you not to bring these tricks home when I'm here? I get so stressed seeing them."

"Yes, Father," she responded. "We are leaving now."

She nodded her head towards the door, still pointing the gun haphazardly at Nat, who stared at the living room entrance. He couldn't see Piti's father, so he stumbled towards the entrance.

"Sir, I want you to know I have honorable intentions towards your daughter," he said as he approached. "I will not besmirch your honor or your family's face. No, I..."

He didn't hear a response. When he peeked inside the living room, he saw Piti's father was asleep on a recliner.

He turned to Piti, who had joined him, still holding the gun. "I think I could have done a better job than him," he said.

44

"She's a pretty girl, isn't she?" Vishal's voice resounded through the Skype video as Lance saw his daughter, Shoquanda, tied up in a chair. "But bad things can happen to pretty girls. If you withdraw your bid from the Long Island City Project, you have my word, she'll go back to school. I'll even pay for private school. You wouldn't believe what my man saw her doing at the public school when he got her."

"Sick fuck!" Lance screamed, pacing around the drawing room uncontrollably. Carty stood directly in front of the laptop, while Lachlan took notes out of camera range.

"Vishal, first let me say that I'm glad you're alive," Carty said. "We thought you were dead."

"Bob told you, right? I thought I could trust him, but I guess I was wrong."

"Problem with your plan, Vishal, is that we know where you are," Carty continued. "We can call the FBI now. They'll arrest you, and this will end fast."

"Then Lance's daughter will die. And Carty, the Feds will know about your involvement in Bob's life and death, your plot to influence the

LIC project, not to mention plenty of other tidbits about your business practices. I suggest we settle this out of court, so to speak."

"What is your specific demand?" Carty asked.

"Tomorrow night, the Community Board will meet again and The Arts and Cultural Affairs Committee will give its recommendations. Withdraw Dekalb's bid by then. If you do, I will release Shoquanda and pay for her private schooling, assuming you keep out until the final vote. You see, I am offering more than I should."

"The philanthropist as always, Vishal," Carty said. "I taught you well."

"You didn't teach me shit, Carty. I want my house back, too, by the way."

"Is that part of the demand?"

"No. But I'll get it back anyway. Have a nice day."

Vishal cut off the line. Lance was cursing. "I'll drive down there and rip out his heart. And slaughter his entire family too."

"No point in overreacting," Carty said. "Vishal's demand isn't so steep. Maybe we should give it to him."

Lance's face twisted up. "You kidding me, my brother?"

"You want your daughter back, right?"

"Yeah, but how that help you? I'm not computing."

"I'll make a phone call and a visit. Come with me. Sometimes, Lance, you have to compromise to get what you want."

45

Niral analyzed the crates of drugs, making sure everything was there. Then he supervised Rahmat's men as they carried them out and stored them inside the trunk. He worried whether they could fit, but the trunk was larger than he thought. Still, as he watched the men working, he began to wonder. How much profit could be made with such a small amount that was so difficult to procure and and would be difficult to distribute? Had Duncan made a stupid deal, just as he had with Thanat's diamonds? The quality was good, but with all the heat, could they keep getting the merchandise from down here in the future? And why be indebted to Talim and his men with these advances before the assassination even took place?

After the crates were packed, Rahmat left Niral in the coffee shop alone to make his phone calls. His first call was to Duncan's new number. Duncan didn't pick up on the first call. He did the second time, but Niral could only hear him through static.

"Where are you?" Niral asked.

"I'm in the Chiang Mai countryside. I'm going deeper, where there won't be reception.

Kan's friend Thon is a member of a Karen hill tribe that's a major distributor of heroin and ya ba through Burma. He's going to hide me until the heat comes off. I've withdrawn all my funds from banks and put it in safe deposit boxes under other names. I've left the keys to the boxes in Lamai's father's house. Thon's spies told me the Narcotics Suppression Bureau visited her, but she doesn't know where I am, and I'm pretty sure they didn't find the keys.

"Drive up to Kanchanaburi and give the product to Kan. That's payment for hiding me. Then drive up to Chiang Rai. Get a hotel room and be inconspicuous. The cops are watching. Find Lamai and let her know I'm okay. When I need it, I'll tell you to get the keys, then the cash from the deposit boxes and the directions to deliver them to Thon's men. If I can't call, I'll communicate some other way."

"Duncan, this is getting complicated. How are we going to make a profit?"

"Don't worry about that. Leave it to me."

"Listen, something else happened in Bangkok I need to tell you about. I had an idea for..."

"I don't care about Bangkok anymore. Focus on this and the assassination. I'm trying to get Talim's product through Thon so we don't have to go south. We'll have a superior product and more efficient distribution."

"So we're really getting another shipment after the assassination? Because this doesn't seem enough to pay for the plans we have."

"Of course! This is just the advance so we can set ourselves up. Talim owes us a lot more when you get the job done, so make sure you do it.

Once you're back, we'll set up, maybe in Burma or Laos. Everything will go smoothly."

He couldn't hear Duncan anymore, so he hung up. He wondered who to call next: Talim, Manu, Mr. Ghosh, or Shekhat's brothers. The whole labyrinth was at his fingertips. He had Rob's old number and Nam's number too. And how about his father? He began to laugh.

Some might be hesitant to pick up after seeing his new number, but Manu might not care, so he decided to call Manu in India first.

Manu did pick up. Niral could imagine Manu driving from Bharuch to Navsari, Mr. Ghosh in the backseat, delivering supplies for Yam Gam. Or at least that's what Niral hoped Manu was doing. After the catastrophic events that included many deaths in Yam Gam and the imprisonment of the former Dubla mayor Prameshbhai and the Brahmin Ravi, Niral had instructed Manu to be his conduit after The Brotherhood had taken over substantial influence over the village by promising to build new homes in the formerly flooded Dubla area that would rival the Brahmin homes. It was being run temporarily by a council, where each member represented the interests of a certain caste, including Narendrakaka for the Brahmins, Meetal for the Dubla, and Lakshmanbhai for the Vaishya and other castes, until new elections were held.

"Yes, everything is going well, Niralbhai," Manu said. "I have followed your instructions. Yam Gam has accepted the temporary council, and elections are set for next month. Only minor conflicts have erupted between Brahmin and Dubla. Prameshbhai is still being held in the Dubla village, but we have moved Ravi to Prameshbhai's old house. His re-education to The Brotherhood way will be finished soon. Then he will marry Lata and be a good father to their child. Meanwhile, Bhai has poured money into the Dubla village and it is being reconstructed fast. Meetal says a private donor is also giving a large amount to help speed the process. So the Dubla are happy about that. The Brahmins are happy that Bhai has refused to redistribute land. Except he has given Prameshbhai's land to Lata."

"Excellent. How about the other part?"

Manu's voice suddenly got lower. "It is going well too. We should be ready by Diwali."

"Good. And he doesn't suspect you?"

"No, Niralbhai, I don't think so."

"You're doing well, Manu. Thank you, my friend."

"It is a question of God's work, Niralbhai. And I will not forget how you clarified my vision of my wonderful daughter, Gayatri."

Niral hung up. Next he called Talim, but Talim didn't answer. So he called Anil Shekhat's brother, Mitesh, who was still working at the warehouse where Niral had killed his brother.

"Remember what we discussed," Niral said. "I'll call you when I think we can move forward. Meanwhile, keep working like your brother Anil is still there. We can report him missing when it's time."

Last, he called his father on the landline at home. He picked up after several rings.

"Deddy," Niral said.

"Niral," his father responded. "Is that you?"

"Yes, Deddy. How have you been? What have you heard?"

"Heard?"

"Yes. About Yam Gam. About Diwali."

His father was silent for a while. Then he said, "I heard Manish died. I am sorry about that."

"But The Brotherhood has taken over the village."

"Yes," his father said cautiously. "Sometimes good things come from bad situations. I never trusted Prameshbhai. But I was surprised he willingly handed over power to a democratic council. And that Bhai now trusts Narendrabhai."

"Strange things happen," Niral said, happy that his father seemed to have heard, and believed, a sanitized version of events. "You should consider donating to the Dubla village reconstruction. Remember that Harshkaka and Kamkaki work for us."

"I love Harshkaka and Kamkaki, but I don't believe in donating directly to causes. I donate to The Brotherhood, and they distribute the money as they feel. But I've heard that Bhai has been generous."

"Yes, but there has also been a private donor. I naively thought it was you."

"Niral, I am glad you have become involved again, both in regards to the protection of our society and to social service. Perhaps it is in our blood. But do not get sucked into politics. You know I avoid politics."

"Deddy, will I see you again in India? Will you be at Shri Diwali?"

"Yes, I plan to be at Shri Diwali. I hope you will be a good boy until then."

"I am trying, Deddy," he said. "I am trying."

46

Nat and Piti passed a few farang and entered the Nutty Park complex. The bars were mostly empty of customers; a few bar girls played pool or sat on stools. Piti led the way towards the end of the hallway, then took a right to the end of the complex. At one of the bars, she asked a girl in Thai to get the owner.

A short, fat woman came out frowning. But the frown became a smile as she recognized Piti. They hugged and chatted a bit. Piti introduced Nat as an old friend.

"I know Apinya from Khon Kaen," Piti explained. "She used to own a bar there. She thought business would be better here. Some girls from there moved up to join her. Is business good, Apinya?"

"This end of the complex isn't so lively," Apinya said. "More farang gather near the entrance, so the bars there do better. I've been trying to change our location, but the competition is fierce and no one will budge. But it is still better here than Khon Kaen."

Nat gave Piti his phone. She showed Apsara's picture and described Som to Apinya. As she did, Nat heard a commotion on the other side of the complex. At the bend in the hallway, two men were arguing in English. Nat thought they had Australian accents and seemed to be discussing crime in Queensland. One of them was vocally anti-Queensland, saying he had been happier in the bush. Nat began walking towards the bar, and as he did, the voice clicked for him, and so did the figure. He began running.

Rob seemed to understand right away. He picked up a chair and hit his fellow Aussie, then bolted in the other direction as Nat yelled for him to stop. Nat pulled out his gun. Farangs and Thais alike ducked out of his way. At the entrance to Nutty Park, Rob jumped into a tuk-tuk. Nat struggled through the crowd, called a tuk-tuk too, and followed Rob.

He could see Rob's tuk-tuk's taillights in the distance. Nat's tuk-tuk honked as Rob's made a turn. As his tuk-tuk turned too, he noticed Rob's tuk-tuk had stopped. Nat told his driver to slow down. He pointed his gun as they pulled alongside. But Nat saw only the driver. Rob had disappeared down a dark alley. It was illuminated by the moon, but Rob was nowhere to be seen. Nat chased for a minute, checking the various depressions and mini-alleys, but he could not see anyone. Rob had eluded him again. Nat cursed out loud, then returned to the tuk-tuk and drove back to Nutty Park.

47

"Nice to meet you," Alicia told Brendan Carty as they sat in her living room. They were sitting with Alicia's Uncle Jerry, Lachlan Carty, and Lance. "I thought I was meeting Bob Macaday, the man who put my people in jail."

"Bobby's dead," Brendan said. "Not on the news yet, but the police will figure it out."

"Dead? Who got to him?"

"He came out of witness protection," Brendan said. "He was helping us with our mutual nemesis, Vishal Patel. Unfortunately, Vishal found out."

"I thought you had done me the favor of killing Bob for me. Then we'd have something to talk about. Now— "

"I come to you with all the cards on the table, Alicia. No gimmicks, no tricks."

She looked at Uncle Jerry, then at the drawer that held the gun she believed had killed Vishal Patel. "Okay. So Bob's dead, but Vishal Patel is alive."

"He is. But he's changed his face, name, and identity to a distant cousin named Ashok Patel."

"And where is he?"

"North Carolina. A town off the coast. Near Apex, I think. He lives with his extended family."

Alicia glanced at Uncle Jerry again. "So you could take him out. Why come to me?"

"The situation has grown complex, my dear. He's taken Lance's daughter hostage. I don't want Lance to lose his daughter. He's valuable to me. Vishal's condition to free her is that I withdraw my bid on the Long Island City property. I don't want to, but I think there's a way we can all win here."

"How is that?"

"I drop my bid, Lance gets his daughter back. Then I go in with you on your bid. Opaque, of course, but you give me equal kick-backs."

"And what's in it for us?"

"Influence. We already have the CFLIC and Board members on our side—and Councilman Vince Stevens. You have influence over the Queens Borough president. Without even suspecting it, Vishal will lose the project easily."

"When he loses, he'll realize he was duped. And he'll come back for us," she said.

"Yes, but by then, we'll have a plan to eliminate his influence in NYC and get the money back he stole from us. Killing him now would be too easy and fruitless. His family has a motel fortune, and he clearly controls that Ozone Construction company and whoever's behind it, whether it's gangs or other businessmen. I suspect that includes the unions, which you used to have influence over. Once we figure out his network, we can work to get them under our control. Then we can have our revenge, plus money and power."

Alicia looked at Uncle Jerry again. "I'll speak to my uncle. We'll get back to you. Soon."

48

"Older vic ID'ed as Franklin Stewart from a North Carolina driver's license in his wallet," Detective Trevor Lawrence said.

He was talking to Detective Manny Sanchez, his old partner from the

108th Precinct in Long Island City. Lawrence had transferred to the 113th precinct in St. Albans, nearer to his home in Cambria Heights, because he had gotten sick of the commute. Plus, he wanted to solve crimes in his old neighborhood, and the NYPD had a shortage of detectives in the precinct. But the old partners were fond of each other and Lawrence missed Sanchez's sixth sense. So he called him up after he responded to this double murder.

"White guy wearing a tuxedo shot in St. Albans?" Sanchez said. "Looking for late-night black pussy?"

"It's cheaper here in southeast Queens, no doubt. But that's not the weirdest part. House he was shot in front of belongs to an old acquaintance of ours. Lance Portman."

"Who?"

"Long Island City fire case. Niral Solanke's friend. The janitor, remember?"

Sanchez thought for a minute. "Yeah, when we found Lorenzo's body. We questioned him."

"I'll admit, I remember him because he was a brother."

Sanchez laughed. "That's why you moved down south, so you can be with your people. But seriously, this could be a complete coincidence."

"Yeah, but this dead guy's mug resonated with me. I was like, I've seen this cat before. So I had my partner, Lewis, dig up some old pics on the internet. Sure enough, this guy looks like Bob Macaday."

"The witness in the Lucchese case. Isn't he in witness protection?"

"That would explain the other name. I'm gonna call the Marshals. They must have fingerprints and DNA on him."

"Good luck with that bureaucracy. And hope they don't take jurisdiction."

"If this cat left Carolina on his own, it's our murder. I'm not letting the Marshals take it."

"Unless it was part of the Marshals' game plan. And if this hits the Daily News, watch out, man, it'll be all over. You remember what happened with the Traglianis. The News is always itching for that mob connection. So what's the theory if this checks out and the Marshals have no idea? Lance recognizes Macaday, lures him to his house, and tries to exact revenge for who? Niral? Stan Lorenzo?"

"Or Lance tries to blackmail Macaday, he comes over, they fight, Lance shoots him. But why wouldn't Macaday be armed? Why's he wearing a tuxedo? And what about this brown kid who's got his head half blown off? He hasn't been identified either."

"Adopted son?"

"Don't see any record of it. Lance has a daughter, Shoquanda. I'm gonna question the ex and see if she knows him. Still, witnesses say Lance shot the kid, but no one confirms he shot Macaday. And there was a white woman too, tall and beautiful. Some say she was crying over Bob and Lance kidnapped her at gunpoint and drove away. Others say she was willing."

"Didn't think you'd get high-end action in St. Albans. Maybe just some stupid kids, wannabe gang activity, junkie murders..."

"Well, we're high class when we wanna be, brother. We got Caribbeans here now. Listen, I'm gonna look up Macaday's wife. I think she was in wit prot too, but she is older than the broad seen here. Still, that could be a lead. I'll be in touch with further developments. And you reach out if you got any thoughts."

PART IV

†

Phang-Nga, Thailand; Near Krabi, Thailand; Udon Thani, Thailand; South Jamaica, Broad Channel, Long Island City, Astoria (Queens), New York; Surat Thani, Thailand; Kanchanaburi, Thailand; The Road, Thailand; Near Udon Thani and Nong Khai, Thailand; Sands Point, New York; Near Erawan National Park, Thailand

49

The Narcotics Suppression Bureau's determination to hunt down remaining Dragon members and cease distribution of the new ya ba at any cost had created an intense dragnet around Bangkok and Phuket. Niral decided to stay in Phang-nga rather than risk a checkpoint stop on his drive up. Leaving the car at Rahmat's village, he borrowed a motorcycle from the man with the scarred face and spent his days moving back and forth between Phang-nga and Rahmat's village outside Krabi, where he knew there were no checkpoints. That's how he lived for a few weeks until the fervor died down.

Inevitably, after spending time with her in the hotel room, he became intimate with Buppha. They didn't fuck, but they did cuddle, fondle, and masturbate each other. She had been the aggressor, and while he felt a bit guilty and uncomfortable, he came to accept the relationship as it was. In his mind, he was still her protector, defending her without exploiting her, as redemption for failing to protect Lauren. Whether the sexual component was payment for services rendered was questionable, Buppha never expressed it as such and never asked for anything in return. Niral would just give her money, and during the day she would go about town and spend it.

He had never envisioned a relationship with a ladyboy; his claims of homosexuality had finally, strangely, become a half-baked reality. Yet despite the odd coupling, he was glad to finally have a relationship with someone who seemed loyal. Compared to his previous women, she was a vast improvement. The prostitutes of Pattaya and Bangkok were only faithful while he could pay them. Apsara had disappeared after their intimate encounter, and he recalled Zaineb's backstab, Chloe's flakiness, Lauren's obsession with Amrat, and Meetal's bitchiness. Of course, he recognized Buppha was a prostitute, like all the rest, and that she was playing a role. But he felt a certain genuineness in her intimacy. He trusted her enough to tell her about the drugs, but not enough to mention Talim and Bhai.

His Muslim compatriots could not know he was housing a ladyboy, let alone that she was his lover. He would often spend the day with them and see Buppha only in the evening. Additionally, he restricted her movements. He wanted her to remain in Phang-nga and expressly forbid her to travel to Phuket, although he suspected she would take occasional trips to Krabi and Phi-Phi. He required her to be back by dinner time, when he would often bring leftovers of Pasat's delicious southern cuisine, but she was told to avoid being spotted entering the hotel. Naturally, this situation caused a strain and led Buppha to tire of their arrangement.

Niral had ameliorated his relationship with Pasat, and Pasat began to trust him as a "good" Indian. Pasat explained that he had encountered many groups of Indians who were rude and didn't pay the full price or argued about small things. When Niral asked why Pasat had claimed to love India initially, he said that was a standard thing he said to all nationalities and ethnicities when he welcomed them.

Niral often ate an early lunch at Pasat's restaurant, then motorbiked to Rahmat's village for the day, staying until evening, when he would return to Pasat's restaurant for dinner. Despite Rahmat's urging, and pointing out that Niral didn't have to waste two and a half hours every day traveling from point to point, he rarely stayed overnight since he wanted to keep his word to Buppha. He also didn't feel comfortable being unconscious around the Muslims, especially in the rural and enclosed atmosphere of the village. Yet, he felt a kinship with the men in the village that he felt balanced his relationship with the feminine kathoey, Buppha. Their being strict Muslims didn't bother him since Rahmat had toned down his rhetoric and spoke to him as a friend. Through this trust, Niral revealed elements of the plot to Rahmat.

Now Rahmat knew there were two complexes: Dwarka and Lamba. That The Brotherhood believed the terrorists would try to infiltrate the primary complex in Dwarka during Shri Diwali, not knowing the actual location of the plot was Lamba. The Brotherhood expected the terrorists to be ambushed, imprisoned, and tortured for information so their security apparatus could eliminate Talim and his co-conspirators. That they would try to keep the operation quiet, but if it did erupt in the media, they would play the coverage to their advantage, painting the Islamic terrorists as a threat to Hindustan itself that only The Brotherhood's leadership could protect the Indian people from.

That was what The Brotherhood believed would happen. But Niral explained to Rahmat that his plot with Talim was different. The conspirators would enter the Dwarka complex as unarmed Hindu pilgrims the day before the event and sleep overnight along with the other pilgrims. The next morning, the buses transporting the pilgrims to Lamba for the event (the pilgrims would also be unaware of the actual event at Lamba for extra security) would take two conspirators to the Lamba complex, leaving two behind to hide at Dwarka. Niral would have a man inside the Dwarka complex to supply arms to those two conspirators in a room without cameras. After the pilgrims were transported to Lamba, the terrorists would wait inside the room until Niral's man gave them the word that the mission at Lamba was complete. Then, avoiding detection as they would know the layout due to a map of the security arrangement, the terrorists would murder everyone left at the complex, eliminating much of Bhai's security apparatus. Then, they would plant bombs in each temple and blow them up.

Meanwhile, Niral would stash arms at the highest temple in the Lamba complex. Because the pilgrims would be strictly organized by who could enter which temple at which time, he would have the conspirators positioned so they could enter the final temple before the final ceremony. Niral would pass them weapons in a spot where cameras did not capture the transaction. They would hide their weapons and wait for Bhai to emerge before murdering him. Almost certainly they would forsake their own lives, but they did not mind. They welcomed martyrdom for Allah.

Rahmat asked why Niral had studied Bhai's movements while staying in the Dwarka complex if he hadn't intend to poison him. Niral explained he was actually mapping the layout of the Dwarka complex so he would know where security would be stationed and where they could avoid camera detection. The Dwarka massacre would be a double event with the assassination that would play much better in the media than a boring poisoning.

Next, Rahmat wondered how Niral could possibly survive the assassination without being suspected as a collaborator. For the Dwarka plot, Niral explained, his inside man could be blamed: he was a former Dubla, and it might be believed that he was influenced by the Muslims. Plus, he would not live to tell his side. Niral could explain he was duped too: he didn't know the terrorists would enter as pilgrims and that the Dubla would provide them information on the Lamba complex. In Lamba, if the exchange was done right, the cameras could not prove his involvement, and they could surmise another person in the security forces provided the weapons, possibly a Muslim named Bilal.

"But no one else has so much influence as an in-between—"

"They respect me and my father. I know they would suspect me, but I have to take the chance that they would believe me initially. That should give me enough time to leave before I'm detained."

Rahmat did not say what he wanted to say: that if Niral became a Muslim it would not matter if he was detained or killed. He had become fond of Niral. He wanted to convert him to Islam, but he realized his best bet was through friendship, not lecturing. Listening to the details of the plot, he was impressed with Niral's deft handling of the two camps and wondered how he had learned those skills.

One day, as Niral drove up to the village in his motorcycle—the man with the scarred face was pissing off in a corner of the adjacent field— Rahmat approached him and, whispering, asked if they could speak in private. Niral agreed, trusting Rahmat as much as he could in his situation—a vulnerable situation.

He parked his motorcycle and followed Rahmat, wordlessly, back the way he had come. They trekked up a grassy path and took a right into a narrow passageway within a field. Niral continued to follow nervously. They entered an empty, circular space. Niral flinched, expecting to be jumped. To the right, in a tight corner, where tall ferns had been chopped away to clear a path to a small stream, Rahmat squatted.

"I buried him right here, peace be upon Ibraaheem, and may Allah be pleased with him."

"Who?"

"My boy Aadil. One morning after breakfast a couple of months ago, he and his cousins were playing, and he got separated. His mother called and told me he had not come home. It rained that night so we waited until the next morning to do a search. While I searched his village, his cousins ventured into this field. They found a topi in the dirt and smelled something foul, so they ran and got me. I found him in the stream. Someone had tried to cover him up, but the rain had washed enough away to reveal him. He had been beaten to death. He should not have died so young. Before puberty, before adolescence, before sin. He had to suffer the shaking in the grave, simply because of our sorrow. But I know that he is in the care of Ibraaheem in Paradise, as any boy would be."

"You think Rob did it?"

"It was only a day after he left. It must have been him. We had tortured Maric and taken his weapons. Aadil was murdered with brute force by someone's hands. Oh, Allah, avenge me!" Rahmat said, weeping, covering his face. "Avenge me, Niral, if you should see the monster again. We do not target children, do we? We do not target women, do we? No, we are the civilized ones."

"Rob's missing, so I won't see him, Rahmat."

"You may. He may elude justice from the police, but he will not elude justice from you. I have seen how you are. You can fool even your closest friends."

"So how do you know I'm not fooling you?"

Rahmat stared at him with dumbfounded fury. He rose to his feet.

Niral kept a steady glare. "You don't," Niral said. "And how do I know your son was killed? You never mentioned a son."

"He was born of my second wife. You have never met her. She keeps herself covered and lives in a nearby village. I don't share my family life with my business partners. But he was my only son. My first wife only gave me daughters."

"And this makes your loss greater?"

"Yes, but for God's sakes!" Rahmat yelled, his fists clenched.

"I thought this was not about revenge."

"Killing Muslims, killing children. It must be."

"Rob is my friend. He's never done anything to me. Why should I kill him for you?"

"I looked into Maric's eyes as he suffered when we tortured him. At that moment, you see someone's soul. I saw nothing. He does not have friends. If he acted like your friend, it was only to gain something."

Niral took out his gun from his holster. "You forgot to unarm me. You probably shouldn't make that mistake again."

Rahmat swallowed as he eyed the gun.

"So what, you will shoot me?" he asked. "To avenge your friend's torture?"

"No, Rahmat. Now I will take my car and my drugs and my ladyboy girlfriend I have stupidly hidden from you and drive up toward Bangkok. If I am caught, so be it. I will shoot my way to freedom or death. If I should meet Rob again, I will look into his eyes and make my decision based on my own sense. Does that sense come from Brahma or Allah or Buddha or some abstract phenomenon we cannot comprehend? I used to sit in a shitty apartment in Brooklyn thinking about such things. I haven't thought about things like that in a while, which is why you would probably see in my soul what you saw in Rob's: an emptiness, a void, nothing at all but fraudulence and foolishness. But when I move up north, maybe that void will fill with something. Maybe I won't be able to fool people so easily anymore. And maybe I won't be of such use to you when I see Rob."

Niral turned around and began to walk back through the passageway. Rahmat tried to understand Niral's words. When he couldn't see Niral anymore, he fell again to his knees and faced Mecca. He put his arms out and prostrated to the ground. "Allah, peace be upon him..." he muttered. "Allah, peace be upon him..."

50

Nat smoked about two packs a day now. For weeks, he had been staying in a hotel room in Udon Thani. Piti would come up and visit him during the day, cruise with him to various complexes to see if Apsara, Rob, or Som had showed up. Occasionally, they visited villages on the northeast outskirts closer to Laos. He had ignored calls from Detective Chan and General Toon. Nat considered himself resigned from the Royal Thai Police force, but armed and active nevertheless.

One day, as Nat lay on his bed, his head bent over backwards off the side of the mattress, blowing smoke up into the air, Piti entered his room. She was excited.

"Did you hear what happened in Phuket, Nat? They found Maric's DNA on the mattress. They say he killed the tourist! So they released the Thai Panit."

"They solved the case without me," Nat responded in a deadpan tone. "But no sign of Maric."

"They will look for him harder now. They found the husband's body—in America!"

Nat sat up suddenly.

"In America?"

"Yes, Natthew. Strange, no? An international case..."

"But still no Maric. And I saw him. I failed to get him for the third time."

"So you will succeed on the fourth try."

"He likely crossed into Laos weeks ago. There's no point."

"So look for him in Laos. Maybe Som is there."

Nat stood. "Piti, when I cremated my parents, I felt their spirits were uneasy. I thought to myself: I must return to Udon Thani and hold vigil until I find my son, dead or alive. By now, their spirits may have passed into a next life after heaven, and I may never find him. Would a rational person move on? Should I return to Bangkok and solve ladyboy murders in Klong Tuey?"

"If you do, take me with you. I've always wanted to live in Bangkok."

He approached her and asked, "Will you dance at Nana? Or Soi Cowboy?"

"I will dance anywhere," she answered. "And you won't have to work if..."

"Don't work for me, Piti," he said, covering her mouth with his free hand while flicking the ashes from his cigarette. "I will work for you. But first, let's take one final shot at the bar, Day & Night. Otherwise, we will give into fate, and let Buddha provide...."

51

Lawrence met Sanchez in a Czech restaurant near the RFK bridge in Astoria, where they had some cod liver, boiled klobasa, and beer as they peered at a foggy and partially obstructed view of Manhattan and the Bronx.

"Why'd you call me here? To look at this damn bridge, making us feel inferior to the other boroughs?" Lawrence asked.

"Felt like some Czech beer. It's the good stuff. So what's the word?"

"Bob Macaday's been identified by the Marshals. We sent over DNA and fingerprints, and they did the ID quick. If that's not amazing enough, Bob's wife, Linda, was killed a couple of months ago while they were on vacation in Thailand, and Bob's been missing since. So the Thais and Marshals have been looking."

"The Marshals just let him go to Thailand on vacation? Isn't Solanke there?" Sanchez asked, drinking his dark brew.

"Yeah, Solanke's been teaching English there, last we heard, but that might be a coincidence. As for Bob, Marshals can't stop 'em from leaving wit prot. Apparently, the couple got sick of their location in El

Paso, Texas. Which means that Carolina is a whole 'nother mystery. His name in wit prot wasn't Franklin Stewart; it was Bob Murphy. Real imaginative."

"So he was living in Carolina under a different name too? Then why come to New York?"

"Those are the trillion-dollar questions, brother. Looks like he got set up in Carolina with a fake SS number and an address on a worthless piece of land with a mailbox on it owned by the federal government for a potential park site. How he got that Social, I don't know, and apparently that license got issued while he was in Thailand. Shady shit. The Marshals said they'd work with the Feds to check the videos and logins at motor vehicles, but I'm not hopeful; it might have been created off-site by a hack. And you know how interagency shit goes."

"Marshals or Feds trying to take the case?"

"Captain says they're gaming. But I leave politics to them. Until they say otherwise, I'm on it. My partner, Lewis, contacted the Carolina State PD to expedite the search, but they only do highways."

"Anyway, back to Macaday."

"So he gets a new identity in Carolina. Must have had someone's help to get it while he was in Thailand. Then he's up in NYC in a fucking tuxedo meeting Lance Portman, along with some white hooker and a Bangladeshi kid. Whatever your theory, here's something to complicate it: the gun left at the scene was in the kid's hand and had his fingerprints on it, but it doesn't match the bullets in Bob. The kid has bullets in him consistent with Lance's registered gun, at least the same make and model. But the bullets in Bob don't match Lance's registered gun either."

"So maybe he used a different gun to shoot Bob."

"Yeah, but we did find bullets in the park apparently fired from the car, and they do match Lance's gun."

"Meaning maybe there was a third shooter? And Lance was shooting at him?"

"Possible, but no witness saw him. I'm still thinking Lance is the shooter using a different gun, or there's a third shooter and Lance was trying to eliminate him just like he eliminated the other kid. Or maybe the bullets in the woods were fired another time."

"Hmm. That is strange. And you're sure the woman was a hooker?"

"Not conclusive, but it fits the theory. I figure she was Lance's bait to get Bob to St. Albans. We found a Texas ID for Robert Murphy on the floor of Lance's daughter's room. The bed was extended by a cot, like someone needed more room to get busy. We've got Bob's DNA, including semen, and an unidentified female DNA on the cot and the bed. Plus, the same DNA in the shower, sink, and on towels in Lance's bathroom downstairs, like they used it before and after they got busy. Bob's got a history of infidelity with young women that came out at the trial. So looks like he got lucky before he got killed."

"Hmm...are you sure they weren't living there?"

"If anything, she might have been staying with Lance, maybe his rent-a-gf, although her DNA wasn't in his room, which makes me think she was hired for this job. We did find a couple of suitcases in the living room, one for Bob and one for her, but they weren't the same type of suitcase, and hers was smaller, more like a day bag she might roll around between tricks. A toothbrush and poof in the shower had her DNA on it, but not clear if they were hers for the day or weeks.

"His bag wasn't huge either, and he didn't have any personal items, like a toothbrush, in the bathroom or upstairs. Everything was in his bag, including his dirty underwear. I figure maybe he's been moving from hotel to hotel or friend to friend, though we don't have any evidence of where he was staying, nor did we find a phone on him, so we can't track any calls. We're still checking on how he got to New York or if he was ever in Carolina at all. Maybe he flew into New York from Thailand because his contact was here. Maybe whoever pulled the strings did it from here but got Carolina involved just to create confusion."

"All possible. Did the wife have a new identity made too? Maybe they both planned to move back to NYC but with different identities. Homesick after their vacation?"

"That's possible. Then his woman gets whacked, maybe by the Traglianis, and he escapes to NYC with that new identity alone?"

"Complicated case. You need me for anything?"

"If you can dig up more stuff from the LIC case and the Lucchese trial, that'd be helpful. I wanna do some homework. I'm gonna check with the Thais on the Linda Macaday murder. And I'm considering who'd have the power and means here to create this fake identity. Might even be an inside job. Maybe the Marshals aren't telling us something."

52

Not only had Shoquanda been released, but she had returned to New York City, began living with her mother, and enrolled in an elite private high school in Manhattan called Corcoran. Vishal had paid the fees and pulled strings fast with the help of Ashley Simmons, who was a board member and donated to the school. Their efforts were aided by the fact that the school year had just begun.

Lance, still hiding at Carty's, visited his daughter one day at her mother's place in South Jamaica, Queens. They knew he was a fugitive and had been responsible for both Shoquanda's brief captivity and her newfound fortune.

"I know you were fooling around with those niggers down south," Lance told his daughter, holding his finger firm. "That's why I put you in this white-boy school. Get some better friends. I see you hanging around with those fucking niggers with their pants down low, I'll take a pistol to 'em like I did to that Pakistani nigger. You got that? Don't fuck with me."

"Why you talking to me like that, Dad? I didn't..."

"We sent you down south so you can behave better, not get HIV from some broke-ass skank. We scared you with the kidnapping, now this the real test. You better pass it, or there ain't gonna be no 'GO' sign when you come around the board again. You got that?"

"That's enough, Lance," his ex-wife said. "I think she got the message."

"She better. Next time she got a blindfold on, it ain't gonna be pretty when it's lifted."

Shoquanda took a taxi to school that Vishal was also bankrolling. Lance's ex-wife pulled him aside.

"Look, like I said before, I don't wanna know where this cash is coming from. After I saw the news stories about this mob witness, I stopped asking questions. Long as I know Shoquanda's safe—"

"Don't worry, she's safe. I wouldn't be doing this if not. She got a good ride now."

This comforted his ex-wife enough. But Lance, driving Carty's limo now, was afraid of their future prospects. He had been profiled in the media, and Bob's true identity had been revealed. The Arts and Affairs Committee had approved the bid from Vishal's front, Ozone Construction, and recommended it over the other bids. But support on the board was illusory. Through multiple channels, Carty and Tragliani planned to pull the rug out at the next meeting.

Carty was hiding Lance, but now that Vishal was helping Shoquanda, it made no sense for Lance to support Carty and Alicia's plan to mount DeKalb Construction. It made more sense for him to override them. He pulled over on Merrick Boulevard and called Vishal's house.

Hemraj answered.

"Man o' the house around?" Lance asked.

"Which one? There are a lot."

"A, brother. A."

"There's only one A."

Lance could sense Hemraj roll his eyes. Hemraj told Dharini to call Ashok to the phone. Since participating in Shoquanda's kidnapping by befriending and tricking her, Hemraj had grown distasteful of Ashok, even as Ashley and Hemraj's family continued to adore him.

"Yup," Ashok said.

"Vishal. We've gotta talk." Lance explained the situation. Vishal wasn't surprised.

"I knew Carty wouldn't give up that easily. And Alicia's got some guido parked out here. He hasn't made a move. I figured there was a reason."

"So what we do, brother? I appreciate your efforts for Shoquanda. That's my daughter right there. Raising her right is my primary concern. Carty made that deal for me, I can't forget that, but he never done nothing like this. You might have tied her up, but now you treating her like a princess."

"And I'm gonna go all the way with that. Look, you keep watch for me. Tell me what they discuss, what goes on. With the two aligned, we've got an uphill battle these next few weeks, but we can make it happen. We've got Bob's wife, don't we? The Russian girl."

"Yeah, but she's been a mess. Your boy killed Bob right in front of her. No way she'll help you. Cops haven't ID'ed her, or at least they ain't saying publicly. Think she's a hooker working for me. They looking for her but don't have no profile."

"Cops aren't too bright. We never put the marriage on paper in case of a situation like this. She doesn't have to like me, but she's switched sides before. Make her understand this is survival. And I know someone she wants to see. If she follows through, tell her she can see him."

"If you mean that cat Rob, Bob told Sveta that he sold her sweet ass to him. Plus, Carty got his wife and daughter on her these last few weeks. She's attached, and she's comatose."

"So wake her up to reality. Does she have influence on the CFLIC?"

"She and Bob met with Cortland, the CFLIC Chair, before your boy jacked Bob. Sounds like they had rapport, and she could talk to him. But if he follows the news, Cortland knows Franklin's dead, and that he's Bob, so he's a liability if he squeals to anyone."

"I don't wanna go around whacking rich white guys if we don't have to. We'll get more heat and never get this development off the ground. But like I said, we've got the Russian girl. Tell her we can get her to Rob. In return, she'll talk to this Cortland guy to make sure he's on Ozone's side. Have her tell him the mob whacked Bob, and that DeKalb's got the mob behind it. If she convinces Cortland that DeKalb's in bed with the mob, maybe he'll convince the CFLIC to vote for us and keep the cops out of it to protect himself from retaliation. Doubt he wants to go into witness protection too. I know it's a risk, but I think that's a better bet than other options."

"It'll have to happen soon."

"Who knows, maybe this Cortland guy is out of the country or doesn't watch the news. But if he does, I agree, you'll have to work fast. Good luck."

53

Niral returned to the hotel in Duncan's car, bypassing Pasat's restaurant. He had called Buppha's cell phone. She had their stuff packed when he arrived. Earlier, after leaving Rahmat and retrieving his car, he had pointed his gun at the man with the scarred face, daring him to shoot the potential hero of Islam in India. The scarred man had opted not to shoot.

The ride up toward Kanchanaburi along the Gulf of Thailand coast was beautiful. They saw limestone crags and lakes against the clear sky, the timeless and magnificent beauty of Thailand that even the epics could not capture. But Niral felt Buppha had grown tired of his company. She played video games on her phone, only occasionally acknowledging the scenery Niral pointed out.

Niral had vowed to protect Buppha, but their relationship seemed destined to end. Two hours into their trip, they entered Surat Thani and stopped at a roadside restaurant. Buppha noticed signs for a ferry to Koh Pha Ngan and Koh Samui.

"Have you been to the full moon party, Niral?" Buppha asked.

"Yes, I went with my boss and my coworker. Long time ago."

"You party all night?"

Niral nodded. "Yes, it's once in a lifetime."

"I am still alive. I have never been to Koh Pha Ngan or Samui. I believe the full moon is tonight. Maybe I will go now."

"So you'll leave me. Just like that?"

"You come too."

"I can't leave the car here, not with what's in it."

Buppha shrugged. "Then I don't go too. I have no money."

"You didn't have much money in Bangkok, either. But you made money how you could."

"Are you telling me to sell my body?"

"I'm not telling you anything. I'm not going to dictate what you do."

Buppha smiled. She enveloped his face and kissed him. "You are good man, Niral. I love you."

"I love you too," Niral said, reaching into his pocket. He gave her a roll of baht. "You call me anytime you need me."

"Thank you, Niral. I will."

"And keep putting makeup on that ring around your neck. Don't let that jerk Nam bring you down."

Buppha smiled. "Yes, Niral. I will not let anyone bring me down."

54

At Day & Night, Nat was drinking a Singha and chatting up a bar girl when Piti approached, holding hands with another bar girl.

"She has a story," Piti said. "I think you should listen."

The bar girl, named Ska, told him about an old woman who had moved to her village a few years ago with a young girl. They claimed they couldn't take the big city and preferred village life. Everyone thought it strange because not only was it the opposite scenario of most, but they claimed to be from Udon Thani, yet their accents resembled the Khon Kaen region. They bought a stilted home from a family that moved to Bangkok once their daughter made it big down there, which was the typical scenario. No one in the village saw the grandmother work, so again, everyone thought it strange. How did they afford to live? Money from Bangkok, too, they assumed.

Later, the grandmother moved to a house on the outskirts of the town, past a few farms, where the other villagers rarely ventured. The girl changed schools to the next town over, a better school, and the other house languished. Finally, it was rented by a village family that needed extra room for an impregnated daughter.

To collect the rent from the family, the grandmother would come to the old house regularly, but more recently, they say a young woman came. The old people said she looked like the grandmother, only younger, and that she was pretty. Ska had never seen the young woman, but when Piti showed her the picture of Apsara, Ska said the general features matched.

"Should we go?" Piti asked Nat. "It could be her. And if it's not, at least we tried."

"Even if it is her, finding Apsara doesn't equal finding Som or Maric," Nat replied in somewhat slurred speech. "But we have no other lead."

"Where is your sense of adventure? If nothing else, we may uncover a good story of a struggling daughter returning to Isan to tend to her child."

"Yes," Nat said, chugging down his beer. "A hero's story."

55

"Bob Macaday might ruin my life again," Alicia said as she was sitting in her living room with Brendan Carty. She had called him over while Uncle Jerry was out. "If this investigation gets bigger and they link him to the Long Island City Project, we all go down. I suffered enough with the last trial. I say we cap Vishal while we can and hope to survive the fallout."

"Don't panic yet, my dear," Carty said, holding a white Russian. "We've still got a good plan."

"They know Macaday's identity. Don't people know he's that Russian girl's husband? And now they're saying his real wife was killed in Thailand? We eliminate the Russian girl, eliminate Vishal, even this black guy you have. We don't leave any traces. His daughter too?"

"You're ruthless, my dear. We can still win without resorting to violence. I've got plenty of connections. So trust me."

"Last time my father trusted a hedge fund guy, he ended up with a bullet inside him from a spic."

"Alicia, my dear, you're not your father, and I'm not Vishal. I agree, the investigation into Bobby is troubling, but it's also pressuring Vishal to clean up on his end. Maybe he already has. He's neutralized for now, so it's better to keep the peace."

"They're looking for the black guy and the Russian girl. They know who he is, and they'll probably figure out who she is soon. You've got them right here. Why take a chance?"

"More bodies will bring more focus. There's a smarter way to handle it."

"I'll trust you for now," Alicia said. "But my patience isn't boundless, Carty."

56

When Niral finally made it up to Kanchanaburi, he texted Kan cryptically from his new number. Kan called him back and suggested they meet at a club within the city. Niral thought it strange, since Kan usually wanted to meet on the outskirts of town.

Niral often stayed on the street Th Mae Nam Khwae, sleeping in raft houses and hanging out in backpacker bars there with Rob, but the club was on Th Song Khwae, where the Thai bars were. The area was relatively serene, devoid of tourists and the noise from all-night karaoke cruises on the Khwae Yai River.

Niral parked his car close to the club. He didn't want the merchandise too far away. As he entered the club, a pretty Thai hostess confronted him with a deep, serious wai, meeting his eyes.

"My friend," he said in Thai, pointing towards Kan, who was seated against a red cushion in front of a large, round table. The club was almost empty; three young Thai men were seated at another table. A single strobe light twirled around, but no one danced. The pop music of Jintara Poonlarp resounded.

Kan had been drinking. A bottle of Johnnie Walker red label was on the table along with a glass. He called the waitress and asked in a slurred voice for another glass.

"Beer for me," Niral said, giving the waitress a mild smile. "Tiger, please."

"You look good, Khun Niral," Kan said, slapping Niral on the shoulder. "I thought you be nabbed by Suppression Bureau."

"Nope, I got out. And I've got more stuff for you. You talked to Duncan?"

Kan smiled. "I speak to Thon. He tell me about Duncan. I feel bad. This would not happen if not for man in Bangkok. Sumantapat."

"Yes. Would I love to get revenge on him. I think we all would."

"It will be tough job. He is often at club these days, where many men are undercover."

"Are you saying you'd be willing to take care of it for a price?"

"Niral, if you take Muay Thai lessons like I tell you, you take care of it yourself." He laughed hard, slapping his thigh. The waitress brought Niral's beer and a glass.

"I like you, Niral," he continued. "You are the only honest Indian. I know, it difficult to describe drug dealer as honest, but I think you are. We do business for a while, so I think you know if I negotiate."

"It would be nice to have him dead. But it might create more problems too."

"We don't like problems in Thailand. Sanuk, sanuk. That is all we say."

Niral sipped some beer from the bottle rather than pouring it in the glass. "Look, Duncan didn't tell me exactly how much to give you. He said part. I don't know what that means, and I haven't been in touch with him in a while."

Kan smirked. "Niral, I am in business with Thon. The product come down here. Duncan's protection lasting for weeks now. Why you give me only part?"

"Well, he said part. I tried to call him on the way up, but he didn't answer."

"He is in mountains near Chiang Mai. Only way the Bureau cannot find him. I hear you are supposed to go up to see Duncan's wife. I don't blame you. I hear she is beauty. But the Bureau is watching. Better if you are here, working with me. Maybe we get you wife, settled, and kill this Sumantapat while we make fortune. So far, the news has not mentioned you. So you are in clear."

Niral didn't answer. He drank down some beer and thought to himself.

"I always told you, lead a balanced life, like that face of yours, like Hanuman." Kan poured and drank another shot. "Okay, let us go to the car."

Niral drank another sip of his beer. He let Kan pay, even though Kan treated him as the poo yai by referring to him as "Khun," but no matter; Niral was his guest so there was no shame.

He followed Kan out. Kan seemed casual. He had no men around him, and they'd been doing business for a while. Yet, he felt strangely uneasy. Kan stood in front of the passenger's seat.

"What are you doing?" Niral asked.

"I won't look at merchandise here, Khun Niral. Let's go."

57

Night had fallen, but Nat drove the ladies to the village anyway. Ska sat shotgun while Piti lounged in the back. Nat had paid a hefty bar fine to take the girl, but he figured it was his only shot.

The village was down a minor route going west towards Nong Bua Lam Phu. They hadn't ventured into that side of Udon Thai at all.

After thirty minutes, he turned and drove north up a rural road illuminated only by his headlights. He drove for a good hour, then Ska signaled they were approaching the village and asked Nat to stop at a small shop. The establishment was closed, but the proprietor sat on the front steps smoking, spotlighted by a bare bulb. Ska got out and spoke to the proprietor. He pointed in the distance and waved his finger around.

When the bar girl returned to the car, she asked Nat if he wanted to show Apsara's picture to the old house's current inhabitants or proceed to the grandmother's house. Nat said they'd start with the grandmother, and if no one was home, they could come back and interview the others.

So they chugged through the village and turned onto a bumpy dirt road between farms. The car's headlights spotted not a single soul but occasionally Nat detected a human shadow on the periphery. Past the farms and a sugarcane field, they approached a small hut on stilts. Nat noticed that at one window a faint light emanated upward, like the rays sourced from a lamp positioned on the floor.

Nat parked, then shut off the engine and the lights. He turned to Piti.

"How should we proceed?" he asked.

"I don't know," she answered. "You're the cop."

"You're a cop?" Ska asked.

"Used to be," Nat responded. "Don't worry about it."

He opened the door, then turned to Piti.

"Wait here," he said. "I will give a signal if you can come up. Probably the lamp."

Nat closed the door softly. He peered between the stilts to see if anyone was living beneath the structure. In the darkness, he made out a clothesline and ceramic jars that usually contained water. He took out his gun, held it ready with his arms out, and then slowly climbed the stairs. On the upstairs terrace, he peered through the window with the light. It was a large room filled with Buddha statues, a spirit house, red carpet, and draperies. A girl slept on a bed holding a doll, and an old woman sat up with her eyes closed, apparently meditating. A lamp with its shade inverted was near her.

He moved on.

He passed a door. The next window was boarded up. Then he noticed another door. The window next to it was blocked by a cloth shade. He went around to the other side of the terrace and peered into an open window next to a tree branch. This time, he could see a woman sitting on a bed in a small room, perfectly still, facing the other door. She was barely illuminated by another floor lamp whose shade was normally placed. Nat could have jumped through and surprised her, but he decided to return to the door on the other side.

He knocked and waited for what seemed like a century, staring ahead at a large full moon. The full moon party was kicking down in Koh Pha Ngan, he thought. All the farang were having fun.

He didn't hear any movement, like her scurrying to the back window, which he was ready for. He knocked again twice. He heard a woman's voice asking for identification. Nat said, "Your friend."

"We don't have any money here," she said. "Please go away. I have a gun."

"I have a gun too," Nat said. "I am the police."

The woman didn't respond. Nat waited. Then he said, "You can't escape. I have people in the back and downstairs too. Open up. I just want to talk."

Then the woman said, "I cannot pay. We don't have contraband either."

"Are you Apsara? Duanphen? Ploy? Tip?"

A long pause endured. Then he heard, "I have a gun. I will kill myself. You have no shame, causing me to lose face."

"Apsara, I will be honest. I am a police detective from Bangkok, but I am retired now. I will not arrest you. I have another agenda. I want to talk. If everything goes well, you won't lose anything. No money, no face, no life."

He waited again. He heard the door unlock. Slowly, it slid open. Nat burst in, holding his gun out. Apsara sat on the bed, holding a knife to her throat.

Nat said, "A knife is not a gun."

"It can still do the job," Apsara said. "What do you want?"

"I want to help you," he said, lowering his gun. "Believe me, I want to help us both."

58

Lance entered Carty's mansion in Sands Point with his key, and proceeded to the upstairs bedroom where Sveta lay, staring up at the ceiling. Judith and Siobhan were not there.

Lance closed the door. He sat next to Sveta on the bed.

"Girl, you awake?" he asked as he waved his fingers over her eyes.

"Obviously," she said quietly, continuing to look up.

"Just wanna ascertain. You're basically comatose these days."

"I saw my husband killed right in front of me. How would you feel about this?"

"Girl, I popped a kid. You don't remember that?"

"You're reminding me. Again."

"Point is, you know shit's fucked up. I wanted to be CEO, but that's not in the cards. And you wanna be a princess, but that's only partial in the cards. We've gotta make adjustments in this life. You should know that more than anyone."

"Why?"

"Let's just say an authority told me your history. Girl, you've been through a lot, and you've been tough. So be tough now. We still got a road ahead."

For the first time, she turned her eyes to him. "Authority? Do you mean Bob?"

"Why you crying over Bob? He beat you and raped you, didn't he? Don't make it right just cuz brothers jumped you in Australia too."

"You won't do the same thing?"

"Not my style, girl. I don't force my way in, I smooth it. I got plenty of bitches on the side, and they got nothing but respect for my black ass. This one girl, Candy, she used to be a stripper at Gigglies, this club that burned down where they wanna build. Now, she married to some boring white accountant guy, but she always begging me to knock her up. Say she want her baby black, she wanna name it Leroy. Ain't that crazy?"

"You are charming guy, Lance," Sveta responded, deadpan.

"I'm saying, none of us perfect. We all got different situations. And a lot of times we think someone screw us over and they really done us a favor or vice versa. Like you remember Bob saying, before he pass, about how that Rob sell you to him?"

Now Sveta had his attention. "Yes?"

"Well, that's not true. I got it on good authority that Rob killed Bob's wife for him. In return, he brought you to America to give you freedom. That's what Rob did for you, girl."

Sveta asked, "How do you know? Who is this authority?"

Lance hesitated. Then he laid it out. "It's all over the news, sister. They found Bob's wife, Linda, in the sea. They thought some Thai guy did it, but now they know it was Rob. And they're after him, Sveta. With Bob killed in front of my crib, they got more pieces. But I tell you who the true authority is, who tells me everything. It's a man in North Carolina. Hemraj's cousin, Ashok. He's in touch with Rob, and he can get you back with him. But this time, you won't be beholden to no one. You won't have to sell your body unless you want to, girl."

"Didn't he kill Bob? Now you are with him? How about Carty and Judith and Siobhan?"

"We've gotta adjust to practicalities. You know that better than anyone."

"I feel I am adjusting all the time in America. Who can I trust?"

"Look, I liked Brother Bob. I knew Linda: she was a nasty woman who'd betrayed him before. I don't blame him for getting rid of her. But he might have done the same to you later. Rob did you a favor because he loved you. Ashok needed Bob and you for that Long Island City Project, and you benefited. But then Bob betrayed Ashok by switching to Carty, so he had to snuff him out."

"And me. And you. And I hear your daughter was kidnapped too."

"Actually, Ashok's helping my daughter now, and he gonna help us too. We're on the run, so we're expendable in Carty's eyes. Carty's allied with Alicia Tragliani now, and she don't take chances. We gotta play this right. Because otherwise..."

"We are dead?"

"Yup. From one side or the other. You and I, we locked at the hip, girl. We've gotta help Ashok get this Long Island City bid, and then I'll take you to Rob myself. We all in the same boat now."

"How do I help? Everyone knows my husband is dead. And the police are looking for me."

"It'll be tricky, but let's put on our thinking caps. We'll get together a plan, and we'll figure it out."

59

When Vince Stevens entered the bathroom at his office building in Long Island City, he slipped inside the stall on cue. Carty was there. While Vince locked the stall, Carty started to kiss him, but Vince fended him off.

"Dear, I'm not in the mood. We've gotta talk about this Bob Macaday situation."

"All right, but first I wanna give Daddy a kiss."

"Dear—" Vince began, but Brendan kissed him strongly. Vince let him first, but then he pushed him back.

"Look, I'm worried," Vince said. "What's up with this Bob, Franklin, whatever his name was? And his wife is on the CFLIC?"

"We're allied with Alicia, which means the Queens Borough president is on our side. And with your people on board, that shouldn't matter for the bid."

"This could blow up on me, dear. If they link you to it, and find out..."

"How would they link me? They don't have anything."

"They suspect Alicia. They know your black man. They know this Russian model."

"She's no model. She's contained, and my man..."

"Can't be seen. I know you've always had a soft spot..."

Carty smiled. "Soft spot? Dear, I'm a kitty."

"Exactly. Which is why you should, maybe, let the grown ups handle this one."

Carty took a step back. "Grown ups? I'm a millionaire many times over, honey. You don't have anything near my net worth."

"Different ballgames. We're talking about politics here. And in this case, criminal enterprise."

Carty thought to himself. "If you think it's necessary...I suppose Lachlan can hire someone."

"I don't see any other way. We can exile them, but where? They still remain liabilities."

"Maybe that's why I lost everything to Vishal. Couldn't get my hands dirty, dear. I didn't want to be a gangster."

"You have to get your hands dirty when you make a deal with the devil, Brendan. You are allied with Alicia now, just like Vishal was allied with her father. We all make our alliances, no matter how shallow or how dangerous."

"Speaking of alliances, can you keep these protesters in line? I imagine they like Vishal's proposal more."

"They'll be angry, and I'll rant and rave against it, but my people will vote for you and hopefully the crowd won't be too suspicious. Then I'll steer their energies to another topic of public ire."

"I like the way you operate. Wanna be my publicity guy?"

"I could always take that if I don't get re-elected," Vince said, smiling and kissing Carty.

60

They drove deep into the countryside, it seemed, past the temple on the hill he had once tried to visit, past acres of woods, and toward Erawan or Sai Yok National Park.

"We've never gone out this far," Niral noted.

"I hear you were with ladyboy," Kan said, smiling mischievously.

"Where'd you hear that?"

"Around."

"Do you have a problem with it?"

Kan laughed. "This is Thailand. Why would I have problem?"

"Others have had a problem. In Thailand."

"We Karen are not like Burmese or Muslims. We are more like Thais, even though they discriminate against us."

"You're Karen?"

"I don't live with my people. I don't practice their ways, but yes, I am Karen."

"That's how you know Thon."

"Yes. We go back. I wish you brought the ladyboy so I can meet her."

"Her name is Buppha," Niral said, uncomfortable with the conversation. "She decided to go her own way."

Kan grunted. "Very unreliable, these ladyboys."

"Maybe I was afraid what you would do to her. You talk about tolerance, but..."

"Khun Niral, Karen respect women. We ask them for judgment, even as men do the work."

He laughed. Niral continued to drive into the black night.

"Where the hell are we going?" he asked. "We've been driving for over an hour."

"Do not worry, Khun Niral. Be happy. Make this right up here."

Kan slouched down. Niral became nervous as they continued to drive up a grassy road. Only his headlights and the full moon's luminescence lit the road. After fifteen minutes, Niral witnessed a yellow blaze on the right. As they got closer, he noticed it was a bonfire.

Several men had gathered around it, their cars parked not too far away. Niral stopped his car suddenly. He took out his gun and held it to Kan's head.

"What is up, Niral?" Kan asked.

116

"These are your men?" he asked.

Kan nodded.

"I don't recognize them," Niral said. "They're not the normal ones."

"They are not the same men, Niral. They are from up north. Please, put the gun away."

"Fuck you," Niral said, waving the gun at the door. "Get out slowly. I'm watching you."

Kan opened the door slowly and got out. Niral exited quickly. He saw men holding rifles approaching him. Kan scurried and took cover behind another car.

"Don't move. I'll shoot," Niral said, pointing his gun at them as the men approached steadily. He prepared to hop back into the car, not knowing if he could make it.

"Niral!" he heard his name resound. A man approached, his hands in his pockets. Niral recognized the familiar walk. The other men lowered their weapons.

"Duncan," he said. "Wow, I can't believe it."

"Relax, Niral," Duncan replied. "You're among friends."

Niral lowered his gun. "I wish Kan had told me. Bringing me out here to this shit."

Kan waved to him mischievously, then began joking around with one of his comrades.

"Nobody knows I'm down here," Duncan said. "Sorry it had to be done this way."

Niral and Duncan hugged. It was a strong hug. They had never hugged before.

Duncan leaned back and held Niral's shoulders. "Remember before Rob, when it was just me and you? Now it is just me and you. You're the person I trust most in this world. No Rob, no Hong, no Nam. No Dragon debt. Just me, you, and Lamai. We're going to survive, and we're going to flourish."

"How? You're on the run."

"I'm living in the Chiang Mai countryside now, but eventually I'll cross into Burma to live among the Karen. I haven't made the trip yet because Lamai will be due any week now. I wanna make sure I can visit her, and after the baby's healthy, we can sneak them over too. Talim will get you there after the assassination. From there, we can decide if we want to change identities and move back to the US, Europe, or somewhere else."

"You still need me to visit Lamai?"

"Yes. You're not on the radar yet, so you can still operate in public. Let me handle the drugs. We're going to have good distribution now. I'll talk to Talim about getting the remaining batch through Burma so we don't have to go south after the hit. You focus on finishing the job on Bhai."

"And this guy Thon? Is he here?"

"Sure," Duncan said. Thon approached and smiled.

"Pleasure to meet you," Thon said. "We are very fond of our new business partner. We look forward to handling your famous merchandise."

"Handling it?" Niral asked, but when no one responded, he decided not to inquire further. "Are we taking a trip up north?" he asked instead.

"Yes," Duncan said. "While Kan sells our merchandise in the provinces, I'm gonna show you my new digs. And then you go see Lamai in Chiang Rai, when the Bureau isn't looking, of course."

"So Kan takes the whole batch?" Niral asked.

"Let me handle the deals," Duncan said, dismissing his question. "You handle Bhai."

61

"It is a long story," Apsara said, sitting on the floor of the small room now with Nat, Piti, and Ska. "I did it for my daughter and my mother. My father died when I was young."

"So you killed Pornopat and his men," Nat said. "You killed Boy. You dealt drugs."

"I did none of those things. Rob did them. I was just his gik."

"Now he has my son. Or he has killed him. He may be in Laos, or he is still looking for you. Did he love you?"

Apsara smiled. "He says he did. But I know men. Prem said the same thing."

"Who is Prem?"

"He is Thanat. Pornopat. Whatever his name was at the moment. He was the father of Hathai, my daughter."

"The gem dealer was the father of your daughter?"

"He was a con artist. I've known him since we were children. He has always been con artist. We were in love for a short time. When I had our daughter, he became scared so he ran away to Chiang Mai. That forced me to quit school and move to Bangkok to support Hathai. At the bus station in Bangkok, I was tricked and forced to sell my body. I escaped, but then, what could I do? I met a woman who told me, instead of working at a club as a dancer or selling myself to random men, I could put myself up for auction. Some men came to buy women for the night, but others would pay handsomely to own a woman. And so I was bought by Mr. Hong. He gave me money I could send to my mother and daughter. I had to pay him back by working at his club Scandal, plus much interest, but I needed money badly, so I did so gladly.

"That is when I met Duncan, my mia noi. I thought Duncan might marry me, but instead he married his proper girlfriend, a Lanna girl named Lamai. So I started sleeping with Rob, his assistant, too. And then, one day, out of the blue, Prem came to me. He said he missed me and our daughter and wanted to provide for our family.

"We started talking, and I told him about Duncan's business. He suggested we rob him by selling him fake diamonds. I told him I was doing well as Duncan's mia noi and didn't want to be involved, but he was determined to succeed, so he introduced himself to Duncan without me, and that is how he brought Duncan fake diamonds and stole his money.

"Duncan and Mr. Hong wanted revenge for the theft. They thought it was best a woman somehow find, seduce, and lure him to his death. I asked Prem for a slice of the money for Hathai, but he only gave me a small share. I felt he was still his greedy, selfish self, but I could work him. So to keep both options open, I volunteered to seduce him for Duncan and Mr. Hong.

"I began working at Sumantapat's club Go-Go Rama and convinced Duncan that I met Prem that way. Prem began to trust me more and brought me in to work on tourist gem scams. He gave my mother access to his bank account in Isan to withdraw money when she needed it for Hathai, including the money he had stolen and deposited. But I knew that his generosity would not last long. It never did. The Dragons were a stronger gang, and my perks were better. I owed Mr. Hong money, but Duncan helped me pay it off. In return, I spied on Rob, who also helped me with money when I needed it. Prem had screwed me over before. But since I had his bank account information, I went along with the plot.

"One day, Prem tried to sell fake diamonds to an American tourist. Rob killed Prem and the dealers, then he blackmailed the tourist. Rob ended up killing the tourist's wife in return for money and his Russian gik, who married the tourist and got a trip to America. The money he gave to me. Boy showed up as he did. I ran away as they fought. I think Rob killed him. I knew things would be bad with Sumantapat, so now that I had this extra money, I decided to split. On my advice, my mother had already moved out of our old village and come here. Then we decided to switch homes. And here I am."

"Why does Rob still want you?"

"Maybe he is in love with me. I don't know that he still wants me. Maybe he wants to kill me. It seems like everyone else does."

"But no one has. No one has found you until now."

"Yes, and I hope you will keep it that way."

"I will, but only if you help me."

"Do what?"

"What you did to Prem. Lure Rob here so I can deal with him. And hopefully save my son."

"How can I do that? You say he may be in Laos?"

"Yes, but I don't think he is. I think he is still out here, in the villages, trying to find you. So maybe you can make it easier for him to find you."

"He is a killer. I want to keep my daughter safe."

"I want her safe, too. I want to save our children. And if you help me, we will."

120

BOOK TWO

PART V

Bushwick, Bay Ridge, Greenpoint (Brooklyn), New York; Near Udon Thani, Thailand; Chiang Rai, Thailand; Sunnyside (Queens), New York; Near Chiang Mai, Thailand; Bangkok, Thailand

62

Suddenly, Lance woke up. He had been dreaming a long and varied nightmare he only partially recalled. He remembered running to Carty's mansion, chased by the mob, except Vishal opened the door, and inside, Lance confronted Niral, half his face scarred, a voice chuckling in the background. Niral stepped aside. Lance entered the hallway. At its end, a guru, whose image he associated with Amrat, was choking the life out of Lauren, who transformed into a naked, sneering Sveta. She vanquished the guru with a push, then opened her mouth and fired a flame at Lance. Lance ducked, only to find himself being whipped by Candy. Then a gaggle of tormentors, including Stan Lorenzo, Bob Macaday, Brendan Carty, and Vishal Patel mocked him as he cowered on the floor and received his punishment.

He was sleeping on a couch. He tried to remember where he was. A slight ray of light peered through an askew opaque glass window. As he examined the worn refrigerator covered with magnets advertising obscure publishing companies, he recalled his location. A week had passed since he had fled Carty's home with Sveta to a lair in Bushwick recommended by Candy. While she had settled down and married an accountant, her stripping days long behind her, Candy still held membership in an anarchist organization, the Brothers of Aesthetic Unity, that she had joined after Gigglies had burned.

The Brothers of Aesthetic Unity had, when formed, one foot in Occupy Wall Street and one foot in Mikhail Bakunin. They were social anarchists who believed in artistic freedom and workers' rights. They detested corporate America, Wall Street, and oligarchic government. But they had been veering from protesting at demonstrations and parades, wearing black masks while shouting down pigs and corporations, to acts of violence and true anarchy towards civilization. It was not enough anymore to form worker cooperatives and collectives, to live and protest peacefully, to work within the system with trusted political representatives. They had tried that, and it had not worked.

The Long Island City Project was especially close to their heart. They saw it as a symbol of potential victory over corporate greed and middle-class regimentation. They had been active, behind the scenes, in protests against the CFLIC and the Community Board. They opposed any contract that didn't include rebuilding the former structure of The Spray Mecca and guaranteeing a place for artists and self-conscious/self-appointed members of the proletariat, run as a collective so the workers could obtain the fruit of their labor. Their leader, Jeremy Svensen, had worked with Vince Stevens, the city councilman, to make this happen. When Stevens had told them a contractor would rebuild The Spray Mecca as a museum with an artist space that would co-exist with low-rent housing at the former Gigglies, the Aesthetic Unity Brothers should have felt victorious. But when Jeremy described the particulars to them, the core members, the true believers, felt betrayed.

Clearly the plan was another trick: the developer would make smaller, crappier units for low income families in that area while building superior, more expensive units on the East River where The Dock had stood, continuing class division. The museum entrance fee would not go to the artists but half to the developer and half to the city, creating a perpetual for-profit motive. Even the donations would primarily pay the contest evaluators, not the artists who received the fellowships. Yet their leader Jeremy had advised practicality, and the members had begrudgingly followed. However, during a recent meeting, Lance had told them about Stevens' working relationship with the capitalist bidder Brendan Carty and even, apparently, the mob, as well as his plan to subvert even this compromised bid. Hearing that, a portion of the group vowed a different course and even vengeance.

Getting up, Lance noticed the apartment was bare. The bathroom door was ajar, and no one was inside. He glanced at a mattress covered by a blue sheet that lay on the floor. Sveta had been sleeping there, but she wasn't there now.

Suddenly, he heard the door to the apartment, up a flight of stairs, open. Lance called out to Sveta, but another familiar figure descended the steps: a skinny white male wearing all black. He looked like a bland yuppie from Seattle until one glared into his dark black eyes.

"Jeremy, where's Sveta at?" Lance asked him.

"She's out with Chloe," he explained as he reached the landing. "She'll be back soon."

"Yeah? She better not be seen."

"We'll need her to be seen soon enough," he said, turning towards Lance. "She's got work to do. Remember, if we don't get what we want this way, there's another way we can go."

"No need, brother. We should go my way first."

Jeremy spread out his arms, but not in a way that made Lance comfortable to approach him. "I'll give it a shot, man," he said in his squeaky, but oddly compelling, voice.

Over the last week, Lance had discovered Niral had been friends with Jeremy and Chloe, his girlfriend, before working for Stan Lorenzo. What a crazy coincidence, but then life was filled with crazy coincidences, wasn't it? Niral had lived in this very basement before renting a proper apartment. Jeremy had lived in an East Village loft at the time, but now he owned this building, buying out the former owner, who had illegally rented the basement to Niral. Jeremy used the basement for Brothers of Aesthetic Unity meetings, related endeavors, and to occasionally let friends crash.

Lance learned Jeremy was from Bronxville in Westchester County but was clearly embarrassed by his wealthy upbringing and elite education, the white privilege that he and his fellow progressives railed against but whose perks they consistently enjoyed. Chloe had attended Smith for two years, then Vassar. Jeremy worked, on the surface, as a software designer in the East Village, whereas Chloe owned a handicraft shop in gentrified Bushwick, next to a collective grocery store, where she sometimes volunteered.

What had led Jeremy to form the Brothers of Aesthetic Unity? Jeremy revealed to Lance that he had always been a radical, but more or less a peace-loving hippie and socialist. When he had known Niral, his subversive activities included smoking weed, sniffing cocaine, writing formless poems, and hanging out at parties in the East Village, Alphabet City, and different parts of Brooklyn, where he would have drunken conversations about revolution. But he never put his money where his mouth was. He was a spoiled and arrogant rich kid, dedicating more to having a fun NYC life than organizational anarchy.

Then something had woken him up. His friends began to get married. Never as wealthy as Jeremy, or at least not as endowed with constant funding by their parents, they moved to the Philadelphia suburbs and bought houses. Even his wealthy acquaintances bought brownstones in Park Slope or Prospect Heights and only associated with other couples with kids. His transient international friends, like Rob, moved upstate or to Europe or Asia. Even Niral, a subject of both admiration and mockery due to his immigrant Queens background, had gone back home. Only Chloe had remained, but her flakiness and cocaine addiction began to annoy Jeremy.

Jeremy felt abandoned and cheated by his generation. The once arrogant yet shiftless youth became determined not to sell out like his friends. He sold his East Village loft, bought for him by his parents, and got accepted to Teach for America in Houston, Texas. But after only a few months, he got tired of teaching English to kids who clearly didn't care about education and would never be freed from social injustice without radical revolution.

He moved back to New York, began reading Mikhail Bakunin more seriously, and got involved in the Occupy Wall Street movement. The controversial aftermath of the Spray Mecca incident, rent risings, and other events led him to meet others like him and form this group. He now considered himself a true anarchist, but one dedicated to occasional social justice, certainly if it meant battling cops, corporations, and other authoritarian figures. Art was a God, but one manifested in anarchy, confusion, disorder, and dysfunction. That was the only way to form it—to unform it.

Chloe, meanwhile, had swerved from party girl to drug addict and conventionalized hipster to small businesswoman and secret anarchist girlfriend. After Niral and Jeremy had tired of her carefree attitude and decadent lifestyle, after her other friends had become suburbanites and bourgeois hypocrites, she found herself alone and partnerless. Her isolation exacerbated her previously stalled cocaine addiction and pushed her towards the extreme. Like Niral, she learned the hard way how people like her cared only about themselves.

For months she lay in her East Village apartment, sniffing cocaine and crashing. Occasionally, she would sit in coffee shops, watching videos on her laptop as she waited for her dealer to arrive with more blow. She stopped going to rehab clinics and meetings. She no longer dyed her hair or wore makeup or nose rings. She seriously considered, at times, ending her pointless existence.

But then Jeremy returned from Houston and his new focus and purpose inspired her. He was a budding leader who needed a follower, and she was an aimless drug addict at the edge. He was principled enough not to get a corporate job, buy a brownstone, or get married, yet wealthy enough that he hadn't been priced out of New York City. They had been on and off fuck-buddies for years, so becoming an item again was natural. He got her to quit cocaine, patiently guiding her through withdrawal. He bought the handicraft shop for her, since she could only withdraw enough from her trust fund to pay for food, binges, and rent. In return, she became his right-hand woman, helping him form the Aesthetic Unity organization and attract members.

Given that strong and loyal relationship, as he waited with Jeremy in the basement for the ladies to return, Lance worried that, while out together, Chloe was trying to influence Sveta towards some unknown aim Jeremy had, or investigating whether Lance's story held up. Lance and Jeremy had already discussed a plan to influence the board through

Sveta for the benefit of Vishal's Ozone bid, which Lance explained Aesthetic Unity could have more influence over and which would result in labor for unions of working people not backed by the mob. While Jeremy knew that Lance and Sveta were on the run, he didn't know about Lance's connection to Vishal. Rather, Lance had convinced Jeremy that he, Sveta, and Bob Macaday had been trying to right the wrong of Lauren's murder under Candy's guidance when Bob, a former capitalist reformed towards socialism by his years in witness protection, had been assassinated, likely by Tragliani and Carty, so of course subverting Carty's bid was of primary importance, both for The Long Island City Project and the larger aims of the revolution. But there was still a question mark about how to deal with the influential political turncoat, Vince Stevens.

"What we do about Stevens?" Lance asked.

"We're having a meeting tonight. We'll decide by consensus."

"Man, he the worst of the worst. Hypocrite."

"Yes. We'll have to ferret out the dirt and expose him somehow."

"I got a smoother plan, brother. Give me a shot at him," Lance said. "I'll turn him to our side."

"Yeah? How are you gonna do that?"

"I got a secret on him. Something the Post don't wanna know."

"And what'll that do?" Jeremy said, seeming to soften on his support for Ozone. "Even with his influence, his people will still vote for one of these crappy proposals, and we'll still lose either way."

"Ozone got a plan for studio apartments, fellowships, museums," Lance said, chopping down on an open hand. "That's as good as we gonna get at this point, but with Ozone, we got influence down the line, plus the better unions. The Arts and Affairs committee recommend Ozone too. It's just Stevens' influence that could tip the scale towards Carty's bid, since they already got the Queens Borough president's people. So you give me a shot at him, and he could turn the tide."

"And Sveta will talk to that chair again?"

"Exactly. We try to take that practical course first. I know ya'll want revolution, but sometimes that quiet game a better bet."

Jeremy laughed. "If you didn't make sense, I might kill you."

"Where's that hippie shit now, brother?" Lance asked, bending over and slapping him playfully. "Where's that hippie shit now?"

63

A tween boy ran across a wide forest, carrying a water bottle in one hand and a map in another. As he rushed toward a large tree, he tripped and fell. He jumped up quickly and scurried around the tree. On the other side was a semi-circular entry into a hollow portion of the tree. Inside it, a man lay down, his feet near the entrance, while a girl lay perpendicular to him, her head on his abdomen.

"Paw!" the boy exclaimed. "Paw!"

The figure shook and grumbled. Then his hand gripped the boy by the neck.

"What you yabbering about, mate?" the man asked.

The tween shook the map. The man pushed the boy back so that he landed on his butt. The girl had woken up too. They both sat up. She fixed her hair as the man took the map.

"What this say, mate? Reckon I told you to yabber with the buffalo boys."

"I did, Paw, and they showed me this map."

"This a drawing, mate. Don't even know where it's at."

"But I do, Paw."

"Spit it out, Som."

"A girl in this village has a mother and daughter. But the mother and daughter are not from the village. They moved."

"From where?"

"Near Udon Thani. They move to this village around here, and then this girl come."

"So how come it took this long to find her? You never saw her in Udon Thani, did you?"

"I did, Paw. She is from a village near Udon Thani."

"Makes sense, I reckon. She got my money, so no reason to go back except to get her lips wet now and then. Still wasted my time there.

Almost got caught by the same pathetic jack. See that wanker again, gonna blow a hole through 'em."

"I did good, Paw?"

"Yeah, mate," Rob said. Rob reached out. Som expressed fear at the lurch, but smiled like a puppy when Rob rubbed his head. Then Rob turned to the girl.

"Boonsri, we might be meeting mum. You wanna meet mum?"

Boonsri shook her head.

"Come on," Rob continued. "Your old man, he was a perverted cunt, but we're gonna be a big happy family now. And once I get my money, I'll provide."

He took his gun from his bag. "This village kinda far, mate? Like motorcycle far?"

"We cannot walk, Paw. But it is not too far."

"So we'll get the old motorcycle. But I'm wondering, Som, how come all this time you going to village schoolyards and me to Udon Thani bars and none of us found this story nowhere? Suddenly, you get a bush telegraph from a couple of buffalo boys in our own backyard. Think it's dodgy, Som? Or you got something to do with it?"

"I would not do that, Paw."

Rob rubbed Som's head again, gun in hand. "I know you wouldn't. I'm just gammin' ya. You've become a good boy, Som. Don't know why I never had kids before. Actually, I do. It's a story you don't wanna hear, but I'll tell you one day."

Som nodded. Then Rob said, "Whatcha waitin' for, mate? Let's get to the cycle. Possible this is nothing, but if it's her..."

Boonsri got up indifferently. Rob wasn't sure what to do about her. He felt more attached to her than Som since he had seen her suffering so often. Yet, he wasn't sure how to take care of her. Either way, he couldn't let her go now. She was his or she didn't exist. He crawled out of the space and into the sun. It was a powerful sun.

64

Lawrence called Sanchez on his way to an apartment in Greenpoint, Brooklyn.

"You do any digging on the LIC case, brother?" he asked.

"Yeah, and some convos with inside bros. The Traglianis definitely had a hit warrant on Macaday and his wife, but not sure if it was satisfied."

"So makes sense if they'd hit the wife in Thailand and finish Bob here. The Thais are being evasive. They might know Linda's killer and theorize a motive but they're not finalizing. Still say the Thai could've done it cuz of some sex thing. I'm thinking our theory's better, so we can try to link Lance with the Traglianis. Is it possible Solanke's working for the Traglianis and did the hit in Thailand?"

"Find that hard to believe, unless he's really gone to the dark side. How about the airports?"

"Marshals still say they got beef with the Feds, but now I'm just thinking they're stalling. We can't get the airport info any other way, so who knows where he came in or if Linda also got a fake identity. They still fighting to take the investigation, but I still got the Bangladeshi kid, even if they claim Macaday. That's St. Albans territory."

"So you're crippled."

"Yeah, but not paralyzed. I'm on a mission to find this Portman. Going over to his old lady's place now. Former dancer from Gigglies named Candy."

"Good luck."

Lawrence found the apartment on a triangular corner in Greenpoint, a few yards from the East River, and rang the bell. Candy interrogated him on the intercom, then buzzed him in.

He took a rickety elevator up to an apartment that opened into a loft. It had a nice view of the Manhattan skyline. Candy walked out wearing a tight black dress, her breasts almost bulging through the top.

"See your assets haven't suffered," Lawrence said.

"Look around, baby, I got plenty of assets now."

"Suckered one of your clients, did you?"

"That was the end game."

"You remember that brother Lance. Used to call him the Iceman."

"Sure, I remember. But I haven't seen him in years, if that's what you're asking."

"Really? Cuz that's not what I heard."

"What'd you hear, Trev?"

"That you've kept in touch."

"Not true. When Gigglies went down, I got what I could in the few clubs left in Queens, and there was no Iceman around. Heard he joined some anarchist organization."

"That's the rumor about you too."

"Do I look like an anarchist?"

"Gentrified liberal."

"There's no politics in money."

"Aight, babe. Another question. You see a tall white chick in the clubs with red-brownish hair?"

"Better description? That describes half the girls on earth."

"Never mind. Guess I meant you ever see him with her, but you ain't seen him either."

Candy shook her head.

Lawrence took out his card. "You call me this time if you hear anything, right?"

"I ain't on the street anymore. I don't need a get out of jail free card."

"Then call me if the tenant ain't around. You dig?"

65

Lamai's sister, Malai, loved to visit the Chiang Rai night market. The entire village would come out on Saturday night. She could meet some old friends who lived in rural villages and only emerged during these festivals. There would be a live music concert on the stage, sometimes featuring ladyboy performances, and every kind of cuisine and merchandise you could think of would be sold.

She had just finished talking to a woman who had sold her live crickets when she had a strange feeling she was being followed. She turned around and saw an Indian man behind her. He had ominous white splotches on his face. He smiled and approached her. She became nervous.

131

"Are you Malai, Lamai's sister?" the man asked in English.

Malai looked around. "Yes," she said cautiously.

"Can we talk? I am a friend of your sister."

Malai hesitated. "Why? How do you know my sister?"

"I know your sister and Duncan. I have a message from him. Can we please talk?"

They went over to the Centre Point Night Bazaar. The place was packed, so they sat at a table next to a family of four, while the parents were yelling at their rambunctious children. Malai was carrying a bag of crickets and a plate of noodles.

"Go ahead and eat if you want," Niral said.

"Do you want some?"

Niral shook his head. "I had some wrapped banana leaves and nya u. Ever try it?"

"What is it?"

"Karen food. Fish paste with rice and vegetables."

"We are Lanna people. I have never met a Karen person. Are you living in the countryside?"

"I have been for the last week. And Duncan's been living there even longer."

Malai closed her eyes a moment. "So he is still alive, and he hasn't been caught. Lamai has been worried sick. He has not sent any messages. I told her, you should have never trusted a farang."

A small table was deserted, and Niral shifted over. Malai followed.

"Too late now," he said. "He wants her to know he's okay, and that he'll take care of the baby once it's born."

"Take care of it?" she whispered. "How? The police are looking for him. He was stupid enough to sell drugs in Thailand."

"That's why he'll have the money to support them. He still loves her. He'll always love her. He did this all for her. I can tell you that's true."

"He is deluded. He can never be a father now. I think he should leave her alone. Live his life in the jungle if he wants. Lamai should get a divorce and marry another man."

"Will she?"

Malai shook her head. "She loves Duncan. She always wonders what he's doing, if he's okay."

"He is."

"But she wants to know more. Why would he do this? I keep on telling her to move on for the baby. But she doesn't want to, the fool. I'm afraid if I tell her about this, she will want to meet Duncan. But if I don't tell her, she will continue to be depressed. Neither is good for her or the baby."

"Tell her she can meet me. At a designated place where the Bureau won't track her."

"Do you think they're watching us?"

"They watch the house, so it can't be there. Maybe on the way to the doctor. I've seen her on that route. Tell her to meet me at the temple on route to the doctor. You know it. Tomorrow, at noon."

Malai nodded. Niral rose. He put his hand in the bag and took out a live cricket.

"I've always wondered what this tasted like," he said, putting it in his mouth and chewing it as he winked and disappeared into the crowd.

66

When they returned to the apartment, Lance saw that Chloe had dressed Sveta up in a kind of simplified buckskin dress like Native Americans wore, except instead of being made of leather or animal parts, it was sewn out of ramie. She also wore a headband with a feather sticking out at the end. Lance joked she looked like a Pocahontas flapper.

"Yeah, I know what a flapper is, brother," he said to Jeremy. "She look like Brett Ashley. See, I go to the lib'ary."

While Jeremy and Chloe stepped out to talk alone about the meeting that night, Lance sat Sveta down on the couch and asked her what, if anything, Chloe had asked her.

"Nothing, she showed me her shop. She has many stupid things in it, but this dress was pretty and so different so I decide that I will try it. Chloe said I can have it for free, that I look like hippie now!"

"She didn't ask you nothing about me or Bob?"

"We talk a little bit, but I say what you tell me. I say Bob like socialism now. He good to me in Thailand and save me from prostitution. Now that he is dead, me and you are here to help them."

"Good girl, that's my lady! She ain't say nothing about doing something else?"

"No, we talk about girl things, first time since Dharini. I didn't like that Ashley. But I like Chloe; she give me this dress. She tell me how Jeremy is great man."

"I see," Lance said. Then he reviewed her role with her and what had transpired with Kirk Cortland. Sveta had spoken to the CFLIC Chair via phone, telling him the Traglianis had killed Bob and were hunting her. She asked him to tell their fellow CFLIC members about the mob influence on DeKalb, but not to mention her or call the police. Otherwise, the Traglianis would find and kill her like they had done to Bob.

She was worried Cortland would call the police anyway or tell someone who would, so Lance told her to follow up and keep in regular contact so he wouldn't falter. She would use different cell phones from different spots in case the cops were tracing it. And if he seemed insecure, she could seduce Cortland to keep him happy. She was willing to do this as long as Lance followed through on his promise to reunite her with Rob.

At the meeting that night, the Aesthetic Unity Brothers came with their "sisters." Despite the trend among many such organizations towards gender expression, gender identity and gender-neutrality, with words like genderfluid, demiromantic, asexual, and non-binary floated often, the Aesthetic Unity operated like many organizations that promoted, on the surface, gender and racial equality, but was dominated by alpha white males who brought along their beta whores—women who would never date a weaker man or even a woman but who, nevertheless, claimed to be subversive feminists.

The men were naturally resistant to Jeremy's proposal for Lance and Sveta to try a sly diplomatic approach. They felt the Aesthetic Unity Brothers had compromised too often, and that radical action was the only means to a solution. Whether that involved a sit-in at the meeting, which most deemed visible but ineffective, to more violent action involving threats or even terrorism, it seemed more natural than having a random black man or Russian woman (with an accent) do their work for them. But after they grumbled and had their say, Jeremy spoke over them.

"If exposing Vince Stevens can sway the vote, why not try it? It's better than getting arrested."

"Aren't you willing to go to jail or die for what you believe in?" a man named Tomas asked. "Isn't that what sets us apart from these other cowards?"

"Yes, I am willing," Jeremy said. "But if we die without solving the problem, what's the point? Gandhi made an exhibition, but he didn't commit suicide."

"We've tried many peaceful methods, trusted many politicians," another man said. "In the end, we always get sold out. Enough with the marches and the masks. Let's blast these bastards."

Jeremy shook his head. "That's a death mission with no purpose. We need to be subversive but also smart."

A girl raised her hand. She was new to the group, a recent college graduate, allowed in only when the group determined she was committed to the cause.

"Yes, Stella," Jeremy said.

"Let's say we embarrass Stevens," she said. "It might take him out completely, and then we've got no allies."

"We'll threaten him but won't go to the press," Jeremy explained. "That way he'll stay in line."

"But in retaliation he could say he'll get his people to vote for us, then pay someone else to go against it and we'll never even know," Stella pointed out. "He's got more influence than us."

"Exactly, sister," Levon said, putting his hand on her back. He was the only black man in the group besides Lance. "Stella's right. No point trusting these cats. They're smart with the under-the-table shit."

Stella smiled at Levon. Even as she tried to retain her anger, she couldn't help but stare at the tall, cute guy with his hand on her.

Jeremy held out his arms. "Look, I don't think we'll go wrong by trying. If we decide it won't work, we can try something else. Why don't we vote on it?"

"One more thing," Tomas said, pointing at Lance and Sveta. "How do we know these two are on the level? Did you check their stories?"

"What do you mean?" Jeremy asked. "We know who they are. Candy's friends."

"How do they know Stevens and this Carty cat?" Levon asked.

"They know Stevens and Carty because they knew Macaday," Jeremy explained. "Bob was in love with Lauren, Candy's friend, our patron saint who was murdered at the Spray Mecca. He was undercover, trying to stop this shit when he was found out and gunned down by our enemies. So yeah, one rich guy saw the light, and yeah, he was willing to die for his beliefs."

They became quiet. Then Tomas asked, "Where's Candy?"

"She said her husband was keeping her. If she doesn't make it tonight, she'll be at the next meeting," Jeremy responded stoically.

Then he announced the vote. Everyone voted by secret ballot. As usual, the papers were collected by Chloe, and as often happened, it was a tie. Jeremy had the deciding vote.

67

From the shop near the entrance to the village, Som ran into the forest and found Rob and Boonsri, who sat on a motorcycle in the shade of a banana tree.

"Paw, he says the house is there. But someone else asked for it a week ago. Do you think it was the police, Paw?"

"Hmm..." Rob said, thinking. "Heaps of cunts after Apsara. Could be that copper or Nam or Niral or Duncan or Sumantapat, I reckon. But if they found her, we might be taking a squiz at a bloodbath instead of a cum dumpster."

Som shrugged. "Should I ask him again what she looked like?"

"Was it a she, mate?"

"I think he said she. And like he knew her."

"Well maybe it's her girlfriend. Still, we'll be careful, mate."

Som hopped onto the motorcycle, in front of Rob, like he always did: Rob's second eyes and ears. Boonsri hung on at the back, arms around Rob, like she always did.

Checking the map, Som directed them to an isolated, bumpy dirt road between farms. Rob saw the house in the distance. Nothing seemed out of the ordinary.

Rob stopped in the middle of the road, then swerved the bike onto a mud path at the edge of a sugarcane farm. He parked, then lifted Som and dropped him into the mud. He turned to Boonsri.

"Stay here, Boonsri," Rob said. "Don't want you to get hurt. There's shade from the sugarcane."

Boonsri didn't respond. She climbed down and sat on the mud, soiling her dress.

"We'll wash that up when I get back," Rob said. He patted Som's shoulder and led him a few steps out. Then he whipped off his duffel bag and opened it.

He asked Som, "Gun or knife?"

Som looked at him. "You are giving it to me, Paw?"

"You deserve it, mate. We'll work together. Which one?"

Som peered inside the bag. He reached for the machete. Then, shuddering, he took the gun instead.

"It's heavy," Som noted, trying to hold it up.

"Point and shoot, mate. Ain't trickier than that. Just make sure you ain't pointing it at old Paw."

Som turned the gun toward the road. "Don't shoot unless you got to," Rob warned. "We don't need nobody getting wise to us."

Som heeded Rob's advice and didn't shoot. Still, watching Som hold the gun made Rob nervous.

"Sure you don't want the machete, mate? Cuts up good."

Som shook his head. Then Rob realized why; he had seen Rob use it to cut up Wat.

"You're right, mate," he said. "Keep the gun. You'll need striking distance."

Rob ran ahead, ducking in and out of the sugarcane field, waving

137

Som forward and implying that he copy Rob's movements, which Som did, but not always with agility or precision.

"It's the Thai way," Rob muttered as they got closer to the home. He continued to analyze the house but saw nothing out of the ordinary. Still, he didn't want to take any chances.

He told Som to check behind the ceramic jars under the stilts and hover around the back of the house in case someone was hanging out, waiting to get the jump on them. Rob saw a spirit house next to a tree. He moved right towards it, analyzing the home from afar.

Then he heard a click. Turning to the tree, he saw Detective Nat emerge from behind it, pointing a gun at him.

"Easy," Nat said. "Drop the machete."

"Detective," Rob said. "I should have known it would be you."

Nat shrugged. "You've shot me and hit me. What else can you do?"

"What do you want from me, mate?" Rob asked, dropping the machete and raising his arms. "I'm trying to enjoy Thailand like every other farang. Don't know why you're chasing me around."

"You kidnapped my son, for one thing."

"Your son?" he asked, genuinely baffled. And then he slowly realized Nat's meaning. "Oh, you mean Som. Small world, I reckon."

"You messed with the wrong guy."

Rob smiled. "Funny thing, mate. Som told me he didn't have an old man. Or a mum. Both left him with his sweet grandma when he was an ankle biter. Sad story. My folks did the same thing to me. That's why Som calls me Paw. He knows we're the same way."

Nat breathed heavily. "Shut up," he said. "Get on your knees."

Rob plopped down to his knees, still holding his hands up. "You don't know how to be a dad, bro. Least I've tried, and I don't even gotta."

"Shut up," he said. "Stay still."

Rob noticed Nat was shaking. He looked for an angle. Then they both heard a shot. Nat glanced around, long enough for Rob to pick up the machete, rise up, and slash Nat across the neck as he turned back.

Nat fired a wild shot as he fell. Then another. Rob stood over him as Nat shook uncontrollably, dropping the gun as he tried to hold his neck shut as the blood gushed out.

"Nothing else, eh?" Rob asked as he sliced Nat twice in the head, the blood splattering on the spirit house and the tree. Then he heard whimpering and looked back.

In front of the stilts, Som lay on the ground, holding his stomach.

Rob ran over. Som had been shot. His gun lay next to him.

"Fuck!" Rob yelled. Som's whimper became a cry.

"It hurts, Paw!" Som yelled in Thai, screaming in agony.

"Shit, mate." He lifted Som and climbed up the staircase. He knocked on the first door.

"You better be home, bitch," he yelled. "And you better have some first aid, you fucking cunt!"

68

The next day, Lamai, pregnant for almost nine months, arrived at the temple on the typical route to see her doctor. She waited at its base, then heard a whistle from the top. She saw Niral peeking out from the entrance.

She removed her shoes. "You can go," she told Malai, who had accompanied her.

"Are you sure?" Malai asked.

"Yes. Just wait in the car. When I'm done, I'll come back."

Malai squeezed her arm and returned to the car. Lamai climbed to the entrance of the temple, an arch carved with ornate images of Buddha.

"Niral, how have you been?" Lamai asked. They hugged warmly, Niral avoiding her bulging midsection.

"I should ask you the same thing," Niral said as he released.

"You can see my belly now," Lamai said, teasing.

"A nice, round belly. I wonder if I can listen to the baby?"

"Of course. You've never heard her, right?"

"It's a her?"

"Yes. Please, get on your knees. Listen."

Niral dropped to his knees and put his ear to Lamai's tummy.

"Sometimes you can hear her kicking," she said. "Can you hear it?"

"Faintly," Niral said, though he could not hear anything. He got up.

"She's strong. Like her father."

"Do you think he is? Strong I mean."

"I would like to know where he is. Is he still alive?"

"Yes. I just saw him. He's in the Chiang Mai countryside, living with a Karen tribe."

Lamai shook her head. "I can't believe he would dishonor Thailand like this. Or me. I am a Lanna. My father was a government official."

"He was looking out for your future. For all our futures."

"By ending up on the run? Or on death row?"

"He's fine and looks forward to reuniting with you," Niral recited. "He still loves you and wants to be with you." Lamai rolled her eyes again. "He says you should have the baby, wait until it's healthy, then the Karen will take you to where he's hiding. By then, he'll be in Burma, where it's safer. They'll find a way to relocate us to another country. We'll live happily ever after."

"Yes, while relying on drug sales to fund our life. It's demeaning."

"It's a life," Niral countered. "Don't be naïve."

"Who is being naïve?" Lamai asked. She looked back at her sister sitting in the car across the street. She pushed Niral further into the temple so they weren't visible. No one was inside during this time of day. Not even a monk.

Niral was pushed against a panel that showed Rama slaying Rakshasas with an arrow that transformed into ten flaming arrows. "Look, my parents have already disowned Duncan," she said. "But I still love him. If what you say is true, that he's in the countryside, I want to see him now. I don't want to wait months after I have the baby."

"What if your water breaks on the way? It's not wise."

Lamai tightened her face. "Is it wise if I throw myself down the stairs?"

"You wouldn't do that. What about your baby?"

"How will my baby be without her father? Take me to Duncan now. We can go out the back way. Where are you parked?"

Niral swallowed. "Maybe I should call Duncan..."

He started to take out his phone but Lamai held his arm. "Last time I took Duncan to a temple, he refused to follow the monks' advice.

He even suggested he was going to visit some gik afterwards. I'm not stupid; I know how men are. But that's why I don't need his advice. Or his thoughts on anything."

Sighing, Niral left his phone in his pocket. He put his hand on Lamai's stomach, and this time he thought maybe he felt something. Then he took Lamai's arm and asked her to show him the way.

69

As Sveta conversed with Kirk Cortland via cell phone from a random deli in Bay Ridge, Brooklyn, Lance chose the personal approach by breaking into Vince Stevens' apartment in Sunnyside, Queens through a slightly ajar window screen in the living room. Wearing all black, he sat on the living room couch and watched Netflix, getting through two and a half episodes of the latest true crime documentary before hearing a key in the lock. He shut off the TV and hid in a closet between the kitchen and a hallway, leaving the door slightly open and holding up his gun.

The light turned on. He heard the door close and lock. Someone approached the kitchen and put a bag of groceries on the counter. Then, the figure neared the couch. Lance was about to leap into action when he realized it was not Vince Stevens but another skinny male wearing a black pullover and skinny jeans. Lance cursed to himself, wondering if he had entered the wrong apartment.

Then he heard another key in the lock. The door opened again, and he heard a familiar voice.

"Dear, there's no reason to lock the door when I'm right behind you."

"Daddy, I know how long it takes you to decide between Yoplait and La."

"No matter how much I fret, honey, you know I always pick La. And when we moved, I told you it's not that kind of neighborhood anymore."

"You should know, Mr. All-Powerful Councilman."

Lance heard Vince Stevens shut the door and saw him approach the couch. The two men kissed, then lay down on the couch to make out. Lance rolled his eyes. Then he remembered a press conference during which Stevens stared down a single, straight male rival, scathingly mentioning his own upcoming marriage to annoy him. So this was Vince Stevens' husband, Lance realized. Lance wondered if he should pop out, scaring the husband too, or bide his time. He decided to be patient.

The husband complained he wanted to watch TV, but Vince was clearly horny. He pulled his husband up, turned him around, and pushed him against the TV. He rolled down his pants and took him, while the husband yelled "Daddy! Daddy!" Lance rolled his eyes again. He hadn't disturbed the shades, so the pair had no worries about peeping toms.

Afterwards, the couple began putting away the groceries, joking and gossiping as they did. The husband, Gerry, complained about being the bitch too often. Stevens said whenever Gerry was horny enough, Stevens would gladly be supine. Gerry gasped and said he was retiring to the bedroom. Stevens laughed. Once Gerry was gone, Stevens continued putting away groceries, and Lance emerged from the closet.

"A safe neighborhood, eh?" Lance asked in a whisper, pointing the gun at Stevens.

Stevens nearly jumped when he saw Lance, but his cool composure returned quickly.

"Lance, right? Brendan Carty's man?"

"Not no more. I've been dismissed."

"Oh. I didn't know," Stevens said, placing some milk in the fridge.

"Why don't you give that a rest? I wanna have a little chat."

Stevens shrugged and shut the fridge with a bang. Then he turned and held up his hands.

"What would you like to discuss? I'm at your disposal."

"If your beau comes out, tell him I'm an old friend."

"Sure, a black man wearing all black, pointing a gun at me. I'm sure he'll believe that."

"Don't talk back. Do something sudden or loud, and I'll blast your ass back to a time before Stonewall."

"So you know the history of gay rights. Hurray. Should I stand here or can we sit?"

"Take your sweet time and do it quiet. Come around."

Vince Stevens made his way to the couch, hands still up, and sat down quietly. Lance backtracked and, still standing, held the gun on him.

"What do you want to discuss, sir?" Vince asked.

"For starters, why you fucking around with Carty if you got a missus?"

"You've never done the same thing?"

"That's different. Now listen, I know all about this Carty business, and you don't want that shit getting out, especially being a married man and all. I'm sure the Post, the local stations and even the Daily News be all over that. I can see the headlines now."

"What do you want in return for this brilliant blackmail?"

"Support the other bid. Make your constituents and your liberal supporters happy."

"And stab Carty in the back?"

"He won't know til after the vote. Then you tell him some believable bullshit like your people change their minds cuz they got self-interest. What's so hard about that? Yo' ass live on bullshit."

"Except that I don't want the other bid to win."

"Why not? That's the best bid. You get your artists, your unions, and your constituents something. Supporting Carty's bid makes no sense, other than you bought off."

"So it seems. Look, if I promise you the other bid will win but it doesn't, despite my efforts, what happens to me?"

"You and your beau end up in the grave. That easy for you?"

"Yes, that is easy for me." Stevens smiled nervously. "Fine. What do I have to lose? A slightly upset mistress. A better development."

"I get it, you worried about the gravy train stopping. Except I got a sponsor too. He'll make it worth your while."

Stevens glared at Lance. "The infamous Vishal Patel. Wherever he is. Whoever he is. Damn. Now you're working for him."

Lance smirked.

"Except everyone he comes into contact with dies. It's like making a deal with the reaper."

"Your choice, Stevens."

Stevens shrugged. "Sure, why not? I'm at risk either way."

Lance heard someone coming down the hallway. He put his gun in his waistband, covered it with his shirt, and stood at attention.

"Dear," Stevens said, turning to Gerry. "Meet Mr. Lance Portman. A friend from the neighborhood. He's been having some problems with the law, and I've been working it out for him. But I forgot to tell him that I accidentally pressed a button calling the cops when I was in the kitchen." He turned to Lance. "So he should probably get going if he wants to avoid them. I think it's better that we leave them out of it for now, don't you think?"

Lance swallowed. He nodded at Gerry and headed for the door. He unlocked it, closed the door behind him, and took the staircase down. As he approached the first floor, he heard talking near the elevator. When he peeked out from the staircase, he saw two cops. Through the front window, he noticed a police car with blinking flashers. He cursed to himself.

70

Rob sat in the big room with Apsara across from him. Between them Som's body lay, a bloody bandage around his abdomen. Eyes closed, he was sweating and breathing deeply. Apsara's mother was washing Boonsri's dress in the smaller room while watching her and Apsara's daughter Hathai.

Rob didn't have any clothes on. He had drawn up his knees and wrapped his arms around them.

"For once, you care?" Apsara asked.

Rob didn't respond at first, staring at the floor. Then he looked up at her.

"I cared about you, you little cum dumpster."

"But never about a little boy. Or a little girl."

"I reckon I've harmed 'em all: the innocent, the guilty, the young, and the old. But Som is different. He followed instructions. He looked up to me. Called me Paw. That's a feeling, you know."

"Now you know why I did what I did."

"For your daughter, you mean? But why'd you have to screw me over?"

"It was not personal, Rob. When Boy attacked you, I didn't think it would end well, so I ran back home. I realized I didn't have to pay Mr. Hong and could keep the money for my daughter. So we moved and hid here."

"So you thought Boy would kill me? You've got no confidence, sweetie."

"I didn't know. I wasn't sure."

"You could have found out. You could have contacted me."

"I was afraid someone would find me. Hong, Sumantapat, the police, whoever. Was I wrong?"

"You expect me to believe you didn't use me the whole time?"

"I love you, Rob. That has not changed. I'm glad you found me." Apsara smiled at him.

"So now we're a family," Rob said, smirking. "You help my little buggers, I'll help yours."

Apsara nodded. "Yes. But honestly, Rob, I don't know if Som will survive without going to a hospital. Mae stopped the bleeding for now, but we have no way to close the wound. We don't know what we are doing. It's a miracle he is not dead yet."

"I can't take him. You can't take him. Your mother can, but how's she going to get..."

"You can drop him at the door. But you'll have to let him go. We can't go back for him."

"How about we cross into Laos and bring him to a hospital there?"

"It will take too long. And it is risky. Better to drop him in Nong Khai."

"That's risky, too, but fuck it," Rob said, stretching out his legs. "Got a pair of men's clothes?"

Apsara shook her head. "No men around, except the dead man outside. Which reminds me, he brought a couple of girls here. He sent them back to Udon Thani before you came, hopping a ride with a village man. But if they don't hear from this detective, they might be back. One girl is from the village."

"Tell me, why'd you let this copper set me up?"

"I didn't think you would come, Rob. I thought maybe Sumantapat's men would come."

"Yeah, but that copper was looking for me. Whatever, I don't wanna waste time. Can you buy me some clothes in town?"

"They might not be big enough, but I will try."

"So I'll wear tight clothes, no worries. Meanwhile, I'll dig a grave under the stilts for our dead friend and my bloody rags."

"No," Apsara said, suddenly. "They might look there. Dig it in the forest. Far from the spirit house. I will clean it, but I don't want more bad luck."

Rob shrugged. "Fine. And get me the directions to the hospital. I'll figure how to get Som there without getting nabbed."

71

Driving a motorcycle, Lamai on the back, sideways and shoeless, Niral cruised past an elephant camp and drove into a dense forest. Kilometers later, he stopped at a tree where a man stood next to a tuk-tuk.

"No one said two people," he said in Thai. Lamai responded to him in Thai. The man shrugged. He radioed someone, then waved his hand.

They boarded the tuk-tuk and were taken deeper into the woods. The path seemed circular. Niral didn't recall his trip out being this convoluted.

They reached a man with a motorcycle. The man, who Niral had met, was dark-skinned and wore a red bandana. He took out a rope and blindfold.

"I don't have enough for two," he said in English. "It will have to be for the lady."

Lamai appeared nervous as she was blindfolded and tied up. She sat in front of the man and Niral mounted the back as they proceeded towards the camp. It was further inside the forest than where Niral had spent the last week. The tribe had moved inwards.

The path was complex, but Niral tried to remember the route, not that it would matter because the tribe would inevitably move again. About forty minutes later, after many stops and starts in the thick woods as they motorcycled over difficult terrain, they reached the camp.

As the man unbound Lamai's hands and took off her blindfold, Niral saw Thon and Duncan emerge from a tent along with the woman he had come to know as Bway Paw and her two helpers, Paw Htoo and Naw Baw. They wore neck-rings that gave the visual illusion of elongating them.

Duncan had a bit of black ash smeared across his cheek, perhaps from making a fire for cooking. He was shocked when he saw Lamai.

He glared at Niral angrily. His eye began twitching violently. Niral shrugged. "Sorry, she insisted on coming," he said. As Lamai saw Duncan, she became emotional.

"Tee rak!" she yelled. "Tee rak!" She opened her arms and ran towards him, still shoeless, closing her eyes as he caught her and held her lightly.

"Be careful for the baby," he said. "Why'd you come?"

She backed up angrily. "Why? To see you, Duncan. You've been gone for how long? Without a word?"

"You know the situation, Lamai. I..."

She slapped his face. "Situation? Dealing drugs behind my back? With Mr. Hong and who knows who else? Getting Niral to help you?"

"I did what I had to do for this family," he responded stoically, rubbing his cheek.

She shook her head. "You had to betray me and abandon me?"

"I gave Niral instructions. Did he give them to you? Have the baby, then..."

"I am your wife, not your whore. You remember that," she said. "Don't you treat me like a mia noi or a gik, or even a faen. I am a wife. That means equal station."

"Yes," Thon said. "In Karen culture, women have even higher station than men. My wife, Bway Paw, runs this operation. All final decisions come from her."

Duncan glanced at Thon angrily but quickly changed his expression.

"Look, I'm sorry, Lamai. I just want to make sure everything goes well with the baby and..."

147

Lamai started flailing her arms and screaming savagely, beating him on the chest, asking how he could do this to them. She went on for a minute. Then she cried, and he held her tightly in his arms.

Thon went back into the tent. The dark-skinned man in the red bandana smiled at Niral.

"Maybe you guys should have some quiet time," Niral said to Duncan. "I'll ask Thon if he can clear the tent for an hour or so."

"I think that's a good idea," Duncan said as he held Lamai. "Thanks."

72

Sveta returned to the apartment with Chloe after her talk with Cortland. Jeremy was there.

"So what happened?" Jeremy asked her.

"He listen to me," Sveta explained. "I tell him about Franklin again. He ask if I am sure I do not want to call the police. I say, they did not protect Franklin, how will they protect me? Then I explain why it is important they vote for the Ozone Construction bid over DeKalb, because mob is in DeKalb and this is best way to beat them. Not the police."

"Excellent," Jeremy said. "So he'll tell his friends and they won't go to the pigs. The Ozone bid will get their recommendation when they vote. Cortland will take that to the board at the final meeting, and we'll get our artist studios and everything else. Then we just have to make sure they follow up on their promises after the vote, but that's a whole 'nother battle."

"What if they decide to delay everything because of this rumor about the mob?" Chloe asked. "Right now there's no evidence, but once they have it and the media gets wind of it, they could say we've had two corrupt bids in succession, Patel's cousin and now the mob. They could decide to re-evaluate everything before moving forward."

"We've waited this long, what's another delay?" Jeremy asked. "As long as an apartment building or a shopping mall doesn't go up there, I'm happy."

"Yes, honey, but we'll have to work longer if there's a delay. We won't have the immediate influence we have now, and they might build an apartment building or shopping mall later anyway. With Ozone, we know we'll get part of what we want."

"Miss Practicality," Jeremy said. "Of course, I agree, we should push Ozone's bid. It's not me you should be worried about; it's our impatient brothers and sisters. They want to blow the place sky-high. Either of our scenarios is better than that."

"My point is we should use our influence to make sure the vote happens sooner than later, while we've got the influence and momentum."

"That's why Lance is putting the screws into Stevens. If we can turn his turncoat ass onto our side, we'll make sure he gets it done for us."

Sveta looked around. "Where is Lance?" she asked. "He should be back by now."

"I called him, but he didn't respond," Jeremy said. "Don't worry, he'll be here soon. I'm sure everything worked out."

73

Lance found himself hiding in the same closet as before while Vince assuaged the police's worries and dismissed them. Vince also told Gerry that Vince needed to speak to Lance further and that Gerry could go to bed.

Then, Lance found himself stuck up by his own gun, which Vince held on him after he had insisted on taking it in return for hiding Lance. Lance emerged from the closet with his hands up, making his way to the sofa and plopping down, Vince standing where Lance had once stood.

"Strange altering of events, Lance. When you're in politics, you see everything as a game where things can go one way or another. You never know how events will turn, but you try to shift them in your favor. And when the key falls in your lap, you've got to take advantage and use it."

"Without that gun, you nothing, Stevens. If you don't kill me now, I'll come back and kill you."

"You could, but you won't, for the same reason you don't want to die right now. Because deep down, you're a politician too. And whether it's now or later, the situation would still be the same: black man tried to rob me, left, came back, and bam!"

"That a legal gun? It registered to you?"

"I took it away from the big, bad black..."

"All right, brother. What you want?"

"I could call Brendan. Or Ms. Tragliani. Maybe she's looking for you too."

"What you want, Stevens?"

"I don't want to be blackmailed, certainly not by you!" he snarled, his face scrunching up. "I've got the power, not you!"

"Okay, brother. Calm down now. What you want?"

"Tell me, what does Vishal have over you? Why'd you switch sides?"

"He convince me Brother Carty want me dead after Bob hit the grave. And I think he right."

"So I'll do Brendan a favor by whacking you. Is that right?"

"You don't need that kinda press, Stevens. Killing me means the end of your career. It's called Black Lives Matter, brother."

The gun shook in Vince's hand. He seemed angrier, but he didn't respond.

"You know I'm right, brother," Lance said. "Now let's discuss this shit calmly. You benefit with Vishal on your side. You'll be winning elections 'til next century. Carty a pretender. And the mob's finished in this city. The Traglianis be holding on by a thread. Ain't Giuliani been mayor for a while?"

Stevens swallowed.

"Vishal got a new coalition for this city," Lance continued. "If you smart, you go along. We got Asians, black folks, gays, and revolutionaries from Occupy Wall Street. We got that wide tent, and even from Timbuktu Vishal can put and keep that coalition together. That's what I'm talking about. That's what I'm feeling. You feeling it, brother?"

The gun continued to shake in Vince's hand. Slowly, Lance stood up.

"Brother, just give the gun to me. I won't bite."

He went over and slowly put his hand on the gun. Then he snatched it away, and rearing back, elbowed Stevens hard in the face. Stevens fell down, holding his face, and screaming in pain.

"That's for being a dick," Lance said.

Stevens got up as Lance heard Gerry asking after Vince from the bedroom. Vince started toward Lance but, seeing the gun, ran towards the door instead and threw it open.

Lance heard two shots. Vince fell back as two streams of blood jetted from his chest. At the open door, Lance saw the shorty who'd capped Bob Macaday. Or at least he wore the same mask and was about the same height.

"Motherfucker," Lance said, pointing the gun at him and firing. The kid ran away as Lance chased him down the stairs. The kid turned and fired. Lance ducked, then checking the staircase, continued down. As he emerged from the staircase, he dodged another bullet. Catching his breath, he sped to the building door and peeked outside. The kid was running down the external stairs and towards a tree. Lance had a clear shot and unloaded three bullets into the kid's back. People on the streets hit the pavement or hid behind cars or doors. Lance didn't care. Incensed, he approached the kid and fired three more bullets into him as he lay with his head bashed against the base of the tree.

"Teenage nigger motherfucker," he muttered. "Pants down-to-here motherfucker."

He put the gun in his waist and ran back into the alleyway of the building.

74

"I'm surprised you're still here," Rob said as he entered the large room after dropping Som off at a hospital in Nong Khai. Apsara was playing with her daughter and her doll. Boonsri sat alone in a corner.

"Did you think I would run away?" Apsara asked. "I meant it when I said I loved you."

Rob didn't respond. He glared at Boonsri, went down to one knee, and tied his shoelace.

"How was the drop off?" she asked.

Rob felt the tight clothes stretch as he tied his laces. Surprisingly, the shirt hadn't ripped en route.

"I could feel he was tired, weak. I held him in front of me with my left arm, careful not to put it around his stomach. I drove fast as I could. I took that roundabout way the shop man recommended to you to avoid that dragnet. Got lost once, and I couldn't forgive myself for twice. When I got there, I put his body gentle on the floor, in front of a man who called inside the emergency room."

"He saw you."

"I don't give a fuck. If it saved Som's life…"

"I am surprised you are the same man," Apsara said. "Don't get me wrong. I'm happy."

"He was like me. Except I didn't have no one to give me mercy. I had to make my own way, deliver my own justice."

"Justice?" Apsara asked.

Rob wiped tears from his cheek with the back of his hand.

Apsara put her daughter on the floor and stood. "What's wrong, baby?"

"Fuck it. Nothing. Thinking about old times."

"In Australia? You never tell me about it."

"I never told nobody. It's not worth telling."

"When you were Som's age?"

"Forget it. Not worth going over."

"Is it about Sveta?"

"Nothing to do with that cunt. Look, can you get your kid to play with Boonsri? She's miserable. And Boonsri's actually human."

Apsara put her hands on her hips. "Hathai loves her luk thep doll, but fine Rob, whatever you say. Do you want to sleep? My mother will make your bed."

"That's a good idea," he said, bending his leg in order to stand. At that point, his pants ripped at the butt crack.

They both laughed.

75

That night, Niral sat at the fire with Thon and the dark-skinned man with the red bandana. Duncan emerged from the tent and approached the fire.

"Good time with wife?" Thon asked.

Duncan smiled, rubbing his hands. "Nothing like alone time with a long-lost woman."

"Too much alone time is not good either," Thon said. "Sometimes women need to be together. Bway Paw will take good care of Lamai. We respect women here. We are not like the animal Thais."

"They say they respect women too," Duncan said.

"Endless whores. It is not like that here." Thon put his hands towards the fire. Then he said, "I don't want to create tension, but if her sister knows she is missing, she may go to the police. That means we should move you to Burma now. At least start that way."

"So you think Lamai should stay?" Duncan asked, sounding surprised.

"If we send her back now, The Bureau may ask her where she was. We cannot risk discovery. Anyway, a husband and wife should be together. We have delivered babies out here. Bway Paw is responsible, and Paw Htoo and Naw Baw are capable. I would not worry. It is actually the safest way."

"I'm sorry for complicating the situation. She couldn't stay away from me, I guess."

"It is understandable. I told you, husband and wife should be together. Actually, this is easier than calling her later. That is more complicated."

Duncan nodded. Thon rubbed his hands.

"You said you would pay us extra for moving you," Thon reminded Duncan. "If possible, I would like that cash now."

"Niral will get it tomorrow morning," Duncan responded. "He needs to hurry, though, as he has a flight the next morning to India from Bangkok."

"He will get the cash from a bank or from Lamai's sister's house?" Thon asked.

Duncan seemed wary about identifying the location, but he said, "A bank."

"Either way, tell him to be careful. Lamai's sister might have identified him to the police."

Duncan turned to Niral. "I hope you can get on that flight."

"Unless I can get to India through Burma, I have no other choice," Niral said.

"Unfortunately, that route's not set yet," Duncan said. "Hopefully on the way back, it will be. The authorities might not suspect you'd get on a flight from Bangkok if they think you're up here."

"I've gotten lucky so far," Niral noted. "I don't think Malai knows my name, just what I look like. Unless Lamai told her."

"Let's hope not," Duncan said, his eye twitching.

"We will move the entire camp tomorrow morning," Thon said. "The Bureau may raid our villages. It's happened before. So Niral, you should not come back here. On your way to Bangkok, go to Kanchanaburi and give Kan the money."

Niral nodded. He looked at Duncan. They moved aside to talk in private.

"The keys for the safe deposit boxes are in Lamai's father's house," Duncan whispered. "They're on a key ring inside the drawer of the guest bedroom. You've gotta figure out a way to break in and get it without anyone seeing you. I'll give you the names and codes for the boxes too."

"I'll review the route with the dark guy right now, get a few hours' shuteye and leave."

"Get all the cash but leave one box full, just in case."

"Fine. Anything else?"

"This is it," Duncan said, taking Niral by his shoulders. "Last time I see you before we get the big shipment. Don't fuck up the assassination, man. That's our key to the good life. Our only escape from this cycle."

"Okay Duncan," Niral said, nodding. "I won't fuck it up."

76

Sanchez looked over the shoulder of a forensics expert at a blood stain on the floor of Vince Stevens' apartment as Lawrence walked inside.

"You called me up this late, brother?" Lawrence asked. "Hope it's for a purpose."

"Good purpose, man," Sanchez said, turning around. "Guess who shot who? Our old friend Lance Portman."

"Shot who?"

"Some kid, again. And maybe one Vince Stevens, city councilman. Or maybe the kid shot him and Lance killed the kid for shooting Stevens."

"First Macaday, now Vince Stevens? The media's gonna have a field day with this one. If the Macadays being whacked a world apart isn't enough, now we got a politician hit. But what's the connection between Stevens and Macaday?"

Sanchez opened his arms. "Long Island City fire? Stevens was speaking up about the new project, and it's his jurisdiction. What else?"

Lawrence nodded. "Brother likes killing kids. He really doesn't like 'em."

"Except his own kid, right? Didn't you tell me she's back up here, attending some tony private school in the East Side?"

"Yeah. How'd the mom come into that type of cash? Unless the brother got it."

"So he's assassinating kids for someone? Or defending the rich and powerful?"

"Not sure. You know it was Portman from eyewits?"

"Yeah, Stevens' husband and another witness description fits the general ID. Hopefully, Stevens might tell us what old Lance is up to. Took two clean shots right through him, but he's still critical."

"Alive for now."

"Better than dead, man. Better than dead."

77

"What happened?" Vishal asked over the phone as Lance stood in the doorway of Jeremy's building.

"You get some kid to shadow me? Or to gun me down?"

"He was there to back you up. What happened?"

"Stevens thought he had the upper hand for a while, got me stuck up after he flipped the situation. Then I flipped the shit again. But as soon as I do, this kid comes in blasting for the second time. Man, that really triggered my ass, so I ran him down and did him in."

"Fuck!" Vishal yelled. "Well, the kid's expendable. I'll just smooth it over with his gang. I thought of wasting him after he killed Macaday, but I figured he could still be helpful to you. But you say he came in blasting. Does that mean..."

"Stevens dead, I think. Two shots right through him. I doubt he survived that."

"Damn! So now what? We rely on Sveta courting Cortland?"

"That might work better than you think, brother. If they know the mob involved..."

"Still doesn't guarantee anything. Can't believe this one project is so difficult."

"What'll you do if Carty gets it?"

"Carty and Tragliani both. It's a blow. I might just make an appearance in NYC."

"I understand that, brother. But I wanna know, Shoquanda's still okay, right? You gonna still..."

"Did anyone see you kill the kid?" Vishal asked, ignoring Lance. "Or see you in the apartment?"

"Gotta say, brother, they did."

"If it's one or two, we can solve the problem."

"I ain't wasting innocent people. I ain't about that."

Vishal paused. "Well, you're on the run anyway. Doesn't change anything. Just stay out of sight as much as possible. I'll have to think about solutions on my end."

"What about Shoquanda? She..."

"When I make a promise, I make a promise. Don't worry about that. Just stay out of sight."

78

In his office at Royal Thai Police headquarters in Bangkok, Commissioner Prongchat hosted General Toon Tomechrin; Narcotics Suppression Bureau member Colonel Nopasit Limwat; General Chaow, who was visiting from Phuket; as well as Colonel Arthit, who was teleconferencing from Chiang Mai; Colonel Dusit, teleconferencing from Chiang Rai; and Detective Chak, teleconferencing from Isan.

"Khun Commissioner," General Toon reported, "my Detective Chan has indicated to me that Duncan Smith's wife has gone missing. He has been helping to track her family in Chiang Rai."

"Apparently, you did not track her very well," the Commissioner said. Toon avoided his eyes. "I hear your other detective, Nat, is still missing?"

"Yes, Khun Commissioner," Toon confirmed weakly. "We have not seen him since the celebration of the Dragon arrests."

The Commissioner shook his head. "Probably a revenge hit on our force from someone associated with the Dragons. Hopefully he will be located so we can deliver justice to the perpetrators. Has this farang Maric been found in Isan, Detective Chak?"

"We still have surveillance on Udon Thani, Nong Khai, and Khon Kaen, as well as more border patrols along the Laos border on the Mekong River," Detective Chak said. "Sightings have been reported in Udon Thani, but none are confirmed. A drunk even described a Thai chasing an Australian in the Nutty Park complex in Udon Thani. We dismissed that to imagination since no one else confirmed it, although the Thai's description was surprisingly similar to Detective Nat. Today, someone fitting Maric's description dropped off a small boy with a bullet wound at a hospital in Nong Khai, but we still have to investigate that to see if it is related. Honestly, our officers are tiring of the surveillance. They say it is mai sanuk."

"This is a serial killer of women and children we are after, Detective Chak," the Commissioner said. "Civilians can complain about mai sanuk, but we are officers of the law, defending Thailand's safety and honor. Tell your men to keep it up. By the way, is it possible Maric came down to kill Detective Nat and is near Bangkok? Or that Detective Nat went up there? Then this sighting might be more credible."

"It is possible, Khun Commissioner," General Toon admitted. "All is possible."

"What are you doing, General Toon?" the Commissioner scolded. "You've lost two detectives in succession. I wanted to promote you after Fan Hong was killed, but now, how can I? General Chaow, how is the investigation into this tourist's murder in Phuket?"

"We have cleared the Thai Panit," General Chaow explained. "The Americans have confirmed that the man murdered in New York City was Robert Macaday, who was our witness to the gem dealer murders, known to us as Robert Murphy. We are doing our best to coordinate with their authorities. The Dragons have a base in New York City, so we are following that angle to see if they finished eliminating the witness there. We believe this Maric killed Robert's wife in Phuket. Both husband and wife were in witness protection in Texas for testifying against Italian mobsters in New York City, hence the different names. Apparently, they visited Thailand while on vacation after voluntarily leaving witness protection in Texas. If they witnessed the murder of the gem dealers in Bangkok, presumably killed by Maric too, they were probably murdered under Fan Hong's authority. But if Robert was involved with the Dragons in New York City too, we might have a larger motive. Who knows?"

"Good work, General Chaow. Keep digging," Commissioner Prong-chat said as General Chaow smiled at General Toon. "Now back to Chiang Rai and this Duncan Smith. So his wife is missing. What else do we know, Colonel Dusit?"

"His sister tells us an Indian man visited her. He claimed to work for Smith. He had burns on his face, she said. He set up a meeting with his wife, Lamai, at a local temple. They disappeared together through the back exit as the sister waited in front. We don't know if Lamai left willingly or was kidnapped, but the sister says that the Indian man mentioned that Duncan Smith was hiding in the Chiang Mai countryside with a Karen hill tribe. We imagine they are ya ba importers and dealers too."

"Good," the Commissioner said. "Let's assume they are in the countryside. We need to raid the countryside to capture them and eliminate the drug routes they have set up there. I think it is safe to assume neither husband nor wife will return home, so we can lighten the police presence over there in Chiang Rai. Focus on the countryside and exterminate this wretched gang. Colonel Nopasit, I assume we can count on overwhelming commitment from the Narcotics Suppression Bureau regarding this matter?"

"Of course, Khun Commissioner," Nopasit affirmed. "I will assemble our forces here and in the northern territories. We will raid the countryside, using logistical support from Colonel Arthit, assuming he will give it?"

"Yes, you will receive our total commitment," Colonel Arthit responded. "These Karen drug dealers are a scourge. I've been trying to rid Thailand—"

"Now you can, Colonel Arthit," the Commissioner said. "This is our opportunity. You will receive maximum support from Colonel Dusit too. We need to stop these dealers now. The Thai people are counting on it."

PART VI

†

Chiang Rai, Thailand; Near Udon Thani, Thailand; Bushwick (Brooklyn), New York; Near Kanchanaburi, Thailand; Bangkok, Thailand; Forest Hills, Fresh Meadows (Queens), New York

79

Moments after dawn, Niral sat watching Lamai's parents' home from the alleyway of the adjacent house. Up front, a detective sat in his car, texting on his cell phone. Every ten minutes, the detective emerged, lit a cigarette, strolled to the backyard, and made his way around the house until he put the cigarette out with his shoe in the driveway. Then, he returned to the car and began the cycle once again. Once Niral had figured out his MO, he waited for one more round. When the detective started back to the car, Niral put on his Hanuman mask and made a break for the house.

He pried open a window and crawled into the kitchen. He bent down and listened for sounds. Then he slipped into the living room, his knees aching. Using Duncan's description of the guest bedroom's location, he navigated his way toward a closed door.

He felt the knob, twisted it slowly, and crept inside. The drawer was to the right, some distance from the bed. He turned on his flashlight. The curtains were drawn so the morning light only entered the room in small slits.

Niral slid open the middle drawer and found the key ring. Then, he felt a motion behind him. He froze. He heard a word uttered. He stood and pointed the flashlight at the bed.

160

Two people lay there. One was sitting up; the other, under a cover, began to rise too. The first individual appeared male, rotund. Perhaps he was wearing a suit and holster with gun, perhaps not, but Niral didn't take a chance. He fired into the man, and then the person next to him, whether man, woman, or both, he didn't know. Then he ran out the bedroom door and to the front door. He heard another door open as he fled the house.

The detective emerged from the car, but Niral fired at him, hitting the car as the detective ducked behind it. Niral escaped into the neighbor's alleyway and made his way through an intricate maze of his own devising to his motorcycle, where he took off his mask and stuffed it in a duffel bag as he rode away.

80

When Rob awoke, he could smell breakfast. He got up and strolled outside the small room to the terrace where he stretched, breathed in the morning air, and witnessed smoke rising above the forest trees from what he assumed were distant villages. Someone sang the Gayatri mantra. He had a deja vu moment, like he was back in Khao San. But then he realized the singer was Apsara's mother.

He entered the larger room, which he called the lounge room, although it contained no couches or other typical amenities. Sitting on the floor, Apsara tried to feed her daughter Hathai, *who seemed at least five years old*, Rob thought. *Was there any reason she couldn't feed herself?*

Apsara's mother prayed to a spirit house filled with Hindu deities. She lit two incense sticks as she chanted and rocked back and forth. Boonsri played with Hathai's doll in the corner.

"Good morning, Rob," Apsara said in English. "We have breakfast of noodles, eggs, some chicken and papaya salad."

Rob saw the food sizzling on pans placed on hot plates. He walked over to Boonsri. She shrunk from him, squeezing the doll.

"I won't hurt ya, sweetie. Som was an accident."

He bent down. She turned away from him. He touched her shoulder.

"I've been the nicest mate to you. I never rooted your ass or nothing."

She turned to him angrily.

"I know, you didn't," she said in Thai, turning again to the wall. Rob looked at Apsara.

"She wants me to rape her," Rob said angrily.

"Don't say that around my daughter," Apsara said. "Your daughter is your business."

Rob stood up. "They're both our responsibility if you love me like you said."

"I cannot take care of another child. I have my hands full."

"No wonder everyone wants to waste your ass, ya cunt."

Rob marched out the door. He returned a minute later.

"You got a phone I can use?" he asked Apsara.

"Why, so the police can figure out where we are?"

"You don't have an encrypted device?"

"Do you?"

Rob went back out. A few minutes later, Boonsri followed. She threw the doll off the terrace.

"Haven't I been a good Paw, sweetie?" Rob asked. "Better than that wanker, Wat?"

"You killed Wat," Boonsri said, turning away from him.

"He used you, sweetie," Rob said, rubbing her head. "I've treated you right."

She turned and hugged his legs. "Root me then," she said.

He smirked. "That ain't right. An old man doesn't root his daughter. Grown man don't root a child."

She looked up at him, tears in her eyes. "I am not a child," she said. "I will get you a phone from the village like Som got you information. You can trust me, Paw."

"Yeah? Get me some new clothes too, while you're at it," Rob joked.

"I will, Paw. You'll see. And then..."

81

It wasn't until morning that Sveta realized Lance was inside the apartment. He was sleeping on the couch rather than the mattress on the floor where sometimes they slept together. She crawled to Lance's side. She was a bit groggy, but still, excited by his sight, she jumped on him.

He awoke with a start.

"Damn, girl," he said, looking around, "you scared the shit out of me. What's up?"

"You're alive," she replied, sliding her hand down his boxers. "I was worried."

"Course I'm alive, girl," he said, closing his eyes again. "No one's bringing down the Iceman. That's what Candy used to call me when Gigglies was still up."

"You bring up another girl as I hold your cock. Is this wise?"

"Woman, we ain't got no ties. Thought you were sweating after Rob."

"I can have fun while I wait," she said, leaning over him.

"Not now, sister," he said, pushing her away. "I got things on my mind."

Sitting upright on his legs, she sighed in frustration. Opening his eyes, he saw her nipples hard through her white t-shirt. He sat up and grabbed her waist.

"That's what you were waiting for all night, bitch? Thought you'd be thinking, 'did that brother do all right with the councilman?'"

"I want baby named Leroy," she purred, rubbing her hand on his package again.

Lance laughed. "All right. After I take a shower. I need to clean my ass up."

"You will get sweaty again."

"That's fine. How'd things go with Cortland?"

"You are talking business this early?" she asked, standing up and walking away, her arms folded. "Yes, I told him again about the mob and all that. How about this councilman person?"

"He dead, girl. So is another boy. You see why I ain't jumping to fuck you?"

She turned around, eyes wide. "What do you mean, he is dead?"

"That stupid-ass nigger shot him, and I paid him back. All Vishal's stupidity."

"Who is Vishal?"

"No one. I meant Ashok."

Sveta swallowed. "Does this mean you will go to jail and I will never see Rob?"

"Don't panic. I told Ashok. He's gonna look into it. Maybe they'll think it was a mob hit. You got to Cortland so that word's spreading. And I'm fucked a lot more than you are, girl. They don't even know who you are. They know me exactly."

"Which means they will find us."

"I hope not. But maybe we should get you to Carolina so you protected. Or hide you with Candy."

"So I will work as stripper again? To make you money?"

"I didn't say that."

"If I go to Carolina, will Ashok send me back to Rob?"

"I think he wants this deal to go through first."

"So then I will stay here and help you. I don't want to be with this strange Ashok and that Hemraj. They give me creeps."

"We'll have to see how this goes. I don't know how Jeremy, Chloe, and the Unity Brothers will react. We might have to formulate something new. You up for that?"

"I am," she said, approaching him and clasping her arm in his. "Whatever you decide."

82

Niral made quick work of the banks, not being questioned or detained despite his looks. Thais suspected Indians had money in secret places anyway, and this time, the stereotype worked in his favor.

Still, getting into the first bank at 8:30 and moving around to the others, strapping the cash onto the motorcycle so it wouldn't fall— that took him until ten. Then he drove as fast as he could down Route 1, knowing it was a nearly eleven-hour journey to the outskirts of Kanchanaburi.

Driving three hours straight was tiring, though he was relieved that he had passed two seemingly-abandoned police checkpoints. A planned half-hour break at a roadside restaurant became an hour due to exhaustion and hunger. But he considered himself lucky. During the latter part of the break, he noticed nearly endless streams of police cars and vans cruising up Route 1.

Then hours of driving. At the next stop, around five p.m., he needed to use the bathroom. He wanted to be quick, so not to leave the motorcycle alone with straps of cash on it, but he collapsed in front of the toilet. As he tried to get up, he began to cry. He dropped his head onto the floor and cried like a baby. Whether it was due to exhaustion or because he had needlessly murdered two more people or because he was in perpetual flux as a prisoner to many factions, he wasn't sure. Perhaps, all of it had finally broken him, but then wouldn't he laugh like a madman, not cry like a woman?

He wiped his eyes with toilet paper. What a long way he had come from his days of writing in his Bushwick apartment. He sat on the toilet and disciplined his mind, thinking about nothing while he relieved himself. As he washed his hands, the thoughts came back again. But this time, he felt energetic and determined to carry out his plans.

He was ready to use his gun as he exited the roadside bathroom, but the bike was still there, the money still attached. What a country, he thought. It wouldn't have been there in New York or in India. He was lucky enough to have lived in Thailand, even if he never saw it again.

He biked continuously for the next five hours until he found Kan and his men in the dark forest, illuminated only by car and motorcycle headlights. Instead of greeting him, Kan made fun of the bags.

"You look like a stupid Vietnamese peasant delivering rice to drug addicts," Kan said. "I can't believe the police did not stop you."

"I guess they don't think much of Indians. Plus, I got lucky. Cops are headed up to Chiang Mai or Chiang Rai for some reason. A whole battalion passed me while I was eating."

Kan looked at his men. "Big raid? Not good. We should tell Thon." Then he surveyed Niral. "Are you okay, Niral? You look like you have seen a ghost."

"I'm tired."

"If only you had your ladyboy. She would relax you." He laughed. "I am trying to lighten the mood, as you would say, yes?"

"Yes, Kan. Thank you."

"You are staying overnight? I put you up in nice hotel in Kanchana-buri, not in this jungle."

"No, I've got a flight to catch in Bangkok. I need to go now."

"Where are you flying?"

"India, Kan. Land of my forefathers."

"Your forefathers. Like Hanuman."

Niral nodded. He slid the duffel bag from his back to his front. He opened it and carefully took out the Hanuman mask.

"I saved this for you, Kan. I thought you would find it ironic. If you know what that means."

Kan took the mask and looked happy. "Yes, I like Hanuman. But you are more like Hanuman," he said, putting on the mask.

"I am. But I already have the face."

"Nice face, Niral. Balance."

"You think?" he asked. "I need to go, Kan."

"When you come back, you bring me sweets from India. I like sticky thing. Orange."

"Yes, jalebi. I will try," he said as he waited for Kan's men to peel off the last of the cash bags. Then he mounted the motorcycle. "Goodbye, Kan. I've enjoyed your company."

83

"You didn't knock it off, did ya?" Rob asked, opening the flip phone. He sat on a pile of loose sugarcanes in the field, wearing his new clothes, which felt a little looser, but not by much.

Boonsri shook her head.

"I reckon ya must have. You don't got no dosh to pay for it."

Boonsri smiled. Rob rubbed her head. She hugged Rob, then lay down with her head on his lap.

"Not exactly what I wanna be teachin' ya, but you've learned well." He dialed the number he wanted. He waited for the rings. Then he got the voice he expected.

"Vishal, I'm still alive. I know it's amazing, mate."

"I imagine Niral's long off your radar. Are you still in Thailand?"

"Border. But yeah, I'm still in."

"I thought you were in Laos if you weren't dead."

"I've still got business here. I lucked out, and now I'm close."

"Women are trouble, Rob."

"How'd you know, you wanker?"

"Experience."

"Getting out might not be so easy. They've got border patrols and they're still after me."

"I'm gonna put you in touch with someone who can help you. You get to Laos, you get a prize."

"What're you gonna shower me with, Vishal? Diamonds? Bullets?"

"A woman, Rob. Just you wait."

84

"This isn't good," Jeremy said as he sat with the Asthethic Unity group. "Can we still influence the board decision without Stevens?"

"Cortland will influence his friends on the CFLIC and Ozone will get their recommendation," Chloe said. "Cortland will pitch Ozone's proposal himself at the final board meeting. He's got some influence on the board itself too since he's prominent in upper Queens society. At first, we wanted to hide the fact that Macaday was hit by the mob, but now that Stevens has also been hit, it might be to our benefit to preempt the news story. If we leak to the press that Macaday was a mob hit and that they're behind DeKalb Construction, maybe we can stop their bid period, or delay the bid process. At first I thought delaying it was a bad thing, but it's better than the bid going to DeKalb."

"Well, the Macaday hit is already being speculated in the media as a mob hit," Jeremy said. "But where's our proof that the Traglianis are behind DeKalb?"

"The tabloids never need proof," Chloe said.

"So we leak something to the papers," Levon said, standing up. "But what if they don't print it? They got their own thing going on. They've focused on all the sensational aspects of this case but never anything too deep. So maybe they don't care, or they're bought off too. And no one trusts the media anyway. What then? We've got to stop this shit no matter what. I'm talking about the larger picture."

"Yeah, we've gotta stop it," Stella concurred, standing next to him. "Any way possible."

"I still say we try the media," Jeremy said. "There have been plenty of articles in the local papers about the negative aspects of this for artists and working people. If they put it out there, the vote might be delayed again."

"But the board doesn't need to listen to the press," Tomas said. "The Queens Borough president can say there's no proof. And the board will give it to DeKalb, which we know is a mob front, and we didn't do anything about it. I'm tired of words and no action."

"Honestly," a kid named Mel said from the corner, "what's so bad if they put up some apartment buildings? I mean if they make them affordable, poor people can live there."

Tomas, Levon, Jesse, Stella, and their followers gave him dirty looks. He looked nervous.

"We don't know if they'll be affordable, Mel," Jeremy said. "Plus, if the mob's involved, they'll be cheating people for sure. And who knows what else they'll put there. They could include all kinds of organized crime fronts."

"Yeah, but that would be anarchy, right?" Mel said. "Isn't that what we're about?"

"It's called organized crime, Mel," Stella sneered. "It's organized."

"We support subversive artists, not middle-class people who claim to be poor," Levon said. "I'm sick and tired of this bullshit. I say we vote now."

"Hold on," Jeremy said, putting his arms out. "I don't think we've talked enough yet to vote."

"You mean you haven't put the wool over everybody's eyes and swayed the vote to you yet," Tomas said. "Like always."

"We vote now," Levon said. "In the open, fuck the secret ballots this time. I wanna see who's who."

"Rule is secret ballot," Jeremy said. "There's been no motion..."

"Here's the motion: one side's for leaking the mob to the press and relying on rich white people to stop this bullshit; another's for radical action. Let me see the hands for the former."

Mel raised his hand. Chloe, Lance, and Sveta followed. Then, Jeremy reluctantly raised his hand. Levon smiled.

"Who's for radical action?" he asked. The four radicals, plus their followers, the girl-toys of Tomas and Jesse, Alexis and Arathi, plus two other guys named Chris and Vaughn, raised their hands. What had been a tie last time, broken by Jeremy, was now a victory for the radical element. Candy hadn't showed up, yet again, and neither had the Asian-American habitual heroin users, Lester and Mahdi, who, when they did show up, usually voted for Jeremy instead of Levon.

"Okay," Levon said. "I also propose we vote for a new leader."

"I think you overstepping, brother," Lance said. "One vote don't demand a recall."

"Shut up, you ignoramus," Levon replied, sneering.

Lance stood up, putting his hand on the gun strapped to his waist. "Who you calling dumb, you stupid nigger? I'm the only one who's ever used violence, I bet. You wanna say that again?"

Levon seemed ready for the fight. Jeremy held up his hands.

"Okay, this is getting out of hand. Fine, my side lost the vote. I'll concede that. But I'm still going to lead effectively no matter what course we decide. That a good compromise?"

Levon looked at Jesse and Tomas. "Yeah, I guess for now that's fine. But we put the vote on the agenda for next time. You bring your other people; I don't mind."

"And who will decide what this radical action will be?" Sveta asked.

"Don't worry, baby, we've got a plan," Jesse said. "We've been talking about it already."

"Is it big, brother?" Lance asked.

"It's big," Jesse said. "It's gonna be grand."

85

"Stevens, tell us, what do you remember?" Sanchez asked Vince Stevens as he lay in bed at a local Queens hospital, barely conscious after life-saving surgery.

"Did a brother shoot you?" Lawrence asked him. "A black man?"

Stevens seemed to shake his head. He was still groggy from the anesthesia.

Sanchez put a picture of Lance in front of Stevens' face. Stevens recoiled.

"Seems like an ID to me," Detective Lacey, Sanchez's partner, said from the back of the hospital room.

"We need to be sure," Sanchez said. "He shot you?"

Stevens opened his mouth. "Yes," he said softly.

"Why?"

"L-I-C," he mouthed.

"Yes, but why?"

Stevens opened his mouth. "M-O-B," he seemed to mouth.

"Mob?" Sanchez asked. "Lance Portman hit you for the mob? Because of the Long Island City Project?"

Stevens seemed to nod.

"Who is the mob?" Lawrence asked. "The Traglianis?"

Stevens didn't respond. His eyes closed.

"Let's come back later, when he's woken up," Detective Lewis, Lawrence's partner, said. "We've got enough to go on."

The four detectives left the room and spoke outside Stevens' hospital room, which was being guarded by an officer.

"So Lance hits Macaday and Stevens, using these two kids, then kills each of them at the scenes," Sanchez speculated. "To cover his tracks? For the mob?"

"Looks that way, brother," Lawrence concurred. "Stevens' husband said Stevens was talking to Lance inside his apartment and even called away the cops to protect him. Maybe Lance was extorting the councilman but called in the kid to do the dirty work when he refused, or maybe to intimidate him? Then he executes the kid to cover his tracks, just like the Macaday job. I bet you when we do the test, the kid's gun actually shot Stevens, and Lance shot the kid, but in Stevens' mind, it was Lance because he was extorting him. Don't know why this brother would kill the kids in public both times though, but I'd take Stevens' ID over some half-baked theory of Lance being a multiple bodyguard and vigilante. Still, I tell you one thing, if Lance is with the mob, he's probably dead by now too. Mob won't take a chance on a live wire, especially a black one."

"Maybe," Sanchez said. "I can see the Traglianis whacking both Linda and Bob Macaday, that's a given. But what's the link to this guy Rob in Thailand and the Dragons? Unless the Thai authorities are lying to us to cover things up for their own people."

"Maybe the Traglianis and the Dragons teamed up for some larger goal. Or this Australian killer is on the Tragliani payroll too."

"Fine, but why hit Stevens? Last I heard, he's supporting the artistic recreation of Long Island City, right? Let's check out if he was supporting a specific bid. Maybe it, or a competing bid, has mob backing?"

"It's possible, brother," Lawrence said. "Mob might be weakened, but it's not out of the game. And if it's construction, and if it's in Queens, that's a pretty good bet. Let's look that theory over. I think you know an old cop who could be helpful with that info, right?"

"Yeah. Savard," Sanchez replied. "He's retired now, but we can pay him a visit at home."

"Doesn't he live in copland?"

"Staten Island's more diverse now. Don't worry, it's not the Howard Beach of the eighties. You'll be fine."

86

By the time Niral reached Shekhat's old warehouse in Bangkok, it was two in the morning. He parked his motorcycle and marched inside. Shekhat's brothers, Mitesh and Amit, were waiting for him. From his duffel bag, he pulled out bricks of cash taken from Duncan's final deposit box and threw them on the table.

"Extra funding for the jewelry-making factory. Your cousins in Surat have been working with Kamalbhai to create it, right?"

"Yes, Niralbhai. It will still take months, but they will construct it," Mitesh replied.

"Good. Then we can sell jewelry directly to the US market through my contacts. Once the factory is set up, declare your brother Anil missing, sell the lease on this place, and move to Surat. Wire me the money from the lease sale. Whenever Anil's life insurance kicks in, send that to me too."

"And this cash?"

"I don't want to enter India with it. Launder it to your cousins through your bank. They'll use it for the factory. Pay me back later."

"Yes, Niralbhai."

"I'm sorry about your brother. But let's face it, he was a sisterfucker, right?"

Niral motorcycled to Sukhumvit. Same Same had not been replaced, but a sign for an upcoming club was up. The kid with no legs was back, begging next to the Skytrain steps. Indian guys were flirting with ladyboys in front of the closed club next door. One of the ladyboys was Buppha.

She was flirting with one of the Indians. Niral approached and poked her arm. She turned and smiled warmly at him. He could tell she was drunk.

She hugged him, wordlessly, then turned back to the other Indian. Niral was angry.

"How was the full moon party?" he asked.

"Good," she said, turning her head to Niral. "Very fun."

"I'm going back to India, Buppha."

"That's nice," she said.

After only a week apart, her carefree attitude shocked him. *I saved your life*, he thought. *I said I loved you. You said you loved me.*

The Indian turned to him and said, in English, "Do you have a problem, boss?"

Niral took out his gun. The Indian's hands went up and he backed away.

"Don't be so...dramatic, Niral," Buppha said, smiling. He turned the gun towards her.

"I might be going away forever, Buppha. Do you understand that? Maybe...maybe I can buy a last-minute ticket for you," he said, though he knew he didn't have the money.

"Thailand is my home, Niral. I love Indians, but I don't want to live in India."

Shaking, Niral put the gun back in his holster. He stumbled away. It began to drizzle.

He drove over to Soi Cowboy. He watched Sumantapat's club, Go-Go Rama. *I wonder if he's inside,* Niral thought. *Another problem solved if I can get in and out.*

It started raining heavily. Niral realized that could help him get away. But what was the point? He was on the precipice of a new life. People like Sumantapat never died, other than of old age.

He pulled over beneath an awning to wait out the rain and saw tourists running through the storm, dancers wearing sailor outfits still hawking, still hustling. And inside the ornate curtains, he knew the bored girls from Isan wore bikinis as they pretended to sway to the music.

87

Detective Chak entered the hospital room. A subordinate updated him on the situation.

"It's Bangkok Detective Nat's son," the subordinate said. "The grand-mother came and identified him. She is in the waiting room. It was probably Maric who dropped him off."

"Who shot him? If it was Maric, why would he take pity on the boy after killing so many?"

"I don't know. But the boy could lead us to Maric."

"Did you ask him if he could?"

"Yes. He refuses to say anything."

"Give me a minute."

Chak approached the bed. Som lay with a bandage around his waist. He was conscious.

"You are a lucky boy," Detective Chak said. "We've been looking for you. Your grandmother is happy you're alive."

Som didn't respond. Chak said, "Your father has been looking, too. Do you know your father?"

Som looked up. He didn't respond, but Chak's question seemed to catch his attention.

"Your father is a policeman. Have you seen him?"

Som didn't speak, but his eyes became larger.

"You have seen him, haven't you? Did he fight with Maric?"

Som swallowed. He said, "Paw is my father."

"Paw? So you have seen him."

"Paw left me here to die," Som said, starting to cry.

"You mean Maric," Chak said, looking at his subordinate. "The Australian. The farang."

Som nodded. "Yes, he is my Paw."

"Have you seen your real father, Som? He is a detective."

Som wiped his eyes. "I think he shot me. After Paw shot him. And then Paw left me here. They both wanted to kill me."

"Som, listen to me. Your Paw is a murderer. He killed your friend, Wat. It sounds like he killed your real father. He's killed many other people too. He kidnapped you and Boonsri. Is Boonsri still alive?"

"I think so," he said softly.

"We can save her before your Paw kills her too. Do you know where they are?"

Som shrugged.

"Can you try to lead us there?" Chak asked.

Som didn't speak. Chak looked at his subordinate.

"I think he'll try," Chak concluded.

88

Night had fallen in Isan. Rob had found a flashlight. He had already searched the ceramic jars and was kicking dirt underneath the house.

Boonsri stood by him, holding the waist of his pants. Apsara descended the stairs, Hathai in her arms, the cleaned doll in hers. Apsara was singing to her daughter.

"What are you doing, Rob?" Apsara asked when she saw him.

"That dosh I gave you, Apsara. Where'd you put it?"

"Safe deposit box, like you told me. But in Isan."

"It's in a bank up here?"

"Yes, that's right."

"So I reckon before we get to Laos, we'll pick it up. That right?"

"Yes."

"Anything else you got in there? Like maybe the dosh Thanat stole from Duncan?"

Apsara paused. "Why would I have that money, Rob?" she asked.

"Don't know. We never found it."

"Thanat probably spent it. Or he hid it."

"And during your lovey-dovey phase, he never told you nothing about it?"

Apsara shook her head. "No."

"All right. I was wondering why you didn't want me burying that cop under here. Maybe something else is buried. Like dosh."

"No Rob. I don't want a body buried under my house for many reasons. First, the police are more likely to search it. But more importantly, it brings more bad luck to us. You already sprayed that detective's blood over my spirit house, and the tree cannot even be cleaned. Also, we are supposed to cremate a body, not bury it. Then the person can be reincarnated. None of the people you have killed have been reincarnated, which makes you even worse than many killers."

Rob put his hands on his waist. "Yeah, none of 'em went on. Most of 'em didn't deserve it anyhow. Let 'em suffer for eternity. If there is such a thing."

"You don't believe in anything, Rob. This is your problem."

"I never had no reason to believe. Never did 'til I came here. 'Til I met you. And then you screwed me too."

"But we are back now."

"Yeah, and we gotta leave Candyland."

"Maybe Laos is better. Isan people are Laotian at heart."

"Maybe."

Apsara put Hathai down next to Boonsri, sneering at Boonsri as she did, though Rob didn't see it. Hathai knelt down and began massaging the dirt with her doll's hand.

Apsara put her arms around Rob. She stared into Rob's eyes.

"My darling, we will live forever. The five of us. In Laos. We will leave as soon as we can."

PART VII

†

Tomkinsville (Staten Island), New York; Mumbai, India; Surat, India; Outside Chiang Mai, Thailand; Mae Hong Son Province, Thailand

89

Detective Denny Savard had retired only a year before. He now lived in Staten Island, where Detectives Sanchez and Lawrence made the long trip on the morning ferry, while their partners, Lacey and Lewis, were at their precincts tracking Vince Stevens' history and current political leanings. Sanchez and Lawrence made their way to a single-family home in Tomkinsville.

Savard's wife Martha brought out lemonade for the two detectives as they sat in Savard's tiny backyard, next to a garden of broccoli, spinach, and brussels sprouts, perfect plantings for the October weather.

"We've picked the lettuce, mustard greens, beets, and radishes already," she said. "Do you fellas want some? I've mixed them into a nice salad with some Italian dressing."

"No, ma'am, but thanks for the lemonade," Detective Lawrence said, holding up his glass.

"I know you fellas are carrying on the tough work," she said. "I'm so glad Denny's back home, away from all that nonsense."

"That's enough, Martha," Savard said. "These guys want to talk to me about something important."

"Don't get yourself mixed up in anything nasty, Denny. I know some guys try to pull you back in, and you don't need all that mess," she said as she sauntered back inside.

"Nice to have a woman like that," Sanchez said. "Can't say Lawrence or me are spoken for."

"I owe a lot to Martha. Some women can drive you mad, but find the right one, and they'll get you through the tough times."

"Speaking of tough times," Lawrence said, "you read over what we sent you?"

"Sure. I remember the Long Island City fire well. One of the biggest cases of my career. I've been following the project off and on. Months ago, the media exposed that one of Vishal Patel's cousins, who had put in a construction bid on the property, was shacking up with some blonde bimbo on the advisory council. Vince Stevens spoke out about it, the bimbo resigned, the cousin withdrew his bid and moved back to North Carolina, as far as I know."

"And we never found Vishal."

"No, we never did. I guess it's possible he was pulling the strings if you believe in ghosts."

"But why would Lance Portman whack Macaday and Stevens? And there's Bob's wife in Thailand too. A tie to the Dragons."

"Portman was friends with Niral Solanke?"

"The janitor at the office building where Solanke worked for Stan Lorenzo. Sorry, custodian," Lawrence corrected himself.

"And Portman's pockets seem to be suddenly full, but not according to his bank accounts," Sanchez said. "His daughter Shoquanda's back from North Carolina, living with Portman's ex-wife and attending Corcoran in Manhattan. That's a tony private school, and it ain't cheap. He's not even a custodian anymore. We have no clue what he does for a living, and the accounts we know about are mostly funding basic child support and property taxes, with nothing going in. So there's no evidence the school funding's from Lance, but I can't figure any reasonable way the ex is getting that windfall."

"Did you ask the ex-wife who's paying the bills?"

"Ex-wife claims a wealthy uncle in Carolina's paying the bills," Lawrence said. "We don't have enough for a warrant to look into her financials or the school's, or even get the info on this uncle. But it's weird because the daughter was already in Carolina living with her aunt, apparently to get her away from the big city and straighten her out, but she lived in a low-income neighborhood, not clear that aunt could pay those bills, and if there is a richer relative, why not just stay with him? And why bring her back up to New York? And then, you said Vishal's cousin is from Carolina too. That's a strange coincidence."

"Convince the judge she might be hiding or financing Portman and there's your in to her financials," Savard suggested. "Once you make a connection to the school, get that warrant too."

Sanchez wrote that down. Lawrence looked uncomfortable.

"To me, Macaday and his wife seem like straightforward revenge from the Lucchese for the prosecutions of their people," Savard explained. "That the Thai police have linked it to a Dragon associate indicates they might be working together. Stevens is more puzzling. But since he's a player in the LIC project, it's likely connected. I made some calls and did some digging from people I know on the inside. The bids are between two construction companies, Ozone of Queens and DeKalb of Brooklyn. Ozone was a late entry and seems favored by Stevens and the artsy crowd. DeKalb is favored by the Queens Borough president and the community. Vishal's cousin dropped out, but so did Vishal's former boss, Brendan Carty, who had returned to NYC and bought up much of Vishal's former assets. It's strange that people connected to Vishal keep dropping out.

"You know, there's a rumor that Niral Solanke didn't go to Thailand to teach English. That he's working there for the Dragons because they did him a favor during the Priya Mehta case, leading to Roberto Tragliani's murder. I don't know what that favor was, but the Dragons are based here in New York too. So that's your Thailand connection, tenuous but there. What if the Dragons and the Traglianis, linked now, have a stake in the Long Island City Project?"

"And Vishal?" Lawrence asked.

"I don't know if he's alive, although I have to tell you, based on something Niral said to me in the hospital room when he got burned, I have suspicions that he's dead, either by Niral's hands or the Mad Priest's, Amrat Mehta."

Sanchez swallowed. He had never told Lawrence about his decision with Savard to blame Vishal for Amrat's arsons to prevent the mob from collecting insurance money on the properties, even though they knew Amrat's actions were likely self-directed. His gaze reminded Savard of this subject, so Savard changed course.

"But Vishal's interests seem to keep fading," Savard said, "while we keep coming up with the Dragons and Traglianis. If they're all working together, we've got bigger problems than these assassinations."

"So what's our thinking now, Savard?" Lawrence asked. "What should we do?"

"Legwork. First, look at this Thailand connection, and that means Niral Solanke. Who sponsored him in Thailand? If it's a real name, maybe it's someone connected to the Dragons? Honestly, I'm surprised you haven't pursued that angle yet."

"Well, I've gotten updates from the Thai authorities, but it's mainly been the Marshals talking to them," Lawrence explained. "They have the national manpower and keep saying the Macaday murder's their case, due to the wit prot program angle..."

"Since when does any cop worth his salt leave the legwork to some federal agency? Man up, detective. Let's get some work done here."

Lawrence appeared shocked by Savard's verbal assault. Sanchez gave him a look suggesting that he not say anything impudent.

"No problem, Denny," Sanchez said. "We'll do the legwork."

"Look up Stevens' calls and logs," Savard continued. "Who's he been talking to? Who's been visiting him? Basic stuff. You know the evidence is hidden in the granules, not the ant hills."

"You really think Niral Solanke is working for the Dragons?" Sanchez asked. "I thought he was a good guy. Look what he did to bring down the Mad Priest."

"I don't want to believe it either. I knew his father at the 110, and he did some good work on the Priya Mehta case. But people change. Maybe that burning did something to his mind. But I'll tell you this: you don't just have to rely on the Thai authorities. You've got a resource right here. Prakash Solanke, Niral's dad. He lives in the same place."

Lawrence hit his head. "Fuck, you're right."

"Gentlemen, you need to eat more beets," Savard said, holding up a finger. "I'll have Martha pack you some for the road."

90

Emerging from the Mumbai airport, Niral went straight to Manu's car in the parking lot.

Manu pulled out immediately and headed for Surat. Niral noticed he had a firearm in a bulging, but concealed, holster.

"Any problems?" Manu asked.

"I thought they would stop me at the gate, but they didn't," Niral responded.

"They know you have nothing to do with that mess with the Dragons."

"But I was sponsored by Mr. Hong, the ringleader. They have that on paper."

"You are an avatar. Whether it was luck or something else that has spared you, your mission is clear."

"Which reminds me, have you done everything I requested?"

"Yes, Niralbhai. The plan is in place. Now it is time for execution."

"You can still back out if you want."

"I will die for you, Niralbhai. Not just because of what you have done for my family, but because I believe you are the avatar."

They reached the outskirts of Surat by five p.m. They ate in the same dosa hut where they had eaten the first time they had met, served by the same waiter wearing the same white apron. But this time, they did not proceed to the basement to meet Bhai.

They finished eating and drove on to Rander. Niral didn't need to get money from the bank as he did the last time he was here. He didn't need to hide Manu. He didn't need to call Talim, or whoever was pretending to be Talim. His instructions were already known and clear. He proceeded to the back of the apartment building, climbed over the fence, and strolled to the open field where he had met the hooded figure once before. He did not see anyone, so he approached the large tree that centered the field. There he saw a man sitting on a thick branch, wearing a white kurta and topi. Upon closer inspection, he noticed it was the same man who had told Talim's story the first time, with one lazy eye and one focused eye. He didn't see anyone else around. And this man was not armed.

"So, you are the real Talim after all?" Niral asked, looking up.

Talim smiled. "Did you think I was someone different?"

"With all the secrecy, who knows?"

"Allah knows us true. He even knows you, Niral Solanke, as much as you try to deny Him."

"I never said I denied Him."

"So will you go to your grave a Muslim? If it must come to that?"

"I don't plan to go to my grave, period."

"But it may happen. And it will happen to us all, one day."

"Talim, are you going to throw me a curve? Because we've have prepared well, my man and I."

"No, no," Talim said, shaking his head. He jumped off the branch and onto the ground. "The men are up in Dwarka already. They have their orders; you have yours. If everything goes according to plan, I will avenge my father, my mother, my sister, my brother, and all Muslims who have suffered under Bhai. I will meet them one day in Paradise, and you will receive a road trip to Burma to join Duncan, along with a massive shipment of drugs the size of which neither you, nor many others, have ever beheld. I may even go myself, to meet my good friend who has delivered this gift for me."

"So why call me here? Simply to say good luck?"

"I have not seen you for six months. Of course I wanted to see you again before the big event. You will not switch allegiance because of some last-minute guilt or affinity for your tradition, I hope?"

"I've killed many people at this point, most for no reason at all. I don't mind killing one more for a reason."

"If you are not driven by faith, then certainly you will be compensated by a good material life. As much as I disagree with it, I will promise it."

"Anything else?"

"I spoke to Rahmat. He told me you might pull a gun on me, like you did on him. He said you were not friendly to him at the end."

"I had to dump my gun before I got to the airport, so no, I don't have a gun to pull on you, not that I have any reason to. Rahmat had a special request that I couldn't fulfill, and that had nothing to do with this mission."

Talim put his hand on Niral's shoulder. "Niral Solanke, you know the phrase to say if you wish to convert to Islam. I would give you the Koran, but I don't want to risk you throwing it away."

"I have no place to keep it anyway."

"Yes, I imagine that is true of many things."

Talim turned and began to climb the tree. "Good luck, Niral Solanke," he said. "Allah is watching you."

91

Colonel Nopasit Limwat stood in the middle of the Karen village, hearing screams coming from the huts as he watched them burn. Next to him, a line of villagers were guarded by soldiers and officers from the Narcotics Suppression Bureau. By them, three women lay dead of gunshots. The people left inside the huts, screaming now in pain and death, were either old people who could not get up when commanded or babies their mothers had left when ordered to line up by the loudspeakers. Those women who had stepped out of line to save their children or parents had been killed as violation of the order to stay still.

Some of the remaining Karen women cried, while other villagers pleaded with the soldiers to put out the fires.

"Colonel, isn't this extreme?" Colonel Dusit from Chiang Rai's police force asked Colonel Nopasit. "We don't need to burn all the huts. We don't need to kill all these people."

"We do if they will not tell us about the drugs," Colonel Nopasit said. "They can stop this mayhem by revealing the location of the merchandise or the path of the dealers."

"Believe me, Colonel Dusit, these Karen deserve it," Colonel Arthit from Chiang Mai said. "They sell poison to Thai children and then complain about human rights. Amazing."

As another hut burned, a man raised his hand and yelled, "Please don't burn the next hut. My son inside is sick. We don't have drugs, but we have money that we will deliver to the dealers. The dealers are headed towards Burma."

As he said that, two men carrying briefcases ran from different huts in opposite directions toward the forest. One was shot in the back as he fled. As the man fell, the briefcase flew open and banded bills of money came out.

"This could be lucrative for us too," Colonel Arthit whispered to Colonel Nopasit.

Nopasit smiled. "You keep this batch," he said. "My men are well-fed. We will take the next batch."

He ordered some men to chase the escapee. Then he commanded the rest of the village be burned down to teach the people a lesson. The man who had spoken up was arrested and held for further questioning. Only his hut was spared.

"Shoot anyone else who comes out of line," Nopasit said. "If they riot, shoot them all. Hopefully, we will create a big enough smoke cloud to warn the dealers that we are coming. They will not escape us."

92

As they continued on their trek to their next location, Thon looked up and noticed smoke in the sky that emerged from the direction of the Karen village and informed Bway Paw. She assumed that if villages had been burned, then helicopters would probably come next. She decided they should move into a heavily wooded area before evening so helicopters would be less likely to spot them.

"You've experienced this kind of dragnet before?" Duncan asked Thon.

"Of course, Duncan," Thon said. "We are professionals. We know how to handle it."

Since Bway Paw believed Lamai should not exert herself in her condition, Paw Htoo and Naw Baw had carried Lamai on a stretcher from the village. The two were exhausted by the time they reached their destination. They lowered Lamai gently to the ground and took deep breaths. Some men began building tents for the night; others looked around for food that did not need to be cooked because a fire would attract attention.

"I hear them already," Thon said an hour later as they sat at a fire. "The helicopters. When night comes, they will have their beams on and their heat sensors too. Better to relieve yourself now and sleep early with heavy blankets on to mask your heat."

"I'm glad I'm with such pros," Duncan said, watching Paw Htoo and Naw Baw carry Lamai into the tent. "I'm grateful you're treating Lamai so well."

"Do not worry, she will receive double respect: that given to any Karen woman and the extra respect we give to any guest. By the way, Mr. Duncan, we have never spoken about your past, and I am curious about you. Tell me, do you have experience escaping from the police like this yourself?"

Duncan laughed. "No, not like this. I never had any problems with the police in Bangkok," he said, lying even as he remembered his assassination of the Bangkok detective Pom who had almost found him out. Then, feeling a little guilty about his lie and not having anything to share further with Thon, he said, "I grew up privileged in America, actually. Until I realized my life was a lie. That's when I decided to restart it in Thailand."

"A lie?"

"Yes," he said, hesitating, wondering if he should reveal anything about his past, but continuing on as he realized it made him feel more human and congenial to Thon, given Thon's own openness and hospitality. "See, I thought the people that raised me were my parents, but after a horrible tragedy, I found out they weren't, and I guess that really messed with my head. The man I knew as my dad, he was a corporate lawyer. He brought in the big bucks, so I thought, and I was raised in this colonial-style mansion in Fairfield County, Connecticut. The woman I knew as my mom had worked as a consultant before I was born, but she hadn't worked in years and was a housewife. I went to private schools, then I went to an Ivy League school for college.

"After graduation I thought I would become an investment banker

185

in New York City. But then the recession hit. Dad lost his job. His investments were high risk and not diversified enough, so he had his savings wiped out too, and we couldn't pay the mortgage. I always assumed we had owned the home, but I was wrong. He couldn't take the shame, so he killed himself by hanging himself inside a closet in his bedroom.

"After that, we were distraught, but we were able to find a new apartment in Bridgeport, and we tried to get jobs to pay the rent and bills. My mom tried hard, but she couldn't get regular work. I figured I would get a job, any job, to help out, and the job market was tough, but after enough pounding the pavement, I got part-time work as a waiter and tutor. Then one day, Mom became frantic and frustrated over some stupid thing and blurted out that I was adopted. She said some Lebanese prostitute in Germany had given me up. Probably knocked up by a client. So I figure I'm half-German, half-Lebanese. But until that point, I thought I was Irish, Welsh, Scottish, and Finnish. I couldn't take that deception. So I left. Applied for a job online as an English teacher here, got my work visa, and flew all the way across the world to Bangkok. I wanted to be my own man here, build my own life, and not be the fake kid I had known over there. I met Mr. Hong in a random bar, and we hit it off, and that started everything. That's how I started building my own life, all by myself, see?"

"We don't adopt in our culture, so I don't know how that would feel," Thon said as she rubbed his hands. "But how was this such a bad lie? Your parents did not tell you that you were adopted so you would not feel out of place, so you would not feel like you were outside of your family and your culture."

"Yes, but I would rather have known the truth."

"If I was you, I would have gone to Germany to find your real mother and father, rather than to Thailand. That would have been more logical, given the circumstance."

"I was really broken up over my dad's suicide. And when I learned that he wasn't my dad, I wasn't sure how to feel anymore. My real mother had given me up; my real father had knocked up a hooker. Why would I want to find either of them? Sometimes I wonder if genetics are stronger than nurture. I've gone into a high-risk business like my fake dad, and I've gone my real father's way too with all the giks I've had. But now, I love Lamai, and I want the best for my family, so that doesn't matter. I'm looking towards the future. I'm raising an honest family of my own now. See?"

"I suppose. But you are on the run."

"She's still mine. My daughter will be mine. And she's not adopted; she's real."

Thon looked at Bway Paw, who seemed to guard the tent where Lamai and the women resided. Inside, Paw Htoo and Naw Baw washed Lamai's feet as she slept.

"The bitch is work," Paw Htoo hissed in S'gaw Karen. "We've never treated anyone this good."

"Because of the white man," Naw Baw said. "That's why Bway Paw will kiss her ass. If she was just Thai, they would put a bullet in her."

"Let's do one better. Let's drop her from the stretcher."

Naw Baw laughed. "We can't. We will be in trouble. I have a better plan. I talked to Thon."

"Yes? He wants to do her?" she asked, thrusting her hips back and forth.

"He thinks it will be fun. She will be too ashamed to tell the white man or Bway Paw."

"But it is riskier than dropping her."

"Why do you keep talking about dropping her? This is not as risky. She is already pregnant."

93

Rob slept in the smaller room with Boonsri, while Apsara, her mother, Hathai, and her doll slept in the lounge room. Lying beside him, Boonsri cuddled up to Rob and put his hand between her legs.

"Stop it, Boonsri," Rob said, whipping it away. Boonsri crawled onto his shoulder.

"Bloody hell, do I need to send you to the other room?" Rob asked.

Boonsri moved away and began to whine. "You said if I got you the phone and the clothes..."

"I didn't say nothing. You've got a screw loose, you know that? I should have chopped Wat into five hundred pieces and fed 'em to a croc for how he fucked you up."

Boonsri lay quiet, but Rob didn't trust her anymore. So he picked her up and took her to the lounge room, knocking on the door and waiting outside while he listened to the crickets chirp.

A groggy Apsara answered. "What is it?"

"Boonsri's sleeping in here with you blokes tonight. That alright?"

"Okay, bring her in. But I'm sleeping with you then."

Rob took her inside. Boonsri frowned at Apsara. She winked at Boonsri.

"Stay here, sister," Rob told Boonsri. Apsara followed him outside and closed the door.

"Come on," she said, taking Rob by the hand. She took him inside the smaller room. She shut the door and pushed Rob against it. She flipped off her robe. She put her hand down Rob's boxers and grabbed his cock.

"Remember this, baby?" Apsara asked.

"Yeah. Long time, sweetie," Rob said, pinching her nipples.

"I am free now, Rob," she said. "Because of you. I don't have to do it for money."

He licked her cheek and examined it like he had months before.

"No bruises," he said.

"I told you to visit my family in Isan one day. Now that day is here. And we can be together."

"To visit your sick mother. Except she doesn't seem too sick."

"A white lie."

"Is that the only one?"

"Are you interrogating me?"

"If you really wanted me, how come you never called?"

"What if it was tracked? Sumantapat or Hong would kill me. I knew you would find me soon."

"Well, I did. Sure you're not keeping something from me? About Thanat?"

"If you want to talk about Thanat," she said, pulling down his boxers and falling to her knees. "We can talk all you want. But first, let us celebrate our reunion, baby..."

94

Detectives Sanchez and Lawrence parked across the street from Niral's house in Fresh Meadows. They rang the bell. Niral's mother, Heenabhen, answered.

The detectives showed their badges.

"Is Prak Solanke here?" Sanchez asked.

"No, he went to India," she replied. "For the Diwali festival."

Sanchez glanced at Lawrence.

"We actually came to ask about your son Niral," Lawrence said. "Have you heard from him?"

"My husband has talked to him a few times. I have not."

"Why not?" Lawrence asked her. "He's your son, isn't he?"

"If his father speaks to him, I know he is okay. I don't need to speak to him."

"Do you know what your son has been doing in Thailand?" Sanchez asked.

"First, he said teaching English to children. Then he started selling diamonds."

"Diamonds?" Sanchez asked, turning to Lawrence.

"I just find it strange, ma'am," Lawrence said, "that you haven't talked to your son since he left. Which was years ago, right?"

"He wrote us emails in the beginning, but then he stopped. We wanted to report him missing, but Detective Savard told us to give it time. Then people we knew told us he was alive. That's all I wanted to know. When he called my husband a few months ago, I couldn't bear to speak to him."

"Because he had done something wrong?"

"Because he had disrespected us by leaving. Of course I want to speak to him. More than anything I want him home, but I am also angry at him."

"Do you know exactly where your son is now, Mrs. Solanke?" Sanchez asked.

She shook her head. Sanchez thought she was lying.

"Can we can get a number to reach Prak Solanke if we need him?" he asked.

After Niral's mother gave them a number, Sanchez and Lawrence handed her their cards in case she was contacted by her husband or son.

As they walked back to the car, Lawrence said, "Notice she didn't ask why we were asking? And why's her ass not in India too?"

"She knows something."

"English to diamonds, brother. Let's call Bangkok and see if we can get his immigration info, see who sponsored him. Maybe that's what we need to start unraveling this weird web."

"Or it could be another superfluous thread."

"Gotta start somewhere. We don't got enough yet to get her phone wired."

"Let's see what Thailand says. How many hours we have to wait?"

"It's late night, brother. That's early morning there. I can call soon after I get back to the station."

95

After his meeting with Talim in Rander, Niral and Manu stopped off at Kamalbhai's diamond polishing factory in the heart of Surat. Manu had called Kamalbhai from Rander to let him know they were coming.

"Good to finally meet you in person, Niral," Kamalbhai said as he performed namaste. "Manu and your uncle Vikasbhai have created a great portrait of you."

"You're probably disappointed by this scarred face, then," Niral joked.

"Nothing makeup cannot solve," Kamalbhai responded with a smile. "We are very advanced and sophisticated today in India."

They sat and discussed plans for the jewelry factory that Shekhat's brothers' cousins' were building. On Niral's behalf, Manu had asked Kamalbhai to help finance the factory since the Shekhat's funds were limited, and they would pay him back once the money began coming in from the jewelry sales. Kamalbhai had agreed as he wanted to sell his product to a more efficient and reliable partner, and a consignment deal was also a possibility. While it had been Kamalbhai's family's business for centuries to sell to middlemen after acquiring the stones from Belgium, he knew diamonds would only be profitable in the future if the process was made more efficient and reliable, and a jewelry factory with a reliable sales partner in the US was key to lessening his headache.

"Are the Shekhats are easy to work with?" Niral asked him.

"Yes, but honestly, based on what Manu explained to me, I don't understand why we need them. I could have borrowed money from the bank and created the factory myself, and you could have paid me back when you get the money they owe you. Then we could be in business directly without them."

"It's better to have them involved right now. I have other business interests, and I would prefer they do the work for me. That could change later. I'll keep you informed."

They finished discussing business and left the factory. Manu thought they would head to Yam Gam, but Niral asked to stop at Niral's cousin Val's house. He wanted to say hello and also to tell Vikasmama, Val's father, that he had gone into business with Kamalbhai on his recommendation after all. On the way, he bought Val's daughter Amrita a present: a figure of Ambamata on a tiger.

As Manu pulled up to the house, Niral saw Amrita on the swing with her mother Sobha. He waved and got out of the car. He began to walk up to her, holding her present, when he saw a man emerge from the door. He did a double take. He had completely forgotten about his father's plans to come to the Diwali celebration, and now he was confronted by him at Val's house.

"Deddy," Niral muttered, stopping in his tracks and dropping the Ambamata figure. His father stood still. Niral knew his father never cried, and he didn't this time either, but his eyes appeared more moist than usual.

"My son," he said, opening his arms. Niral did not move at first. He felt a surge of emotion he had not felt in some time. And then he found himself, almost helplessly, in his father's arms.

96

A few minutes before going to sleep, Paw Htoo and Naw Baw left the tent to allow Duncan and Lamai some brief time alone. The two held each other in a crescent shape. Duncan rubbed her belly. He suggested making love, but Lamai just wanted him to hold her.

"I'm sorry for putting you through this, honey," he said.

"What went through your mind, Duncan, when you decided to sell drugs here? Did Mr. Hong talk you into it?"

"Don't blame him, Lamai. He didn't know about the drugs."

"Then why? And don't tell me you wanted to provide for this family because you could have done that without breaking the law or ruining people's lives."

Duncan didn't respond.

Lamai asked again, "So?"

"I guess I had a hole in my heart," Duncan said immediately. "I wanted to fill it. I thought you would fill it. But it wasn't enough. I needed more. I needed to provide more than my body. Because I did that for the giks too."

"So you're saying the giks made you do it. That sleeping with other women, cheating on your wife, made you want to sell drugs, to provide for me?"

"Yes, Lamai. I know it sounds stupid, but that's what I'm saying. I'm being honest now."

"That's ridiculous."

"You know my parents are dead."

"Yes. So you told me. Is it true?"

"My father is dead. My mother is alive, but she is dead to me. But neither were my real parents."

Lamai turned towards him and put her hands on his face.

"What do you mean?"

Duncan told her what he had told Thon shortly before.

"So you ran away to start a new life," she said. "And you just happened to find me. A nice girl."

"I wanted to be a husband and a father."

"But you ruined the situation, like both your fathers did. Maybe we can live in Burma, but what will our life be like? Duncan, you know the Burmese try to come to Thailand."

"We'll go somewhere else. I'm expecting a new shipment once Niral does his job in India. Then we'll be on easy street."

"More drugs? Duncan..."

"We have no choice. That's all we have now. But you can leave at any time if you want to, I don't want to hold you down. I don't want to abandon our child either, but I'm not telling you what to do in this situation. I know it's tough."

Lamai shook her head. "You give me no choice, Duncan Smith. I love you." She kissed him for a long minute. Then she pulled away. "I will stay with you and our baby to the end. But promise me that once we have the money, you will try to make a living a different way."

"If it's possible, I will, Lamai," he said as Paw Htoo peeked inside. "I promise."

97

Colonel Nopasit Limwat sat in a tent beside another village they had raided after receiving a lead the delivery man had fled there. They had not found him, but had impounded some ya ba from the homes before burning the village to the ground.

Nopasit ate a simple dish of flat noodles, eggs, and lentils, drinking a Chang beer with it. Colonel Arthit entered and greeted him with a wai.

"Any news?" Nopasit asked, continuing to eat.

"The helicopters have not spotted anyone, but I suspect the Karen are hiding under the heavy foliage blocking the thermal heat sensors."

"Or they are in Burma already."

"I doubt that," Colonel Arthit said.

"But it is possible. Has that one villager mapped out a route for us?"

"It's a strange route he has drawn. I don't know how reliable it is, but we can try to trace it tomorrow. More importantly, we now know their drug route within Thailand. It runs all the way down the border with Burma to Kanchanaburi. Apparently, the Karen leader is a woman named Bway Paw. Her husband Thon runs the day to day operations."

"Good, that's important. I will give the drug route information to my people at the Bureau, and they will stamp out this scourge within Thailand."

"Will you tell Khun Commissioner about my good work?"

"Of course, Colonel Arthit. But I don't plan to speak to him until I can report total victory against this cancer."

"We should keep him abreast of developments, Colonel."

"I thank you for helping us in Chiang Mai, Colonel Arthit, and I know you have come here and been very helpful in our assault against the Karen drug dealers. I understand you want to inform Khun Commissioner about the status of the operation and your extra role in it, but as a member of the Narcotics Suppression Bureau, I have a greater responsibility to Thailand: to stop the flow of poison into our entire nation. You benefited at the first village — I made sure of that — and you will benefit again during later searches. So I would appreciate it if you defer to me on this matter, considering the important subject at hand."

Colonel Arthit felt anger at this request, but he showed cool heart and diffused the conflict with a smile and wai. Colonel Nopasit offered him some noodles and beer. Colonel Arthit accepted and was going to sit when Colonel Dusit marched inside. He was sweaty.

"I am sorry for interrupting," Colonel Dusit stated, greeting them both with a wai. "But Lamai's parents have been murdered in their home."

Nopasit looked at Arthit.

"How?" Nopasit asked Dusit.

"A man in a Hanuman mask broke into their house early this morning. He was looking for something in the drawer of the guest room, but we don't know what. The parents were sleeping inside. They thought if their daughter returned, it was the first place she would go."

Nopasit thought. "We can use this to our advantage," he said. "If we

194

convince Lamai that her husband ordered their murder, she may leave him and make it easier to capture or kill the dealers."

Dusit seemed shocked by Nopasit's cold calculation.

"But how do we tell her?" Arthit asked. "By yelling it from the helicopters?"

"No," Nopasit said. "Is the sister still alive?"

Dusit nodded.

"Wonderful. Bring her to the camp tomorrow morning," Nopasit said. "We will bring her with us."

PART VIII

†

Outside Udon Thani, Thailand; Surat, India; Long Island City, St. Albans, Flushing, Sunnyside, Forest Hills (Queens), New York; Mae Hong Son Province, Thailand; Yam Gam, India; Bushwick (Brooklyn), New York; Near Nong Khai, Thailand; Near Chiang Mai, Thailand

98

Rob woke up early the next morning in the small room and found his hands bound together and tied to the bedpost. His legs were also bound and tied the same way. He spit out some water. His face was wet. Apsara stood over him, holding a gun and an urn. She poured water on his face again.

Rob spit it out again. "What the fuck, ya cunt?"

"Why do you keep on asking me about Thanat?"

"What, you fucking—"

She poured more water. He shook his head furiously.

"Okay, you fucking..." he yelled, coughing. "I heard Thanat was your lover, and maybe you still had the dosh he stole from Duncan."

"Who told you that?"

"This man I've been working for."

"So Duncan was right," Apsara said. "You did have some other agenda."

"He said that to you?"

"I was reporting on you. That's how I first started with you. But I actually did fall in love with you, Rob. I did not lie."

"So you were spying on me?"

"Duncan thought you would steal the drugs and drive to Malaysia. But you didn't."

"My boss isn't in Malaysia, ya bogan cunt."

"Where is he?"

"Goes all over."

"And how does he know about Thanat?"

"He has ways of finding out, I reckon."

"And he told you when?"

"I called him yesterday. Boonsri stole a phone for me."

"What Boonsri will do for her Paw."

"So it's true about Thanat?"

"Thanat was named Prem when he gave me Hathai and left for Chiang Mai. When I found him in Bangkok, I got my revenge and the money he owed me as an absent father."

"And the money is buried under the house?"

"No. It was in Prem's bank account. Mae took it out and put it in our account. Then I withdrew it from a Nong Khai branch and hid most of it near the Laos border. So when we escape there, we will have it."

"And the money I gave you? Both times?"

"It's there in two other briefcases, all US dollars like you gave me. Some of Thanat's money is here in Thai baht, but it is just enough to live on."

"So you were planning to go to Laos anyway?"

"Yes, Rob. But first I was waiting for you to find me. Like a true Romeo. Like Odysseus."

"You expect me to believe that, you backstabbing cum dumpster?"

"If you don't believe it, you don't love me. And we can't be a family, can we?"

Rob struggled. He closed his eyes. "It's just like when that Muslim tortured me. I won't break. Not after what I've been through."

"I don't want to torture you, Rob. I just want you to trust me."

"You know why I loved Som? Why I wanted to save Boonsri and Sveta and you?"

"Why, Rob? Tell me."

"Nat!" they heard someone call outside.

Apsara moved to the window and, opening the cloth shade slightly, she saw Piti and Ska near the spirit house, calling up.

"The girls are back," Apsara said, her eyes moving back and forth from Rob to the window.

"Untie me!" Rob commanded.

Moving the shade again, Apsara pointed the gun at the two girls. "I could hit them from here."

"Ya can't hit nothing if you've never handled a weapon," Rob said.

"Your son did. Little Som."

"You fucking cunt. I'll kill ya."

"Oh, I will really untie you now, Rob."

She heard the girls call again. They were still near the spirit house.

"Why don't they come to the door?" she asked. She lifted the other side of the window shade and peered at the edge of the sugarcane field. She saw another body, dressed in brown, hiding inside.

"It is a trap," she whispered. "The police."

Then she heard another voice. Her mother was out on the terrace talking to the girls.

Apsara rushed to release Rob, using his machete that lay on the floor nearby to slice at the rope, leaving the gun next to him on the bed. She heard the girls asking her mother for Nat and Apsara.

Her mother opened the door as Apsara cut the rope to the bedpost.

"Mae!" Apsara yelled. "Come in and close the door."

Her mother stood there, uncomprehending, as she watched Apsara cutting the rope that held Rob to the bed.

Then Rob heard Boonsri outside, asking for him.

"God, come on, ya cunt!" he yelled as he saw Boonsri come next to Mae. She was holding Hathai's doll. Then they heard a loudspeaker.

"Come out with your hands up," the voice said in imperfect English. "We will not hurt you if you come out without weapons. We mean you, Maric, and anyone else you have inside."

"Boonsri, come in," Rob commanded, but Boonsri froze and dropped Hathai's doll. She thought she saw Apsara cutting Rob's hands with a machete.

"Close the door," Apsara shouted at her.

Boonsri rushed and tackled Apsara. Rob shouted for her to stop, but the two began pulling each other's hair and screaming as Apsara dropped the machete. Rob ripped the rope tying his hands apart as a police officer entered the door armed with a shotgun. Rob quickly grabbed the gun on the bed and fired, hitting the officer in the chest. The officer lost his balance and fired straight into Mae's chest, spraying blood and guts on all of them.

Rob heard Apsara scream loudly. He grabbed the machete and sliced his leg ropes with three forceful thrusts. Then, holding the gun too, he jumped up and rushed to the door. He saw a few officers climbing up the stairs and shot them down with three blasts. Then he ducked inside before a hail of gunfire hit the doorway from afar. He picked up Hathai's doll and threw it over the terrace in an effort to create confusion. Seeing his duffel bag, he emptied it quickly and hung it around his neck. Then, running towards Apsara and Boonsri, holding the gun and machete, one in each hand, he grabbed each by their hair using his free fingers and dragged them to the back of the room, Apsara continuing to scream loudly.

Rob let go of Boonsri, then smacked Apsara hard across the face with the gun. Then he grabbed her by the collar.

"Is there another way out of here?" he asked her. "A back exit?"

"Mae," she responded weakly. "Hathai."

"Fuck, you wanna live, ya cunt?"

He looked out the back window. A tree was close by the ledge of the terrace.

"Boonsri, get on my back," Rob commanded. She jumped onto him, her arms around his neck, her legs clasping his chest.

"It's up to you, Apsara. You wanna live or die? Now's the time to decide," he said, climbing out the window and onto the terrace.

"Hathai!" Apsara yelled, climbing out too.

"No time. Live or die?" he asked, climbing onto the railing, putting the machete in his mouth and the gun in his waistband.

Apsara heard Hathai crying from the lounge room window, but she didn't see her. She glanced back and saw the shadow of an officer in the doorway. She climbed onto the railing and held onto Rob as he jumped onto the tree.

99

Lying between his father and Manu, in his cousin Val's guest room, on the same bed he had slept on when he had visited Surat last year, Niral woke up with a start. He recalled a strange dream where he was confronted by an oddly friendly Amrat, who told him he was wrong in predicting, as he had before his self-immolation, that Niral was not equipped to be an avatar. In fact, Niral's devious and murderous streak had proved he was one. Amrat mentioned Rama, Parashurama, Narasimha, and Krishna. All murderers who had killed for righteous causes. But Niral had countered, 'What was my righteous cause? I've killed for no reason and benefited each time.'

Amrat had laughed. 'You have transformed from a human being to an unfeeling, detached individual,' he said. 'That is progress in our time. Did you benefit from the village's restructuring or Thanat's death or the murder of two random people in Lamai's house? Even after Shekhat's murder, will you become such a great businessman by making diamond selling more efficient?' 'Bhai,' Niral had muttered. 'Bhai!' Amrat had howled back. 'That is the funniest remark of all. Come, I have misjudged you,' he said. 'You have followed the righteous path of dharma, not adharma.'

Niral wanted to adamantly disagree, but he had woken up instead. Now he shuddered at the dream. Then, he saw his father sleeping next to him and remembered crying in his father's lap the night before. His father had been sitting on this very bed and Niral, positioned with his knees on the floor, his hands together and face down, had let out all the anxiety, frustration, anger, and pain, which he had never released before.

Now as he watched his father sleep, he wanted to unburden his conscience completely, not only by revealing his evil deeds and associations, but also the plot. Yet he could not. Despite his release of human emotion the night before, it seemed Amrat was right: he was still detached and dead inside, and no degree of crying could alter the changes inside him that had occurred.

He rose, took fresh underwear from Manu's bag, left the room, and locked himself in the bathroom. He took out the balled janoi, which he had kept in his pocket since leaving India the last time. He stared at it for a while. Then he removed his clothes, put on the janoi, turned on the heater, and bathed, using the bucket and glass. When he dressed and emerged, the others had woken too. They took turns bathing, then ate the nasta Sobha had prepared. Outside, Amrita, surprisingly subdued, played with her broken Ambamata figure. Three of the figure's arms had broken off when Niral had dropped her upon seeing his father. Amrita tapped the areas where the arms had broken, until she cried out in pain; a sharp section had pierced her finger. Sobha brought her a bandage. Niral entered the living room where Val and Vikasmama sat.

"Still buying and selling diamonds?" Vikasmama asked him.

"Yes," Niral said. "But I took your advice. I'm working with Kamalbhai now."

Vikasmama was shocked. "Really, you know him now. How?"

"Don't worry, Vikasmama," Niral said, touching his shoulder. "I have my ways."

Vikasmama smiled. The phone rang. Sobha picked up. She called Niral's father to it.

"No more trips to Rander for you?" Val asked Niral.

"Not in the near future," Niral answered.

"So now you will go to Dwarka to protect Bhai," Vikasmama said. "May God protect you all. I hope you enjoy the festival. We were considering coming, too."

Niral looked uncomfortable. "You would be near the back of the procession if you did," he said, "and the wait is long. The order to get into the last temple is already set—"

"Don't worry," Vikasmama responded, waving his hand. "We already decided not to come. Only the true devotees should attend. Like you and your father."

Niral looked uncomfortable again. Then Niral's father called to him. Niral entered the kitchen, where his father gave him the phone.

"Do you know me, Niral?" the voice asked.

"It's been years," Niral replied nervously.

"Why have you never spoken to me all these years?" she asked. "Remember how I cried and stayed with you when you were hurt?"

"There's no reason for words," Niral said. "I know you love me. That's never been in dispute. What else is there to say? You don't want or need to know anything else. That's why I never called."

He heard his mother crying on the other side. He handed the phone back to his father.

"Niral loves you in his own way," his father said, then went into the bathroom with the phone.

100

"I think we hit pay dirt," Lawrence said to Sanchez on the phone. He was sitting in the St. Albans precinct, while Sanchez was at his own precinct in Long Island City. "At least we've got pieces of the puzzle now."

"Hit me," Sanchez said, marker in hand, ready to write on a large piece of oak tag paper.

"All right. Niral was sponsored by Fan Hong, head of the Dragons in Bangkok. The first time Hong wrote that Niral would teach English at an English language school he owned. But when he renewed the work permit, he wrote Niral was working in Hong's jewelry factory."

"How'd the Thais not spot that?"

"Not sure. Maybe the English school made them less suspicious since it's a pretty typical occupation for a young American there. Hong does own a jewelry factory, and he sponsored plenty of other workers too. But the Thai authorities looked at his work permits again when an Indian guy with scars on his face was spotted with a missing Thai girl in northern Thailand who is connected with the Dragons."

"Niral works for a jewelry factory in Bangkok, right? Which is not in northern Thailand?"

"Right. But while on paper Niral worked for Fan Hong, the Thais believed he worked for another American named Duncan Smith, who was also sponsored by Hong many years ago after arriving in Thailand on a tourist visa. Duncan is now a Thai permanent resident and is married to a Thai woman. On paper, Duncan buys gems from a middleman, Hong makes them into jewelry, then Duncan sells the jewelry to an American seller and pays Hong for the assistance. Now here's the kicker: Duncan sponsored Borisslava Maric, a.k.a. Rob Johnson, our resident murderer of Linda Macaday et al. to help him with his jewelry business. Both Smith and Johnson are on the run now, suspected of drug dealing and, in Johnson's case, murder. And the Indian guy was spotted with Duncan's wife, who is missing too. That was the missing girl in northern Thailand."

"So Niral's in northern Thailand?"

"Not sure. They're checking if his passport was used recently and other public transportation travel logs. If he hasn't left the country, it's a fair bet he's in northern Thailand, where the Thais suspect Smith and his wife are probably hiding out."

"Hmm...okay. Let's assume they're all Dragons, right? They kill Linda Macaday, a pay hit for the Traglianis. But Bob escapes to New York and they finish the job here?"

"Well, the Thais are saying Macaday was a witness to a triple murder in a gem store there, part of some gang war between the Dragons and some Thai gang, and that's why Bob and his wife were murdered, but I'm thinking that's cover for the real purpose. Either way, since the Dragons are well-represented here too, it's a strong possibility the Dragons are working with the Traglianis, unless Alicia put the hit out to Johnson independently, which seems unlikely."

"And the Dragons sent Niral from here to Thailand, why? Because they've got something on him? Or because he was a Dragon before we met him?"

"You believe that?"

"No. But now Lance is making hits, too. Maybe on Niral's orders?"

"Is the hero of the Long Island fire now a mafioso, too?"

"We've gotta investigate the Dragons here first and the Traglianis second. Figure out their intentions and their connections, if any, to the Long Island City Project."

"Seems like a promising avenue to tie things up, brother."

"Let's meet up tomorrow morning and hit the pavement, man."

101

After Duncan left, Lamai was under heavy blankets, sandwiched between Paw Htoo and Naw Baw all night. But when she awoke, she noticed Paw Htoo and Naw Baw were near the tent entrance. They were opening the flap, and through the slight opening, she could see the sun had just come up. She heard soft rummaging outside. She took her eye off the opening and peered around the space. Bway Paw wasn't sleeping in her bed.

Lamai was about to sit up on her elbow and ask her attendants what was happening when she noticed Thon enter the tent through the open flap holding a knife. He was sweating too, his knees were bent, and his eyes were wide and intent.

Shocked, she remained speechless as he rushed at her. He fixed her hand over her mouth before she could scream, then thrust away the blanket. He placed the knife near her neck, his hand shaking violently.

"I've always wanted a Lanna girl," he said in Thai. "Now you're going to give it to me, or else."

Her eyes were wide. She felt a chill shoot up her torso. She tried to say, "Please, don't make me," but through his hand, she only mumbled.

He licked his lips. "Turn around. That's the easiest and fastest way."

Lamai wouldn't move.

"What do you care?" he said. "You're pregnant anyway. The farang won't know."

She glanced at Paw Htoo and Naw Baw. They were chuckling.

He pushed the knife against her neck. "Do you think I am joking?" he said. "Hurry up."

Lamai realized there was no other option, so she complied, turning onto her hands and knees. She felt him flip up her nightgown and lower her underwear. Then the sharp entrance and the quick painful thrusts.

She put her hand over her mouth to avoid screaming as he slapped her butt cheeks. She felt tears hit her hand. He was done in only a minute, but it felt like hours.

When he had finished, he callously pushed her dress back down, and she could hear him zip his pants. She stayed in the same position while slowly lifting her underwear. She closed her eyes and prayed to Buddha.

Suddenly, she felt her hair being violently pulled. She turned her head towards him.

"No one will know," he commanded. "Not the farang or Bway Paw. Understand?"

He let go of her head and stood up. He walked to the tent entrance and spoke to the two Karen women briefly. Lamai was crying, still in the same position, when they approached her.

"Remember what Thon said," Paw Htoo reiterated in imperfect Thai. "No one. Okay?"

Lamai turned her head angrily. "Why?" she asked.

Paw Htoo slapped her butt from behind. "Look what you Lanna do to our people," she said. "This is like nothing compared to how we suffer. You will still have your baby; you will still live with the farang. What will we have? This rural life and nothing else. Don't feel sorry for yourself. Feel sorry for us. Now stop crying. We will make and give you your breakfast."

102

As their men cleared out another village, Colonel Nopasit and Colonel Arthit discussed their upcoming route. Then Colonel Dusit arrived in a Jeep with Lamai's sister Malai. She appeared upset.

Nopasit lent his hand to help her out.

"Khun Malai," he said, "I am sorry to hear about your sister's—"

"I don't want to hear your fake words, officer," she said, catching her tongue just as fast. She forced a smile and performed a wai as she stepped out of the Jeep without his assistance. "I am sorry to be disrespectful. I want justice for my parents. And I want my sister safe."

Nopasit and Arthit regarded each other with curiosity. Dusit smiled.

"Of course," Nopasit said, forcing a smile too. "I did not mean to be condescending. If we find the entourage, we will need your help to save your sister. Trust me, we will not forgive these drug dealers for their affronts against the Thai people."

"I will not forgive them either," Malai responded. "Don't worry, I will help. But please, find her. And make sure you get that Indian man. I believe he killed my parents."

"How do you know he killed your parents?" Nopasit asked.

"He kidnapped my sister, didn't he? And Duncan did not like my parents. He was nice to them because he knew my father had been in the military, but he didn't like how Lamai was close to them."

"So you think the farang ordered the Indian man to assassinate your parents?"

"Yes, I do," she said.

Dusit, still sitting in the Jeep, showed respect to Nopasit with a wai. "Colonel, General Toon has discovered the identity of the Indian Niral Solanke," he said. "Apparently, he is from New York, where that old man was murdered, the husband of the woman murdered by the farang Duncan Smith's associate in Phuket. We believe he was a witness in the gem scam murders here and a witness in a mob case in New York earlier."

Nopasit smiled. "I knew this was part of a wider web. We are important even beyond Thailand. This makes our work here that much more crucial. Colonel Arthit, make sure these villagers are thoroughly questioned. We will find this scum no matter what strategy we need to take."

103

Rob carried Boonsri in his arms as he and Apsara trekked through the forest, the duffel bag on his back, the gun and machete inside it. Apsara was sullen. She hadn't spoken since Rob had skidded them down the tree. The police had shot at them as they ran into the forest, but they had escaped.

Rob's arms were bleeding, and his blood was on Boonsri's dress. She was sleeping.

"You gonna say anything, sweetie?" he asked Apsara. "You gonna be mute for the rest of eternity?"

"My mother is dead, Rob," she said quietly. "My daughter may be dead too. I should be dead."

"That's no way to squiz it, sweetie. Hathai's just with the coppers. Som's there too. Reckon I know the feeling, but still, could we have raised all those kids right?"

"We will have the money to do so when we get to the border. In Laos, it is a lot."

"Yeah, well, we still got one..."

"Who hates me..." Apsara muttered.

"...and even though you ditched me and tied me up, we still got each other," Rob continued.

Apsara stopped and turned to him. "If you want to kill me, go ahead. I deserve it."

"I wouldn't do that, sweetie."

"Everything I did, I did for my mother and my daughter. And now they are gone."

"Sorry to burst your bubble, but it's always you first. That's the number one interest."

Apsara laughed bitterly. "You are saying this, of all people?"

"Look, you made your decision when you jumped on me. The right one. Coppers would've mowed you down if ya hadn't."

"I didn't do anything wrong. They would've let me go."

"Deadset they would've shot you, but if not, they'd have pinned Thanat or someone else on you. Or later, Sumantapat or some Dragon would have got revenge on you. Don't think they wouldn't have, that's the way these wankers are. But you're safe now, and don't worry about nothing. Hathai's in..."

Rob stopped. He swallowed and looked down at Boonsri.

"What?" Apsara asked. "Why do you look like that?"

He sat on the ground, putting Boonsri on his lap. She continued to sleep as he rubbed her head.

"Just realized what I said's a bunch of bollocks. They gonna put

Hathai in some kinda foster care. That's what happened to me after my grandma died. Never knew my oldies at all."

Apsara sat down too. "So now you know how I feel."

"I always felt this way, sweetie. Just rationalizing, I reckon. And Som's gonna go through the same shit."

"So we are both failures."

"No sweetie," Rob said. "We'll go back and get 'em. We'll chop up all those coppers and Sumantapat too. We'll get 'em all. I've gotten 'em all since that day in Noosa."

"What day in Noosa?"

"Don't matter. We'll get 'em all right, but after we get the money and settle down in Laos. We gotta make sure Boonsri's safe and fed. We'll have a good life in Laos, you'll see. You'll treat Boonsri like your own and she'll love you for it. Then I'll come back like the avenger. And I'll get Som and Hathai back for us."

Apsara looked back.

"We better keep moving, Rob," she said, getting up. "They are probably still after us."

"Good thinking, sweetie," he replied. He tried to rise while holding Boonsri, but he couldn't.

"Too heavy," he said, laughing. "Getting old."

104

"Niral," his father said to him as Manu drove them to Yam Gam, "your mother told me that detectives came to the house asking about you. They were the two detectives from the Long Island City fire case: Sanchez and Lawrence."

"Yeah, what'd they say?" Niral asked nonchalantly.

"They wanted to know where you were. Why would they ask about you?"

"Maybe something new came up in the case. I don't know."

"Something new did come up. You do not know about it?"

"What came up, Deddy?" he asked.

His father's face suddenly became stern.

"That witness in the trial of the mobsters. The adulterer that Stan was tracing. I think his name was Bob? He was murdered, Niral."

"They found his body?" Niral asked.

He immediately realized his mistake. His father didn't seem to realize the full implication of his words.

"How could they not find the body? He was murdered in the street. In St. Albans. In Queens."

"In St. Albans? That's impossible."

"Why?" his father asked. "Why is it impossible? Do you know something about it?"

"No," Niral said, backtracking.

"He was murdered in front of Lance Portman's house. They say Lance Portman did it with an accomplice. This Lance Portman was a friend of yours, right?"

Niral swallowed. "Lance?"

"Yes, Lance. Do you know him?"

"Yeah, but I haven't spoken to him in years."

"It has been in the news. And I have other sources, Niral. This Bob Macaday was using a fake name. He had returned to New York. They say he was in witness protection in Texas. And his wife Linda was murdered in Thailand. Do you know about that too?"

Niral didn't answer. He tried to think fast. "No. That's insane."

"Is it, Niral? Is that why you were crying in my lap? What have you gotten yourself into?"

Niral looked at Manu, who glanced back at him, then peered forward again quickly. "Deddy, I—"

"You are not going back to Thailand or America, do you understand?" his father commanded. "You will stay in the wadi if you have to. Even the Diwali—"

"I promised Bhai I would help at Shri Diwali, Deddy," Niral insisted.

"Your safety is more important than that. The NYPD or FBI can come arrest you here. India has an extradition treaty with America."

"I didn't do anything wrong, Deddy. I've been buying and selling diamonds. That's all."

"Yes, you have just been buying and selling diamonds," his father said, shaking his head. "Do you think I am that stupid?"

Niral didn't respond. He glanced at Manu again, who continued to drive stoically.

"Your mother does not know, thankfully, and I don't think the police do yet either," his father continued. "But Bhai knows, and I know what you are, Niral. You can still save yourself, but it can only be in India. It can only be with The Brotherhood. Do you understand?"

"Yes, Deddy," Niral said.

"Look, we will discuss this more in Yam Gam," he said, turning to Manu. "I believe we are almost there, right?"

Manu didn't say a word.

105

Sanchez and Lawrence met with Sergeant Barry Chen of the Asian Crime Investigation Unit at the 109th Precinct in Flushing, Queens. He specialized in gang activity in the area.

"This unit was created in the early '90s when gang problems were out in the open and particularly bad," he explained. "As the city became safer, funding decreased, and then September 11th put the Muslim watchdogs on the top of the funding priority list among the NYPD's Intelligence Divisions. So we got shafted twice, even as the Asian population in Flushing grew and grew. Now it's spilled over into all of northeast Queens and out west through Elmhurst and Jackson Heights too. So we're talking about a huge population and not much manpower on it. I've got two Chinese detectives and two Korean ones. No Indians, no Bangladeshis or anyone else. Thankfully those groups haven't been a significant problem in these parts yet."

"Does that mean you don't know much about the Dragons' operations?" Lawrence asked.

"You have to understand that there are tons of small, extremely local gangs here, mainly Chinese and some Korean. They run the spas that double as prostitution parlors, human trafficking, and small gambling dens, along with some extortion and business fronts for money laundering. Most of the activity is unseen. You no longer see them beating people in the streets or sticking up women like in old days, not as much drug activity with these people either, so far. But the Dragons are a much bigger and more complex operation, so yes, to answer your question, we do know more about them.

"First of all, they are international in scope and they have many different divisions. While we don't have a firm sense of the organization's structure, we believe most of their top leadership is from mainland China, primarily based in Shanghai and Hong Kong, but here, many of the foot soldiers are Korean. They don't care much about ethnic tensions or loyalties, they'll do anything to make money. When they can get along with people to further their goals, they will. They don't create friction for no reason. Usually it's just the young undisciplined types who get into trouble. They don't have a huge network in prison because most don't get caught, so there, they'll often work with black, Hispanic, and other ethnic gangs in the hole. And that means those networks can be utilized for broader purposes on the outside."

"Is it possible they are working with the Italian mob?" Sanchez asked.

"These days, yes, it's certainly possible," Sergeant Chen said, shrugging. "I assume you mean the Lucchese crime family, specifically the Tragliani faction, since that's the file you sent over?"

"Yeah, did you look it over?" Lawrence asked. "Do you think there's a connection?"

"Well, the Dragons and Lucchese have no history of tension. We heard off the grapevine that before the Long Island City fire case, they used to get along, but it's just a vague rumor, and we don't know what their connections or business dealings were. When the Tragliani henchmen went on trial for land fraud, bribery, and other offenses, the Tragliani family was basically cut off from the larger Lucchese operation and forced to fend for themselves. Roberto Tragliani had been an 'under the radar' member, so with him dead and no support from the bosses, they took it particularly hard and severely downsized. I think Alicia Tragliani and her Uncle Jerry, Roberto's daughter and brother respectively, still head what's left of their operations. They still have limited interests in construction, I think."

"So it's possible they might have influence over a bidder for the Long Island City Project," Sanchez said. "And that the Dragons could be supporting them?"

"I haven't heard of Dragon interests in construction, but they've been expanding their reach and the type of businesses they've got their talons into recently. They seem to be pumped with money and ambition. So I wouldn't be surprised if the Dragons were financing all kinds of rackets we don't know about yet. The Traglianis already had the influence on construction, so that's certainly possible. Who are the construction companies?"

"Brooklyn-based operation Dekalb Construction and Queens-based Ozone Construction."

"Hmm...don't recognize them off the top of my head, but I can have one of my detectives look into it, see if he can sniff out gang influence one way or the other."

"Good," Sanchez said. "How about the Dragons' leadership in Queens? Do you know who's in charge here?"

"We suspect it's a man named Ken Wei Chang, mainland Chinese. From Shanghai originally, who manages a bank in downtown Flushing. But we don't have proof of that. Otherwise, we know of a Mr. Byung-hoon Yoon, of Korean origin, who runs some local operations for the Dragons in Flushing. If we can corner him and get him on a smaller charge, maybe he'll talk?"

"Hope so. We're also looking for a connection to an Indian guy named Niral Solanke."

"An Indian guy? That wouldn't be typical. Indians around here are usually straight-laced, even the illegals."

"He's a confirmed Dragon in Thailand. He's an American citizen, natural-born, sponsored by a Dragon boss in Bangkok. We think he made initial contact here. Used to be a good guy, but sold his soul to the devil, we assume."

"Interesting. Again, we'll look into it. As I said, I've got limited staff, so it might take a while."

212

"That's okay," Lawrence said. "This info is important, so we'll wait. And if needed, we'll help too."

106

The Karen tribe continued to move in the daylight, slowly and deliberately, on a roundabout route covered by heavy foliage.

"How long will it take to get to Burma at this point?" Duncan asked Thon.

"This is a much longer route. It will take longer."

"But you've taken it before?"

"Not many times, but we have."

Thon looked back at Lamai. She avoided his eyes as Paw Htoo and Naw Baw carried her, while Bway Paw led them.

"I hope your wife is enjoying our hospitality," Thon said.

Duncan looked back at Lamai too. He noticed she appeared uncomfortable.

"She likes doing things on her own," Duncan said. "She probably wants to walk."

"Nonsense. We can't allow a woman to miscarry. We respect women too much."

"Yes, and I'm grateful. You are so much nicer than anyone else I've ever dealt with."

"If you mean your parents, at least your mother, did not abort you. Adoption gave you a life."

"Yeah, what a life," Duncan said, trying to change the subject. "Is that a helicopter I hear?"

Thon stopped and held up his hand. The entourage ceased too.

"Yes, you are right," he said after listening a while. "They are looking for us, Mr. Duncan. We must be extra careful."

He turned and said something softly to Bway Paw in S'gaw Karen, who nodded and answered him. Then he said something to the group too.

Everyone stopped moving. Lamai was placed down.

"Our messenger who carries the money, he has not arrived yet," Thon said to Duncan. "We hope he has not been detained."

"What money?" Duncan asked.

"The money we transfer in and out of the country. Money earned from drug sales."

"And he takes the same route as this?"

"The same basic route, yes. We have veered into the complicated path, but he should know it."

"How about drugs coming in? Do they follow the same path?"

"We have alternative routes in place, but we told them to hold the merchandise for now in Burma."

"Do we stay here?" Duncan asked. "Or do we keep moving?"

"Relax, Mr. Duncan," Thon said. "We will stay still until we no longer hear the helicopters. Then we will move. Very simple, yes?"

"Except if they know we are here, they can bomb us."

Thon laughed. "Sure, if they believed we were only Karen scum, they would bomb, shoot, rape, pillage, plunder, and incinerate us. But we have a Lanna princess with us. And even a farang. They won't dare use such tactics now. Trust me, you are our greatest assets."

He held up his hand again. They listened. Duncan didn't hear the helicopter anymore.

"You see, poof! Gone like the wind. Let us go, Mr. Duncan. We have a long way ahead."

He whistled, and the others began moving again. Paw Htoo and Naw Baw picked up Lamai. She appeared sweaty and sick to Duncan.

Duncan moved towards her, but Thon stopped him with a light hand on his shoulder.

"Do not worry, Mr. Duncan, the women will look after her," he said. "Women understand the afflictions of other women better than we do. Let them tend to her. You will get a chance to comfort her tonight."

107

The sun was setting. Rob stopped near a tree and set Boonsri down. He gathered kindling to make a fire, then ran down a rabbit and killed it with his machete. He brought it back to the tree, hung it from a branch, skinned it, began a fire, then looked for a way to cook the rabbit.

"Is this how the bush was?" Apsara asked.

"You tell me. Wasn't it like this in Isan?"

Apsara shrugged. She was sitting with her calves tucked underneath her thighs, pointed away from the fire, watching Boonsri sleep. "My distant cousins had farms, but my parents had a small store. Like 7-Eleven, but not chain. They could barely make the rent."

"And your father ran away too?"

"No. He died. I remember his death. I was little."

"How'd it happen?"

"Heart attack. He wasn't old, but maybe he ate too much meat."

"Thought you blokes didn't have enough to eat? Don't even know how to cook a proper rabbit."

Apsara stretched her legs towards the fire.

"I am sorry I tied you up, Rob," Apsara said. "I needed to know what you knew about Thanat. But I meant what I said. You are not like Thanat. I knew you would come back for me."

"So Thanat got what he deserved, but I'm different?"

"Prem was his real name. It means 'content' in Thai, happy with what you have. He was happy until he could trick someone else for more. You are different, Rob. You have good side."

"That's why you didn't set me up? Or maybe you did. Maybe you're a mole."

"How can you say something like that, Rob? I would not do that."

"You didn't tell those girls where I was, who then told the coppers?"

"Som probably told them at the hospital. If he lived."

Rob had built a stand out of two pieces of wood dug into the ground, connected by a branch over the fire. On the branch, he attached the rabbit, turning it so he could cook each side.

"See, ingenuity. Of course that little wanker survived. He's a Maric man. We'll get him back. Hathai too."

"Yes," Apsara said, folding her arms, thinking. "My mother needs to be properly cremated."

"I'm sorry about that, sweetie. At least I killed that cunt copper who killed her."

"Rob, tell me, what happened to you in Noosa?"

"Why you ask, Aspara?"

"You kept trying to tell me. Like it meant so much to you. But you could not."

"Yeah, well, bygones."

"You can tell me, whatever it is."

"It's a long story, sweetie."

"You can tell me as we eat, no?"

"Might make you throw up. But sure, sweetie. I guess I can do that."

108

Manu drove up the hill to Niral's faliya. The constructions were complete: each home, including Niral's, was now three stories high. Even Prameshbhai's old house had a new paint job, bright pink.

This time, as he emerged from the car, Niral didn't see Kauntiaunti there, rolling rotli in the small kitchen. Instead, Meetal, Kauntiaunti's daughter, stood on the porch in front of two majestically large and ornate doors covered by inscriptions of Om and swastika symbols varied with short scenes from the Ramayana that were open to a vastly larger interior. It was clear that the home next door, the one on the right, had been purchased or combined and a larger home had been rebuilt as one.

Meetal was dressed in a sparkling red and gold sari, her hair cut and done up into a modest bun, her lips caked with rich lipstick, her cheeks bathed in blush, reddening her light skin. Gold bangles were around her wrists, and they descended halfway down her forearm when she waved to him as she came out of the car.

"Where is everyone?" Niral asked as she approached him. "I thought there was an election today."

"It's in the former Dubla district," she said, smiling as she touched her face. She seemed to hesitate to hug him and just stood there, unsure. "Even the Brahmins are not afraid to go there anymore. It's been quite the turnaround."

"Shouldn't you be campaigning?"

"I'm not worried. I'm the only one running."

Niral smiled. "A true politician."

As Niral's father got out of the car, Meetal saw him, immediately put her palms together, approached him and bowed. He caught her mid-stride and lifted her up, smiling, as she hugged him.

"Prakashuncle. I'm so glad to see you!"

"Dikri, please, I should say the same thing. It has been so long. How have you been? How has Yam Gam treated you?"

Meetal wiped away a tear as she released herself from the hug.

"Well, Prakashuncle...I am doing good work now."

Niral rolled his eyes and entered the home. In only two months, the old structure inside the home had been totally reconstructed. A staircase, visible as he entered the home, was now on the left side. The kitchen had been moved deeper inside. A swing and coffee table were in the living room to Niral's right.

"Nice, Manu," Niral said as he examined the walls, which were now painted with a bluish tinge. "Your pick of color?"

Manu smiled.

"How is your daughter, by the way?" Niral asked as he climbed the stairs.

"Excellent, Niralbhai. Happy, because of you."

"I didn't do anything for her."

"You clarified my vision of her. The right vision. That's all I needed, Niralbhai. A clarification."

"Is she in Mumbai or at home?"

"In Mumbai right now, but she may make it up to Dwarka for the Diwali celebration if she can. I am very happy about that."

Niral stopped halfway up the stairs.

"You sure that's a good idea? Given—"

"She will be at Lamba, Niralbhai."

"Of course," he said stoically.

"Don't worry, Niralbhai. Everything is in God's hands. You are the avatar."

Niral rolled his eyes again and continued up the stairs. On the second floor, he saw another living room and a hallway leading to what he assumed were two or three bedrooms, but he did a double take when he saw a man sitting on a swing in the living room between two large Indian men dressed in suits, who were clearly carrying weapons. The seated man was also dressed in a black suit and wore a black tie. He held a cane in his right hand, which shook uncontrollably. His face looked awkward and slightly grotesque, like a mask that hadn't been put on straight.

"Hello," Niral said. "Who are you?"

The man smirked. The guards put their hands on their guns, ready to draw.

"Who am I?" the man asked. "I'm your friend, Niral."

The voice made Niral shudder. He turned to Manu, who got ready to draw his gun too.

"We should speak alone, Niral," the man said. "My bodyguards can escort Manu downstairs so they can converse with Meetal and your father. Go ahead," he said, waving to them.

The bodyguards straightened up and approached them. Niral hesitated, then, moving aside, nodded at Manu, who took his hand from his holster and waited for the bodyguards to descend before following. The man gestured to a single sofa seat across from a coffee table.

"It's not as cool as the swing, but it's a good cushion," the man said.

"Your voice is deeper now, but I can still tell it's you," Niral said, sitting across from him.

"It's that specialized education from New York. Are you unhappy to see me?"

"Considering I thought I killed you, more like surprised."

"Juan did me a favor before hitting the grave. I was lucky. But then all life is luck, isn't it?"

"I haven't been so lucky. I feel like I've descended down a deep well, but I haven't hit hell yet."

"We don't believe in heaven or hell, remember? But don't worry, even if you do believe in such a Semitic concept, you will redeem yourself at Diwali, so we know where you will end up despite your sins if you die. I'm an insider, Niral, I know all about the plan and the set-up.

218

I talk to Bhai. I donate to The Brotherhood. Perhaps Bhai or Mr. Ghosh mentioned me. I am Ashok Patel from North Carolina now."

"My father doesn't want me to go to Shri Diwali anymore."

"You've already set it up. You don't have to go for it to work."

"The Muslims will be suspicious if I'm not there."

"So I'll convince your father that you'll be under my protection."

"Does Meetal know that it's you?"

"A sister can tell. Always. It's impossible to fool them."

"Your parents?"

"They are wise enough not to ask."

"Not even your mother?"

"My mother has not seen me yet, Niral. She went up to Dwarka already. But she knows her son, and she knows her place. Niral, you know I'm a good son. Even when I disappear for eons, I always return in glory, money showering from my palms upon those who need it most."

Niral bent over and laughed a deep, ironic laugh. Then he straightened up and looked serious. "So you are the secret individual donor too."

"I've built this village more efficiently than can be done anywhere in America. For people who need it. No more castes, no more division. Now we have quality of life. We will have an equal playing field where men and women will be judged by more than their backgrounds. And we will have justice."

"I recall a sermon from you on Masoch: if there's a hammer and anvil, you might as well—"

"Hasn't your vision of the world changed since we last met? I know you've grown and changed. So have I. I believe in The Brotherhood. I believe in diplomacy and the chance for equality, despite all the obstacles. Maybe in some twisted way I'm the Brahmin now, in the American sense."

"I'm afraid to ask where the money came from. Other than the money you stole from your investors in Coleman and Ledacorp."

"There are many avenues for funding. A wise philanthropist mines all, and he has no qualms about his means because he knows his ultimate mission is legitimate and good. I can teach you that and more. I'm not

219

your enemy, Niral. I want to be your friend. Your actions began the transformation of this village, but even though you've grown, you will still need some coaching. I'm willing to provide that. I can even sneak you into North Carolina where I live with two warring families I've somehow transformed into one. You have the same skills for diplomacy; you just need to hone them."

"How do you know I haven't already honed them?"

"I'm not saying you haven't honed some."

"But you seem to know all about me. Do you know why they're looking for me?"

"That you're a multiple murderer? I know that. You killed me too. Who have I killed, Niral? And don't say Priya."

"You don't do anything yourself. That doesn't mean—"

"I didn't set up Stan. It wasn't me. That was Bob Macaday if I had to guess. His nice guy act was just that. But you would know, since you ran into him in Thailand."

"How'd you know that?"

"I have my ways. You shouldn't try to escape me, Niral."

"Bob's dead. Apparently, Lance killed him."

"Working for the Traglianis, maybe. Allied with my old boss, Brendan Carty."

"But how'd Bob get to New York? I thought my friend Rob killed him in Phuket."

"Your friend Rob has additional interests, let's just say. He let Bob go so I could use his services," Vishal said. "Alicia Tragliani didn't like that."

"You know Rob?"

"I employ him, Niral. He watched you for me. Don't blame him. He liked you. I don't think he would have killed you if I had asked him to. But I didn't ask him to. You're valuable to me, Niral. I have no reason to harm you. I want you to work with me."

"You tried to kill me. You did that yourself with your own hands."

"But I failed. And I'm glad I did."

"I failed too."

"Bygones be bygones be bygones. Let's talk about now. This village is a testament to my family and yours. Together, with Bhai, we can work to extend that legacy."

"I should see it for myself."

"Sure, let's go," Vishal said, switching his cane to his left hand so he could use it to rise. Niral noticed he walked with a limp, and that his crotch didn't bulge, but he didn't say anything or inquire if his own handywork had made Vishal a eunuch.

"I wonder if your father will recognize me," Vishal said.

"He always thinks of the Other as the good son," Niral replied. "Will it matter?"

Vishal laughed, "Let's go see him and find out."

109

Sanchez and Lawrence returned to their respective precincts to complete paperwork and speak with their partners, but they were called back to the 109th Precinct later that evening. Sergeant Barry Chen introduced them to Detective William Kwon, his best expert on the Dragons. Detective Kwon took them into a tiny office littered with boxes and papers. Then, with difficulty, he closed the doors.

"Wanted to talk to you in here because the noise doesn't travel out," he said. "I've gotta be honest with you guys; I don't trust anybody in this precinct. Rats everywhere. We've had multiple cops arrested for bribery and working with the gangs here, getting payoffs from massage parlors and karaoke shops. So what I say to you stays between your ears."

"Sure, Detective," Lawrence said. "What you got?"

"Okay, so I did some digging, and I found out a number of men we suspect to be Dragon members took a flight to Thailand a couple of months ago."

"So there's the solid Thailand connection," Sanchez said. "But we already knew there was a general connection. Maybe we can figure out the specific connection to Niral?"

"That's where I'm going. So I assume they needed extra muscle because, according to my international contacts, they also got people from Korea, mainland China, and Hong Kong. Later, the Dragons' operation in Bangkok got raided, and a number of these Dragons were found dead or are now considered missing, according to our Thai sources. One guy I had on my radar as a possible lieutenant was Ricky Wong. We believe he's been a Dragon since high school, mainly shaking down Korean businesses in Flushing. We can't get him because none of his victims will complain. He wasn't logged among the dead in the Bangkok raid, so he's still missing. But this led me to look into his past. And guess who he went to junior high school with?"

"Niral Solanke."

"Exactly. There's your connection, gentlemen."

"Okay, but this Ricky is either in Thailand or he's dead, so he's unavailable to us," Lawrence said. "How do we find out info, visit his family?"

"There's another possibility, a guy by the name of Wan, who fell off our radar because he was in prison for ten years to life for murder. Now he's out on parole so we figured he'd lay low, but he has been spotted with Byung-hoon Yoon, a suspected local Dragon boss, a few times. Yet, we can't connect him to criminal activity, so we can't bring him in."

"Hanging out with known criminals is a violation of parole," Lawrence reminded him.

"Problem is, Yoon doesn't have a record. These Dragons are smart."

"Okay, but we've still got something, potentially, to lean on him with. What's his connection to Ricky?"

"Ricky and Niral Solanke both. All three went to junior high together. Plus Wan went to high school with Niral too, at least til Wan dropped out. He committed the homicide shortly after and went away for a decade, but when he was released, he settled back in Flushing, and guess what? Niral was living in Fresh Meadows nearby at the time, and this was right before the Long Island City fire fiasco."

"So he might be a stronger connection to Niral than Ricky, potentially."

"It's possible. His full name is Wan Kim."

"Who's his PO?" Sanchez asked. "We'll visit him first."

110

When Thon and his crew set up camp again, Duncan was allowed to visit Lamai alone in the tent. Duncan held Lamai and rubbed her belly as they lay in their usual crescent shape.

"You're quiet," Duncan said. "Did the trip exhaust you?"

Lamai shook her head. She said, "Tee rak, do you really think we're going to make it out alive?"

"Why not? Thon has experience. He'll get us to Burma."

"But do you really trust them? I mean, why do they need us?"

"Lamai, we're just as valuable to them as they are to us. Maybe more."

"I was thinking, maybe we could escape and make it on our own."

"We'll die out there on our own, Lamai. We don't know the land or the layout. Don't worry; Thon and his people will get us out of Thailand and help us deliver the baby. Plus, our business depends on them. Once Niral carries out the plan in India, we'll be getting loads of merchandise, and we'll need their connections to sell it in Thailand."

"To my people."

"Not any more, Lamai," he said, rubbing Lamai's belly. "Our people number just three now."

"And Niral?"

"Sure, and Niral too. Assuming..."

Lamai turned to him. "Assuming what? Are you going to double cross him?"

"No, Lamai. I'm hoping the plan will succeed and he'll join us."

"But you don't think he will live?"

"I don't know, Lamai. I'm not worried about the shipment itself, but I'm not going to lie to you; Niral is on a dangerous mission. If things go according to plan, he should be okay. But almost nothing goes according to plan these days."

Lamai put her hands on Duncan's cheeks and watched his eyes twitch. "You are lying to me, aren't you? I can tell when you do."

"I'm not lying. I don't know what will happen. That's the truth. Why do you care about Niral so much anyway?"

"Why do you think? He's done so much for us. Like Rob did."

"Yes, but he works for us, just like Rob did. Bottom line."

"They are not our family?"

"Not exactly."

"And me? Do I just exist so I can pop out a baby for you? So you can prove to be a father like your real father never was?"

Duncan turned away. "I knew I shouldn't have told you about that. Now you're going to psychoanalyze me until the end of time."

"Duncan, I'm just worried. I'm worried about me and the little girl in my belly."

"It's not your job to worry, tee rak. Let me worry for you. Trust your man, honey. You have to trust your man."

111

Having finished their meal of hare and mangoes—the mangoes picked by Boonsri from the ground of a nearby tree—Rob and Apsara sat beside the fire. Rob was shirtless, the fire enlightening the many tattoos on his chest. A few were acquired in Melbourne, like the one with Sveta's name on his ass, but most were marked in Alphabet City, Hong Kong, Jakarta, and on Khao San Road. They were varied enough, but each one represented a certain feeling or object of affection he had at the time they were carved. Boonsri was asleep again, lying on Rob's lap while sucking her thumb like a little girl. Rob wiped her hair from her brow.

"Are you sure you want to hear it?" Rob asked Apsara.

"You're all I have left, Rob. My mother is dead. My daughter is gone. So yes, I want to understand you."

"Not sure you'll understand me from it. How will ya even know it's true?"

"I will know, Rob. I trust you."

"All right. Well, you remember how my mum and dad left me, and then I lived with my grandma in the bush. Then she died, so I started staying in foster homes in Queensland. I'd make life miserable for whoever and get sent to another home; it's just the way shit was. I went to school once in a while, and I did my homework sometimes, but I'd always be getting into fist fights with nasty wankers who didn't like me using combo slang with bogan. Reckon I had this dream of living on my own in the forest. I read Huck Finn in school, and it really inspired me. So last time I was living with a woman kinda like that widow. I mean she wasn't bad, but I didn't like someone trying to reform me and stuff. So I figured why not run away and be on my own? I had nothing to lose anyhow.

"So I took a bus to Noosa. I'd gone there on a school trip. I remembered the forests between the beaches where we went hiking, so I set up camp there. I was just a little older than Boonsri here. I remember that first night, making a small fire and laying out in a donna I'd bought at a local op shop, hearing the crickets and feeling that cool air. I felt so terrified and alive at the same time.

"A few days passed like that. I made a knife and went hunting. The first thing I caught was a rabbit just like this. I remembered eating it in the bush and how my grandma would prepare it. Sure, I was young, but I remembered. I always had a good memory.

"I never had real dosh besides change, so I'd go into town and knock off the registers from the swanky restaurants and some shops. Wasn't easy but I usually managed to get in through the back way when blokes were turned. It was Oz, and no one noticed much.

"When I wasn't out in town or in the forest, I'd walk along the beaches. I'd pass by a nudist crowd that hung out, mostly older blokes with beer bellies and nasty dongers, and once in a while an old lady with sagging knockers. I didn't pay them no mind. But one morning, I was lying in the forest wondering which store on Hastings Street to try when this bloke comes up to me. He's wearing a hat, a thong, shoes and nothing else. He's a big guy, much bigger than me, and he says good morning and makes small talk about how I'm getting on. He keeps standing by the fire and yabbering and yabbering 'bout all kinds of bullshit, and finally I tell him what's what. So he says he admires me, wishes he did the same thing when he was my age. Instead, he went the wanker route and got a college degree and went into business. But it never made him happy. He kept coming back to the beach.

"And then he tells me how to really free myself. But I says no thanks. He hangs around a bit longer, tells me his name is John, and then he goes. A few days later, he comes back, but by that time I'm glad to see him. Knocking off the shops was getting tougher, and I got to worrying I'd get caught. Plus, I was tiring of the same old routine. Figure I'd have an adventure. So he brings me down to the beach and I tear off my clothes and veg out. The old fellas like my look, and I feel proud and free. I start hanging there more.

"Long story short, I get on with these guys, and it turns out John has this beach house right there, and he invites me over. Gives me some drinks. Gets me full of piss.

"Never thought of myself as a poofter or nothing else. Never kicked one's ass but didn't mind it either. But when it happened to me without me wanting it, I didn't know how to feel. I felt violated by John, I reckon, but also ashamed of myself, and I thought maybe it meant I was that way and I never knew it before. I avoided John and stayed in the forest for a few days, moving around, but I was back soon enough, cuz I didn't know where else to go, and he was my only mate.

"But me coming back made that cunt more bold. I thought he loved me or something but he just started treating me like this plaything. Because one day I was full of piss again and the whole crew comes through the door, no clothes and hard as hell. I start screaming, but they stuff a sock in my mouth and tell me to shut the fuck up. And that's when they take me down to the cellar and do it.

"Afterwards, I'm lying in his cellar, my ass sore as shit, shaking like hell and crying myself out, when John comes down and throws this blanket on me. Says I was a good fuck, and we'd do it again, like it was the most natural thing in the world. Says I could sleep there or go back to the forest. He should have tied me up, but it was Oz; he didn't think of that. So I made my way back to the forest. I got my knife. I was depressed and shocked. I felt humiliated, but I was also spewin'. I marched around the forest for a while. When I got back to the house, no one was around. But in the distance, I saw they were at the beach, standing around a fire.

"That's when I did it. The first guy didn't see it coming. A knife right through his gut. Felt so good. And then the next. You'd think they would've run away, but they just stood there, like zombies. The first three let themselves get massacred, then the next three tried to fight but lost their fingers or their hands or their arms, fixing 'em long enough for a gut and a carve. Six of them, including John. I loved how he begged and screamed as I chopped off his balls and his cock. That felt good.

"You have to imagine the cleanup job. After that, I was set. Threw everything into the sea. That was a beginner's mistake, because shit washed up, or so I read, but by that time, I was in Melbourne working for Sasha, and I reckon they never connected me. Next time I dumped in the sea I used garbage bags, but then that copper spotted me. Took care of him too. Everything seems to come around eventually. Reckon I've been lucky in my own way."

"You are like me, Rob. I can't believe you did not tell me before."

"Yeah, but my story is true."

"Mine is true too."

"About you getting lured from the Bangkok bus station and made into a sex slave?"

"Yes. And about Thanat selling me to another man for money before he gave me Hathai."

"So that's why you killed him?"

"You killed him, Rob."

"I killed him for you. You and Duncan, who was using you to spy on me?"

"That was before I fell in love with you."

"Yes, and you still are, ya say?"

"You don't believe me?"

"I have to believe ya, Apsara. For me and for Boonsri."

"I have nothing left, Rob."

"Yes, you have me. And Boonsri."

"And you will get back Hathai? And Som?"

"Yup. Once we get to Laos. We'll get 'em back, for sure."

112

After Meetal introduced Ashok to Niral's father, Prakash, and portrayed him as a prominent member of The Brotherhood in North Carolina as well as her distant cousin, the two greeted each other with a respectful namaste. Meetal couldn't explain the exact relation herself, but Ashok helped her out by describing a simplified family tree. Prakash did not seem to suspect Ashok was Vishal. Certainly, he may have wondered about the grotesque face, and he may have felt uncomfortable at Ashok's armed bodyguards, but he did not ask questions.

The six headed towards the Dubla village. Ashok limped along, flanked by his bodyguards. He congratulated Niral's father on being a good steward of the village from afar, though Prakash denied having anything to do with the rebuilding. Then Ashok asked why Niral's mother, Heenabhen, had not come, considering he had heard she was raised in the village and was a devoted Brotherhood member herself. Niral also wanted to hear the answer to that question, but he suspected he knew it—that she did not want to see him and the failure that he had become.

But his father responded that she had God's work to do in New York City: one of them had to continue spreading The Brotherhood way. And then Ashok and Prakash conversed about The Brotherhood structure in North America, where Sureshuncle headed the operations now with the help of Premuncle and Alkeshuncle. Ashok seemed bitter that Sureshuncle controlled the entire North American funding scheme and implied that he was corrupt. But Prakash defended the structure and said that while all funding did go into one pot, Sureshuncle didn't control the fund himself like Narendrabhai had controlled the northeastern US fund in New York before the changes. Bhai and Mr. Ghosh oversaw the fund, and Sureshuncle was merely the point person. The funds were funneled to the central Indian account and then used for collective projects like this. Ashok didn't respond to that description but laughed sardonically.

Niral, meanwhile, wanted to berate Meetal for transforming seemingly overnight from a penniless sadhu to an ornamented mistress, but he didn't get the chance because Manu and Meetal got on famously and couldn't stop conversing about the village. His only option to socialize was with Ashok's bodyguards, an option he chose to reject.

Upon approaching the village entrance, Niral noticed the slope had risen so that the village stood on a plateau as Mr. Ghosh had promised.

And, as promised, the village had been renovated completely. One-story shacks had been replaced with two or three-story homes, which rivaled the Brahmin houses in quality and elegance. The communal building was gone too, replaced by four smaller buildings. In front of each, village members had lined up to vote.

The middle of the village looked like a small square, outlined by benches where people relaxed and gossiped. Niral saw Brahmin men hanging out with Dublas, when only months earlier they had been ready to beat each other with hammers and boards.

"They must have been brainwashed," he said, speaking to nobody. Only Ashok seemed to hear him and snickered in response.

Niral turned to Manu. "How did you manage this?" he asked.

"Just as I told you on the phone, Niralbhai; it happened by itself," Manu responded. "Once we removed the false barrier of caste distinctions and gave everyone a reason to work for something, people came together. You saw this in a small way after the massacre. The Brotherhood way works."

"Yes," Niral responded. "Except I imagine *you* did not change this fast."

"Sorry, Niralbhai?" Manu asked, but Niral didn't continue the conversation. Instead, he walked forward and continued to observe. Harshkaka stood by one of the small buildings, holding a clipboard and making sure all voters were counted once and only once. He smiled at Niral. Then Niral saw Kamkaki, Lata, and Ravi together, sitting on a bench.

"Niral, I will say hello to Kamkaki," his father said. "Do you want to come?"

Niral shook his head.

"Why not?" his father asked angrily. "She helped raise your mother."

"We've already met, Deddy," he said, remembering how his father had refused to donate directly to her cause. His father scoffed and went on.

Niral turned to Manu again. "Where is Prameshbhai?" he asked. "Is he still alive?"

"Of course, Niralbhai," Manu replied, pointing to a large, three-story building in the corner of the village with a clock on top of it. "He is in the building over there, in the cellar."

"And Narendrakaka?"

"Probably in the same building but on the ground floor with Lakshmanbhai, waiting for the results of the election. That building is our courthouse and jail, the main dispenser of justice."

"And Narendrakaka and Lakshmanbhai are the only candidates running for their positions?"

"Yes, Niralbhai," Manu said. "But we have also created a new position of president. It is only ceremonial and exists in case certain policies voted on by the board are not able to be implemented. Then the president can use his power. Two candidates are running for that."

"Who?"

"Me and Ramonbhai, the father of one of the murdered children."

"And yet you are not campaigning either?" Niral asked.

"I rely on God for votes," Manu stated.

Niral smirked. He glanced at Ashok and Meetal.

"Shri Diwali is only two days away," Niral noted aloud. "When will we travel up there, Manu?"

"We can leave whenever you like, Niralbhai," Manu stated.

"We are leaving tonight," Ashok said. "Driving all night. We will meet Bhai and Mr. Ghosh and participate in the pre-ceremony before the event."

"With or without bodyguards, Ashokbhai?" Niral asked. He glanced at Meetal, who seemed perturbed. "Will you be taking Meetal and her father? If not, we can provide transportation."

"Meetal and Narendrabhai say they will not be present at the event," Ashok replied. "Both are too preoccupied with the village's affairs. But I believe Kauntibhen is already there."

230

"We will go whenever you want, Niralbhai," Manu said again after a namaste to him. "Now or later, it does not matter."

"Are you sure you don't want to stay behind to take care of the village?" Niral asked sharply.

Manu looked offended. "No, Niralbhai, we have a mission," he replied softly.

Niral nodded. "Come, Manu, let's say hello to Narendrakaka and Lakshmanbhai."

They headed towards the courthouse, leaving Meetal, Ashok, and his bodyguards behind. He greeted Kamkaki, Lata, and Ravi from a distance with a namaste but did not heed their wave to join them and his father.

"We'll leave as soon as possible," Niral whispered. "I don't care if we get there late at night."

"Yes, Niralbhai."

"Are you serious about this president thing?" he asked.

"If am elected, I will start my duties after Diwali. The people know I did a lot. I brought in money from Mr. Ghosh and Ashokbhai. It was distributed fairly by the council with my input. They might feel sympathy for Ramonbhai, but they can trust me."

"Spoken like a true leader," Niral said. "But then how loyal are you to me?"

"Why do you continue to test me, Niralbhai? My duties are temporal. You are immortal."

"What if we are found out and murdered, Manu?" Niral asked. "Will we be immortal then?"

"I trust in the mission, Niralbhai. I trust in you."

They entered the courthouse and saw Narendrakaka and Lakshman-bhai sitting next to a couple of armed young men. Niral greeted all with a namaste and a bow. Manu imitated him.

Narendrakaka stood, elated, and hugged Niral.

"I am so glad you are here," Narendrakaka said. "You have returned as the hero of this village. Have you seen what you have wrought?"

"I don't feel like a hero. No one has treated me like one."

"They are busy with the election. If you talk to them..."

"I want to speak to Prameshbhai, actually," Niral said.

Narendrakaka was taken aback. "Why?"

"I just do. Can I?"

Narendrakaka nodded. He gestured to the young men, who showed Niral and Manu down to the dungeon, opening gates along the way. The two men stayed two gates away as Niral and Manu entered a small, plain cell where Prameshbhai sat on the floor, his hands bound behind his back, wearing a cream kafni that appeared surprisingly clean.

"So they dress you in fresh clothes," Niral said, approaching, Manu behind him. "Your favorite, if I remember correctly."

Prameshbhai smiled at him. "You have come back for the third time, Niralbhai. Do you like what you see?"

"Everyone seems happy."

"Yes, they do seem so. I was never a fan of the caste system, you know. I rose from being a Dubla myself. And granted, I have not seen what has become of the place with my own eyes, being down here, but I do not believe this experiment will succeed in the long run. The people are happy and willing to join because they do not have to pay for the lila, the fantasyland, that has been created for them. But once The Brotherhood stops pumping money in, laziness will rule, the same divisions will form, and someone else will reap the rewards. Perhaps that is natural."

"I guess we will see."

"You are smart enough to envision that reality. Look, why have you come down here? To gloat about killing Satish or watching my daughter and Pranam burn?"

"No. I wanted to know your take on the situation."

"I gave it to you without you asking. I must be a psychic, as you Americans say."

"How about the Muslims? Do you know any sympathizers among the men here?"

"I would not tell you if I did."

"You only have to lie and say you believe in The Brotherhood way and they might let you out. You would have done that in the old days. Why not now?"

Tejas Desai

Prameshbhai shrugged. "I guess I am ashamed of my past and seek to be a principled man. Or maybe, like Napoleon, I believe I will escape and rise again."

"With the help of the Muslims?" Niral asked.

"With the help of people who understand the true nature of man. I don't think Muslims count."

"I want you to know the trajectory of this country is about to change. Whether it will be to your liking, you will have to see."

"Playing people against each other always ended in a bang for me, usually with me receiving money. But your prediction sounds more exciting. I like a good mystery. And a good thriller."

"You might see me again; you might not. If you do, you might learn something more."

"Okay, my guru," Prameshbhai responded. "I would namaste to you if I could move my hands."

"I'll imagine you did," Niral said, taking his leave with a namaste. "Let's go, Manu."

113

The detectives found Wan Kim at a construction site in Sunnyside. He hadn't been at his Flushing home when the detectives had knocked on his door, but he had listed this site with his parole officer as his latest place of employment. The company written down was Ozone Construction, which Sanchez and Lawrence knew was one of the bidders on the LIC reconstruction. Previously, Wan had been employed at a karaoke parlor in Flushing.

"Now we know it's got something to do with the LIC project," Sanchez whispered to Lawrence as they headed over to the parole office.

"Yeah, but do we know Wan's still a Dragon?"

His parole officer, a sweet but tough African-American woman named Linda German, had visited the construction site last when Wan had reported his job switch. She said he seemed hardworking and that his bosses seemed professional.

"How about his job at the parlor?" Lawrence asked Linda as they drove over to the construction site. "Those are usually fronts for prostitution and other rackets."

"I'm aware, detective. But when we investigated, everything seemed on the up and up."

"You knew he was hanging out with this Mr. Yoon?"

"Yes, but we can't do anything about that. Yoon doesn't have a criminal record."

"So he was present at this parlor the entire time he was supposed to be working?"

"I can't check where he is all the time, detective. Anyway, deliveries could be part of his job. As long as they don't involve liquor."

At the site, the detectives accompanied Ms. German to a trailer. Wan was inside, wearing a hard hat. He was talking to his boss, an Irish-American man named McCarthy. Miss German had met Mr. McCarthy before, and they exchanged pleasantries. Lawrence displayed his badge quickly to both of them, breaking up their conversation, and asked Wan if they could talk in private. McCarthy and Ms. German left the office. Sanchez closed the door.

"You might fool this sweet lady, but you don't fool me," Lawrence said right away to Wan. "We know you're still working with the Dragons."

"I'm not—"

"You know Niral Solanke?"

"Niral?" He paused. "Yeah, we went to high school—"

"And Ricky Wong?"

He shrugged. "Sure, we were buddies a long time ago."

"But no recent contact?"

"No way. I steer clear of known criminals."

"Niral's not a criminal, is he?"

"I don't know. I—"

"Look, I'll be honest, we don't give a fuck about you," Sanchez said, approaching. "We want the whole network. The connection to bring down the latch on whoever's involved. We've got mob witnesses dead and politicians in the hospital. So unless you want to spend the rest of your life in Sing Sing, I suggest you tell us whatever you know."

"I don't know anything, detectives, scout's honor. I feel bad about what I did, and I'm trying to make amends. I even send money to the widow of the guy I capped. Simple life."

"Really?" Sanchez asked. "Maybe we should ask her about that because I'm not sure you're supposed to be going near her either."

Wan appeared nervous for the first time.

"How do you get her the money, Wan?" Lawrence asked.

"I mail it," he said.

"Yourself?" Sanchez asked.

"I got someone to send it to her, all right?"

"Who?" Lawrence asked.

"Look, why are you hassling me?"

"Tell me, are the Traglianis in with the Dragons on this Ozone Construction deal for the LIC project?" Sanchez asked. "We know it's a front, so don't bullshit us."

"Traglianis?" Wan asked with a snicker.

And with that, Sanchez's question was answered. "Didn't think so," Sanchez said.

"Wan," Lawrence said, "you did time with Tyrone Williams, right?"

Wan was tightlipped.

"Answer the question," Lawrence said, although this reference had thrown Sanchez.

"Yeah, I did time with Tyrone," Wan replied. "So what?"

"Word on the street says the kids who died at both the Bob Macaday and Vince Stevens hits were in Tyrone's gang in South Jamaica. How's it that you did time with Tyrone, and both these cats got connections with Ozone's bid on the Long Island City Project? Plus, you went to high school with Solanke, and his fingerprints are all over Dragon murders everywhere. Pretty coincidental."

"I don't know anything about some project or any murders. I knew Tyrone in the hole, but I don't know him now. Same thing with Niral. No go," he said, making a cut sign at his neck.

Lawrence laughed. He looked at Sanchez.

"Okay, Wan," Lawerence said. "Let's say I believe you. We got coincidences coming out the wazoo, but I believe you. You're a reformed bad guy who did the wrong thing years ago and now you've gone straight. Can't help it you're connected to gangsters, right? But if one of them decides to cut a deal by pointing the finger at you, forget evidence; you're going back to Sing Sing. Forever. Remember that."

Lawrence gave Wan his card and told him he'd be in touch. Outside, as they waited for Ms. German to finish talking to McCarthy, they whispered to one another.

"What the fuck, Lawrence, why you didn't tell me about those kids?" Sanchez asked.

"We did our own research, brother. Lewis connected Wan to Tyrone and the kids to Tyrone's gang. Latter's hearsay, but we can get gangbangers to turn and reveal easy. Now Lewis'll look up the widow and figure out the sender. Bet you it's Ricky Wong or Yoon. And if it's Wong and that cat went to Thailand, we got yet another coincidence. Plus, I think Wong's got a minor rap sheet from years ago. Known criminal's easier to prove."

"Did you see Wan's reaction when I mentioned the Traglianis?" Sanchez asked. "We got it all wrong before. This is a battle between the Dragons and the Traglianis. I'll have Lacey look into a DeKalb and Lucchese connection."

"Well, if Wan was the go-between and hired Tyrone to waste Macaday, then why? And then Stevens too? I'd think the Traglianis would have the biggest motive."

"Looks to me like the Dragons tried to waste Macaday in Thailand but just got the wife. Finished the job here. Then Stevens stands in the way of the bid too, maybe blackmailing them, saying he'll side with DeKalb, so they try to waste him and turn the dials back. Either way, I'm not sure Lance Portman was involved. He killed the killers but maybe he was a bodyguard for both."

"I'm more confused than ever. I'm not sure we'll get to the bottom of it all, but we don't have to. We can get the principals. This LIC project is at the center of the storm. That Community Board meets tomorrow to grant the contracts. We either solve this case by then or we see what goes down on that front. We need to investigate these board members. If your people can't do it, maybe the Feds can."

"I'll give my Captain a call. We'll be all hands on deck. I'm surprised the Feds or Marshals haven't bucked in on either of us, but we'll keep riding this wave while we can."

"In the meantime, we follow this Wan cat, and I bet you he leads us to something. Maybe it'll confuse us even more, but it'll be something."

"Amen, brother," Sanchez said, slapping Lawrence's arm. "This is why I love being a detective, man. The whirl of the mystery and the thrill of the chase!"

114

"The criminals are near the border now," Colonel Arthit was telling Colonel Nopasit in the tent. "They are not too far from it, so if we want to act, we should act now. We are pretty sure they are hiding under the foliage. I say we blast them with bombs."

"Khun Commissioner does not want that," Nopasit said. "Lamai's father was respected in the military. He doesn't want her harmed if it is not necessary. And it will be bad press."

"We've had the sister for a couple of days now. We haven't used her. You want them to escape into Burma and continue—"

"We've got the drug transportation route determined now. That was the main goal. The dealers in Kanchanaburi are under surveillance. Even a mole is inside. It will probably lead us to their Bangkok operation too. We've spotted the man with the money, and we're tracking him as he approaches the camp. We will nab the criminals the normal way."

"You didn't tell me that," Colonel Arthit said, outraged. "You said you had lost him."

"We can't reveal all things to all people, Colonel Arthit. Would you respect us if we did?"

Colonel Arthit stood. "I have withstood your slaps out of respect. But this disrespect—"

"Relax, Colonel," Colonel Dusit said, coming out of the corner of the tent where he had been hiding. "You can also be a key component of our enterprise."

"Colonel Dusit?" Arthit asked, shocked. "What enterprise? Of all people, you—"

"You know I'm a rational man, Colonel," Colonel Dusit said. "I don't believe in brute force unless it is truly necessary. I favor sensible tactics. Your actions towards the Karen repulsed me. But I must admit that, due to them, now the Karen will respect us more, and the Thai public will be happy about our tough stance. Either way, if we want to move up to be the Khun Commissioner's right-hand men or replace him ourselves one day, we cannot just stop this drug trade. We need to know its procedures and perhaps control it ourselves. We have significant competition in that arena. We need to beat our competition at their own game."

"What do you mean competition?" Arthit asked. "Are you saying we should be drug dealers?"

"I am saying we need to have dealers in our pocket, and on our side, to compete against our rivals to ultimately stop the trade. That does not mean dealing it ourselves. But let's face it, unless we intervene to control it, it will go on anyway, and it will be worse than before. Wiping out the Dragon organization in Thailand was a brilliant play by General Toon Tomecherin to hide his own control over the ya ba market in Bangkok and Pattaya. He controls it through his man Sumantapat. And now General Chaow has signed on to join the operation with his own drug contacts in the south. We believe that's where Duncan Smith was getting his merchandise originally. That's why they needed to connect the Dragons down there too, and to blame Maric for the murder of the farang's wife. Now they've decided to change the main method of transport of their supply from the north to the south."

"Khun Commissioner does not like General Toon after failing to protect his detectives," Arthit noted.

"Yes, but General Chaow is closer than ever to the Commissioner. That was another reason for Tomecherin to make a deal with him."

"So we control the drug trade up here once we nab the Karen. We have them work for us. And that means we can compete with General Toon?"

"If we do not do this, Sumantapat's merchandise will be all over Thailand and the scourge will never end. This way we can counteract them and ultimately control the trade ourselves. Then, with the Narcotics Suppression Bureau on our side, and the entire system identified, we will be able to stop it."

"How did you find out about Toon?" Arthit asked, glancing at Nopasit, who was smiling.

"Nopasit has been watching him for a while, completely undercover," Dusit said. "Even the Khun Commissioner does not know. But we did not want to act until we were sure what we were dealing with. Now we have a better chance at victory."

Colonel Arthit sat down. "I feel like I have been completely fooled. I have lost all face."

"Smile, Colonel Arthit," Colonel Dusit said, resting his hand on Colonel Arthit's arm. "Think of it as a rebirth, into an all-knowing Buddha."

115

At the next meeting of the Brothers of Aesthetic Unity, Jeremy was replaced as leader by Levon. After the meeting, the moderate wing stayed in the basement to counteract Jesse's radical action plan for the Community Board meeting, if possible. Candy had finally joined the group, as had Lester and Mahdi. But the seven hadn't been able to outvote the eight radicals.

"Jesse's plan is going to set us back decades," Jeremy said, sounding resigned. "But I don't see how we can stop it without breaking the Unity Brothers apart. Stevens is still hospitalized, so I don't know how the mayor's side of the board will vote. Plus, the radicals stopped us from publicizing DeKalb's mob connection in the media. Cortland did convince the CFLIC to vote for Ozone, so he'll be there pitching it. He's pulling some strings on the board with mob gossip, but Jesse and Levon could make sure nothing happens in LIC for a while."

"We got no choice but to set up Levon and his crew so nothing exciting happens," Lance said. "Ozone bid's gotta win out for our values to go forward. Only way that's gonna happen is if we stop these crazy cats."

"How are we going to do that?" Jeremy asked. "Call the police? What if the cops get onto us too?"

"I'm the one who stands to lose, brother. They're already after me. So follow my plan or don't; it's up to you."

"I think we should hear Iceman out," Candy said. "He's always been solid on strategy."

"He messed up Stevens," Chloe said, her arms folded.

"That was on account of a little brother," Lance said. "Would've gone fine if he hadn't showed."

"Even if we stop them, how do we know the bid will go to Ozone Construction?" Chloe asked. "The CFLIC is only a recommender to the board. We need the mayor's people and one other to vote for the contract to swing in our direction, and without Stevens putting pressure on them—"

"Don't worry, Chloe," Lance said. "I got people working on that."

116

Brendan Carty acknowledged a police officer, signed in, and, holding a bouquet of roses, entered the hospital room of Vince Stevens.

"Long time, Daddy," Brendan said, placing the roses on Vince's chest as he lay in bed.

"Thought you'd never show up, dear," Vince replied in a soft deadpan voice.

Brendan wiped Vince's hair from his brow. "Gerry's been around?"

"Twenty-four/seven in the beginning. But he went back to work today."

"We all have to, right? You know the vote is tomorrow."

"One stupid project," Stevens said, shaking his head. "Don't you rich people have better things to worry about?"

"If Vishal beats me, that'll be twice. I can't stand that. Can't allow it."

"So it's all about pride. Your ego. I'm glad I'm a politician. I don't need ego or pride."

"Really?" Carty asked, laughing.

"If not for you, that Lance wouldn't have showed up. I told you to get rid of him earlier."

"Well that ship's sailed. Police are still looking for him."

"And the kid?"

"What kid?"

"The one that shot me, dear. Didn't Lachlan hire him? He shot the wrong guy, dummy!"

"Of course not, Daddy. You didn't tell the cops that, did you?"

"Why would I tell them about you?"

"If you thought I hired the kid."

"I thought Alicia Tragliani did, through Lachlan. She capped Macaday too, didn't she?"

"No, it was Vishal. Maybe he hired the kid."

"Why would he hire both the kid and Lance? Lance was trying to blackmail me for Vishal, using my relationship with you!"

"Police'll figure it out. You've gotta hold strong, Daddy. You need to rally your people."

"From here? Fuck you."

Brendan picked up the roses.

"What do you want from me, Brendan?" Stevens asked. "I'm weak."

"Yes, you are," Carty said. "I thought you were a Daddy. You want to see me again, you better do the right thing. Gather up the votes for DeKalb."

Stevens shook his head.

"It's your call," Carty said, walking out with the roses. "But expect consequences for inaction."

BOOK THREE

PART IX

†

Yam Gam, India; The Road, Gujarat, India; Dwarka, India; Near Lamba, India; Mae Hong Son Province, Thailand; Nong Khai, Thailand; Outside Vientiane, Laos; Karen State, Myanmar; South Jamaica, Forest Hills, Sunnyside, Flushing, Long Island City, St. Albans (Queens), New York

117

In conversation, Ashok told Niral's father that Bhai had informed him about Niral's troubles in Thailand and America, but that Niral was now a true devotee dedicated to reforming himself. His role at Shri Diwali would be the ultimate redemption for his sins and, despite his father's reservations, he had to be present. But Ashok offered to lend one of his bodyguards so Niral would not be nabbed by the police on his way to Dwarka. After the ceremony, they could consider hiding him in Yam Gam or the wadi until the heat went away.

Since Prakash insisted on going up to Dwarka with Niral and Manu despite Niral's suggestions that he stay in the village to help Narendrakaka and Meetal, Niral was forced to acquiesce and allow Ashok's bodyguard Parthu to accompany them, although he made it clear he was only accepting protection on the ride up. They drove up that evening.

Meanwhile, Ashok had changed his mind and decided to wait until early the next morning to leave, telling Niral he wanted to spend more time with his father and sister before he left, and informing Prakash that he had things to take care of in the village.

Niral slept most of the way up. Parthu dozed half the time too. Only

Niral's father spoke to Manu all night, keeping him awake. With stops, during which Parthu looked out for Niral, it took until just after noon the next day to reach the Dwarka complex.

Upon arriving, their car and bodies were searched, but Parthu was allowed to keep his gun after Mr. Ghosh was called. The four entered the complex. Manu parked in the official security parking lot.

Coming into the square, they were astonished at the number of pilgrims who filled it. They did not pack the entire square but enough of it that the wide alleys between the three large temples and even the spaces between the smaller temples were full of pilgrims. The pilgrims were reciting the lunch prayer, men and women separated, most wearing simple white kafnis and saris. He didn't see anyone in a wife-beater as he had on his first visit, and unlike the first time, he did not see either Bhai or Mr. Ghosh in the crowd, at least not near the stage next to Bhen's statue, which in this case was in the middle of the large crowd.

Mr. Shah approached them as they walked over to the residence wing on the right side of the hexagonal structure.

"A good turnout so far, but we are not overwhelmed," Mr. Shah said. "The last batch arrives tonight, then tomorrow is the main event. Are you ready?"

"Yes, Mr. Shah," Niral said. "This is my father, Prakashbhai Solanke."

"An honor," Mr. Shah said with a namaste. "I have heard great things about you, and I respect your son. I believe the heads of North America—Sureshbhai, Prembhai, and Alkeshbhai—are already here."

"Yes, I see them," Prakash said.

Niral saw them too now, in the distance, at the head of the praying pack past the large temples. Further down, he noticed more familiar people, and to the far right, he noticed Kauntiaunti among the women.

"Sureshbhai is the head," Niral's father clarified. "Prembhai and Alkeshbhai are only the assistants."

"I thought that man from North Carolina, Ashok Patel, would be here too," Mr. Shah said.

"He will be arriving later," Prakash answered. "He is a wonderful gentleman. He gave us his bodyguard to protect Niral."

"Niral is supposed to be our protector," Mr. Shah said, snickering as he analyzed Parthu. "Please, Prakashbhai, would you like to join the prayer or have lunch in the private quarters? Bhai may join you."

"Manu and my father need sleep," Niral said. "Perhaps they can meet Bhai tonight. I would like to meet him sooner than that, if possible."

Manu turned to Niral. "It is okay, Niralbhai, I can—"

"Get some rest, Manu," Niral said, putting his hand on Manu's shoulder. "We have a long day tomorrow."

Manu entered the residence quarters and went upstairs with Mr. Shah's security guards, but Prakash ignored his son and joined the prayer, dressed as he was in a dress shirt and pants.

"You can't stop a true devotee," Niral said to himself.

Niral and Parthu entered the residence quarters with Mr. Shah and, going downstairs to a basement, ate a Gujarati thali meal with chai in a small dining room. Then they waited alone in a small prayer room nearby to meet Bhai and Mr. Ghosh.

When Bhai entered, he was wearing a bullet-proof vest on his chest and a dhoti wrapped around his loins. Bhai's security guards, including the Sikh guard and slightly bearded guard, followed, then Mr. Ghosh entered, carrying a black binder.

"Why isn't he wearing the vest under a kafni?" Niral asked.

"Bhai's not comfortable wearing a kafni right now," Mr. Shah said. "And if people see the vest, they will know that he's protected."

"That's a joke, right?" Niral asked. "Then they know shooting him in the head is their only option. With it underneath, they figure it doesn't matter where they get him."

"Who is they?" Mr. Shah asked. "The plan is to capture the assassins here at Dwarka while Bhai is at Lamba. This is just an extra precaution."

"He will wear a kafni tomorrow," Mr. Ghosh clarified. "This is more comfortable for him now."

"I hate wearing it," Bhai said. "I don't want people to think I am afraid."

"So why wear it now?" Niral asked.

"People with guns are here," Mr. Ghosh noted. "Parthu is armed, isn't he?"

"You're the one who allowed him to keep his gun," Niral noted.

Bhai told everyone to leave but Niral. That included Parthu and Bhai's security guards.

Mr. Shah objected.

"It's okay," Bhai said angrily. "I don't need to be surrounded by people all the time."

Everyone but Niral left. The door was closed. Bhai took off the vest and threw it on the floor.

"If only I could wear it under my skin. I know I am not invincible, Niral."

"Manu seems to think I am."

"Manu is dedicated. I respect him more than myself. You should consider yourself lucky."

"I've treated him better than The Brotherhood did. I gave him a position of importance and responsibility, not simply that of a driver."

"Yet he drove you here," Bhai noted. "And Mr. Ghosh gave him the responsibility, not you."

"But I made him part of this mission."

"I agree, that was you. Sleeping on his floor, saving his life, protecting his daughter. You have a talent for making people think you are not manipulating them."

"He will feel a pride he's never felt. His daughter will be here."

"I saw her in the crowd with her mother. I remember meeting her as a girl. Did you see your men in the crowd?"

"Yes. They are here."

"So everything is set. Do you know which ones will be heading to Lamba?"

"I believe so. Manu will stay here and be the hero of Dwarka," Niral said.

"Mr. Shah will enjoy some glory too. Which is why your role is so important. You must be the man who delivers in the final act of the play."

"How about Bhavesh, Bilal, Paul?"

"They will be inside the Lamba complex. But no one, not even my guards, is aware but you."

"Oh," Niral said. "I didn't realize that."

Bhai put his hands on Niral's shoulder.

"Niral, when we set this plot in motion, I was skeptical you could follow through on it, even enough to make it here. But I knew that you were the only person who, if he did, could keep this secret. If they know, there is no surprise, and we cannot be effective in the larger mission."

"Then I am the expendable one," Niral said.

"No, Niral. I am the expendable one. It is very possible I will not survive despite the protection. This is the risk I take for Hindustan. You, Niral, have a thousand lives. I would count on a thousand and one."

"I might not make it out either. Or they could blame me afterwards. Especially if you don't survive."

"I have faith in you, Niral. And don't worry, I have procedures in place to make sure the latter does not happen. You think like Talim if you believe I would harm anyone who didn't deserve it, let alone one of my own. We are not gangsters or terrorists like them."

Niral closed his eyes and lowered his head. "But I am, Bhai. I've done horrible things."

"Yes, I know what things you've done."

"How could you tell my father?"

"So you have another reason to carry through the mission and not return to Thailand. We will protect you here, and we will reform you here."

"You told me nothing about Vishal."

"I cannot inform you about all things, Niral. You should be glad Vishal is alive. He's done tremendous good for Yam Gam and The Brotherhood. He wants to protect you too."

"My friend in Thailand was just a spy for Vishal. And maybe for you."

"I am not a perfect man and neither is Vishal. Neither are you. Was Krishna a perfect man? Or Rama? All made mistakes. But we try to do the right thing for society when we can. You've seen the world; you know how things are. You know this is the right thing to do, don't you?"

Niral nodded.

"Now let's bring in the other men and discuss the particulars of the Dwarka operation," Bhai said. "You will inform Manu about it afterwards?"

"Yes, I will tell him," Niral answered.

118

After night fell, Rob, Apsara, and Boonsri stealthily entered Nong Khai on foot. They avoided the patrols and blended into the unusually large crowds. It was Okk Paan Saa—or Vassa—the last day of Buddhist Lent, when many people flooded the city from the provinces to watch the dragon boat festival, attend the street fair near Wat Lam Duan, and see naga fireballs in the night sky.

The dragon boat races were finished, but Apsara advised the border patrol would be less likely to check if they saw someone rowing across the Mekong on a deserted stretch. They hung out among the crowds, then walked along the Mekong River, away from the Friendship Bridge. Many people had waited on the Mekong's banks for a mile across to see the famous naga fireballs and little hot air balloons launched by locals. The show was long over, and the crowds were receding. But the full moon was still bright in the sky.

"Shouldn't we wait til tomorrow night?" Rob asked. "Lots of wankers still about."

"Have faith, Rob," Apsara said. "This day Buddha comes down to earth from heaven after teaching his mother about dharma. We are protected."

Rob rolled his eyes. With Boonsri on his front, holding him around his neck, and the duffel bag on his back, Rob followed Apsara. They reached a stretch of river with fewer people. About a ten-minute walk later, the shore was deserted. He spotted a small beach where two longtail boats were docked. He checked his flip phone. It was two o'clock.

"Two fishermen here rent their boats to people who want to cross without going through immigration," Apsara explained. "That is our passport."

"All right, so where are the briefcases stashed?"

"I buried them behind a short hill next to the beach."

"You sure those blokes didn't take 'em?"

"I buried it when they weren't here."

He followed Apsara to the back of the hill. A Singha beer bottle stuck out of the dirt behind a slight ridge. She pointed at it.

"Real subtle," Rob said. "You got a shovel?"

"Do I look like I have a shovel, Rob?" Apsara asked, putting out her arms. "We can ask the fishermen."

"No worries," Rob said. He told Boonsri to hop down. Then he took off the duffel bag and removed the machete. He started digging with it. Apsara rubbed Boonsri's hair. Boonsri stepped away.

"Let me fix your hair, Boonsri. Don't you want to look pretty when we reach our new country?"

Boonsri seemed hesitant, but then, to Apsara's surprise, she nodded. Apsara ran her fingers through Boonsri's hair to smooth it out, then tied it into a natural bun.

Rob finally dug deep enough, about a foot down, to hit the briefcase.

"You dug this yourself?" Rob asked.

"I did not want the rain to wash it away."

"Surprised the beer bottle stayed," Rob said, taking out the briefcase. "You got the combo?"

Apsara came over and opened the briefcase. Rob's eyes went wide.

"All right, we're happy. All Thai baht though, must be Thanat's cash. Where's the other two in dollar bills, the ones I gave you?"

Apsara pointed towards a spot near the ridge.

"I did not mark it because it is a lot. So you will have to search a bigger area."

Rob shrugged. He handed the briefcase to Apsara and went to work. About fifteen minutes later, he had unearthed the other two briefcases. They were the same cases he had given to Apsara months before, without combinations.

"Bloody hell," he said after opening them to check their contents. "This'll be plenty to live on in Laos."

"Yes. Me, you, Boonsri, Hathai."

"And Som. Damn that Duncan. Never would've guessed we'd be richer than him."

"Duncan was not a good man. I am sorry I spied on you for him."

"No worries, sweetie. Past is past."

He looked up at the moon, then at the briefcases again.

"Carrying three is a bit much. Lemme see if I can fit one stash into the duffel bag," he said.

He emptied the first briefcase and fit the money into his bag, then added the machete and his gun. He threw the empty briefcase into the hole. Then he put the bag on his back and lifted the other two briefcases in each hand.

"Boonsri, you'll have to hold Miss Apsara's hand, all right?"

"Yes, Paw," Boonsri replied, taking her hand.

Apsara led, and he followed them down to the bank. Apsara spoke to the driver of the boat on the left. He smiled and nodded. The man in the other boat, who sat on his boat's tail drinking a beer, appeared dour.

"Okay," Apsara said. "He'll take us across."

"Now?" Rob asked.

Apsara smiled. Then there was a flash. Rob ducked and hit the floor. When he looked up, the driver was laughing. Apsara and Boonsri were watching the sky.

"The naga fireballs," she said. He saw thin bolts of orange lights rising into the sky.

"Fucking amazing," he said.

"No one has seen them this late," Apsara said. "Normally, they appear around dusk."

"But you sure we should cross with this light on?"

Apsara asked the driver in Thai. He gave his assent.

"No problem," Apsara said. "The undercover border patrol is busy watching the fireballs too."

Rob felt his phone vibrate. He put down one briefcase and checked it. He told Apsara it was almost three.

"Soon we are in Laos," Apsara said, "where they use dollars."

"Come on," Rob said. Apsara helped Boonsri into the boat, then climbed in herself. Rob put the briefcases in first, then followed. The driver revved up the motor. The other driver continued to watch them, drinking his beer.

The boat launched. Rob saw people on a distant hill, cheering while watching the fireballs. The Friendship Bridge was in the far distance, and other longtail boats were docked down the river.

Boonsri trotted to the edge of the boat to look over, but Rob grabbed her before she reached it.

"Don't fall in, sweetie," he warned.

"It should not be too deep, Rob," Apsara said. "Around this time, the water level is low."

Then Apsara stopped speaking. She tapped Rob's shoulder and pointed at the shore. Rob saw another flash, but it didn't startle him like before. This time a man was pointing a flashlight at them, while another was speaking to the other boat's driver. They were close enough that Apsara recognized one of them.

"It's Nam," Apsara said. "He actually found us."

"Still wants revenge for Hong, I reckon. I'll get my gun."

Apsara grabbed Boonsri, covering her with her body as Boonsri fought her.

"Hold still, Boonsri," Rob said as he opened the duffel bag and took out his gun. The driver suddenly became startled.

"Keep calm, mate. Get us to the other side fast. Otherwise we're all dead."

The men boarded the other boat. It started to follow them.

"Good thing the crowds'll drown out the shots, no?" Rob said, pointing the gun at the boat.

"I didn't think they would find us," Apsara said. "Why are they still looking?"

"Stubborn fucks. He put that ring around your neck, yeah? I'll put a hole in his fucking head for you."

119

"We'll be in Burma tomorrow," Thon had told Duncan as they sat around the fire the night before, eating lychee from a knife. Now, it was around dawn, and as he lay in bed inside his tent, Duncan was excited beyond his wildest dreams, yet also nervous about India. Anything could happen, but even if Bhai was not killed, the Muslims could gain significant PR around the attempt, and he could still benefit from the shipment. He felt he was on the precipice of a new life, a life that he had earned, and only him.

That's what he was thinking when he heard a scream, a shot, and a voice on a loudspeaker. He sat up and scanned the tent. He didn't see Thon, but the other men were up and awake. Then he heard the loudspeaker again. The voice was in Thai. It was ordering them to surrender.

The men began fleeing the tent, taking weapons with them if they could. Duncan grabbed the man who normally wore the bandana, asking him frantically for a weapon. He shrugged Duncan off, taking a gun with him as he fled the tent too.

Duncan heard gunfire outside. He looked around desperately for a weapon but couldn't find one. Then he felt he shouldn't wait any longer, so he ran out.

He could see Karen men lying dead close to the base camp. Others were firing into the forest. Then he noticed Thon standing outside the tent for women, shirtless and holding a knife.

"Where's Lamai?" Duncan shouted as he ran towards Thon. Thon didn't answer. He was staring at the spot where the campfire had been the night before. Beside fresh wood, Bway Paw lay dead of a gunshot wound, along with two Karen men. He guessed she had been about to light the fire when the shooting had started.

Soldiers approached the camp, but they were shot down by Karen bullets. Paw Htoo and Naw Baw ran towards Thon.

"Thon, where's Lamai?" Duncan repeated, shaking him, his eye twitching. "What do we do?"

Thon grabbed Duncan and placed the knife to his throat. His eyes appeared fierce and murderous. But then he seemed to regain his senses and released Duncan.

"There's one way out," Thon said. "Follow me."

Thon began to lead Paw Htoo and Naw Baw, but Duncan shook his head and entered the tent. Lamai was sitting up on her elbow, sweating, listening to the gunfire. Her nightgown was done up, her stomach and vaginal hair exposed. Her underwear lay on the ground by her, sliced up.

252

"What happened?" Duncan asked.

Lamai stared at him coldly. "We're going to die," she said.

"No, we're not," Duncan replied, lifting her up by her shoulders. He continued to hold her up as her legs seemed powerless.

"Get a grip, Lamai," he said, shaking her. "We need to get out of here."

"About time you were a man," she said.

He kissed her fiercely, at which point her legs came to life. She cupped his cheeks and forced his head back.

"Come on, tee rak," she said, staring into his twitching eye. "Let's go."

As they left the tent, they heard the loudspeaker again. This time the voice was Malai's.

"Lamai," she said in Thai. "Please surrender. Save the baby and yourself. The police will be lenient. They know you did nothing wrong."

Duncan looked at her. "You can stay if you want," he said. "But we'll never be together again if you do."

"I chose you long ago," she responded tearfully.

Suddenly, Thon approached. He pointed his gun at Lamai. Duncan blocked her with his body. Thon touched Duncan's shoulder.

"Come if you want to live," he said, firing the other way as soldiers entered the camp. "Both of you."

120

Detective Lewis and fellow officers raided Tyrone's gang in South Jamaica, bringing them into the 113th precinct in St. Albans for questioning. Meanwhile, Detective Lacey visited Vince Stevens again and began calling Community Board members to assess their knowledge of the situation. Detectives Sanchez and Lawrence, with Linda German in the vehicle, tailed Wan Kim as he was picked up by Byung-hoon Yoon and driven to a bank in Flushing. As they were waiting, Sanchez received a call from Detective William Kwon.

"I talked to the widow," Kwon said. "She used to get payments from Ricky Wong. Even got to know him. Then, lately, she got a visit from Byung-hoon Yoon. This time he gave her the cash, apologizing for Wan's deed. So we got them both."

"Should've used the mail," Sanchez said.

"These gangsters find the personal touch works better on locals. Makes them seem human."

"Speaking about the personal touch, we're outside Ken Chang's bank. Wan Kim and Yoon went inside, presumably to meet the boss. Can we do anything?"

"Sergeant Chan's trying to get a warrant for Wan Kim. We can bring Yoon in for questioning. We've got nothing on Chang, but we can bring him in too."

"Sounds thin."

"Yeah, but you just want to exert pressure for today, right, and keep them occupied? At least until the vote passes."

"We've got Wan's PO with us. Does that give us leverage?"

Sanchez heard a pause. He assumed Kwon was checking with Sergeant Chan.

"Sure," Kwon finally said. "German's got authority over Wan. You can go in now. Sergeant Chan and I will come down to bring in the others."

121

Lance and Sveta parked near the Church Building in a used car, waiting to see if their plan would succeed. Lester and Mahdi had bought the car for Jeremy in Willet's Point, paying cash to a strange Armenian.

Cortland and the board members had just entered. The meeting was about to start.

"Are you sure they will vote for A's bid?" Sveta asked. "I want to see Rob again."

"It's not just the CFLIC now on board Ozone's wagon, so we should be good. With the phone calls A's people made, the entire mayor's side of the board should think the Traglianis shot Bob and Stevens, and that DeKalb's got that mob footprint."

"But what if they are afraid of being killed too?"

"Putting word in the media about the mob connection could've helped that, but it's too much to do now. Could stall the entire operation. So we'll have to hope for the best."

A beat-up van drove up to the block opposite the Church Building. Lance knew it was Levon's van. The door slid open, and Jesse slipped out. He marched briskly towards the Church Building.

Suddenly, a police car rounded the corner and blocked his way. Jesse rushed around the hood and towards the building. Two police officers emerged from the car and commanded Jesse to halt, kneeling to shooting positions. Several plainclothes officers exited the building and rushed towards him. Jesse stopped—cornered—and, his hands up, began laughing.

"Jeremy, you fucker!" he yelled. "How do you like this?"

Suddenly, Lance saw a huge flash, followed by a deafening blast. Lance and Sveta ducked as they felt the car and their bodies shake. When Lance came up again, he heard a whooshing sound. A huge cloud of smoke emerged from where Jesse had been. The police car was half-gone, the rest was on fire. The plainclothes officers had either been obliterated or their wounded bodies lay on the ground, writhing. One uniformed cop lay dead, the other was on fire, staggering in the street.

"Fucking hell," Lance yelled. "Let's get out of here."

As he put the car into drive, the other radicals exited the van. Stella aimed a semi-automatic rifle at the upstairs floor where the board members were meeting.

"I did not know about this," Sveta shouted.

"Me neither," Lance said, turning the car around. As he did, he saw Levon point a rifle at them.

"Duck, baby," Lance shouted, bringing Sveta's head down. A successive round of bullets hit the car's trunk and pierced the windshield as Lance ran the light and turned the corner.

"A fucking bomb and guns?" Lance asked. "Thought they were just gonna throw paint on 'em."

"They knew we would try to stop them," Sveta said.

"When'd these hippies even learn to shoot?" Lance asked. "Shit, we gotta get out of this city. And never look back."

122

Late that night, in their room on the third floor of the complex residence wing that looked over the complex square through a large window, Niral spoke to Manu about the mission. Niral had insisted on the two sharing a room with two equally large and comfortable beds, so they would not repeat the unequal arrangement of their first stay.

Manu, standing near the window, told Niral he was prepared.

"We will stop these Muslims," Manu said. "We will protect Hindustan, The Brotherhood, and everything we hold dear."

"Your daughter is here. Did you meet her?"

"I will meet her when I am a hero. But don't worry, Niralbhai; I will not act out of pride."

"Of course not."

Niral tried to hug Manu, but Manu avoided it and instead bowed to Niral. Niral tapped Manu's head in response.

"You are the avatar, Niralbhai," Manu said. "Tonight my daughter sleeps among the other pilgrims. Tomorrow she will be proud of me and so will all of India."

Niral left the room and saw Parthu outside the door. Niral reminded him he did not need a bodyguard anymore. Parthu shrugged and followed him anyway. Instead of taking the longer internal hallway to reach the north wing of the hexagonal complex where the offices were and where he believed Mr. Ghosh was meeting with Sureshuncle, Niral decided to go downstairs, leave the complex residence wing, and cross the eastern part of the square in between the pilgrims who slept on the ground because he wanted to see if he could glimpse whether the assassins had arrived yet. But as he did, he saw Ashok in the distance in the security parking lot on the south side of the square, walking away from his car with his other bodyguard, Kavi, and after eyeing Parthu, Niral decided to meet him.

"We arrived late, but we are here," Ashok said to Niral as the four met at the southern edge of the area where the pilgrims slept. "I hope Bhai is not asleep yet. I wanted to see him before the big day."

"He probably is," Niral said. "But Mr. Ghosh is awake. He's meeting with Sureshuncle now."

Ashok smirked. "Yes, the Big Brother who took Narendrabhai's place. Do you know him?"

"We met briefly in New York, before the big events occurred. But no, I don't know him personally."

"A medical doctor. Thinks it gives him the right to lord over everyone."

"You know everyone's expected to be a doctor in our culture. By that standard, we're all failures."

"By that standard?" Ashok laughed, hitting Niral's arm. "Come on, let's see if Mr. Ghosh is still awake. And where is your father?"

"Asleep. In the crowd with the pilgrims. He declined a room. He'll get up early for the sun prayer. You know how he is."

They crossed the square, Niral noticing his father sleeping but still without sign of the assassins, and entered the northern wing of the complex. Niral led Ashok and his bodyguards to the room where he believed Mr. Ghosh was speaking to Sureshuncle.

"Niral, we need to do something about that face," Ashok said. "Look how well I've fixed mine."

"Unlike yours, mine has character, Ashok. It's real. You can have your bodyguard back, by the way. I can protect myself."

Ashok didn't respond. Mr. Shah was personally guarding the door to the room. Niral introduced Ashok as they approached.

"At long last, we meet," Mr. Shah said to Ashok. "I have heard much about you from Mr. Ghosh."

They greeted each other with a namaste and, apparently, equal admiration. The door was opened by a guard from inside, and Sureshuncle came out.

"Ashokbhai," Sureshuncle said, offering his hand. Ashok shook it limply. "I am glad to see you."

"Sureshbhai, you are the head of all heads in North America. How can I not see you?"

Sureshuncle smiled. "It is only a position, Ashokbhai. A selfless duty. You know that."

"A position and duty that controls all donations from the entire continent."

"We keep it safe for God's work and only God's work. Money from outside the fund being spent for alleged Brotherhood interests might be used for any purpose and be from any source. So Bhen herself advised against such uncontrollable and unaccountable spending."

"Yes, but Bhai is in charge now, is he not?"

"He is the one who put me in charge as the point person of the fund from North American sources, and he made clear rules and conditions of transparency so that Narendrabhai's theft could not happen again. But you were not part of The Brotherhood at that time. It takes time to learn and to appreciate the work of your elders, Ashokbhai."

"Yes, and it takes talent to heal the wounds of warring families, to make them adhere to the ideals of The Brotherhood movement. It takes skill to rebuild entire villages and point them towards the ideals of God's way. That work necessitates more intelligence than mere monetary maintenance."

"I can ponder that point tonight in my sleep, Ashokbhai," Sureshuncle said, shaking Ashok's hand again. "And next time I see you, maybe I will give you a response to these claims of skillful engineering. Will you be inside Bhen's temple when Bhai speaks?"

"I am supposed to be. Unless another worshipper has bumped me."

"I will see you then, if not during the climb."

Sureshuncle left after a namaste to Ashok. He didn't say anything to Niral, didn't even seem to notice him. Ashok appeared disconcerted by the conversation. By then, Mr. Ghosh had come to the door and was urging Ashok to enter with his bodyguards.

"Come, come," he said, waving him inside.

Ashok turned to Niral, who had stood on the side, deciding not to interfere with any potential conference.

"We will see you tomorrow, Niral," Ashok said, as he entered the room with both Kavi and Parthu.

Niral nodded, and then the door closed in front of him. He took the internal hallway back to his room.

123

Rob pointed his gun at the other boat. He hadn't fired yet.

"I wanna get the right shot," he explained to Apsara. "No wasted bullets."

They heard a shot. Rob ducked.

"Stupid cunts," he said. "I'll get 'em."

Rob got up and fired a single shot. Then he ducked down again.

Apsara was sitting on the boat's floor, holding Boonsri. They were both shaking.

"I can't believe they're still after us," she said. "I thought the police were—"

"Maybe they got an order from the top. Or maybe it's personal. They got nowhere to go without a boss."

"We didn't kill Mr. Hong or anything."

"No, but you fucking robbed that wanker by leaving like ya did."

They heard another shot. Rob got up and fired again. He ducked back down, then turned around and looked at where the boat was headed.

"We're near the shore," he said. "Better if we dock and get out. Then we can use the boat as a shield."

"Just shoot them," Apsara insisted.

"Don't wanna waste the bullets. Let 'em waste 'em, and we'll be alright. Trust me."

The boat neared the shore. Rob grabbed his machete and crawled towards the driver.

"No worries, mate. Just dock it easy. I got you covered."

The driver turned off the motor. Rob jumped into the water and pulled the boat towards the shore at an angle so they could hide behind it as the other longtail boat docked adjacent. Apsara heard another shot. Then she heard Rob's voice on the other side of the boat.

"Come on," Rob said to her. "Climb out this side."

Apsara held Boonsri and jumped into the shallow water. The driver followed. Rob had the gun in one hand and the machete in the other. They all bent down, shielding themselves with the boat.

"Rob, give me the knife," Apsara shouted in a whisper, but he didn't respond as he snuck around to the other side of the boat. Suddenly, Apsara saw a gun in front of her face held by Nam.

Nam grabbed Boonsri's arm. "Let go, bitch," he said to Apsara. "Or you'll be sorry."

Apsara let go. Crying, Boonsri ripped Apsara's tanktop as Nam forced her away.

"No need to be rough with the little one," Rob said, coming around the corner of the boat. Boonsri ran over to Rob and hugged him. He rubbed her head with the hand that held the machete.

"What the—" Apsara yelled as Ricky grabbed her from behind and put his gun to her head.

"Go on," Rob told the driver, who ran toward the other boat.

"Why?" Apsara asked, finally grasping the situation. "Why, Rob? I love you."

"Like you loved Thanat? Like you loved Duncan and Mr. Hong?"

"I didn't love them. I didn't love them like you!"

Rob rubbed Boonsri's head. "I can't afford to believe ya. There's only one woman I love now."

"You're making a mistake," she cried hysterically. "I will be a good mother to Boonsri. I'll—"

"She hates you, ya cunt! Don't you, Boonsri?"

She looked back at Apsara. She hesitated, then nodded.

"She hates you, and so do I."

"So why did you look for me then?" Apsara asked wildly. "Why did you come back to me?"

"To get my moolah back, what'd ya think? It's in the boat, Nam. Two briefcases and one duffel bag."

"So they work for you now? The man who put the ring around my neck?"

"I would've done worse than that if I didn't have to get paid."

"Don't worry, girl, our boss has plans for you," Ricky said, squeezing the barrel into Apsara's cheek. "Laos is a land of opportunity too."

"What plans?" Apsara asked. "What plans, Rob?"

"I don't know," Rob said, shrugging. "I'm not the boss."

Ricky pulled Apsara back towards the trees at the edge of the shore.

Nam emerged from the boat carrying the two briefcases and wearing the duffel bag. Apsara was yelling Rob's name at the top of her lungs, but Rob ignored her.

"There's a car over on that hill," Nam said. "It'll take us to the house our man bought. Should be a good life for you."

"You guys can't go back to Thailand either."

"There are plenty of other destinations for Dragons."

"I've still got a piece of business back there," Rob said.

"There's time for that."

"One briefcase for the boss. You get your cut out of that. Rest is earned money."

"No worries," Nam said, putting down one briefcase and slipping off the duffel bag. "Isn't that what you say? We work for a good boss now."

Rob put the machete under his armpit, slipped the gun into his waistband, and took out his phone.

"I'll text him and tell him the operation was a success," he said.

124

An hour after the escape, Duncan, Lamai, Thon, Paw Htoo, Naw Baw, and a few others reached the Karen camp in Burma.

As his people emerged from their huts as well as a large building that dwarfed the others, they asked Thon questions about the fate of Bway Paw and the others. Thon answered gravely, and briefly, in S'gaw Karen. Then he turned towards Duncan and Lamai. He opened his arms.

"You have made it!" he shouted. "You have survived!"

He cackled maniacally. His people appeared shocked by his behavior, but they did not react.

Duncan and Lamai were both exhausted. Lamai was leaning on Duncan for support.

"Can you get her into bed now?" Duncan asked. "I hope the baby will live."

"You have all the luck, white man!" Thon said. "You will be rich, and we will survive. Isn't that the way it works? And if this baby doesn't live, you can fuck and create another one."

Lamai dropped to her knees. Both men and women from the camp rushed to her aid.

"We did make it," Duncan said, smirking, his eye twitching slowly. Then he collapsed too.

125

"They escaped!" Colonel Arthit shouted in anger. "I knew we should have bombed them."

"Always so dramatic, Colonel Arthit," Colonel Dusit said. "We got what we wanted: the drug routes, the contacts, even an inside informant now. All will lead to a showdown with General Toon and Chaow. A battle for the heart and soul of Thailand."

"And will we win, given the way this operation was conducted?" Arthit asked.

"Muscle is only needed sometimes, Colonel Arthit. Brains will be more important on this mission. We Thais are not known for that."

"We Lannas are known for that," Arthit responded.

"The kingdom was forged by the Siamese, Colonel Arthit," Colonel Nopasit said, entering. A hooded figure followed him, led in by soldiers. He was seated forcefully. "We know how to wage battle, whether undercover or on the ground."

He removed the hood, revealing the face of Kan. "An informant who knows the players and the routes. We will turn more and more, until we control the trade and force the hand of the other players. Then we will crush it. For Thailand."

"For Thailand!" Colonel Arthit and Colonel Dusit yelled.

126

"We've got them all here," Sergeant Chan said to Detective Lawrence over the phone. Chan was at the 109th Precinct in Flushing, while Lawrence was at the 113th in St. Albans. "Wan, Yoon, Chang. I know

Tyrone and his gang are in your precinct, but we've got thin shit on all of them."

"You got Wan on suspected parole violation, enough to hold him a bit. Meanwhile, use the threat of him turning to tie up the two kingpins as long as possible. In the meantime, Detective Lewis is trying to get someone in Tyrone's gang to squeal on the Macaday and Stevens shooters. One of 'em cracks, and it all comes tumbling down."

"What's going on in Long Island City? I hear there was an explosion."

"All over the news, brother. Sanchez just told me over the phone that the FBI's taking this one. Too big now. Just hope they don't swallow us too."

"What happened?"

"Some radicals, looks like art fanatics or anarchists, set off a bomb in the square, taking out some of our guys who got a tip there was something going down. Then these nutjobs took machine guns to the windows where they were holding the Community Board meeting to vote on the bid. The board members hit the floor. But here's the funny thing: they actually finished the meeting. After backup gunned down these anarchist clowns, this board member, Cortland, stands up on the table and says, 'Are we gonna be intimidated? Mob's not gonna intimidate us.' Tells them the mob's behind DeKalb's bid, so they gotta vote Ozone. All confident about it. But when the vote comes down, it goes for DeKalb! Queensboro pres people and some mayor people got it over the hump. Don't know if it was intimidation from outside or if they knew by then the violence was from the arts guys so they wanted to screw Ozone, or something we know nothing about. But whatever it was, DeKalb got the bid. Queensboro president's crying on the news saying we won't let terrorists win and the like, but she must be happy. Now she's got more support for a regular development and can take away concessions from the arts crowd, I guess. Whatever. I just hope we don't get taken over by the Feds before we crack these cats.

"Hold up, it's Lewis," Lawrence said after a pause. "I think someone broke."

PART X

†

Dwarka, India; Near Lamba, India

127

The morning had arrived. Niral was up early, standing at the window of his room on the third floor of the complex residence wing, watching thousands of devotees, more than the day before, exercise and recite the sun prayer together. He was wearing a gold-colored kafni, but he had put on a bullet-proof vest underneath it, and his pajamas were held up by a belt. Manu stood behind him. He was also wearing a kafni and a bullet-proof vest underneath, which Niral had recommended, though Manu was nervous the vest would show through.

"The terrorists are anticipating it," Niral had told him. "Obviously, they want to kill everyone but you."

Now his heart was beating fast too. The followers would be told after the sun prayer about the exodus to Lamba, although the buses and trucks had already gathered in front of the complex for that purpose.

He closed his eyes, then opened them. He turned to Manu.

"I'm going to head off. Sure you don't want to see your daughter before they leave for Lamba?"

"I'm afraid that if I see her she will want to stay with me here, and I don't want her here. What if the plan is not successful? She will be killed. It is too risky."

"I wasn't going to—"

Manu bowed a respectful namaste to him. "That is okay, Niralbhai. I should not have doubted an avatar. Whatever you recommend—"

264

"I recommend you do what you feel is right. That is what a free man does."

"Yes, Niralbhai."

"The men are in the right corner. I didn't spot them last night, but they are there now in the right spot. I will signal them as I leave. Then stand in the foyer. Once the announcement has been made and the people begin moving towards the gate to pick their numbers and settle into their groups, they will sneak into the designated room in the complex."

Niral hugged Manu, then left quickly. He descended the stairs and moved towards the square. He saw Mr. Shah there. They nodded to each other in acknowledgment.

He marched quickly towards the complex exit. As he did, he eyed the men, the Muslims he had met the first time he had traveled to Surat, the men Talim told him had been wronged by Bhai, their families massacred, butchered, simply because of their background and faith. One of them was the bearded man, now clean-shaven for the feat at hand. The others had been in camouflage that first meeting. He knew the formerly-bearded man and one other would be at Lamba.

He acknowledged them with a wink, then looked back. Manu stood in the foyer, his hands behind his back, ready to act, or so Niral hoped.

128

Niral drove Manu's car to the Lamba entrance. His car and person were checked. Then he was cleared by Bhavesh, radioing down to security from upstairs, and drove through. This time, he skipped the other temples by driving up the secret internal road to the top temple. Once parked, he was met by Bhavesh and Bilal. Bhavesh shook his hand; Bilal greeted him with a namaste.

"Good to see you again, Niralbhai," Bhavesh said. "Are you sure you do not want to monitor the situation at Dwarka?"

"Bhai wanted me here. And since Mr. Shah will direct the capture, they don't need me there."

"But you have your man there to coordinate it?"

"Yes. Manu. But he is not my man."

"Will the terrorists come to the complex after the pilgrims leave?"

"No, they are already embedded within the crowd. They will sneak inside the complex office building area once Manu gives the sign to them. And then the procedure will commence."

"Excellent. Thank you for setting this up, Niralbhai. You have saved us much hassle."

"I've done it at great peril too. People will want me dead."

"You must make choices, Niralbhai. We are glad you have made this one."

"Is Bhai here? I'd like to see him."

Niral was taken into the temple and led to the back room on the first floor. Two bodyguards manned the door. Inside were the other two bodyguards, the Sikh guard and the slightly bearded guard. Bhai was seated between them, his eyes closed, praying.

Niral waited respectfully until he finished. Bhai was dressed in a saffron dhoti and nothing else but his janoi and owl glasses.

He stood slowly and told his security to leave the room. The door closed.

"Niral, you are ready."

"Yes. Where is the room with the guns?"

"So fast to ask. You know only I could have secured the weapons."

"I can't believe you didn't tell your staff. Now they'll definitely blame me afterwards, no matter what happens."

"We have an elevator, and an escape hatch here. You can leave afterwards that way, if you wish."

"Very funny."

"Niral, you must trust me. You have nothing to worry about."

"Anything could happen. I have plenty to worry about."

Bhai took Niral by the shoulders.

"You don't have enough faith. I should have used someone else, maybe."

"Do you think I would have done this without faith?"

"Your motive, if I had to guess, is a larger version of dharma that has little to do with faith. Perhaps to subconsciously please your father, or

266

maybe it is in your blood, that special mix of your Kshatriya and Brahmin heritages."

"Again with caste."

"We cannot escape duty, or our blood, as much as we try to erase the wrongs and divisions of the past. Look, Niral, I don't doubt your courage. This has been tested. But your feelings and your loyalties... you know we cannot control what happens in Thailand. To any of your former associates."

"I'll live with it. Now show me the room."

Bhai smiled. "If you go down the hall and curve into the corner, past the staircase to the cellar, you will see an Om sign scratched onto the door of a room in a tiny alcove on the right. That is the only room without a camera, and the alcove is not visible either. The weapons are hidden behind a bucket and mop. It is where I bathe, and me alone."

"So I can check now."

"No. It is too risky. Only when the moment arrives."

"I know where the room is. Bhavesh showed me last time. But I have to trust the weapons are there?"

"If you don't trust me already, why are you here?"

"And the exchange? We can make it—"

"You will have to go into the crowd and brush against the men to deliver them. As we discussed."

"The snipers won't bring me down?"

"More risk."

"How do we know they will be here? What if something—"

"Remember, you gave them the numbers in advance so two of them will be part of the top VIP group. And they will line up that way. That is enough. If they are not braindead, they will make it."

"And that's it? We just wait all day for this?"

"Patience, Niral. That is a virtue too."

"How about my father? Is he in the top VIP group?"

"He, Kauntibhen, Sureshbhai, Ashok...all the most devoted people. I don't see how we can keep them out."

"They could be killed in the crossfire—"

"You must have faith, Niral," Bhai said. "Develop it. It is now or never, isn't it?"

129

As the pilgrims began to proceed towards the entrance to the complex, being cordoned into groups by security, VIPs were herded into one corner and told to form lines to take numbers from men with predetermined lists, which had been finalized by Manu, determining which of the four groups and therefore the temples they would be accorded access to. The other temple entrants would be determined by lottery amongst the crowd as they were given numbers for which groups they would enter the Lamba complex by. The two assassins were already in the regular crowd, but they had been given their numbers already, designating them for the group headed inside the final temple.

Meanwhile, as this occurred, the other two Muslims assigned for the Dwarka plot saw their chance and rushed towards the designated room on the first floor of the complex residences where Manu stood alone—Mr. Shah had moved towards the complex entrance to direct his men. But as they did, a girl ran up to Manu and hugged him fiercely. It was Manu's daughter, Gayatri. Her mother, Sita, who had finally reconciled with her at Manu's insistence, lagged behind.

"Finally, Pappa!" she screamed.

The two Muslims were not sure what to do. They froze and glanced around. Manu stared at them while trying to engage his daughter.

"Dikri," he said. "You made it."

"Yes, Pappa! I am so glad to see you. We have been surrounded by unfamiliar people."

"Your daughter is not enjoying the trip," Sita said, folding her arms. "She is not used to the simple life."

"I don't like praying all the time and wearing white saris, that's all," Gayatri exclaimed.

Manu moved Gayatri into the square, his wife following. This allowed the two Muslims, who believed themselves seconds away from being shot by snipers, the ability to sneak into the foyer.

"Leave her here," Sita said. "She will not enjoy Lamba. Like the time we visited Tirupati. She cannot tolerate a long wait or climb, especially for something spiritual."

"I don't like dirt and rude women, Mummy," she said.

"It's not good for you to stay here," Manu said, noticing the men enter the designated room. "You should go to Lamba with your mother."

"I want to be with you."

"I need to stay here, dikri."

"So I will stay here too."

Manu noticed the crowds of people receding as pilgrims boarded the buses.

"Okay, but you will stay in my room upstairs," he said.

"And what will you do?"

"We have exercises to run here."

"With other men?" she asked, smiling.

"She likes being around men, she told me," Sita said in a frustrated voice. "Stay here with your father, Gayatri. I will go to Lamba."

She marched off towards the complex entrance to join one of the crowds.

"Father, why do you seem so nervous?" she asked, noticing her father sweating as he watched his wife walk away.

"Nothing, dikri," he said, staring at her. "Let me show you your room."

130

"We are already experiencing problems downstairs," Bhavesh told Niral in the control room. "The VIP groups are entering in different orders than planned, and we don't have the room or time to rearrange them."

"But you're screening them thoroughly?" Niral asked, watching the monitor.

"Of course. One by one. It will take a while."

If the assassins' group wasn't assigned to the final temple, or at least wasn't in the order that allow them to enter the right temple at the right time, Niral would have to act somehow to make sure that would happen, but he had no idea how to accomplish that feat, considering they would be packed among thousands of pilgrims. Niral didn't want his father and Kauntiaunti in the final group anyway. but he wasn't sure how to remove them without disturbing the plot. Their devotion wouldn't allow him to talk them out of it anyway.

He left the control room and descended to the first floor through the door at the end of the hallway. Bhai's guards let him inside his room. This time, Bhai was wearing a saffron kafni pajama. Niral assumed the bullet-proof vest was underneath the kafni, but he didn't check.

Again, Bhai asked his guards to leave. Niral told him the problem.

"This is why I have you, Niral. You are a problem-solver."

"The entire plan might be ruined."

"Worse comes to worse, we can still triumph. You know who the assassins are. They won't get out without being detained. At the least, we will gain information."

"You might have nothing to lose, but..."

"I have everything to lose," Bhai said angrily. "No one will lose more than me!"

"Yes, Bhai," Niral said. "You're right."

131

Manu was staring out the window of the third-floor room, rolling a few bullets around his fingers, when he noticed the square had cleared. All the buses were gone. The only people left in the complex were him, Gayatri, the complex's security, led by Mr. Shah, and the two terrorists.

Manu checked the time on his phone. He put the bullets in his kafni pocket.

"Pappa," Gayatri said, sitting on his bed. "Is there something going on?"

"Nothing, dikri. I just need to go out and speak to the people in charge."

"I felt your vest, Pappa. I know there is something happening."

Manu turned.

"And you did not say anything until now?" he asked, putting his phone back in his pocket.

"That's why I did not want to go with mummy."

"That is why?" Manu asked. "It is not because you are a whore who wants to bed the guards?"

Gayatri laughed defensively. "What?" she asked.

"I thought Niralbhai told me the truth," Manu said, shaking his head. "But he lied to me."

"Who is Niralbhai?"

"Your protector, dikri. Someone who thought that, by lying to me, he was doing the right thing. Someone I thought was the avatar. But maybe not."

"The avatar?"

"How do you afford your life in Mumbai, dikri? Do men call you and ask you for fun?"

Gayatri froze. She opened her mouth, but Manu raised his finger. "Do not lie to me, Gayatri. I will know."

"Pappa—"

He smacked her across the face. She fell on the ground, shocked. Then he kicked her hard in the side. She grunted.

"You whore!" he yelled. "We refused the Backwards Class benefits because we believed in you, in your intelligence, in your honor! And you betray it simply because you want to live in a nice Mumbai apartment? Do you care at all that my principles, that everything we have lived our lives for, have been ruined because of your actions?"

Gayatri didn't respond. She was coughing blood and crying intermittently.

"Damn you!" he screamed, opening the door and rushing out. He proceeded down the stairs to the foyer and accessed the room where the terrorists hid.

"Come," Manu told them, "I will show you where your guns are."

"Already?" said one of the men. "I thought we were waiting until the Lamba operation was complete."

"Better for you to be armed now. You can go back to the room after you collect your weapons and then wait until I tell you the Lamba operation is done to act."

He took them a few rooms down and opened the door with a security code. Inside were many stashed weapons, including pistols, shotguns, semi-automatic rifles, and automatic machine guns.

The assassins smiled. Each picked out a machine gun.

"Where are the bombs?" one terrorist asked.

Manu pointed at two contraptions in the corner. The terrorists strapped them around their chests. Manu held up a pistol.

"Show us where the top security guards are," one of the terrorists commanded.

"Niral explained the layout to Talim, didn't he?"

"Yes, but we don't—"

Manu laughed, turned, and ran back towards the staircase. The terrorists looked at one another.

"I guess he will show us later," one said to the other. They each picked up another pistol, closed the door, and headed the other way, towards the other room. But when they reached it, they realized it was locked.

132

Bhavesh entered the kitchen. Niral was drinking tea.

"It's done," Bhavesh announced. "Dwarka is saved."

"Already? The terrorists were taken alive?"

"No. It seems Manu didn't inform Mr. Shah once he had armed the terrorists like he was supposed to. But our men saw them on surveillance in the foyer. When they surrounded them and warned them to surrender, the terrorists said they would blow up the bombs if they were shot."

"As planned, that should have led to their capture."

"Yes, but we assumed they would drop their weapons. They did not. So our men informed the terrorists the bombs were fakes, and that they should drop their weapons if they wanted to live. The terrorists decided to go out shooting."

"But there were no bullets inside the guns."

"The guards reacted by their training."

Niral sighed. "Oh well. I suppose they are in Paradise now if what they believe is correct. I don't know what happened with Manu. He wasn't supposed to arm them until later, and he should have kept Mr. Shah informed of the operation either way."

Bhavesh became silent and appeared nervous. Niral stared at him.

"What?" Niral asked. "What is it?"

"I didn't want to tell you until the event was over, but you may be angry at me if I don't tell you now."

"Tell me, Bhavesh. It's now or never."

Bhavesh swallowed. "Niralbhai, Manu is dead. Mr. Shah found him in your room after the terrorists were killed. Based on the position of his pistol, he believes Manu shot himself. A young woman was found by him, also dead. We think it might be his daughter. It appears he may have shot her before he killed himself."

"My God," Niral responded, shaking his head. He began to think, then finally said, "Are you sure?"

"I am sorry, Niralbhai. God bless him. Maybe he could not take being part of the plot. Maybe he did not have the capacity for violence, except on himself and his child."

"Yes," Niral said, standing up. "Yes, maybe that's it."

As he stared at Bhavesh, his brooding expression transformed into something more concrete.

"Where is the top VIP group?" he asked Bhavesh. "Where is the ceremony occurring now?"

"Niralbhai?" Bhavesh asked.

"We cannot brood on Manu's demise," he said. "We must move forward. We must protect Bhai and The Brotherhood. Do you understand?"

Bhavesh didn't respond. Then Niral repeated his previous questions.

"I will ask Bilal," Bhavesh replied, then left the room.

Niral pounded the table with his fist, bursting into tears, but as Bilal entered, he quickly regained his composure and stood upright.

"Are you okay, Niralbhai?" Bilal asked.

"Yes," he said, wiping his tears. "What is the report?"

"The top VIP group is one group back. They are slated to be inside the third temple, where Mr. Ghosh will be conducting the ceremony. At this moment, the second temple ceremony is being conducted by Sureshbhai."

"We need to make sure that top VIP group will be inside the last temple. Although if you can take my father out, that would be better."

Bilal regarded him strangely.

"How can we do this, Niralbhai? There are such crowds."

"Don't worry," he said. "I'll go myself. Down the elevator."

133

He exited the elevator into the black temple. As he opened a door leading to the back area, he was confronted by a temple maintainer and showed his badge to pass. Peeking into the passageway, he saw Sureshuncle leading prayers to a massive crowd of seated onlookers Niral did not know. A security guard noticed him and turned his gun on Niral. But Niral held up his badge and whispered his identity. Meanwhile, Bilal had called down, telling the guards the situation through their earplugs, so Niral was allowed to pass out of the temple.

Out the double doors, between the statues of Shiva and Ganesh and beyond the serpent staircase, he saw a mass of devotees seated butterfly-style on the black gravel, watching Sureshuncle on the screen. The crowds were so massive there was no way to separate the men and women, inside or outside the temples.

Spiraling through the immense crowd and approaching the lingam fountain, he was surprised to see Paul, the Christian guard he had met during his trip to the temple, standing with other guards.

"Paul, we need to make sure the top VIP group makes it into the last temple," he said. "Right now, the order is switched up."

"Point them out," Paul commanded.

He perused the crowd and located Ashok, Parthu, Kavi, and Kauntiaunti seated near Alkeshuncle and Premuncle. Then he searched for the formerly bearded Muslim and his comrade. He didn't want to point to them, but he wanted to make sure they were in the right group.

And they were. Far enough away from Ashok's cartel but close enough to be part of the same formation.

Then he looked for his father but couldn't find him. He didn't want to wait too long, so he gave up and pointed directly at Ashok.

"That's the group," he said. "They must be in the last temple."

"Yes, I see they are the next group scheduled. They will be in the third temple, the limestone temple."

"So delay them. Make the last VIP group go ahead so they will make it into the third temple."

"That will be a tough maneuver with the size of these groups, but I think we may have enough people to make it work."

"It must work, Paul," Niral said. "It is essential."

Paul turned to him. "We will make it work, Niralbhai," he responded with a namaste.

Niral nodded. He turned and weaved his way back towards the black temple.

134

Niral sat in the control room in front of the surveillance footage, flicking his thumb and forefinger in nervous anticipation as he watched Paul and his guards try to maneuver the two groups around after the ceremony in the black temple had ended. Bilal was standing next to him, trying to ascertain the situation by asking Paul through his headset.

"The second group has been switched," Bilal confirmed, tapping his headset, as Niral saw Paul nodding at the camera. "That was tough. We're lucky Paul was selected to be part of the second temple's guards. He's good with formations."

"So now the next group is filling into the limestone temple, and the top VIP group is awaiting the final climb," Niral noted as he watched the massive movement unfold. "How about Sureshuncle?"

"Sureshbhai is taking the elevator up. He will be conferring with Bhai before the final ceremony."

"Really?" Niral asked.

"Yes. He will stay here until the last group arrives. Then Mr. Ghosh will come up the elevator too. And Mukeshbhai, the Big Brother from Singapore who officiated at the Kama temple, will join them. He has been taking a short nap at that first temple. But those three will be in the top row as Bhai speaks. Mr. Ghosh, I believe, will introduce Bhai."

In one of the screens, Niral saw Sureshuncle emerge from the elevator. One of Bhai's bodyguards escorted him to Bhai's room.

Niral switched his attention to another camera, watching as the third temple filled up. Meanwhile, Mr. Ghosh stood at attention in the back passageway, and the top VIP group was positioned close to the screen and next to the final climb.

"Damn," Niral said. "My father is in the top VIP group."

"Your father?"

"Yes. Never mind."

"Oh, I remember. Why do you want to take him out?"

"That climb may be too much for him. It might be better if he stays in the third temple."

"He can take the elevator, though I'm not sure we can pluck him from the crowd at this point."

Bilal pressed his headset to talk, but Niral put his hand on Bilal's shoulder.

"Forget it," Niral said. "He'll want to climb anyway. He's got too much pride."

"Are you sure?" Bilal asked.

"Yes, Bilal," Niral replied. "Thank you for your assistance."

135

As security waited for the limestone temple ceremony to end and the climb to the final temple to commence, Niral noticed Sureshuncle exit the temple and stand above the massive staircase.

Niral left the control room and slipped through the second-floor balcony where sages made the final preparations for the deities as guards watched them. Swiping his security card, he descended to the first floor and passed under the stained-glass dome with its searing multicolored light from above clashing with the white light from the glass floor underneath. He noticed the two stages and the massive amount of security personnel. When he looked up, he saw the snipers were already positioned on the second landing. The top landing, under construction when he had last visited, had been completed, but he could not see what was up there. He made a mental note to check the cameras when he returned to the control room, but he wasn't sure he would remember.

Outside the massive doors, he stood next to Sureshuncle, who smoked a cigarette under the suspended statue of Sarasvati, listening to the shlokas emanating from the marble walls of the temple and staring at the sun as it neared a setting position. The square, featuring the statue of Bhen, was laid out in front of them, like Indra's barren court in heaven.

"I thought doctors didn't smoke," Niral commented.

Sureshuncle seemed surprised to see him.

"This one never kicked the habit," he replied.

"Addictions are what Bhen preached against," Niral said.

"You don't have addictions, Niralkumar?" Sureshuncle asked. "I recall your father telling me about some."

"My father told you?"

"Long ago. What have you been doing in Thailand? I assume it has not been good."

"Thailand is a holy place. I used to wake up to the Gayatri mantra."

Sureshuncle laughed. "Somehow, our ancestors spread the faith. Just as we have done and will continue to do in our time. A faith of peace and freedom, not war."

"Is that what you spoke about with Bhai? The peace and freedom of Hinduism."

"I reported about the congregation at the Artha temple where I presided. I wished him luck with his ceremony here at Moksha."

"That took that long?"

Sureshuncle smiled. "If you must know, Niralkumar, we also discussed the security of The Brotherhood fund and my concern over other monies distributed in The Brotherhood's name that don't have to be funneled through the fund. That defeats the entire point of the fund being consolidated and centralized."

"I see."

Sureshuncle blew smoke in Niral's direction.

"I noticed you with Ashok," Sureshuncle said. "I imagine that is why you ask."

"I didn't think you did notice."

"People like me don't always act like we know what we know."

"What kind of person are you?"

"A good person. But one with an eye towards practicality. The only reason I don't call the police on Ashok."

"Why would you do that?"

"We both know he is Vishal. You do know that, don't you?"

"So who doesn't know?"

"Most people. Bhai knows, but he doesn't care. As long as the money is directed the right way, he doesn't care where it comes from or how it is acquired, it seems."

"You would think he would."

"Bhai's plan was always to centralize the fund after Bhen died, and that's why, even before she died, he had it audited and discovered Narendrabhai's fraud, but his purpose was to make it more controllable from India. His first initiative after Narendrabhai's deception was uncovered for us all to see was to complete the centralization of the fund, with all monies ultimately deposited in India, with the express purpose of preventing another theft and to make expenditures transparent and based on social need. But Bhai was also the one who did not make Narendrabhai's theft public in the first place as long as Vishal had recovered the money by the scheduled timeframe. He didn't care where it came from then either."

"So he is consistent. What's your point? And that was Bhen's reason for making the donations anonymous, so no one would feel anybody in the organization was higher than any other member based on the amount they gave. No one, except maybe Narendrakaka, knew how much, or really even who, paid the money that went inside, and that was only because he was often present at the Donation Nights."

Sureshuncle smiled again. "Yes, but there was no separate, unaccountable funding stream outside of The Brotherhood accounts at that time. Look, we will see where this organization heads. Just because I smoke does not mean I don't have other virtues. Recall the virtues of Vasistha, who was pure and did not cheat."

"I think he was pure on many levels, Sureshuncle. So what do you mean, that you will take over The Brotherhood to save it?"

"I am saying perhaps some decentralization may be in order now, so that North American donations go into one fund there and we can spend it on our needs. Every system or framework eventually becomes corrupted and must be altered and refreshed. The Indian leadership does not understand the situation in North America. I think our funds should be used there first, not simply be funneled here. They think just because we Americans make money and educate our children, because we are doctors and lawyers and politicians, that we don't need help, that we should simply pay to improve life here in India. But we have problems there too. You should know that."

"Yes, I do know that."

"Think about your values and where your loyalties should lie, Niral. Your father is a good, honorable man. Follow his path, not Vishal's. I leave you with those words," he said, dropping his cigarette, smashing it with his shoe, then picking up the butt. "Now, let's prepare for the ceremony."

136

The cameras picked up the details of the tough climb, especially for the older ladies. Yet, Kauntiaunti was able to make it, helped up by Ashok and his bodyguards. Niral's father, Premuncle, and Alkeshuncle huffed their way to the top, but they seemed spiritually pleased with the exercise.

Once together, the group headed up the marble staircase. They were checked again for weapons, then began to trickle inside. Niral told Bilal he would head downstairs to attend to Bhai and make sure everything else proceeded smoothly. Bilal handed him a headset and showed him how to talk into it and turn it off if necessary.

"Sorry, we should have given you a headset or earplug from the beginning," he said.

Niral put the headset on. Then he headed downstairs to Bhai's room. He heard many instructions from Bilal and reports from security staff, mostly frivolous, so he turned off the headset.

Meanwhile, Mr. Ghosh had taken the elevator up, and he saw him outside Bhai's room, standing between two of Bhai's bodyguards, the Sikh one and the slightly bearded one, the door closed.

Mr. Ghosh took Niral aside and hugged him.

"Dwarka is saved," Mr. Ghosh said. "The plan worked, except we don't have anyone alive to interrogate. Do you know where Talim is?"

Niral shook his head. "That part of the plan never took off. We could have found him with the information of the assassins, but—"

"He moves around a lot. But at least this plot has been foiled. I'm sorry about Manu."

"You've known him a lot longer than me."

"It doesn't make any sense. I saw his wife Sita in the last temple. She does not know yet. And his daughter Gayatri. Oh God!"

"You never truly know anyone, right?" Niral said.

"After this is over, we will investigate this horrible event. Maybe the Muslims had something to do with it. I can't imagine why Manu would take his own life or kill his daughter. They both had everything going for them. Perhaps it is an inside job."

"Yes," Niral said flatly. He heard people muttering through the walls. Suddenly, he became very nervous. He could feel himself sweating. He knew he had to get away from Mr. Ghosh.

He heard Bhai calling his name. Niral turned around. Bhai's head was sticking out the door, between his bodyguards.

"Can you get my cologne from the bathroom, Niral?" he asked. "I showed you where it is, right?"

Niral took a second to process the request. Then he nodded and slipped towards the bathroom.

Behind the bucket, he saw the two pistols. He picked them up and placed them in his belt, under his kafni. The bulge of the bullet-proof vest elevated the kafni enough to make the outline of the weapons invisible.

Then Niral searched for the cologne. He didn't see it. He began to panic.

"Did you find it?" he heard a voice behind him. It was the Sikh bodyguard.

"No," Niral said. The Sikh bodyguard took it from a ledge near the sink.

"He doesn't wear deodorant, but he likes to smell good," the bodyguard explained.

Niral smiled cautiously.

He followed the Sikh bodyguard towards Bhai's room. Mr. Ghosh was still there.

"Niral—" he started to say.

"Sorry, Mr. Ghosh, I need to attend to something," Niral said. "Security just called me."

He rushed through the front door and into the public space. He noticed Ashok, his bodyguards, Kauntiaunti, and his father along with Sureshuncle and the other North American leaders near the front stage. The guards were positioned, three on the right side, one guarding the door to the offices.

He searched the crowd discreetly, knowing they were watching him up in the control room. He saw the formerly-bearded Muslim dressed in a kafni. He was standing near the second, round stage, the wrong one. Beyond him, he saw Bilal, who had apparently come down to supervise the guards.

Niral remembered his headset and turned it on. He heard Bhavesh giving instructions to the outside guards. He rushed towards Bilal but bumped into the Muslim first. During the bump, he reached into his waistband, took out the gun and, shielding it with his own kafni, slid it under the kafni of the Muslim. The Muslim grabbed it and put in his own waistband, tightened for the purpose. But the second gun was still in Niral's belt, and he didn't see the other Muslim.

Niral raised his hand to command Bilal's attention, but in the commotion, Bilal did not see him. So before leaving, he patted the Muslim on the back, apologizing for the bump, and with the Muslim's back turned towards where the cameras should have been, Niral handed him the other gun, which the Muslim also placed in his waistband.

"The other stage," Niral whispered without looking, hoping the Muslim had heard him.

Niral raised his hand again and ran up to Bilal.

"Are we ready?" Niral asked.

"Yes, I was calling you on the headset, but I'm sure you were busy with Bhai."

"Too many people talking at once. I turned it off to concentrate."

"Bhavesh is commanding the control room now. Everything is going according to plan. A few pilgrims tried to rush forward so they could be part of the last group inside the temple, but our massive guard presence calmed the situation. Honestly, I cannot believe it has gone so well."

"Yes, it is amazing. God has smiled down on The Brotherhood."

"Brahman is with us. And don't worry, the top VIP group is in here, as you can see."

Niral perused the front of the room. Once again, men and women were sitting together. Mr. Ghosh and a few other men joined Prakash and the North American leaders in the front row. Niral assumed the other men were Mukeshbhai and regional leaders of The Brotherhood from around the world. Ashok, his bodyguards, and Kauntiaunti were now seated two rows behind them. Niral noticed Parthu and Kavi's sides were bulging through their suits.

"They are armed," Niral said, pointing at them.

"Mr. Ghosh insisted, and Bhai consented. Ashokbhai needs special protection, they say."

When Niral tried to locate the formerly-bearded Muslim, he was no longer in his former place. He had moved up to the second row, behind The Brotherhood leaders, but in front of Ashok and his bodyguards. Now he saw the second Muslim seated next to the first. He had received the message, but Niral wasn't sure if he had received the weapon.

The crowd was seated, the doors shut. Mr. Ghosh came to the front, stood on the rectangular stage, and led a short prayer. Then he thanked everyone for coming and noted the event had gone better than any of them had imagined.

"This love for Bhai, this grace of God, this devotion to The Brotherhood," he said. "We are all moved, and I am thankful. It is a powerful testimony to how strong this movement has become. We all remember Bhen and her example, and we all act based on her message. We have done wonderful things, rebuilt lives, villages, forgiven and forgotten, and moved to forge a new society based on inner and outer peace, based on a brotherhood and equality of man. We still have far to go, but we know that we will continue to fight until The Brotherhood is in the heart and soul of every man. Only then will we have a pure and fair society.

"Now, I am sure you want to see Bhai. But before he arrives, I ask you to reflect on how you have symbolically climbed the stages of life. Through Kama, Artha, and Dharma, you have successfully traversed. Now, we reach the toughest stage of all, Moksha, that oneness with God, that transcendence, that only a few of you may achieve in this lifetime but which Bhai will address today. He will speak about the importance of spirituality and oneness with the immortal being as the final goal of all life, that only the Perfect Man can achieve, and what qualities a person must possess and acquire in order to reach that status. We have had many ceremonies, speeches, and prayers during this New Year, this Festival of Lights. Here is the final light, the greatest act of all. Here is Bhai."

Mr. Ghosh moved aside, then stepped off the stage. Everyone was quiet in anticipation. Suddenly, they heard an electronic unlocking. The door opened. Over the headset, Bhavesh told the guards to be ready.

The Sikh and the slightly bearded bodyguards emerged first, followed by Bhai, who wore his saffron kafni pajama. Then his two other direct bodyguards emerged, followed by two more. Bhai greeted the crowd with a namaste as he climbed the stage and stood in front as he made eye contact with Niral.

He dropped his hands and began to say "Welcome." But as he did, Niral heard the shout of "Allah Akbar!" and then gunfire. Bhai was hit and fell back. The Sikh bodyguard shielded him and seemed to be hit too. Then the rapid fire of guns sounded from both stage and ground, as Bhai's bodyguards, Ashok's bodyguards, and security guards fired upon the assassins. The crowd erupted in terror, rushing towards the shut doors. People struggled to open them and were crushed by their brethren when they failed.

Niral glanced at Bilal. He seemed to be frozen. Through the headset, Niral could hear Bhavesh asking what was happening and demanding that the guards protect Bhai.

It seemed like as soon as the shooting had started, it was done. Blood was everywhere, and several people were dead or wounded. The assassins lay face down, riddled with bullets front and back. The body of the Sikh bodyguard was draped over the edge of the stage. On the stage, the slightly bearded guard, apparently hit in the arm, and the other bodyguards tended to Bhai.

And in front, below the stage, two other men lay dead too: Sureshuncle and Premuncle. Alkeshuncle, wounded in the leg and screaming in pain, was being tended to by Ashok's bodyguards. The other security guards stood around, trying to get information from upstairs through their earplugs, but the communication had apparently gone dead and they were tapping their earplugs furiously. Niral looked at Ashok, who was comforting his crying mother as she rolled up into a ball. Meanwhile, Niral continued to hear the shouts and grunts of people trying to open the door and being crushed against it. Then he realized he didn't see his father.

"Deddy!" he screamed. He rushed forward among the bodies. He saw Mr. Ghosh, Mukeshbhai, and others. The blood on their clothes were not theirs, and they seemed to be alive. Then he scrambled around the left side of the stage, trying to find his father.

"Deddy!" he screamed.

No response.

"Deddy!" he screamed again. Then he heard a grunt in the corner next to the stage. His father was face down, huddled within the curtains that draped down the walls. Niral ran up and turned him. That's when he saw the dark blood on the left side of his chest and a gaping wound.

"Deddy!" he screamed again, clutching his father. He heard a voice behind him. It was Ashok.

284

"I'm sorry, Niral," Ashok said. "But he'll be okay."

Niral turned. He attacked Ashok, choking him ferociously, hearing a groan ring through that expressionless mask, until Parthu and Kavi wrestled him off.

"Deddy!" he screamed again.

EPILOGUE OF VOLUME 3

†

Yam Gam, India; Outside Yam Gam, India;
Outside Vientiane, Laos; Karen State, Myanmar;
Broad Channel, Long Island City,
St. Albans (Queens), New York

137

A week had passed. Niral and Ashok sat on the porch of Pramesh-bhai's former home, now a meditation center, a safe space for those who needed silence and solace.

"You should thank me," Ashok said. "My money bought the helicopters to the Moksha temple that saved lives, including your father."

"You also shot my father," Niral responded.

"We'll investigate who shot him. We all hope he will wake up."

"So Sureshuncle and Premuncle were accidents?"

"It was a terrible scene. Our spiritual leader was being shot. People were being trampled. My bodyguards reacted. We regret if bullets went askew. But Bhai is alive because of them."

"He's alive because he was wearing a bullet-proof vest, and by luck, none of the bullets hit him in the head."

"Who advised his undercover uniform, Niral? Mr. Ghosh will run the investigation into how these Muslims got inside and received their arms. His determination won't just be approved by Bhai. He'll also ask me."

"What are you getting at?"

"Bhai got what he wanted. Ahmedabad, Surat, even Mumbai, burned. Thousands of Muslims butchered. They won't dare attack us again, at least not for a while. You can never hold them down for long, but we've bought time. And more importantly, Bhai is a celebrity, and The Brotherhood is now the premier Hindu organization in India. Forget about the fasts of other pretenders. The assassination attempt is the king of religious persuasion."

"So you're saying Bhai planned his own assassination?"

"I'm saying he benefited from it. And if he had help, I can look the other way, and so can Mr. Ghosh and the security apparatus."

"How noble of you."

"Niral, you are meant for great things. I can help you get there. But first we need to take your father's advice and hide you away so you're out of the spotlight until the right time comes. Because as you know, many people want to find you."

"By 'great things' do you mean replacing Sureshuncle as the North American head?"

"You can't, and neither can I. But others can act for us."

"Alkeshuncle will be your limp puppet once he recovers?"

"Maybe. Or another. But that's not so important. We have greater goals than that."

"Such as?"

"We'll talk about it another time. First, let's get you situated in the wadi. My sister can take you. It's past where she told me she used to pray. Your mother's cousin lives there. The police won't check that far in."

"Muslims were killed by the thousands. But they were innocent, Vishal. The true perpetrator, Talim, still lives."

"You should have considered that when you planned this with Bhai. I still don't understand what you got out of it, Niral."

"Maybe you're looking at it, Vishal. But I don't think you'll ever understand that."

138

At the camp in Karen State, Duncan sat in a large building used as an administrative headquarters as well as a place to store supplies. He was holding his daughter in his arms. Lamai had given birth to her only a day before, and she was resting now in the makeshift hospital across the road.

Thon entered with the bandana man and Paw Htoo.

"Mr. Duncan, are you enjoying your daughter?" he asked.

"Of course," Duncan said, smiling. "I see the world in a whole new way."

"I imagine so. I would not know as I never had children with Bway Paw. But she was so respected that she continued to lead us even though she was barren. Now, it seems I must lead our tribe until another woman is appointed. Meanwhile, our business proceeds unhindered. Kan continues to receive our product and distribute it near Bangkok. Our supply lines haven't been disrupted as I feared. The product is still arriving from Bangladesh, and despite the money and lives lost from the manhunt, we are getting it across to our customers. But Duncan, there is a problem. We have not received your shipment yet."

"I haven't been able to get through to my man," Duncan replied. He had heard of the events in India: that Bhai had been shot but not killed, and that riots had engulfed India once again, with Muslims bearing the brunt of the violence.

"No. Yet your man is here to visit you."

"What?" Duncan asked, standing up slowly as Talim entered the building. He was alone. His lazy eye was covered by an eye patch, his focused eye intent. Duncan had never seen him, so he simply guessed his identity when he said Talim's name.

"Good to finally meet you, Duncan," Talim said. Paw Htoo took the baby from Duncan's arms.

"Wow, you made the trip," Duncan responded, excited. He approached and put out his hand to shake Talim's hand, but then realized he wasn't sure of the correct gesture. Talim smiled and shook Duncan's hand, placing his other hand over them to clasp the union.

"Yes, and I have brought a present," he said, releasing his two hands after a moment. "Come."

Duncan followed him outside. Supply trucks had pulled up and parked on the road. On their open beds were piled heaps of bags.

"Heroin and ya ba," Talim said, waving to them. "All you wanted."

"Wonderful," Duncan exclaimed as men exited the trucks and came forward. "So the shipment is here, Thon."

"Yes," Thon said, shrugging as he approached. "I guess I was wrong."

"We can talk about the price particulars later," Duncan said. "Now that we know the supply routes are fine."

"Talim mentioned he might want to forge a continued partnership beyond this shipment," Thon said. "Come, let us walk down the road to discuss it."

"Coming through me," Duncan clarified. "Right?"

"Well," Talim responded, "once you sell the latest batch and your daughter and wife become healthy enough to travel, I thought I would take you back with me to India, then to Pakistan, where you can escape to Dubai or Qatar and live there. You are still wanted. And with the money earned from this batch, you can live under our protection for a while."

Duncan turned to Thon. "Am I not safe here in Burma?"

"No one is safe in Burma," Thon replied. "We have battles with the military and our other enemies. Either way, it is better for your family if you do not live in Karen State. The Middle East is a better place."

Duncan smirked. "I get the feeling this is not meant to protect me but to get me out of the picture. So I can't be a middleman."

They reached the edge of the camp, where a short wooden cross connected telephone and cable wires.

"Why do we need a middleman, Mr. Duncan?" Thon asked. "You don't have that value anymore."

Duncan swallowed. His eye began twitching. "I can provide a useful function in the future."

"In the future?" Talim asked. "You are a wanted man. Plus, you failed at your task. Bhai is not dead. And Dwarka is still operational."

"Bhai was shot. You still got your shock and awe."

"I wanted Bhai dead. I wanted the Dwarka complex destroyed. Instead, thousands of Muslims have perished. Like my parents, my sister and brother. And your man Niral has disappeared too."

"He didn't come back to you?"

"No, he did not. Otherwise I would have brought him with me. And I have no evidence that he was disposed of by The Brotherhood."

"Maybe he was."

"But I have no evidence of it."

"So you'll find the evidence later. Your men failed, not us."

"You are responsible," Talim said.

"And for Bway Paw's death," Thon added, "and for the deaths of many good Karen people."

"What?" Duncan asked. His eye stopped twitching.

Talim waved his finger. The men who had left the trucks grabbed Duncan. He was too shocked to struggle as they pushed him against the cross. The bandana man approached with some rope, and they began to tie Duncan to the cross, his arms extended and his feet on top of one another.

"What is this?" Duncan asked, now struggling to get away, but it was too late as the men held him in place.

"I was going to wait until India, so I could show you what you've done, but Thon convinced me we should get it over with," Talim said. "Actually, you convinced me now."

"Thon, what is this?" Duncan asked desperately. "Talim?"

"Don't worry," Talim said, "your daughter will be raised right, as a Muslim girl, a potential martyr of God."

"And your wife will make a great concubine," Thon said. "She will be better off than any Isan girl, I assure you."

Duncan was tied to the cross. Then one of Talim's men approached, carrying a hammer in one hand, and some large nails in the other.

"Oh God!" Duncan screamed. The other Karen tribe members emerged from their huts and began watching.

"I will give you the option of converting to Islam before you perish," Talim said. "I gave Niral the same option, but he did not take it."

"Please, good God!"

The bandana man took the hammer and nails from Talim's man. Talim's man held the fingers of Duncan's right hand out as the bandana man placed one nail on Duncan's palm.

"You can die a Christian or a Muslim," Talim said. "You choose."

"I'm not either!" Duncan screamed as the bandana man hammered the nail into his palm. Duncan yelled a deafening cry, then began to whimper and breathe rapidly as he watched the blood spirt out, and then drip down. The bandana man, his shirt sprayed with dark blood, smiled and moved to the other side.

"A Christian or a Muslim?" Talim repeated.

"Okay, okay!" Duncan yelled, as the bandana man positioned the next nail.

"Say the words, 'There is no true God but Allah, and Muhammad is his messenger.'"

The bandana man hammered in the next nail. Duncan, his eyes closed, screeched in pain.

"Say the words before you perish, Duncan. And you will be rewarded by Allah."

The bandana man bent over and attended to Duncan's feet.

"There is no true God but Allah, and Muhammad is his messenger," Duncan screamed as his eyes opened wide.

The nail went through one foot, then the other with successive hammers. Duncan began gasping with deep breaths, his eyes towards the heavens. Talim approached him and placed his fingers over Duncan's eyes.

"Because you have seen the light," Talim said, "I will show you God's mercy." The bandana man placed a nail on Duncan's forehead, then pounded.

139

"Tyrone gave up Wan as the point person for the contract on the Macaday and Stevens hits," Detective Lawrence told Detective Sanchez on the phone. "Wan still hasn't said a word to Chan or Kwon, but they're confident they can break him once they unload Tyrone's confession in full. No way he's going to Sing Sing for life. He'll deal and give up the whole Dragon command if we convince the Marshals to give him protection."

"Same thing they did to Macaday, and he's dead now," Sanchez noted. "Why not have Tyrone talk to Wan if he doesn't fold on info alone?"

"Bring him over to the 109. It's an idea."

"It's a good idea. Meanwhile, we've still got a total mess in Long Island City, and the Feds are taking over. This is gonna get even more complicated."

"Traglianis get the farm; Dragons gotta swallow the manure. But the noose is tighter on everyone."

"And still a long way to go 'til the execution, brother."

140

Carty had a drink with Alicia Tragliani in the living room of Alicia's home in Broad Channel. Uncle Jerry was in the kitchen taking a call.

"Here's to you, Alicia," Carty said, holding it up. "I can't believe we won."

"Your politician was successful," she said, glancing at the picture of her father and herself on the adjacent drawer. "He's a good weapon."

"I was shocked myself, I have to say. He's more loyal than I gave him credit for."

"We'll need him. The battle isn't over yet. Even with the approval, we could face hurdles if we don't keep influence over the mayor's people. We've got the Queensboro pres, but Vishal won't quit."

"I thought you were going to finish the job on him."

"Easier said than done. My man was found murdered in North Carolina a few counties away from the Patel home."

"So send down another posse."

"We'll find a better way. Your black man is still missing, right? Maybe on Vishal's side?"

"Probably. And he's a wanted man. But whatever his interests now, Lance is a solid weapon. If he's in Vishal's good graces now, it might be advantageous to have him back on our side. And now that you mention it, I can think of a way to get him back on board."

"Which is what?"

"His daughter, Shoquanda, attends Corcoran. Remember, I've got a big family. And my son Seamus, he's got a daughter at Corcoran too."

141

Rob stood on the shore of the Mekong River with Boonsri, on the Laotian side, watching the sun setting in the distance by the Friendship Bridge. She was seated on his shoulders, and he held her legs.

"Your brother's still out there," Rob said. "We're going to find him and bring him back."

"We will go back to Thailand?" she asked.

"We'll find a way. We've got plenty of resources. And who knows, Boonsri...maybe we'll get you a mum too. A good one this time."

142

Niral followed Meetal as they left the meditation center that was Prameshbhai's former home. They passed the grazing fields and wheat farms, the long section of yellowed grass and weeds where the funeral pyres of the dead had laid months ago, then the stump where Meetal had once prayed. Eventually, they approached a terrain that appeared more like a proper jungle.

"Here's the entrance to your uncle's wadi," she said, standing at the edge of the woods. "He lives deep inside it with his family. Go straight and you will find it after a long time walking. Don't be discouraged, you will hit it, and they know you are coming. It is deep enough that the police won't track you here. You'll be safe there."

"How do you live with it?" Niral asked. "This big change backwards. Going from spirituality to money and politics?"

"If my brother can combine all the qualities of life, so can I."

"Your brother killed Priya. He killed Sureshuncle and Premuncle."

"He saved The Brotherhood financially and morally," she responded. "He sowed up the wounds of a warring family in North Carolina. He upgraded the Brahmin, Vaishya and Dubla villages here and united Yam Gam. Now he's helping you. And you are hardly in any position to judge others or to criticize personal change. Sureshuncle and Premuncle were killed in the crossfire. Priya and her father were greedy. They basically killed themselves, and don't forget Amrat's role. My brother does good works; he helps people. Just like he's doing for you."

"He shot my father."

"No one believes that. Look, you can stay here if you want. Run away if you want. It's your life. Just don't blame my brother for all of your problems. Take some responsibility for yourself, for once, Niral."

"You'd think becoming a sanyasi would make you see the world more clearly."

"It's another phase of life, Niral, but I realize now that it was one of escape. Maybe I needed it for a while. And now I've moved onto another phase. That's what Hinduism is not correct about. The phases are not set. They don't move from Kama to Artha to Dharma to Moskha. Often they mix around and come back again. It's never a set course. We both know that."

Niral breathed deeply and stepped into the jungle. He turned back toward Meetal.

"Maybe I'll ask my father about the right course," he said. "When he wakes up."

GLOSSARY OF TERMS: THAI

Arahant (also known as Arhat)—Someone who has achieved Buddhist enlightenment and/or nirvana, the ultimate goal of the Buddhist path.

As-salamu alaykum—A greeting in Arabic meaning "Peace be with you." It is a common greeting among Muslims as well as many Arabs.

Auction—In Thailand, often done in the late hours at illicit bars or warehouses to "auction" women. During the event, women are seated on a stage and wear numbers. Men can bid on them to either take them home for sex or "own" them in other ways, depending on the type of auction. Often, the women do this voluntarily to pay bills or debts, but sometimes force may be applied.

Baht—Monetary currency of Thailand.

Baht bus (also known as a songthaew)—A pickup truck with an open back and two long seats that picks up passengers for a fee. They usually take set routes and sometimes don't leave until a certain number of passengers are aboard.

Bar fine (also known as compensation fee)—A fee paid to take away a bar girl, go-go dancer, or masseuse from her establishment to have sex with her. This is in addition to the fee paid for sex and sometimes may be added even if going to a short time room (see below) within the establishment. The room might have its own fee, too.

Boom boom—Slang for sex at Thai bars, usually in exchange for money.

Buddha (originally named Siddhartha Gautama)—An Indian prince from the 5th or 6th century BC, who gave up his royal lifestyle and escaped society to become a monk and reach enlightenment. Through his life and teachings, his followers created Buddhism, one of the major religions of the world and the primary religion of Thailand.

Buddhism—The major religion of Thailand, derived from the teaching of Buddha. There are two major strains of Buddhism: Theravada, which is the one prominent in Thailand, and Mahayana, which is prominent in countries like Japan.

Buddhist Lent (also know as Vassa)—A three-month period during the rainy season in Thailand, usually July to October. It is used as a retreat by practitioners of Theravada Buddhism to either meditate or follow other ascetic practices. Many Thai boys and young men who are encouraged to become monks for a short period in their lives will often practice as monks during this period. The last day of Buddhist Lent is Okk paan saa (see definition) when a festival is held.

Buffalo boy—Slang term referring to young men in Isan who herd water buffalo.

Burma—Now known as Myanmar, a nation to the west of Thailand where many illegal immigrants in Thailand come from. These immigrants are still colloquially known as Burmese.

Chocalee—Slang for ya ba (see below) in northern Thailand due to the strong chocolate smell and taste it often leaves in the mouth.

Compensation fee—See "Bar fine."

Cool heart (also known as Jai yen)—In Thai, it means keeping a cool and composed manner in a tense situation, often dissolving the situation through laughter, diplomacy, or compromise.

Dai people—An ethnicity in Thailand.

Dragon boat festival—While there are similar festivals throughout

Asia, this refers to a rowing boat competition in Nong Khai during Okk paan saa, the last day of Buddhist Lent.

Faen—A boyfriend or girlfriend.

Farang—A foreigner. It literally refers to those of Caucasian race, although it can be used colloquially to refer to any foreigners.

Friendship Bridge—A bridge connecting Thailand and Laos in Nong Khai, Thailand.

Full moon party—An all-night party that usually takes place on Hat Rin beach in Koh Pha Ngan. It takes place once a month the night of the full moon, or close to it.

Gaeng sohm—A sour orange curry from southern Thailand made with fish, turmeric, and pineapple. It is often eaten with roti, a flat bread.

Gem scam—A confidence scam prevalent in Bangkok where a tout, or team of touts, tries to cheat tourists into buying fake gems, gold, or jewelry.

Gik—A casual mistress or "fuck friend." A gik is less formal than a mia noi (see definition). Often, a male or female has multiple giks they can call to hang out with.

Golden Triangle—An area near the borders of Thailand, Laos, and Myanmar (formerly Burma) where opium and ya ba is made and trafficked.

Gooay deeo—Wide rice noodles, usually fried with chicken, egg, squid, and/ or garlic oil. Typically, you can get this dish or some variation of it at street stalls in Bangkok.

Grand Palace—A complex of buildings in Bangkok where the Kings of

Thailand have had official residence since the 18th century. It includes panels of mythological drawings from the Ramakien, the ancient Thai epic.

Hanuman—A central figure in India's epic Ramayana and Thailand's similar Ramakien. Hanuman is an ape-man who is a strong devotee of Rama. He is the God of celibacy, a yogi who can control his senses, and a Brahmachari (devotee of Brahma) who can perform selfless actions (bhakti).

Ibraaheem (also spelled Ibrahim)—Islamic name for Abraham, considered one of Allah's prophets and messengers in the Koran.

Isan—A large area of northern Thailand often regarded as the poorest section of Thailand. Many prostitutes, bar girls, go-go dancers, and masseuses in Bangkok and other larger Thai cities originate from Isan.

Jintara Poonlarp—A Thai pop music singer.

Johnny Walker—An American whiskey often drank in Thailand.

Kanom jeen nam ngeeo—Northern Thai dish consisting of noodles in a pork and tomato broth.

Karaoke boat—Essentially a river cruise, either for a few hours or an entire day or night, where you can listen to music and participate in karaoke.

Karen—A hill tribe in northern Thailand that also lives in Myanmar's Kayin State.

Kathoey (also known as a ladyboy)—A transgender Thai.

Karen State (also known as Kayin State)—An area of Myanmar (colloquially known as Burma) where Karen tribal people primarily reside.

Khao yum—A traditional spicy, southern Thai rice salad dish.

Khon Kaen University—A public research university in Khon Kaen, Thailand.

Khua kling—A southern Thai dish of roasted meat and curry paste. It is usually spicy and dry.

Khun—Thai honorific or courtesy title.

Khun yai—Term for grandmother.

Korp khun krap—Thank you; said by a male.

Krap/ka—Krap is often used after a phrase to connote that a male is saying the phrase. Ka is used for females.

Ladyboy (also known as kathoey)—A transgender Thai.

Lady drink—A special drink a patron buys for a bar girl that usually costs twice as much, or more, than a normal drink. This usually suggests that the patron is interested in buying the girl's time, possibly leading to short time or long time (see below) later in the night.

Lanna—A Thai ethnic group from northern Thailand, named after the ancient Lan Na kingdom.

Lao—Of ethnic or national origin from the nation of Laos, north of Thailand. Many northern Thais and Thais from Isan have Lao cultural attributes, and some prostitutes in northern Thailand originate from Laos.

Larb—Lao meat salad also widely eaten in Isan.

Long time—Paying a prostitute for her time where the patron will keep her overnight or through the next day, depending on negotiation.

Long time fee—Fee paid for sex with a prostitute for a "long time." The patron may also have to pay a bar fine to take her from the establishment where he met her (bar, go-go club, massage parlor, etc.).

Lose face (also known as sia naa)—Loss of honor for a Thai. In a public situation, causing a Thai to lose face could result in them behaving in an unexpectedly violent manner.

Luk thep doll—Life-like plastic dolls that are popular in Thailand. Some believe that they can be possessed with human qualities after being blessed by Buddhist monks, so they may treat them like people, and various other superstitions have been attributed them. Interestingly, a Thai airline even started selling seats for them, and they have been used in association with Kuman Thong, a Thai folk religion. However, many Thais just use them as typical dolls.

Lychee—Small round fruit with rough skin and a soft white interior.

Mattayom—Name of secondary educational institutions in Thailand that usually starts at age twelve. Mattayom 1-3 is three years of lower secondary education, and is compulsory, followed by three years of upper secondary education, Mattayom 4-6, which is voluntary and leads to either university preparation or vocational programs.

Meter kap—"Meter, please." Said when in a taxi, especially from the Bangkok airport. Taxi drivers often deliberately don't put on the meter and charge exorbitant amounts of money when they get their (usually foreign) passenger to their destination, so it helps to insist on the meter. Another common scam is taking the highway and charging a fee, so a passenger can also insist on not taking a highway.

Mia noi—A minor wife, or mistress, common among men in Thailand of various backgrounds.

Middle Way (also known as the Middle Path)—Major doctrine of Buddhist philosophy that emphasizes a middle way of moderation between sensual indulgence and asceticism. It is the route that leads to the Noble Eightfold Path to nirvana, which is right understanding, right thought, right action, right speech, right effort, right livelihood, right concentration, and right mindfulness.

Monk—A priest in Buddhism. Every Thai male is expected to be a monk for a short period of time in youth. Monks are highly respected in Thailand.

Naga—In Southeast Asian mythologies, primarily rooted in Hindu, Buddhist, and Jain traditions, these are divine or semi-divine beings that are half-human and half-serpent. They are celebrated, among other times, during Okk paan saa, which is the last day of Buddhist Lent.

Naga fireballs—Pink or orange balls of light that rise in the sky in Nong Khai on the banks of the Mekong River during Okk paan saa, the last day of Buddhist Lent, or Vassa (see definition). It's not clear if this is a natural occurrence or some kind of hoax.

Naga show—A performance featuring Naga (see definition) creatures at Okk paan saa (see definition).

Nam prik num—An appetizer consisting of garlic, green chilies, rice, and pork.

Nirvana—The ultimate goal of the Buddhist path. Enlightenment or liberation.

Noble Eightfold Path—See definition within "Middle Way."

Nya u—A dish eaten by the Karen hill tribe where fermented fish is pounded into a fish paste and served with rice and vegetables.

Offal—The internal organs of a butchered animal, eaten commonly in a variety of dishes in Isan and Thailand. Their culinary origins are typically linked to the arrival of Chinese immigrants in Thailand more than 200 years ago (see definition for Thai-Chinese).

Okk paan saa—The last day of Buddhist Lent, usually celebrated in October, although the date can change. There is usually a full moon and a large festival, which includes a Naga Show, dragon boat races, the launching of floating lanterns and other events. When celebrated in the city of Nong Khai in northeast Thailand, on the bank of the Mekong River, across from Vientiane, Laos, there are usually fireballs (called naga fireballs, see definition) that arise from the sky. Crowds of people usually gather opposite the Friendship Bridge that separates Thailand and Laos to watch this occurrence.

Paradise (also known as Jannah or the Garden of Eden)—In the Islamic religious tradition, the place where good people and believers in Islam go after they die.

Payasam—A rice pudding known in India as kheer.

Peace be upon him (also alayhi s-salam in Arabic)—A complementarily phrase attached to prophets of Islam.

Pha nung—A cloth worn along the lower body that resembles a long skirt.

Poo noy—Within a hierarchical social position in Thailand, it is considered the junior position (literally "little person"). Poo noys are supposed to show obedience to elders, known as poo yai (literally "big person") and not question them. Poo yai, in turn, sponsor poo noy, buy things for them, etc.

Poo yai—The elder in a hierarchical relationship in Thailand, the Poo yai sponsor the Poo noy and give them favors when possible.

Pussy pong—A demonstration in Thai bars where a woman shoots a ping pong ball, and other objects, including bananas, out of her vagina. This could be shot at other performers or at the audience.

Ramakien—Thailand's national epic, similar to and derived from India's Ramayana.

Red Shirts—Slang for a Thai political movement called the United Front for Democracy Against Dictatorship, initially favoring the policies and government of former Prime Minister Thaksin Shinawatra.

Roti—A flat bread, usually eaten with a curry in southern Thailand. It could also be filled with fruits and other things and eaten as a dessert or snack.

Same same—A common phrase in Thailand, used to suggest that something is similar, whether a hotel, meal, etc.

Sanuk—Fun. It is a major aspect of Thai culture where even work is meant to be a pleasant activity. The opposite is mai sanuk, meaning one is not having fun. Often, this will be rectified by Thais with an activity that is sanuk.

Sanuk mai krap—A question asking "Are you having fun?"

Sawat dee krap—Hello; said by male.

Sen yai noodles—Wide rice noodles used in a variety of Thai dishes.

Sharia—Islamic law.

Short time—Paid sex with a prostitute that lasts one to three hours.

Short time fee—Fee for "short time" sex with a prostitute (bar girl, go-go dancer, or masseuse).

Short time room—A private room where a prostitute from a bar or go-go club will take a patron for sex. Short time connotes that there will be a brief sexual exchange. There may be an additional fee for using the room, in addition to a bar fine and short time fee.

Sia naa—Losing face in Thai society or a Thai social situation. Also see "losing face."

Siamese—A Thai originating from central Thailand. Siam was the former name of Thailand, and the Siamese ruled many of the ancient kingdoms of Thailand.

Singha—A Thai beer. Other Thai beers are Tiger and Chang.

Som tum—Green papaya salad, a staple dish in Isan.

Songthaew—See "baht bus."

Spirit house—A shrine to a spirit that is supposed to protect a place and provide shelter to spirits. It is usually small, mounted on a pillar, and has a small roof similar to a home. They can be anywhere and be any size. Inside spirit houses are usually images, offerings, and carved statues of people, animals, and gods.

Sticky rice—Glutinous rice, grown mainly in Southeast Asia and used in many dishes.

Stupa—A structure, usually with dome and a pointed top, that is a Buddhist shrine. However, it can have a variety of designs.

Sucky—Slang for blowjob.

Suffer the shaking in the grave—Here, Rahmat likely refers to the period between death and the next world in Islam, a complicated journey where it meets angels, sees Paradise and Hell, re-enters the body during burial, then endures the torture of the submerged grave until it is ascertained where the soul will head. However, as Rahmat notes, since his son died before puberty and before sin, Allah should grant him mercy and he should go to Paradise. Notably, many Muslims believe that martyrs who die for Islam or in some horrific way are spared this process and go immediately to Paradise.

Sujata—In Buddhist history, a milkmaid who gave Buddha payasam, ending his seven years of fasting and leading to him to develop The Middle Way as a philosophy.

Tatami mat—Flooring material used in Japanese-style rooms.

Tee rak—Thai slang for sweetheart.

Thai-Chinese—Thai people who are ethnically Chinese. They are the largest minority group in Thailand, have been integrated into the country for over 200 years, and play a role in the Thai economy, military, and political class.

Theravada—The tradition of Buddhism prominent in Thailand.

Tom yam soup (also known as tom yum soup)—A hot and sour soup often cooked with shrimp.

Toot—Derogatory slang for homosexual.

Tuk-tuk—Similar to a rickshaw in India, a small, three-wheeled taxi.

U-Tapao—Now a Thai Navy Airfield, it was once a base of US military operations during the Vietnam War.

Vassa (also known as Buddhist Lent)—A three-month period during the rainy season in Thailand, usually July to October. It is used as a retreat by practitioners of Theravada Buddhism to either meditate or follow other ascetic practices. Many Thai boys and young men, who are encouraged to become monks for a short period in their lives, will often practice as monks during this period. The last day of Buddhist Lent is Okk paan saa (see definition).

Wai—Similar to a namaste in India, a wai is a Thai greeting where the giver holds their palms together and bows.

Wat Lam Duan—A Buddhist temple in Nong Khai, Thailand located along the Mekong River on Rim Khong Alley. A large Buddha sits on top of it, and visitors can see a panoramic view of the city from it.

Wat Pho—Buddhist temple complex to the south of the Grand Palace in Bangkok.

Wittayayon—Slang for Khon Kaen Wittayayon School, which is a public middle/high school in Khon Kaen, Thailand.

Ya ba—Tablets that include a combination of methamphetamine and caffeine.

Yellow Shirts—Slang for a Thai political movement called the People's Alliance for Democracy that initially opposed the policies and government of former Prime Minister Thaksin Shinawatra.

GLOSSARY OF TERMS: AUSTRALIAN

Ankle-biter—A small child.

Back-door bandit—A male homosexual.

Bloke—A dude, a general term for a man or friend, usually with positive connotation.

Bogan—An unsophisticated person, a hick.

Bogged in—To eat heartily.

Boys in blue—The police.

Brass razoo—An antiquated coin, but usually used in the phrase "I haven't got a brass razoo," which means the speaker is out of money.

Bugger—To sodomize, to have intercourse anally. It could also be used to refer to someone who is annoying, either derogatory or affectionate, or as a general expletive.

Bugger buddies—Homosexuals.

Bush telegraph—Information spread through word of mouth or by some unofficial communication network, often criminals or rural people.

Busy boy—Someone who is very active or is going to be very busy.

Chunder—Vomit.

Chunder-fuck—Someone who vomits and can't hold their liquor.

Coit—Asshole, someone's asshole.

Coit dumpster—Promiscuous homosexual.

Cooee—A call or shout used to find people. When used in a phrase "within cooee" it means within manageable distance.

Copper—Police officer.

Cum dumpster—Slut, a promiscuous woman.

Cunt—Literally the female vagina. While it is typically a derogatory word used for a woman, and usually is used this way, in Australian slang, it could also be neutral or positive, especially when used with a modifying adjective ("sick cunt," for example).

Deadset—Without a doubt, for sure.

Dipstick—An idiot.

Dob in—To inform on someone.

Dodgy—Suspicious or untrustworthy.

Donger—Penis.

Donna—Blanket or quilt.

Dosh—Money.

Fair go—Generally a term that connotes someone is being given a fair chance. It could also imply that something is done fairly or without discrimination.

Fart knocker—A male homosexual, or generally a stupid or heinous person.

308

Fit—Good for something.

Full of piss—Drunk, intoxicated with alcohol.

G'day—Good day, hello. Often used in the phrase "G'day mate!" meaning "Hello friend!"

Gab—To talk.

Gammin—Joking, lying, deceiving.

Get on—To get along with someone.

Growler—A hairy and unkempt vagina.

Heaps—A lot.

Heifer—A heavy, fat woman.

How ya going?—How are you doing?

Hezza—Slang for heroin.

Jack—Police officer.

Johnson—Penis.

Knock off (also spoken as "knock it off")—This could have several meanings in Australian slang, but in this case, Rob means "to steal."

Knockers—A woman's breasts.

Mate—A friend, an amicable form of address to another person.

Moolah—Money.

Mum—Mother.

Mut—Vagina.

Oldies—Parents.

Op shop—A thrift store. A store selling used goods at low price, often run by a charity or a non-profit organization.

Paw—Informal term for father.

Pay them no mind—Not paying attention to someone or their comments on purpose.

Pimp—A man who prostitutes a woman or makes money off of a prostitute's earnings.

Poofter—Homosexual.

Randy—Showing sexual attraction or arousal.

Reckon—Think; I think.

Rennie—A heartburn medicine similar to Tums, used more often in Commonwealth countries.

Root—To fuck, sexual intercourse.

Rubbish—Bullshit, nonsense.

Shonky—Shoddy or fraudulent.

Spewin'—In this usage, Rob means "very angry." It could also mean "vomiting."

Squiz—To take a look.

Swanky—Elegant.

Sweetie—Darling, sweetheart.

Swipe—Steal.

Tucker—Food.

Veg out—To relax, to chill out.

Wanker—Literally meaning "one who masturbates." It is used as a common and general insult for people meaning they are a jerk-off. Sometimes, it is combined with a hand gesture mimicking male masturbation.

Wog—An ethnic slur, usually someone of Mediterranean origin, but can also be used on people of southern European or Middle Eastern origin.

Yabber—To talk a lot.

Glossary of Terms: Indian

Act of the play—Here Bhai refers to the concept of lila (see definition) where life is a kind of play.

Adharma—The wrong way of performing one's duty or immoral action. Antonym of dharma, which is one's righteous duty or the right way of action.

Ahimsa—Nonviolence in the Hindu tradition.

Amba (also known as Ambamata and Ambika)—Hindu goddess, usually a form of Durga.

Arjuna—Character in the Indian epic Mahabharata, and the character to whom Krishna narrates the *Bhagavad Gita*. Arjuna is the third of the five Pandava brothers, who are the rightful heirs to the throne of the Hastinapura kingdom. Krishna is his cousin. Arjuna's doubts about fighting the Kurukshetra war against his family members is the basis for the *Bhagavad Gita*.

Artha—In Hinduism, one of the four major aims in life, dealing with wealth, status, and career. The others are Kama (pleasure), Dharma (duty), and Moksha (renunciation).

Atman (also known as Brahman, although in some definitions they are different. See definition)—God, the divine life force, as well as one's true self or inner soul, which is part of the divine life force and becomes one with it once the individual attains enlightenment. It is the combination of the three main Gods (or the Trimurti): Brahma (The Generator), Vishnu (The Operator), and Shiva (The Destroyer). Atman can be obtained through enlightenment in successive reincarnations, though beliefs vary. In some beliefs, Atman and Brahman are identical;

in others, they are mirrors where Atman is the true self and Brahman is the metaphysical self.

Aunti (also known as Auntie)—A respectful Anglo-Indian term for an elder woman.

Avatar—The form a god, usually Vishnu, takes when he or she incarnates on earth. This being, including humans like Krishna and animals like Matsya (a fish), profoundly alters world events. Most Hindus count ten avatars for Vishnu, but these beliefs vary. Some Hindus believe that Moses, Jesus, and Muhammad, among others, were also avatars.

Ayodhya—City in India where the epic Ramayana is based and also where there has been much conflict between Hindus and Muslims, especially over the Babri Mosque, or Babri Masjid, which was allegedly built over a temple of Rama and was destroyed in 1992 by Hindu nationalists, leading to riots.

Backwards Class—See "Other Backwards Class."

Batata poha—Gujarati snack made with potatoes and beaten rice flakes, known as poha.

Bhagvan—Gujarati word for God.

Bhagavad Gita (also known as the Gita)—The text of the dialogue that Arjuna, the third of the Pandava brothers, and his cousin Krishna had on the battlefield of Kurukshetra in the epic Mahabharata. It is considered one of the holiest texts in Hinduism.

Bhai—Respectful term for brother.

Bhajan—Holy Hindu songs, usually sung by groups of worshippers.

Bhajiya—A fried snack, also called pakora. Could contain a number of ingredients including onions, potato, and cauliflower, then dipped into a gram flour and fried.

Bharat natyam—A type of Indian dance performed by one dancer.

Bhat—Boiled rice, often eaten with dal (dal-bhat).

Bhen (also known as Ben)—Respectful term for sister.

Bhima—The second eldest of the Pandava brothers in the Indian epic Mahabharata, and the fiercest rival of Duryodhana.

Bhinda shak—Okra cooked in oil and with spices, often eaten with rotli.

Bhishma—One of the central characters in the Mahabharata, a relative of both Pandavas and Kauravas, who takes a vow of celibacy and is given the ability to end his life whenever he wishes. He fights in the Kurukshetra War on the side of the Kauravas and dies on a bed of arrows at his wish.

Bollywood—The large, popular contemporary Indian film industry.

Brahma—One of the three major gods in Hinduism, known as the "Generator" because he is thought to have created the world.

Brahman—See "Atman."

Brahmacharya—Of the four stages of life in Hinduism, this is the first, the bachelor stage. It is from childhood to twenty-five years of age. In ancient times, a brahmacharya would attend an ashram where he would learn from a guru/teacher and maintain celibacy until marriage and the householder (grihastha) stage of life. The other two stages are forest dweller (vanaprastha) and sannyasa (renunciation). Those priests who practice celibacy and/or worship the god Brahma can also be referred to as Brahmacharya.

Brahmin—One of the four major castes in Hinduism. Brahmins are the priests and scholars. If ranked hierarchically, they are the highest caste in terms of status and respect, though ideally, they are supposed to have little material wealth or power.

Brahmin (American)—In the passage in question, Ashok likely refers to the Boston Brahmins, as well as their counterparts in other American cities, who were members of the traditional upper class, or the eastern establishment of old money, wealthy families that were primarily of British Protestant origin (also known as WASPs), although some were of other European origins (like the Dutch in New York). They were highly influential over American educational and cultural institutions and were at the heyday of their power in the 19th and early 20th century. Today, their power and influence has waned and is less represented in traditional media, but they still exist and have a disportionate influence over American culture and institutions.

Chaas—A drink made from yogurt and water.

Chai—Black tea with milk, herbs, and spices.

Chandlo (also known as a tilak)—A red dot or smudge placed on a forehead using kum kum powder. Usually applied when worshipping God in the temple or at home, during religious ceremonies, or on auspicious days. Signifies, among other things, the worship of intelligence.

Chaniya choli—A colorful, ornately embroidered and mirrored dress for women featuring a short top and skirt, including a decorative scarf called an odhni.

Chutney—A sauce used as a condiment for Indian snacks and cuisines.

Dabbawalla—A lunch box and/or the lunch box delivery system or deliverer for the lunch boxes in India.

Dal—A soup made from split peas and lentils, a staple of a Gujarati meal. Often eaten with bhat (dal-bhat) or boiled rice.

Dalit—Descendants of the "untouchable" caste in India. This "untouchable" caste did laborer jobs that were often considered un-clean. Although, traditionally the Indian caste system has four castes, the "untouchables" were a submerged fifth caste.

Deddy—Short or affectionate Gujarati (see below) term for Father.

Desi—Slang for people of Indian descent or diaspora.

Desi daru (also known as daru)—An alcoholic beverage often prepared in India's rural and impoverished areas, what would be referred to in the US as "moonshine."

Dharma—One's righteous duty or the right way. Contrasts with ad-harma, which is the wrong way or immorality.

Dhokla—Snack made from chickpeas and rice. It is similar to Khaman but usually whiter, thicker, and not as sweet.

Dhoti—A cloth that is wrapped around the groin and thighs.

Dikra (when said to a male or Dikri when said to a female)—Dear child.

Divo—A hand-created candle made of ghee.

Diwali (also spelled Divali, known as Deepavali and Festival of Lights)—Hindu festival of lights, celebrated over five days during the Hindu Lunisolar month Kartika. Dates can differ, but this is usually between mid-October and mid-November. It represents the victory of light over darkness, good over evil, and knowledge over ignorance. It is widely associated with the goddess Lakshmi, but various traditions also associate it with Rama and other gods and goddesses.

Dosa—A fried crepe of rice and lentil batter that serves as a wrap for potatoes and other fillings. There are different types of dosas, depending on the flavor and content of rice batter, fillings, and spiciness. The most popular is masala dosa, which contains spicy potatoes. Mysore masala dosa includes a red chutney filling. Pondicherry dosa is similar but sometimes includes vegetables. In a rava masala dosa, the crepe is made from wheat and rice flour.

Dubla (also known as Halpati)—A caste of laborers in Gujarat, India.

Durga—Hindu goddess of war.

Duryodhana—In the Mahabharata, he is the son of Dhritarashtra and crown prince of the kingdom Hastinapura, who fights the Pandava brothers for the throne in the Kurukhetra war.

Dwarka—Ancient Indian city in Gujarat that was Krishna's kingdom.

Faliya—A housing cluster in Gujarat that links people of a similar caste.

Gandhari—In the Mahabharata, she is the mother of Duryodhana and wife of Dhritarashtra. She is also the mother of all the Kauravas, meaning Duryodhana and his 99 siblings. She conceives these children with the assistance of Veda Vyasa, who incidentally is also credited as the author of the epic.

Ganesh (also known as Ganapati)—An elephant-headed god, son of Shiva and Parvati, often worshipped as the God of intelligence, knowledge, wisdom, the arts and sciences, and the remover of obstacles.

Gayatri—Hindu goddess, personification of the Gayatri mantra from the Rigveda, one of the four canonical Vedic texts.

Gayatri mantra—A widely recited and revered mantra in both Hindu and Buddhist traditions.

Ghee—Clarified butter.

Godhra—City in Gujarat, India where a train was burned in 2002, followed by communal riots.

Gopi—A female cowherder. In ancient times, they were devoted to the avatar Krishna.

Grihastha—The second stage of life in Hinduism, the householder stage dealing with marriage and fulfillment of social duty.

Gujarat—A state in northwest India where the major language spoken is Gujarati.

Gujarati—People from the Northwestern state of Gujarat in India and the language they speak.

Guru—Sage or teacher.

Guru dakshina—In ancient India, a gift given to a teacher after a period of service.

Halpati (also known as Dubla)—A caste in Gujarat of laborers.

Hanuman—Devotee of Rama and one of the central characters in the Indian Ramayana and Thai Ramakien, Hanuman is often depicted as a monkey-man and is considered a master of celibacy, an ideal brahmacharya and yogi, has mastery of over his senses, performs selfless work, and achieves devotion to God. In the Ramakien, he is considered God-king of the apes.

Hastinapura—In the Mahabharata, the kingdom fought over by the Pandavas and the Kauravas.

Hijra—In India, the transgendered and eunuchs. Hijra often live in communities and come around during weddings to demand money. Not giving to them is considered a sin and can have bad consequences and omens. Some believe hijra have divine powers.

Hindustan—Colloquial name for India, emphasizing its Hindu majority.

Hindustani—Technically related to Hindi language or Hindu people, generally used to refer to having a Hindu cultural aura.

Hindutva—A form of Hindu nationalism emphasizing that a Hindu way of life should be central to Indian national identity.

Hiranyakashipu—Corrupt king who received divine powers by praying to Brahma. He was not able to be killed, day or night, by man or beast, in earth or space, inside or outside, by animate or inanimate objects. Seeing Vishnu as his enemy, he became upset by his son Prahlad's unswerving devotion to Vishnu. After various methods of killing Prahlad failed, Vishnu incarnated himself as Narasimha, a half-man half-lion, and killed Hiranyakashipu with his claws at twilight, in the middle of a doorway, on his lap.

Holi—A spring festival inspired by Prahlad's triumph over Holika (see below). Participants usually throw colors at each other and dance around a huge bonfire.

Holika—Hiranyakashipu's sister, who had the gift of not being burned by fire. Hiranyakashipu had her sit on a lit pyre with his son, Prahlad, on her lap, hoping to burn him to death, but when Prahlad prayed to Lord Vishnu, Holika died and Prahlad survived. It is the mythological inspiration for the Hindu holiday/spring festival Holi.

Idli sambar—A meal combination of a rice cake (idli) and a lentil stew (sambar).

Indra—Hindu God, and the king of heaven.

Jalebi—A sticky Indian sweet made by deep-frying maida (a white flour made from wheat) batter and soaking it in sugar syrup. It is usually shaped like a pretzel or in various circular shapes and is often yellow or orange in color.

Janoi—A simple, multi-threaded string that is worn across the chest, over the left shoulder and under the right arm. It is received by brahmin and kshatriya (see below) boys after a janoi ceremony, usually when they are teenagers. It represents their passage into their rightful role in society and their knowledge of prayers expected of their caste. Today, it is often merely given as a symbolic passage into manhood.

Kadhi—A drink made from yogurt and gram flour. Often eaten with khichdi, a kind of rice made with lentils or pulao.

Kafni pajama (also known as a kurta pajama)—A male dress featuring loose pajama bottoms and a long pullover shirt. The female version is called a salwar kameez or panjabi.

Kafir—An Arabic term used by many Muslims meaning infidel or un-believer of Islam.

Kaka—Respectful Gujarati term for blood uncle, though sometimes it is used for respected non-relatives in place of "Uncle."

Kali Yuga—In Hinduism, the last of the four eras of time the world goes through. During Kali Yuga, humanity degenerates spiritually and morally. The other three yugas are Satya Yuga, Treta Yuga, and Dvapara Yuga.

Kama—Desire, pleasure in life.

Kama Sutra—An ancient Sanskrit text on the pleasure aspects of life, including desire, love, sexuality, and marriage.

Kamwali—A maid.

Karma—A complex Hindu concept regarding one's actions and their cause and effect relationship to one's fate and reincarnation.

Kartikeya—Hindu god of war, son of Shiva and Parvati, and brother of Ganesha.

Kauravas—In the *Mahabharata,* the one hundred children of King Dhritarashtra who claim the throne of the kingdom Hastinapura.

Khaman—A Gujarati snack similar to dhokla but softer and often sweeter, made from chickpeas and gram flour.

Khichdi—A kind of rice made with lentils. Often eaten with Kadhi, a yogurt-based drink, and together called Khichdi Kadhi.

Kohl—A black powder used as eye-makeup by Indians.

Kshatriya—One of the four major castes in Hinduism. Kshatriyas are the warrior and kingly caste. If ranked hierarchically, they are considered the second highest caste after Brahmins.

Krishna—One of the incarnations of Vishnu and a major character in the *Mahabharata*. A cousin of the Pandavas, he recites the *Bhagavad Gita* to Arjuna and serves as his charioteer during the battle of Kurukshetra.

Kum kum powder—A red powder used by Hindus for chandlos and other religious markings.

Kurta pajama—See "kafni pajama."

Kurukshetra—Battlefield where the major battle in the *Mahabharata* occurs.

Kurukshetra war—The major battle in the *Mahabharata* where the Pandava brothers and their allies fight the descendants of Dhritarashtra and their allies for the crown of the kingdom Hastinapura.

Laddu—A round sweet made of flour, sugar, and ghee.

Lakshmana—In the epic *Ramayana,* the younger brother of Rama.

Lakshmi (also written Laxmi)—Hindu goddess of prosperity. She is the wife of Vishnu and also, along with Parvati and Saraswati, part of the Tridevi.

Lila—In Hindu philosophy, the divine play of all reality, the human and cosmic drama of life.

Lingam—A phallic symbol usually associated with the god Shiva.

Mahabharata—The longest epic written in human history. It was authored by Veda Vyasa, who is also a minor character in it. Scholars differ on when it was written, but it was probably passed down orally by generations for thousands of years. The epic concerns the fate of the Kuru dynasty, from King Bharat to the death of Krishna. It features the *Bhagavad Gita* and the Kurukshetra war.

Mama—Uncle on the mother's side of the family.

Mandir—A Hindu temple.

Mantra—Words or phrases uttered that have sacred value.

Masala—A mixture of spices.

Masi—Aunt on the mother's side of the family.

Masjid—Mosque or worship hall for Muslims in India.

Mata—Respective term for mother or female goddess in Gujarati.

Mehndi—Body art, usually applied to the hands using paste derived from the henna plant.

Methi—Fenugreek seeds, often used as an ingredient when cooking Indian food.

Moksha—In Hinduism, liberation, perfection of consciousness, or becoming one with God. Can be obtained by human beings through four different methods: jnana-yoga (knowledge), bhakti-yoga (love, devotion), raja-yoga (meditation), and karma-yoga (action).

Mosal—In Gujarati, a person's mother's village.

Motimasi—Oldest aunt on the mother's side of the family. Moti means oldest and masi means aunt on the mother's side.

Motobhai—Big brother.

Mummy—Short or affectionate term for mother used by Gujarati people.

Namaste—A Hindu action used for both greeting someone and taking their leave, similar to the Thai wai. Usually, it is performed with palms together and a slight bow.

Nasta—Snack.

Odhni—A scarf worn with many Indian dresses, including a chaniya choli, sari, and punjabi.

Om—An Indian holy symbol, meaning, among other things, God.

Other Backwards Class (also known as Backwards Class)—The socially disadvantaged castes as defined by the Indian government. Public schools and government positions often will have a certain quota of this caste to fill. They also receive other benefits, sometimes colloquially described as OBC benefits. Another classification is Schedule Castes or Scheduled Tribes, which usually refers to Dalits, or the former untouchables.

Paan—An areca nut snack that is wrapped in a betel leaf, with tobacco and other substances often added. It is often placed in the mouth whole and then the juices are spat out during chewing.

Palathi—Sitting position with legs crossed and feet either sticking out or under the thighs (butterfly-style).

Pandavas—Five brothers who are primary characters in the *Mahabharata*.

Pandu—A character in the *Mahabharata*, descendent of the Kuru dynasty and father of Arjuna and the Pandavas.

Panjabi—See "salwar kameez."

Pappa—Short or affectionate Gujarati term for Father.

Parashurama—The sixth avatar of Vishnu, considered to be the first warrior saint.

Parvati—Hindu goddess of marriage, children, fertility, and love. Part of the Tridevi with Sarasvati and Laxmi, and wife of Shiva.

Patra—An Indian dish made of crushed chickpeas wrapped in big Taro leaves.

Perfect man—A person who has reached moksha after successive births and whose soul is thus ready to rejoin Atman upon death. This person sees the universe as God's lila, or playground, and is mentally detached from all things.

Phalguna Purnima—The last full moon day of the lunar month Phalguna, usually in February or March, when Holi is celebrated.

Prahlad—Son of Hiranyakashipu and a devotee of Vishnu. His father tries to have him killed, but he survives due to his devotion.

Pulao—A rice dish usually mixed with lentils and vegetables.

Puri—Small, round, thin, and puffy deep-fried bread often eaten on special occasions with shak (see below).

Rakshasa—A demon in Hindu mythology.

Rama—Seventh avatar of Vishnu in Hinduism and the hero of the Indian epic the *Ramayana* and the Thai epic *Ramakien*.

Ramayana—Indian epic authored by the sage Valmiki. It narrates the adventures of Lord Rama and his family, including Lakshmana, Sita, and his disciple Hanuman.

Reincarnation—The Hindu belief that human beings, and other life, are reincarnated into other forms during successive rebirths until they reach unity with Atman through Perfect man (see definition) consciousness.

Rickshaw—Similar to a tuk-tuk in Thailand, a three-wheeled taxi.

Rigveda—One of the four canonical texts of the *Vedas*, called Samhitas, or collections of mantras. *Rigveda* is primarily filled with hymns. The other Samhitas are *Yajurveda*, *Samaveda*, and *Atharvaveda*.

Rishi—A Hindu sage.

Rosary—A ring of beads used to assist in praying.

Rotli—A thin, round, flat, unleavened bread made of flour that is rolled, then heated.

Sadhu—A Hindu ascetic.

Salwar kameez (also known as a panjabi)—A combination of pants and long shirt worn by women. The male version is the kafni pajama.

Sambar—A lentil and vegetable soup.

Sanskrit—Ancient Indian written language. Many of the ancient prayers are in this language, and most Indian names derive from it.

Sanyasi—One who renounces worldly desires and concentrates on a spiritual life of detachment.

Saraswati—Hindu goddess of art, knowledge, and education. Along with the wives of Vishnu and Shiva, Lakshmi and Parvati, she is part of the female trinity of gods, or Tridevi.

Sari (also known as saree or shari)—A traditional Indian dress for women consisting of a blouse, or choli, a petticoat, or lehenga, and a single cloth wrapped around the body.

Semitic—Referring to the Abrahamic religious tradition. In the passage in question, Ashok contrasts the Jewish/Christian/Islamic concept of the soul's ascension or descent into a heaven/paradise or hell after death with the karmic conception of reincarnation and rebirth after death in the Hindu/Buddhist religious tradition. Yet, in Hindu mythology, there actually is a heaven of gods that is depicted, reigned over by the god Indra, though the souls of the dead do not go there.

Sev—Thin, crunchy noodles made of chickpeas and eaten as a snack.

Shak (also spelled shaak)—The main staple of Gujarati meals. It consists of a single or multiple vegetables cooked in oil. It is usually eaten with a rotli or other type of bread.

Sherwani—A long, decorative coat worn in India.

Shiva—One of the three major gods in Hinduism. Known as the "Destroyer" because he has the power to destroy the world when it has become too corrupt.

Shiva Sena—A Hindu nationalist political organization in India.

Shloka—Indian epic poetry, usually rehearsed or chanted at Hindu functions.

Shrikhand—Sweet made of strained yogurt.

Siddhartha (also known as Siddhartha Gautama)—Original name of the Buddha, an Indian prince from the 6th or 5th century BC who gave up his royal lifestyle and escaped society to become a monk and reach enlightenment. From his life and teachings, his followers created Buddhism, one of the major religions of the world and the primary religion of Thailand and other Asian countries.

Sikh—A devotee of the religion Sikhism, an offshoot of Hinduism started in the 15th century.

Sisterfucker—A general insult or curse in India similar to "motherfucker" in the United States. In this case, it literally means having sex with one's sister.

Sita—The wife of Rama in the Indian epic *Ramayana*.

Sudarshana chakra—A spinning disk with 108 sharp edges that is spun on a finger and flung to cut off heads and limbs. One of Vishnu and Krishna's weapons. Vishnu is often depicted with one in pictures and statutes. It also represents the wheel of time.

Swastika—An ancient symbol of spirituality and godliness, often found around doorways in Hindu homes and other places to be blessed. Unfortunately, after its usage by the Nazi Party in Germany, it has a negative and antisemitic connotation in the West.

Sudra—One of the four major castes in Hinduism. Sudras are the labor caste. If ranked hierarchically, they are the lowest caste but theoretically carry the least responsibility.

Thali—A round dish usually made of steel, with many pockets for different types of Gujarati food.

Thousand lives—Here Bhai likely refers to reincarnation (see definition).

Tirupati—A city in the Indian state of Andhra Pradesh where an important Vaishnavite shrine is located.

Topi—Hat.

Trinity of Gods (also known as Trimurti for the male gods, and Tridevi for the female goddesses)—The trinity in Hinduism are the forces that generate, operate, and destroy the world, as represented by Brahma, Vishnu, and Shiva among the male gods, and Saraswati, Lakshmi, and Parvati among the female goddesses.

Uncle—A respectful term for an adult male.

Uttapam—A type of dosa with toppings.

Vada—A fried snack, usually made of potatoes or legumes, often eaten with chutney.

Vaishya—One of the four major castes in Hinduism. Vaishyas are the tradesmen, artisans, and merchants of society. If ranked hierarchically, they are the third highest caste.

Vasistha (also spelled Vasishtha)—A revered Vedic rishi. He is mentioned in many Vedic texts, plays a role in the *Ramayana* and is famous for his conflicts with the sage Vishvamitra.

Vedas—The ancient Hindu texts written in Sanskrit that are often cited as the oldest scriptures of Hinduism.

Vedic—Related to the teachings and traditions stemming from the Vedas.

Veena—An ancient musical instrument shaped similar to a violin or guitar.

Veg—A sign posted in India indicating an establishment serves vegetarian food.

Vishnu—One of the three major gods in Hinduism. Known as the "Operator" because he keeps the world running and steps in through incarnation when things are not going right.

Wadi—An orchard.

Yagna (also spelled Yagya or Yajya)—A Hindu ritual with fire, normally officiated by a guru or rishi who leads the singing of prayers, or mantras.

Yoga—Physical exercises from ancient Hindu scriptures.

Yogi—A practitioner of yoga.

Yudhishthira—Eldest brother of the Pandavas, rightful heir to the throne who ascends it after the Kurukshetra War.

GLOSSARY OF TERMS: AMERICAN

All hands on deck—Needing everyone in a group or organization involved for an operation.

Alpha—A dominant person.

Beta—A weak person, usually a follower of an alpha.

Black Lives Matter—A social justice and human rights movement campaigning against systematic racism and violence against black people, particularly in regards to their treatment by police and within the justice system. It began in 2013 as a hashtag movement.

Brett Ashley—A major character in Ernest Hemingway's 1925 novel *The Sun Also Rises*, she is of British origin and has affairs with many of the male characters in the novel. Some consider her a typical flapper (see definition) of the 1920s.

Bring down the latch—Sanchez likely means locking perpetrators in prison, using the metaphor of a latch on a garage door.

Broke-ass—A person who has no money or is in financial trouble.

Bucked in—Could have many meanings, but in this case meaning they are trying to charge in and dislodge the detectives from their case or territory.

Buckskin—The preserved hide of an animal, usually deer, that is often tanned to imitate deerskin clothing worn by Native Americans.

Capped—To be shot.

Carmelo Anthony—A basketball player who used to play for the New York Knicks.

Cat—A dude. Could have other meanings.

Chink—An ethnic slur that refers to a person of Chinese descent but is often used against anyone who has an East Asian appearance.

Come around the board—Referring to the board game Monopoly, where on certain turns you need to go around the board and pass "Go" to achieve some directive.

Coming out the wazoo—A lot, an excessive amount.

Digs—Slang term for a person's living area or home.

Dog—Slang term for a friend or associate.

Don Corleone (also known as Vito Corleone)—A fictional mobster in Mario Puzo's 1969 novel *The Godfather* and the associated films based on it.

Feminism—Movement advocating for women's rights. There have been many waves of feminism, and approaches to it vary widely.

Fifth Avenue—A street in Manhattan that his known for its elegance and being the home of expensive real estate and cultural institutions.

Flapper—A generation of 1920s women primarily in the United States and Europe who flouted previously conventional behaviors and roles expected of women.

Gender expression, gender identity, and **gender-neutrality**—Generally defines a large umbrella of gender issues and identities that were in vogue as of this publication, and are legally protected/codified, especially in urban areas in the US. Specific definitions are below.

Gender expression—Relates to a person's behavior and mannerisms in relation to accepted stereotypes in a particular culture.

Gender identity—The ability for one to express their gender belief regardless of their sex at birth. There is a large umbrella of gender identity terms including genderfluid, demiromantic, asexual, and non-binary. As the definitions of these terms are complex and involve a plethora (and commingling) of other terms, they won't all be defined here but are easily available to look up.

Gender-neutrality—A legal movement that tries to eliminate bias over gender. This includes the implementation in New York City of All Gender bathroom identification for single-sex restrooms.

Hearsay—Information that can't be substantiated, usually based on rumor or gossip.

Herb—A bullying and insulting slur used primarily in early 1990s New York City essentially meaning the recipient is a weakling or coward.

Knicks (also known as New York Knicks or New York Knickerbockers)— A professional basketball team based in New York City.

Jersey—A uniform worn by a professional sports player, or its imitation as worn by a fan.

Lucchese—One of the five major crime families in New York City of the American Mafia. Roberto Tragliani, Alicia Tragliani's father, was a "made man" or fully initiated member of this crime family, although he operated his own minor faction primarily with the assistance of his own family members.

Mikail Bakunin—A Russian proponent of anarchism and social anarchism as well as a founder of collectivist anarchism. He is best known as being an opponent of Karl Marx's brand of communism, particularly the dictatorship of the proletariat.

MO (also known as modus operandi)—Someone's habits of working.

Motherfucker—A general insult or curse, literally meaning to have sex with your mother.

Native Americans—The original people living in what is now the continental United States of America before settlers, primarily from Europe, arrived.

Nigga (also spoken as nigger)—Slang term meaning "man" or "brother," usually spoken by some young men and women in America of all ethnicities, particularly in urban environments but not limited to them. Originally it derives from the racist/ethnic slur "nigger," historically used by White Americans in the US to oppress African-Americans and other blacks, but it was reappropriated starting in the 1970s and is widely used colloquially by a subculture of people who have adopted their own form of "black culture" or other forms of "ghetto culture" which can include wearing low-hanging, baggy pants and other attributes. Many still consider both terms offensive.

Occupy Wall Street—A movement protesting economic inequality, capitalism and corporate greed that began in 2011 with an "occupation" of Zucotti Park in Manhattan's downtown financial district. Occupants lived in tents, created their own decision-making bodies through consensus, played music, and even had a portable library. They were forced out by police after several weeks, but the occupation inspired similar occupations and demonstrations across New York City, the US, and the world.

OTB—Off-track betting on horse racing which is offered in New York State legally by a few government-owned corporations. However, it is also an illegal enterprise run by criminal gangs.

Pants down-to-here motherfucker—Here Lance refers to the practice of some young men wearing low-hanging, sagging and usually baggy pants, often below their asses. Many say the practice originated in prison, but the reason is less clear. Perhaps convicts were banned from wearing belts so their uniforms naturally hung low. Others say it was to let other inmates know they were available for homosexual intercourse. Since Lance is of a slightly older generation and is worried about young urban men corrupting his daughter, it's likely this is why he is so offended at their fashion choice.

Pig—Insulting term for police officer.

Pocahontas—A well-known Native American woman from the 17th century associated with the colonial settlement in Jamestown, Virginia.

Ramie—A fiber crop used as a fabric.

Rap sheet—An individual's record of criminal history or arrest.

Riding this wave—This could have several meanings, but in this case, Sanchez means they want to follow the momentum of the investigation while it lasts, like a surfer riding a wave in the ocean.

Right of first night (also known as lord's right)—Referring to the medieval European practice of jus primae noctis or droit du seigneur, the legal right of a feudal lord to have sexual relations with subordinate women particularly on their wedding nights.

Rock the boat (also known as upset the apple cart)—Phrase meaning to cause problems or trouble, to ruin plans or spoil an arrangement. Here Tyrone uses it to mean not doing anything unconventional or extreme to cause undue surveillance on his gang's criminal operations.

Shorty—This could have several meanings, but in this case means a young, usually preteen or teen gang member.

Sing Sing—A maximum-security prison in Ossining, New York, about thirty miles north of New York City.

Skank—A sleazy or promiscuous person.

Sticks (also known as The Sticks)—Slang term for prison.

Timbuktu—Technically a city in Mali on the African continent, but often used to mean some far away place. Lance likely means here that Vishal can control his people from anywhere on earth.

Turn and reveal easy—Meaning criminals will give evidence and "turn" on one another in regards to their mutual crime, often to get a lesser sentence.

Tween (also known as a pre-teen)—An individual between the ages of nine to twelve, between early childhood and adolescence.

Acknowledgments

To my parents, friends, extended family, acquaintances, and team.
Thank you!

Made in the USA
Monee, IL
26 May 2021

69536027R00197